KU-575-398

Classics

## THE FORTY-FIVE GUARDSMEN

YOU have read, or will read, "Chicot the Jester" (also in this series), there met the debauched Henri III, the traitorous Duc d'Anjou, the lovely Dame de Monsoreau, and that brave chevalier Bussy d'Amboise, noble victim of jealousy and love. In TIE FORTYFIVE GUARDSMEN D'Epernon survives all the rapier-thrusts of that wonderful tale to form the King's bodyguard and set going yet another wonderful weaving of war, intrigue and love.

Now excitement flares about the wars of the King—at the sieges of Antwerp and Cahors. Now intrigue snakes its way about the feet of D'Anjou whom Diane de Monsoreau has never forgiven for the death of her beloved Bussy d'Amboise. Long before the usual mysterious death—it is a period skilled in all the most evil and cunning devices of assassination and revenge—have removed d'Anjou, we feel fully satisfied that this is one of Dumas' finest historical romances. This new edition compresses the pure essence of the tale to the last drop of excitement.

# THE
# FORTY-FIVE
# GUARDSMEN

*By*

ALEXANDRE DUMAS

MELLIFONT PRESS LTD.
1 FURNIVAL STREET, LONDON, E.C.4

# THE FORTY-FIVE GUARDSMEN

## CHAPTER I

### THE PORTE ST. ANTOINE

On the 26th of October, 1585, the barriers of the Porte St. Antoine were, contrary to custom, still closed at half-past ten in the morning. A quarter of an hour after, a guard of twenty Swiss, the favourite troops of Henri III., then king, passed through these barriers, which were again closed behind them. Once through, they arranged themselves along the hedges, which, outside the barrier, bordered each side of the road.

There was a great crowd collected there, for numbers of peasants and other people had been stopped at the gates on their way into Paris. They were arriving by three different roads—from Montreuil, from Vincennes and from St. Maur; and the crowd was growing more dense every moment.

There were, besides this mass of arrivals, some groups who seemed to have come from the city. These, instead of looking at the gate, fastened their gaze on the horizon, bounded by the Convent of the Jacobins, the Priory of Vincennes, and the Croix Faubin, as though they were expecting to see some one arrive. These groups consisted chiefly of bourgeois, warmly wrapped up, for the weather was cold, and the piercing north-east wind seemed trying to tear from the trees all the few remaining leaves which clung sadly to them.

Three of these bourgeois were talking together—that is to say, two talked and one listened, or rather seemed to listen, so occupied was he in looking towards Vincennes. Let us turn our attention to this last. He was a man who must be tall when he stood upright, but at this moment his long legs were bent under him, and his arms, not less long in proportion, were crossed over his breast.

"Yes, Maître Miton," said the little man to the tall one, "yes, I tell you that there will be 100,000 people around the scaffold of Salcède—100,000 at least. See, without counting those already on the Place de Grève, or who came there from different parts of Paris, the number of people here; and this is but one gate out of sixteen."

"100,000! that is much, Friard," replied M. Miton. "Be sure many people will follow my example, and not go to see this unlucky man quartered, for fear of an uproar."

"M. Miton, there will be none, I answer for it. Do you not think so, monsieur?" continued he, turning to the long-armed man.

"Do kings ever know when a tumult will take place?" replied the other, shrugging his shoulders with an air of pity.

"Oh, oh!" said M. Miton; "this man talks in a singular way. Do you know who he is, compère?"

"No."

"Then why do you speak to him? You are wrong. I do not think he likes to talk."

"Hush! he is listening."

"So much the better; perhaps he will answer. Then you think, monsieur," continued he, turning again towards him, "that there will be a tumult?"

"I did not say so."

"No; but I believe you think so."

"And on what do you found your surmise, M. Friard?"

"Why, he knows me!"

"Have I not named you two or three times?" said M. Miton.

"Ah! true. Well, since he knows me, perhaps he will answer. Now, monsieur, I believe you agree with me, or else would be there, while on the contrary, you are here."

"But you, M. Friard, since you think the contrary of what you think I think, why are you not at the Place de Grève? I thought the spectacle would have been a joyful one to all friends of the king. Perhaps you will reply that you are not friends of the king, but of MM. de Guise, and that you are waiting here for the Lorraines, who they say are about to enter Paris in order to deliver M. de Salcède."

"No, monsieur," replied the little man, visibly frightened at this suggestion; "I wait for my wife, Nicole Friard, who has gone to take twenty-four tablecloths to the priory of the Jacobins, having the honour to be washerwoman to Dom. Modeste Gorenflot, the Abbé."

"Look, compère," cried Miton, "at what is passing."

M. Friard, following the direction of his friend's finger, saw them closing yet another door, while a party of Swiss placed themselves before it. "How! more barriers!" cried he.

"What did I tell you?" said Miton.

At the sight of this new precaution, a long murmur of astonishment and some cries of discontent proceeded from the crowd.

"The Lorraines! the Lorraines!" cried a voice in the midst of this tumult.

"Oh!" cried Miton, trembling, "let us fly."

"Fly! and where?" said Friard.

"Into this inclosure," answered Miton, tearing his hands by seizing the thorns of the hedge.

While M. Miton was vainly trying to climb the hedge, and M. Friard to find an opening through which to push himself, their neighbour quietly opened his long legs and strode over the hedge with as much ease as one might have leaped it on horseback. M. Miton imitated him at last after much detriment to his hands and clothes; but poor Friard could not succeed, in spite of all his efforts, till the stranger, stretching out his long arms, and seizing him by the collar of his doublet, lifted him over.

"Ah! monsieur," said he, when he felt himself on the ground, "on the word of Jean Friard, you are a real Hercules; your name, monsieur? the name of my deliverer?"

"I am called Briquet—Robert Briquet, monsieur."

"You have saved me, M. Briquet—my wife will bless you. But àpropos; mon Dieu! she will be stifled in this crowd. Ah! cursed Swiss, only good to crush people!"

As he spoke, he felt a heavy hand on his shoulder, and, looking round and seeing that it was a Swiss, he took to flight, followed by Miton. The other man laughed quietly, then turning to the Swiss said:—

"Are the Lorraines coming?"

"No."

"Then why do they close the door? I do not understand it."

"There is no need that you should," replied the Swiss, laughing at his own wit.

## CHAPTER II

### WHAT PASSED OUTSIDE THE PORTE ST. ANTOINE

One of the groups was formed of a considerable number of citizens. They surrounded four or five of a martial appearance, whom the closing of the doors annoyed very much, as it seemed, for they cried with all their might: "The door! the door!"

Robert Briquet advanced towards this group, and began to cry also: "The door! the door!"

One of the cavaliers, charmed at this, turned towards him and said: "Is it not shameful, monsieur, that they should close the gates in open day, as though the Spaniards or the English were besieging Paris?"

Robert Briquet looked attentively at the speaker, who seemed to be about forty-five years of age, and the principal personage in the group. "Yes, monsieur," replied he, "you are right; but may I venture to ask what you think their motive is for these precautions?"

"Pardieu! the fear they have lest some one should eat their Salcède."

"Diable!" said a voice, "a sad meal."

Robert Briquet turned towards the speaker, whose voice had a strong Gascon accent, and saw a young man from twenty to twenty-five, resting his hand on the crupper of the horse of the first speaker. His head was bare; he had probably lost his hat in the mêlée.

"But as they say," replied Briquet, "that this Salcède belongs to M. de Guise——"

"Bah! they say that!"

"Then you do not believe it, monsieur?"

"Certainly not," replied the cavalier, "doubtless, if he had, the duke would not have let him be taken, or at all events would not have allowed him to have been carried from Brussels to Paris bound hand and foot, without even trying to rescue him."

"An attempt to rescue him," replied Briquet, "would have been very dangerous, because, whether it failed or succeeded, it would have been an avowal, on the duke's part, that he had conspired against the Duc d'Anjou."

"M. de Guise would not, I am sure, have been restrained by such considerations; therefore, as he has not defended Salcède, it is certain that he is not one of his men."

"Excuse me, monsieur, if I insist, but it is not I who invent, for it appears that Salcède has confessed."

"Where? before the judges?"

"No, monsieur; at the torture."

"And what did he say?" cried the cavalier impatiently. "As you seem so well informed, what were his words?"

"I cannot certify that they were his words," replied Briquet, who seemed to take a pleasure in teasing the cavalier.

"Well, then, those they attribute to him."

"They assert that he has confessed that he conspired for M. de Guise."

"Against the king, of course?"

"No; against the Duc d'Anjou."

"If he confessed that——"

"Well?"

"Well, he is a poltroon!" said the cavalier, frowning.

"Bah!" interrupted the Gascon, "the boot and the thumb-screw, nonsense; if Salcède confessed that, he was a knave, and his patron another."

"You speak loudly, monsieur," said the cavalier.

"I speak as I please; so much the worse for those who dislike it."

"More calmly," said a voice at once soft and imperative, of which Briquet vainly sought the owner.

The cavalier seemed to make an effort over himself, and then said quietly to the Gascon: "Do you know him of whom you speak?"

"What do I care?"

"What!"

"Mayneville! Mayneville!" murmured the same voice.

"Yes, mordieu! what do I care?" continued the Gascon. "I came to Paris on business, and find the gates closed on account of this execution—that is all I care for."

At this moment there was a sound of trumpets. The Swiss had cleared the middle of the road, along which a crier proceeded, dressed in a flowered tunic, and bearing on his breast a scutcheon on which was embroidered the arms of Paris. He read from a paper in his hand the following proclamation:—

"This is to make known to our good people of Paris and its environs, that its gates will be closed for one hour, and that none can enter during that time; and this by the will of the King and the Mayor of Paris."

The crowd gave vent to their discontent in a long hoot, to which, however, the crier seemed indifferent. The officer commanded silence, and when it was obtained, the crier continued:—

"All who are the bearers of a sign of recognition, or are summoned by letter or mandate, are exempt from this rule. Given at the Hôtel of the Provost of Paris, 26th of October, 1585."

Scarcely had the crier ceased to speak, when the crowd began to undulate like a serpent behind the line of soldiers.

"What is the meaning of this?" cried all.

"Oh! it is to keep us out of Paris," said the cavalier, who had been speaking in a low voice to his companions. "These guards, this crier, these bars, and these trumpets are all for us; we ought to be proud of them."

"Room!" cried the officer in command; "make room for those who have the right to pass!"

"Cap de Bious! I know who will pass, whoever is kept

out!" said the Gascon, leaping into the cleared space. He walked straight up to the officer who had spoken, and who looked at him for some moments in silence, and then said:

" You have lost your hat, it appears, monsieur?"

" Yes, monsieur."

" Is it in the crowd?"

" No. I had just received a letter from my sweetheart, and was reading it, cap de Bious! near the river, about a mile from here, when a gust of wind carried away both my letter and my hat. I ran after the letter, although the button of my hat was a single diamond; I caught my letter, but my hat was carried by the wind into the middle of the river. It will make the fortune of the poor devil who finds it."

The officer shrugged his shoulders slightly, and said: " Have you a card?"

" Certainly I have one—or rather two."

" One is enough, if it be the right one."

" But it cannot be wrong—or, no, cap de Bious! Is it to M. de Loignac that I have the honour of speaking?"

" It is possible," said the officer coldly, and evidently not much charmed at the recognition.

" M. de Loignac, my compatriot?"

" I do not say no."

" My cousin!"

" Good! Your card?"

" Here it is;" and the Gascon drew out the half of a card, carefully cut.

" Follow me," said De Loignac, without looking at it, " and your companions, if you have any. We will verify the admissions."

The Gascon obeyed, and five other gentlemen followed him. The first was adorned with a magnificent cuirass, so marvellous in its work that it seemed as if it had come out of the hands of Benvenuto Cellini. However, as the make of the cuirass was somewhat old-fashioned, its magnificence attracted more laughter than admiration; and it is true that no other part of the costume of the individual in question corresponded with this magnificence. The second, who was lame, was followed by a grey-headed lackey, who looked like the precursor of Sancho Panza, as his master did of Don Quixote. The third carried a child of ten months old in his arms, and was followed by a woman, who kept a tight grasp of his leathern belt, while two other children, one four and the other five years old, held by her dress.

The fourth was attached to an enormous sword, and the

fifth, who closed the troop, was a handsome young man, mounted on a black horse. He looked like a king by the side of the others. Forced to regulate his pace by those who preceded him, he was advancing slowly, when he felt a sudden pull at the scabbard of his sword; he turned round, and saw that it had been done by a slight and graceful young man with black hair and sparkling eyes.

"What do you desire, monsieur?" said the cavalier.

"A favour, monsieur."

"Speak; but quickly, I pray you, for I am waited for."

"I desire to enter into the city, monsieur; an imperious necessity demands my presence there. You, on your part, are alone, and want a page to do justice to your appearance."

"Well?"

"Yes, I know you are not rich, M. Ernanton de Carmainges," said the young page. The cavalier started, but the lad went on, "therefore I do not speak of wages; it is you, on the contrary, who, if you grant what I ask, shall be paid a hundredfold for the service you will render me; let me enter with you, then, I beg, remembering that he who now begs, has often commanded." Then, turning to the group of which we have already spoken, the lad said: "I shall pass; that is the most important thing; but you, Mayneville, try to do so also if possible."

"It is not everything that you should pass," replied Mayneville; "it is necessary that he should see you."

"Make yourself easy; once I am through, he shall see me."

"Do not forget the sign agreed upon."

"Two fingers on the mouth, is it not?"

"Yes; success attend you."

"Well, monsieur page," said the man on the black horse, "are you ready?"

"Ventre de Biche!" said Robert Briquet; "what an arrival of Gascons."

## CHAPTER III

### THE EXAMINATION

The process of examination consisted in comparing the half card with another half in the possession of the officer.

The Gascon with the bare head advanced first.

"Your name?" said De Loignac.

"It is on the card."

"Never mind; tell it to me."

"Well, I am called Perducas de Pincornay."

Then, throwing his eyes on the card, M. de Loignac read: "Perducas de Pincornay, 26 October, 1585, at noon precisely. Porte St. Antoine."

"Very good; it is all right," said he, "enter. Now for you," said he to the second.

The man with the cuirass advanced.

"Your card?" said De Loignac.

"What! M. de Loignac, do you not know the son of your old friend, whom you have danced twenty times on your knee?"

"No."

"I am Pertinax de Montcrabeau," replied the young man, with astonishment. "Do you not know me now?"

"When I am on service, I know no one. Your card, monsieur?"

He held it out. "All right! pass," said De Loignac.

The third man approached, whose card was demanded in the same terms. The man plunged his hand into a little goatskin pouch which he wore, but in vain; he was so embarrassed by the child in his arms, that he could not find it.

"What the devil are you doing with that child?" asked De Loignac.

"He is my son, monsieur."

"Well, put your son down. You are married, then?"

"Yes, monsieur."

"At twenty?"

"They marry young among us; you ought to know that, M. de Loignac, who were married at eighteen."

"Oh!" thought De Loignac, "here is another who knows me."

"And why should he not be married?" cried the woman, advancing. "Yes, monsieur, he is married, and here are two other children who call him father, besides this great lad behind. Advance, Militor, and bow to M. de Loignac."

A lad of sixteen, vigorous and agile, with an incipient moustache, stepped forward.

"They are my wife's sons, monsieur."

"In Heaven's name, your card!" cried De Loignac.

"Lardille!" cried the Gascon to his wife, "come and help me."

Lardille searched the pouch and pockets of her husband.

The card was looked at and found all right, and the family passed on in the same order as before.

The fourth man advanced and gave his name as Chalabre. It was found correct, and he also entered.

Then came M. de Carmainges. He got off his horse and presented his card, while the page hid his face by pretending to adjust the saddle.

"The page belongs to you?" asked De Loignac.

"You see, he is attending to my horse."

"Pass, then."

"Quick, my master," said the page.

Behind these men the door was closed, much to the discontent of the crowd. Robert Briquet, meanwhile, had drawn near to the porter's lodge, which had two windows, one looking towards Paris, and the other into the country. From this post he saw a man, who, coming from Paris at full gallop, entered the lodge and said: "Here I am, M. de Loignac."

"Good. Where do you come from?"

"From the Porte St. Victor."

"Your number?"

"Five."

"The cards?"

"Here they are."

De Loignac took them, examined them, and wrote on a slate the number five. The messenger left, and two others appeared, almost immediately. One came from the Porte Bourdelle, and brought the number four, the other from the Porte du Temple, and announced six. Then came four others. The first from the Porte St. Denis, with the number five; the next from the Porte St. Jacques, with the number three; the third from the Porte St. Honoré, with the number eight; and the fourth from the Porte Montmartre, with the number four. Lastly came a messenger, from the Porte Bussy, who announced four. De Loignac wrote all these down, added them to those who had entered the Porte St. Antoine, and found the total number to be forty-five.

"Good!" said he. "Now open the gates, and all may enter."

The gates were thrown open, and then horses, mules, and carts, men, women, and children, pressed into Paris, at the risk of suffocating each other, and in a quarter of an hour all the crowd had vanished.

Robert Briquet remained until the last. "I have seen enough," said he; "would it be very advantageous to me to see M. Salcède torn in four pieces? No, pardieu! Besides, I have renounced politics; I will go and dine."

# CHAPTER IV

### HIS MAJESTY HENRI THE THIRD

M. Friard was right when he talked of 100,000 persons as the number of spectators who would meet on the Place de Grève and its environs, to witness the execution of Salcède.

The spectators who succeeded in reaching the Place saw the archers and a large number of Swiss and light horse surrounding a little scaffold raised about four feet from the ground. After the scaffold and the horses, what next attracted all looks was the principal window of the Hôtel de Ville, which was hung with red velvet and gold, and ornamented with the royal arms. This was for the king. Half-past one had just struck when this window was filled. First came Henri III., pale, almost bald, although he was at that time only thirty-five, and with a sombre expression, always a mystery to his subjects, who, when they saw him appear, never knew whether to say "Vive le Roi!" or to pray for his soul.

Behind the king came Catherine de Medicis, almost bowed by age, for she might be sixty-six or sixty-seven, but still carrying her head firm and erect, and darting bitter glances from under her thick eyebrows. At her side appeared the melancholy but sweet face of the queen, Louise de Torraine. Catherine came as a triumph, she as a punishment. Behind them came two handsome young men, brothers, the elder of whom smiled with wonderful beauty, and the younger with great melancholy. The one was Anne, Duc de Joyeuse, and the other Henri de Joyeuse, Comte de Bouchage. The people had for these favourites of the king none of the hatred which they had felt towards Maugiron, Quelus, and Schomberg.

Henri saluted the people gravely; then, turning to the young men, he said: "Anne, lean against the tapestry; it may last a long time."

"I hope so," said Catherine.

"You think then, that Salcède will speak, mother?"

"God will, I trust, give this confusion to our enemies."

Henri looked doubtful.

"My son," said Catherine, "do I not see some tumult yonder?"

"What clear sight you have! I believe you are right. I have such bad eyes, and yet I am not old. Yes, here comes Salcède."

"He fears," said Catherine; "he will speak."

"If he has strength," said the king. "See, his head falls about like that of a corpse."

"He is frightful," said Joyeuse.

The king heard nothing; he was all eyes. They were lifting Salcède from the car on to the scaffold, round which the archers had cleared a large space, so that it was distinctly visible to all eyes.

Salcède was about thirty-five years of age, strong and vigorous; and his pale features, on which stood drops of blood, were animated alternately by hope and anguish. He was no vulgar assassin; he was of good birth, and even distantly related to the queen, and had been a captain of some renown. Those bound hands had valiantly borne the sword, and that livid head, on which were depicted the terrors of death, had conceived great designs. Therefore, to many of the spectators, he was a hero; to others, a victim; some looked on him as an assassin; but the crowd seldom despises those very great criminals who are registered in the book of history as well as in that of justice. Thus they told, in the crowd, that Salcède was of a race of warriors; that his father had fought against the Cardinal de Lorraine, but that the son had joined with the Guises to destroy in Flanders the rising power of the Duc d'Anjou, so hated by the French.

At this moment, an usher, raising the tapestry of the royal tent, announced that the president Brisson and four councillors desired the honour of an instant's conversation with the king on the subject of the execution

"Good," said the king. "Mother, you will be satisfied."

"Sire, a favour," said Joyeuse.

"Speak, Joyeuse; and provided it be not the pardon of the criminal——"

"Sire, permit my brother and me to retire."

"If you will remain, Joyeuse, you will see that it is interesting."

"I do not doubt it, sire; I only think that the interest will be carried to a point that I cannot bear;" and he turned towards the door.

"Go, then," said Henri, sighing; "my destiny is to live alone."

"Quick! Du Bouchage," said Anne to his brother. "The king says yes now; but in five minutes he will say no."

"Thanks, my brother," said Bouchage; "I was as anxious as you to get away."

## CHAPTER V

### THE EXECUTION

The councillors entered.

" Well, gentlemen," said the king, " is there anything new?"

" Sire," replied the president, " we come to beg your majesty to promise life to the criminal; he has revelations to make, which, on this promise, we shall obtain."

" But have we not obtained them?"

" Yes, in part; is that enough for your majesty?"

" No," said Catherine; " and the king has determined to postpone the execution, if the culprit will sign a confession substantiating his depositions before the judge."

" Yes," said Henri, " and you can let the prisoner know this."

" Your majesty has nothing to add?"

" Only that there must be no variation in the confessions, or I withdraw my promise; they must be complete."

" Yes, sire; with the names of the compromised parties."

" With all the names."

" Even if they are of high rank?"

" If they were those of my nearest relations."

" It shall be as your majesty wishes."

" He will speak, sire," said the queen; " and your majesty will pardon him. See the foam on his lips."

" No," said Catherine; " he is seeking something. What is it?"

" Parbleu!" said Henri; " he seeks M. le Duc de Guise, M. le Duc de Parma, and my brother, the very Catholic king. Yes, seek, wait; do you believe that there is more chance of rescue on the Place de Grève than on the route from Flanders?"

Salcède had seen the archers sent off for the horses, and he understood that the order for punishment was about to be given, and it was then that he bit his lips till they were covered with blood, as the queen had remarked.

" No one," murmured he; " not one of those who had promised me help. Cowards! cowards!"

The horses were now seen making their way through the crowd, and creating everywhere an opening which closed immediately behind them. As they passed the corner of the Rue St. Vannerie, a handsome young man, whom we have seen before, was pushed forward impatiently by a young lad, apparently about seventeen. It was the Vicomte Ernanton de Carmainges and the mysterious page.

"Quick!" cried the page; "throw yourself into the opening, there is not a moment to lose."

"But we shall be stifled; you are mad, my little friend."

"I must be near," cried the page, imperiously. "Keep close to the horses, or we shall never arrive there."

"But before we get there, you will be torn to pieces."

"Never mind me, only go on."

"The horses will kick."

"Take hold of the tail of the last; a horse never kicks when you hold him so."

Ernanton gave way in spite of himself to the mysterious influence of this lad, and seized the tail of the horse, while the page clung to him. And thus, through the crowd, waving like the sea, leaving here a piece of a cloak, and there a fragment of a doublet, they arrived with the horses at a few steps from the scaffold.

"Have we arrived?" asked the young man, panting.

"Yes, happily!" answered Ernanton, "for I am exhausted."

"I cannot see."

"Come before me."

"Oh, no! not yet. What are they doing?"

"Making slip knots at the ends of the cords."

"And he—what is he doing?"

"Who?"

"The condemned."

"His eyes turn incessantly from side to side."

The horses were near enough to enable the executioner to tie the feet and hands of the criminal to the harness. Salcède uttered a cry when he felt the cord in contact with his flesh.

While this was passing, the page, seizing the hand of Ernanton, cried: "Monsieur, take me in your arms, I beg you, and raise me above the heads of the people who prevent me from seeing."

"Ah! you are insatiable, young man."

Ernanton raised him in his arms at this last appeal, and was somewhat astonished at the delicacy of the body he held. Just as Salcède had taken the pen, and looked round as we have said, he saw this young lad above the crowd, with two fingers placed on his lips. An indescribable joy spread itself instantaneously over the face of the condemned man, for he recognised the signal so impatiently waited for, and which announced that aid was near. After a moment's hesitation, however, he took the paper and began to write.

"He writes!" cried the crowd.

"He writes!" exclaimed Catherine.

"He writes!" cried the king, "and I will pardon him."

Suddenly Salcède stopped and looked again at the lad, who repeated the signal. He wrote on, then stopped to look once more; the signal was again repeated.

Salcède signed, with his eyes still fixed on the young man. "For the king alone," said he, and he gave the paper to the usher, though with hesitation.

"If you disclosed all," said Tanchon, "you are safe."

A strange smile strayed over the lips of Salcède. Ernanton, who was fatigued, wished now to put down the page, who made no opposition. With him disappeared all that had sustained the unfortunate man; he looked round wildly and cried:

"Well, come!"

No one answered.

"Quick! quick! the king holds the paper; he is reading!"

Still there was no response.

The king unfolded the paper.

"Thousand devils!" cried Salcède, "if they have deceived me! Yet it was she—it was really she!"

No sooner had the king read the first lines, than he called out indignantly: "Oh! the wretch!"

"What is it, my son?"

"He retracts all—he pretends that he confessed nothing; and he declares that the Guises are innocent of any plot!"

"But," said Catherine, "if it be true?"

"He lies!" cried the king.

"Well, then, if he will have it, order the horses to pull."

Henri, in anger, gave the sign. It was repeated, the cords were refastened, four men jumped on the horses, which, urged by violent blows, started off in opposite directions. A horrible cracking, and a terrible cry was heard. The blood was seen to spout from the limbs of the unhappy man, whose face was no longer that of a man but of a demon.

"Ah, heaven!" he cried; "I will speak, I will tell all. Ah! cursed duch——"

The voice had been heard above everything, but suddenly it ceased.

"Stop, stop," cried Catherine, "let him speak."

But it was too late; the head of Salcède fell helplessly on one side, he glanced once more to where he had seen the page, and then expired. Tanchon gave some rapid orders to his archers, who plunged into the crowd in the direction indicated by Salcède's glance.

"I am discovered!" said the page to Ernanton. "For pity's sake, aid me! they come, they come!"

"But who are you then?"

"A woman. Oh, save me! protect me!"

Ernanton turned pale; but generosity triumphed over fear. He placed his protégée before him, opened a path with blows, and pushed her towards the corner of the Rue du Mouton, towards an open door. Into this door she entered; and she seemed to have been expected, for it closed behind her. Ernanton had not even time to ask her name, or where he should find her again; but in disappearing she had made a sign full of promise.

Meanwhile, Catherine was standing up in her place, full of rage.

"My son," said she at last, "you would do well to change your executioner; he is a leaguer."

"What do you mean, mother?"

"Salcède suffered only one draw, and he is dead."

## CHAPTER VI

### THE BROTHERS

MM. de Joyeuse had, as we have seen, left this scene, and were walking side by side in the streets generally so populous but now deserted, for every one was in the Place de Grève. Henri seemed preoccupied and sad, and Anne was unquiet on account of his brother. He was first to speak.

"Well, Henri," said he, "where are you taking me?"

Henri took his brother's hand affectionately. "You are more than a confessor to me, my dear Anne—more than a father; you are my friend."

"Then, my friend, why, from so gay as you used to be, have I seen you become sad? and why, instead of going out by day, do you only go out at night?"

Henri hung his blond head sadly.

"Come," continued Anne, "we are quite alone here; have you anything to tell me?"

"Nothing, but that I love."

"Diable! that is not a very serious affair; I also am in love."

"She never spoke but once before me, and since then I have not heard the sound of her voice. She is a woman, tall and beautiful as a nymph, serious and grave as the angel Gabriel!"

"When did you meet her?"

"One day I followed a young girl to the church of La Gypecienne, and I entered a little garden close to it, where there is a stone seat under some trees. Do you know this garden, Anne?"

"No; but never mind—go on."

"It began to grow dark; I had lost sight of the young girl, and in seeking her I arrived at this seat. I saw a woman's dress, and held out my hands. 'Pardon, monsieur,' said the voice of a man whom I had not noticed, and he gently but firmly pushed me away."

"He dared to touch you, Henri?"

"Listen; he had his face hidden in a sort of frock, and I took him for a monk. Besides, he impressed me also by the polite manner of his warning; for, as he spoke, he pointed out to me the woman, whose white dress had attracted me, and who was kneeling before the seat as though it were an altar. It was towards the beginning of September that this happened; the air was warm, the flowers planted by friends around the tombs scattered their delicate perfume, and the moon, rising above the white clouds, began to shed her silver light over all. Whether it were the place, or her own dignity, I know not, but this woman seemed to me like a marble statue, and impressed me with a strange respect. I looked at her earnestly. She bent over the seat, enveloping it in her arms, placed her lips to it, and soon I saw her shoulders heave with such sobs as you never heard, my brother. As she wept she kissed the stone with ardour; her fears had troubled me, but her kisses maddened me."

"But by the Pope, it is she who is mad, to kiss a stone and sob for nothing."

"Oh, it was a great grief that made her sob, a profound love which made her kiss the stone. Only whom did she love? whom did she weep for? whom did she pray for? I know not."

"Did you not question this man?"

"Yes."

"What did he reply?"

"That she had lost her husband."

"Bah! as if people weep like that for a husband. Were you content with such an answer?"

"I was obliged to be content, for he would give me no other."

"Well, Henri?" said Anne, interested, in spite of himself.

"Oh! it is nearly finished, brother. Her servant whispered something to her, and she lowered her veil; doubtless he told her I was there, but she did not glance towards me. I saw her no more, and it seemed to me, when the veil concealed her face, as if the sky had become suddenly overshadowd—that it was no longer a living thing, but a shade escaped from the tomb, which was gliding silently before me. She went out of the garden, and I followed her; from time to time the man turned and saw me, for I did not hide myself; I had still the old habits in my mind—the old leaven in my heart."

"Well, and where does she live? You found her again?"

"Chance did it. Listen; it is really strange. I was going along the Rue de Bussy, a fortnight ago, about midnight; you know how strict the regulations are about fire; well, I saw, not only light in the windows of a house, but a real fire, which had broken out in the second story. I knocked at the door, and a man appeared at the window. 'You have fire in your house!' I cried. 'Silence! I beg; I am occupied in putting it out.' 'Shall I call the watch?' I asked. 'No! in Heaven's name, call no one!' 'But can I help you?' 'Will you? I shall be very grateful,' and he threw me the key out of the window.

"I mounted the stairs rapidly, and entered the room where the fire was burning; it was used as a chemist's laboratory, and in making I know not what experiments, an inflammable liquid had been spilled, which had ignited the floor. When I entered, the fire was almost got under. I looked at the man; a dreadful scar disfigured his cheek, and another his forehead; the rest of his face was hidden by a thick beard. 'I thank you, monsieur,' said he; 'but you see all is finished now; if you are as gallant a man as you seem, have the goodness to retire, for my mistress may return at any moment, and will be angry if she sees a stranger here.'

"The sound of his voice struck me instantly. I was about to cry: 'You are the man of La Gypecienne!' for you remember that I had not seen his face before, but only heard his voice, when suddenly a door opened, and a woman entered. 'What is the matter, Rémy, and why this noise?' she asked. Oh! my brother, it was she! more beautiful than ever, by the dying light of the fire. It was she!—the woman whose memory had ever lived in my heart. At the cry which I uttered the servant looked narrowly at me. 'Thanks monsieur,' said he again; 'you see the fire is out; go, I beg of you.'

"'My friend,' said I, 'you dismiss me very rudely.' 'Madame,' said he, 'it is he.' 'Who?' 'The young man we met in the garden, and who followed us home.' She turned towards me and said: 'Monsieur, I beg you to go.' I hesitated; I wished to speak, but my words failed me. I remained motionless and mute, gazing at her. 'Take care monsieur,' said the servant, sadly; 'you will force her to fly again.' 'Heaven forbid!' cried I; 'but how do I offend you, madame?' She did not reply; insensible, mute, and cold, as though she had not heard me, she turned, and I saw her disappear gradually in the shade."

"And is that all?"

"All; the servant led me to the door, saying: 'Forget, monsieur, I beg of you.' I fled, bewildered and half crazy, and since then I have gone every evening to this street, and, concealed in the angle of the opposite house, under the shade of a little balcony, I see, once in ten times, a light in her room; that is my life, my happiness."

"What happiness!"

"Alas! I should lose this, if I tried for more."

"But in acting thus, you lose all the amusements of the world."

"My brother," said Henri, with a sad smile, "I am happy thus."

"Not so, mordieu! One monk in a family is enough."

"No railleries, brother."

"You shall see her this evening."

"I!"

"Yes! Be under her balcony at eight o'clock."

"I am always there."

"Well, give me the address."

"Between the Porte Bussy and the Hôtel St. Denis, near the corner of the Rue des Augustins, and a few steps from a large inn, having for a sign, 'The Sword of the Brave Chevalier'."

"Very well, then; this evening at eight o'clock."

"But what do you intend to do?"

"You shall see: meanwhile, go home; put on your richest dress, and use your finest perfume, and I hope that you will enter the house to-night."

"May you be a true prophet, brother!"

"Well! I leave you for the present, for my lady-love waits for me; and I confess, that after your account, I prefer her to yours. Adieu! Henri, till the evening."

The brothers then pressed each other's hands, and separated.

## CHAPTER VII

### " THE SWORD OF THE BRAVE CHEVALIER "

During the conversation we have just related, night had begun to fall, enveloping the city with its damp mantle of fog.

Salcède dead, all the spectators were ready to leave the Place de Grève, and the streets were filled with people, hurrying towards their homes. Near the Porte Bussy, where we must now transport our readers, to follow some of their acquaintances, and to make new ones, a hum, like that in a bee-hive at sunset, was heard proceeding from a house tinted rose colour, and ornamented with blue and white pointings, which was known by the sign of "The Sword of the Brave Chevalier," and which was an immense inn, recently built in this new quarter.

About a month before the execution of Salcède, the host and hostess, all of whose rooms were then empty, were looking out of the window, sadly, and were watching the exercises of some soldiery on the Pré-aux-Clercs, when they saw an officer, followed by a single soldier, advancing towards their hotel.

He was a man of about thirty-five years of age, but he did not look more than twenty-eight, so carefully was he dressed. He was tall, with a fine countenance and a distinguished air.

" Ah! good!" said he, " a large room and not a single guest. But there must be something," he added, " either in your house or conduct that keeps people away."

" Neither, monsieur," replied Madame Fournichon; " only the place is new, and we choose our customers."

" Oh! very well."

" How many people can you lodge here?" asked the captain of the hostess.

" Thirty."

" That is not enough."

" We have often eighty soldiers here, on Sundays."

" And no crowd before the house—no spying by the neighbours?"

" Mon Dieu! no! our nearest neighbours are a worthy bourgeois, who meddles with no one, and a lady who lives so retired, that although she has been here for three weeks, I have not seen her."

" And in a month from to-day——"

" That will be the 26th of October."

" Precisely. Well, on that day I hire your inn."

" The whole of it?"

"Yes, the whole. I wish to give a surprise to some countrymen, officers—or at least—soldiers; they will be told to come here."

"But if it be a surprise——"

"Oh! if you are curious, or indiscreet——"

"No, no, monsieur," cried she.

M. Fournichon, who had heard what had passed, added: "Monsieur, you shall be master here; and all your friends will be welcome."

"I did not say my friends, I said countrymen," replied the officer, haughtily.

"But, monsieur, how shall I know these gentlemen?"

"That is true; parfandious! I forgot. Give me paper, light and wax."

When they were brought, the captain made a seal on the paper with a ring he had on his finger. "Do you see this figure?" said he.

"A beautiful woman."

"Yes; a Cleopatra. Well, each of these men will present a similar one, on which you will receive him. You will have further orders afterwards."

The captain then descended the stairs and rode off, leaving the Fournichons delighted with their thirty livres in advance.

## CHAPTER VIII

### THE GASCON

We dare not affirm that Dame Fournichon was as discreet as she had promised to be, for she interrogated the first soldier whom she saw pass, as to the name of the captain who had conducted the review. The soldier, more cautious than she, asked her why she wished to know.

"Well, my good woman, he who conducted the review is simply Monsieur le Duc Nogaret de Lavelette d'Epernon, peer of France, and colonel-general of infantry. What do you say to that?"

"That if it was he, he did me great honour."

"Did you hear him say 'parfandious'?"

"Oh! yes."

We may now judge if the 26th of October was impatiently expected. On the evening of the 25th a man entered, bearing a heavy bag, which he placed on Fournichon's table.

"It is the price of the repast ordered for to-morrow," said he.

"At how much a head?"

"At six livres."

" Will they have only one meal here?"

" That is all.

" Has the captain found them a lodging, then?"

" It appears so," said the messenger, who went, and declined to answer any more questions.

At last the much-desired day arrived; half-past twelve had just struck when some cavaliers stopped at the door of the hotel. One, who appeared to be their chief, came with two well-mounted lacqueys. Each of them produced the seal of Cleopatra's head, and were received with all sorts of courtesies, especially the young man with the lacqueys. Nevertheless, excepting this young man, they all seemed timid and preoccupied. Most of them dispersed, however, until supper-time, either to swell the crowd at the execution of Salcède, or to see Paris.

About two o'clock, others began to arrive. One man came in alone, without a hat, a cane in his hand, and swearing at Paris, where he said the thieves were so adroit that they had stolen his hat as he had passed through a crowd, without his being able to see who had taken it. However, he said, it was his own fault, for wearing a hat ornamented with such a superb diamond. At four o'clock, forty people had arrived.

" Is it not strange," said Fournichon to his wife, " they are all Gascons?"

" Well, what of that? The captain said they were all countrymen, and he is a Gascon. M. d'Epernon is from Toulouse."

" Then you still believe it was M. d'Epernon?"

" Did he not say three times the famous ' parfandious '?"

Very soon the five other Gascons arrived; the number of guests was complete. Never was such surprise painted on so many faces; for an hour nothing was heard but " saudioux," " mordioux!" and " cap de Bious!" and such noisy joy, that it seemed to the Fournichons that all Poitou and Languedoc were collected in their room. Some knew, and greeted each other.

" Is it not singular to find so many Gascons here?" asked one.

" No," replied Perducas de Pincornay, " the sign is tempting for men of honour."

" Ah! is it you?" said St. Maline, the gentleman with the lacqueys, " you have not yet explained to me what you were about to do, when the crowd separated us."

" What was that?" asked Pincornay, reddening.

" How it happens that I met you on the road between Angoulême and Angers without a hat, as you are now?"

"Ah! my hat had fallen. I sought for it, being my only resource, as I had come out without money."

"But how could your hat be a resource?"

"Saudioux! it was a great one, for I must tell you that the plume of this hat was fastened by a diamond clasp, that his Majesty the Emperor Charles V. gave to my grandfather, when, on his way from Spain to Flanders, he stopped at our castle."

"Ah! ah! and you have sold the clasp, and the hat with it. Then, my dear friend, you ought to be the richest of us all, and you should have bought another glove; your hands are not alike; one is as white as a woman's, and the other as black as a negro's."

"But listen; as I turned to seek my hat I saw an enormous crow seize hold of it."

"Of your hat!"

"Or rather of the clasp; attracted by the glitter, and in spite of my cries, he flew away with it, and I saw it no more. So that, overwhelmed by this double loss, I did not dare to return home, but came to seek my fortune in Paris."

"Good!" cried a third, "the wind has changed into a crow. I heard you tell M. de Loignac that the wind had carried it away while you were reading a letter from your mistress."

Several stifled laughs were heard.

"Ah! gentlemen," cried the Gascon, "do you laugh at me?"

They turned away to laugh again.

Perducas threw a glance around him, and saw a young man near the fire-place hiding his face in his hands. He thought it was to laugh, and, going up to him, struck him on the shoulder, saying:

"Eh! monsieur, if you laugh, at all events show your face."

The young man looked up; it was our friend Ernanton de Carmainges.

"I beg you will leave me alone," said he, "I was not thinking of you."

Pincornay turned away, grumbling; but, at this moment, an officer enterd.

"M. de Loignac!" cried twenty voices.

At this name, known through all Gascony, everyone rose and kept silence.

## CHAPTER IX

### M. DE LOIGNAC

"Supper!" cried M. de Loignac; "and from this moment let all be friends, and love each other like brothers."

"Hum!" said St. Maline.

"That would be difficult," added Ernanton.

"See," cried Pincornay, "they laugh at me because I have no hat, and they say nothing to M. Montcrabeau, who is going to sup in a cuirass of the time of the Emperor Pertinax, from whom it probably came. See what it is to have defensive arms."

"Gentlemen," cried Montcrabeau, "I take it off; so much the worse for those who prefer seeing me with offensive instead of defensive arms;" and he gave his cuirass to his lacquey, a man of about fifty years of age.

"Peace! peace!" cried De Loignac, "and let us go to table."

Meanwhile the lacquey whispered to Pertinax: "And am I not to sup? Let me have something, Pertinax, I am dying of hunger."

Pertinax, instead of being offended at this familiar address, replied: "I will try, but you had better see for something for yourself."

"Hum! that is not reassuring."

"Have you no money?"

"We spent our last crown at Sens."

"Diable! then try to sell something."

A few minutes after a cry was heard, in the street of "Old iron! who wants to sell old iron?"

Madame Fournichon ran to the door, while M. Fournichon placed the supper on the table, and to judge by its reception it must have been exquisite. As his wife did not return, however, the host asked a servant what she was doing.

"Oh, master," he replied, "she is selling all your old iron for new money."

"I hope not my cuirass and arms," said he, running to the door.

"No," said De Loignac, "it is forbidden to buy arms."

Madame Fournichon entered triumphantly.

"You have not been selling my arms?" cried her husband.

"Yes, I have."

"I will not have them sold."

"Bah! in time of peace; and I have got ten crowns instead of an old cuirass."

"Ten crowns! Samuel, do you hear?" said Pertinax, looking for his valet, but he was not to be seen.

"It seems to me that this man carries on a dangerous trade. But what does he do with them?"

"Sells them again by weight."

"By weight! and you say he gave you ten crowns—for what?"

"A cuirass and a helmet."

"Why, even if they weighed twenty pounds, that is half-a-crown a pound. This hides some mystery."

Voices rose, and the mirth grew loud with all, except Carmainges, who still thought of the mysterious page. He sat by M. de Loignac, who said to him:

"Here are a number of joyful people, and they do not know what for."

"Nor I, neither; but at least I am an exception."

"You are wrong, for you are one of those to whom Paris is a paradise."

"Do not laugh at me, M. de Loignac."

"I do not; I distinguished you at once, and that other young man also who looks so grave."

"Who?"

"M. de St. Maline."

"And why this distinction, if this question be not too curious?"

"I know you, that is all. You and he, and all here."

"Why?"

"Because a chief should know his soldiers."

"And all these men——"

"Will be my soldiers to-morrow."

"But I thought that M. d'Epernon——"

"Hush! do not pronounce that name here."

Then rising, M. de Loignac said: "Gentlemen, since chance unites here forty-five compatriots, let us empty a glass of wine to the prosperity of all."

This proposal gave rise to frantic applause. "They are almost all half drunk," said De Loignac; "it would be a good opportunity to make them repeat their histories, only time does not permit of it." Then he added aloud: "Hola! M. Fournichon, dismiss from the room all women, children, and lacqueys."

Lardille retired grumbling, but Militor did not move. "Did you not hear, M. Militor?" said De Loignac; "to the kitchen!"

There remained only the forty-five men, and M. de Loignac then said: "Now, gentlemen, each knows who called him to Paris. Good! that will do; do not call out his name. You know also that you have come to obey him."

"Yes, yes," they cried.

"Then, to begin; go quietly out of this hotel to the lodgings prepared for you."

"For all?" asked St. Maline.

"Yes, for all."

"We are all equal here," cried Perducas, whose limbs felt rather doubtful under him.

"Yes," replied De Loignac; "all are equal before the will of the master."

"Oh!" cried Carmainges, colouring; "I did not know that M. d'Epernon would be called my master."

"Wait, hot head! I did not tell you who was to be your master."

"No; but you said we should have one."

"Everyone has a master; and if you are too proud to acknowledge him we spoke of, you may look higher; I authorise you."

"The king!" murmured Carmainges.

"Silence!" said De Loignac. "But first will you do me the favour to read aloud this parchment."

Ernanton took it and read these words: "Order to M. de Loignac to take the command of the forty-five gentlemen whom I have sent to Paris with the consent of his Majesty.

"NOGARET DE LA VALETTE,
"Duc d'Epernon."

They all bowed at this.

"Thus," continued De Loignac, "you have to follow me at once; your equipages and servants will remain here, M. Fournichon will take care of them: we will send for them; but now, be quick! the boats are ready."

"The boats!" cried they.

"Certainly; to go to the Louvre, we must go by water."

"To the Louvre!" cried they, joyfully. "Cap de Bious! we are going to the Louvre."

De Loignac made them all pass before him, counting them as they went, and then conducted them to the place where three large boats were waiting for them.

## CHAPTER X

### THE PURCHASE OF CUIRASSES

As soon as the valet of Pertinax heard the words of Madame Fournichon, he ran after the dealer, but as it was night he was doubtless in a hurry, he had gone some little way and Samuel was obliged to call to him. Seeing that Samuel was laden with merchandise, he stopped.

"What do you want, my friend?" said he.

"Pardieu! I want to do a little business with you."

"Do you not know that it is forbidden to buy arms?"

Samuel thought it best to feign ignorance, and said: "I

know nothing; I have just arrived from Mont-de-Marsan."

"Oh! that is another thing; but how did you know that I bought arms?"

"I was at the door of 'The Brave Chevalier'."

"Well, come under that portico; it is too public here. Now, let me see this cuirass," said he, when they were there.

"It is so heavy."

"It is old and out of date."

"A work of art."

"I will give you six crowns."

"But look at the chasing."

"Of what use is the chasing, when I sell by weight?"

"The gilding alone is worth ten crowns——"

"Do not call out so loud."

"Oh! I am not afraid."

"Come, then, take ten crowns and begone."

"I told you the gold was worth more. Ah! you want to escape; I will call the guard," and he raised his voice.

At the noise, a window opposite was opened.

"Come," said the dealer; "I see I must give you what you want. Here are fifteen crowns; now go."

"That will do," said Samuel; "only these are for my master; I want something for myself."

The dealer half drew his dagger.

"Yes, yes, I see your dagger," said Samuel; "but I also see the figure in that balcony, watching you."

The dealer, white with terror, looked up, and saw a man who had witnessed the whole scene. "Oh!" said he, affecting to laugh; "you get all you want out of me: here is another crown. And may the devil take you," he added to himself.

"Thanks, my good friend," said Samuel, and he made off.

The dealer began to take up his wares and was also going, when the bourgeois opposite cried out:

"It seems, monsieur, that you buy armour."

"No, monsieur," said the unlucky dealer; "this was a mere chance."

"It is odd how I seem to know you."

"Know me!" cried the dealer, trembling.

"Look at this helmet," said the bourgeois, showing it from the window.

"You say you know me?" asked the dealer.

"Well, will you buy all my armour?"

"No, I only want the cuirass."

"That is odd, for if you buy and sell by weight, one sort of iron is as good as another."

"That is true, but I have preferences."

"What a catch!" thought Poulain, "learned, strong, bold, and rich!" Then he added aloud: "Well! let us enter," and he conducted Briquet to the door of the hotel. The court was full of guards and men wrapped in cloaks, and eight horses, saddled and bridled, waited in a corner; but there was not a light to be seen. Poulain whispered his name to the porter, and added: "I bring a good companion."

"Pass on."

"Take these to the magazine," said Poulain, handing the cuirasses to a soldier. "Now, I will present you," said he to Briquet.

"No, I am very timid. When I have done some work, I will present myself."

"As you please. Then wait here for me."

"What are we waiting for?" asked a voice.

"For the master," replied another.

At this moment, a tall man entered. "Gentlemen," said he, "I come in his name."

"Ah! it is M. de Mayneville," said Poulain.

"Ah, really!" said Briquet, making a hideous grimace, which quite altered him.

"Let us go, gentlemen," said M. de Mayneville, and he descended a staircase leading to a vault. All the others followed, and Briquet brought up the rear, murmuring:

"But the page! where the devil is the page?"


## CHAPTER XI

### STILL THE LEAGUE

At the moment when Robert Briquet was about to enter, he saw Poulain waiting for him.

"Pardon," said he, "but my friends do not know you, and decline to admit you to their councils till they know more of you."

"It is just, and I retire, happy to have seen so many brave defenders of the Holy Union."

"Shall I reconduct you?"

"No, I thank you, I will not trouble you."

"But perhaps they will not open for you; yet I am wanted."

"Have you not a password?"

"Yes."

"Then give it to me. I am a friend, you know."

"True. It is 'Parma and Lorraine!'"

"Thanks; now return to your friends."

Briquet took some steps as if to go out, and then stopped to

"Well, then, buy only the cuirass, or rather—now
again—buy nothing at all."

"What do you mean?"

"I mean that in these times everyone wants his arms.

"What! in perfect peace?"

"You enchant me!" cried the bourgeois, stretching
long arm over the balcony and seizing the hand of the de

"Then who the devil are you?" cried he, who felt his h
held as if in a vice.

"I am Robert Briquet, the terror of schismatics, the frie
of the Union, and a fierce Catholic; and you are Nichol
Gimbelot, the currier."

"No, no! good-bye."

"What! are you going?"

"Yes!" and he ran off.

But Robert Briquet was not a man to be foiled; he jumped
from his balcony and ran after him.

"You are mad!" said he. "If I were your enemy, I have
but to cry out, and the watch is in the next street; but you are
my friend, and now I know your name. You are Nicholas
Poulain, lieutenant to the provost of Paris. I knew it was
Nicholas something."

"I am lost!" murmured the man.

"No; you are saved. I will do more for the good cause
than ever you would; you have found a brother. Take one
cuirass, and I will take another; I give you my gloves and
the rest of my armour for nothing. Come on, and Vive
l'Union!"

"You accompany me?"

"I will help you to carry these cuirasses which are to
conquer the Philistines. Go on, I follow."

A spark of suspicion lingered in the soul of the lieutenant,
but he thought: "If he wished me ill, he would not have
acknowledged he knew me. Come on then!" he added aloud,
"if you will."

"To life or death!" cried Briquet, and he continued to talk
in this strain till they arrived near the Hôtel Guise, where
Nicholas Poulain stopped.

"I fancied it would be here," thought Briquet.

"Now," said Nicholas, with a tragic air, "there is still time
to retire before entering the lion's den."

"Bah! I have entered many. Et non intremuit medulla
mea!" exclaimed Briquet; "but pardon me, perhaps you do
not understand Latin?"

"Do you?"

"As you see."

B

BOOKMARK

THE FORTY-FIVE
GUARDSMEN

ALEXANDRE DUMAS

DAVID B C SCOTT

explore the locality. The result of his observations was that the vault ran parallel to the exterior wall, and terminated in a hall destined for the mysterious council from which he had been excluded. What confirmed him in this supposition was that he saw a light at a barred window, pierced in the wall, and guarded by a sort of wooden pipe, such as they placed at the windows of convents and prisons, to intercept the view from without, while the air was still admitted.

Briquet rapidly climbed on to the cornice which ran towards the window in question, and ran along the wall like a monkey, holding on with his hands and feet to the ornaments of the sculpture.

He then saw a great hall, lighted by a torch, and filled with armour of all sorts. There were enough pikes, swords, halberts, and muskets to arm four regiments. He gave less attention, however, to the arms than to the people engaged in distributing them, and his piercing eyes sought eagerly to distinguish their faces.

"Oh! oh!" thought he, "there is M. Crucé, little Brigard and Leclerc, who dares to call himself Bussy. Peste! the bourgeoisie is grandly represented; but the nobility—ah! M. de Mayneville presses the hand of Nicholas Poulain; what a touching fraternity! An orator, too!" continued he, as M. de Mayneville prepared to harangue the assembly.

Briquet could not hear a word, but he thought that he did not make much impression on his audience, for one shrugged his shoulders, and another turned his back. But at last they approached, seized his hand, and threw up their hats in the air. But though Briquet could not hear, we must inform our readers of what passed.

First, Crucé, Marteau, and Bussy had complained of the inaction of the Duc de Guise.

Marteau was spokesman, and said: "M. de Mayneville, you come on the part of M. le Duc de Guise, and we accept you as an ambassador; but the presence of the duke himself is indispensable. After the death of his glorious father, he, when only eighteen years of age, made all good Frenchmen join his project of the Union, and enrolled us under this banner. We have risked our lives, and sacrificed our fortunes, for the triumph of this sacred cause, according to our oaths, and yet, in spite of our sacrifices, nothing progresses—nothing is decided. Take care, M. de Mayneville, Paris will grow tired, and then what will you do?"

This speech was applauded by all the leaguers.

M. de Mayneville replied: "Gentlemen, if nothing is decided, it is because nothing is ripe. Consider our situation:

M. de Duc and his brother the cardinal are at Nancy—
the one is organising an army to keep in check the
Huguenots of Flanders, whom M. d'Anjou wishes to oppose
to us, the other is expediting courier after courier to the
clergy of France and to the Pope, to induce them to adopt
the Union. The Duc de Guise knows, what you do not, that
the old alliance between the Duc d'Anjou and the Béarnais is
ready to be renewed, and he wishes, before coming to Paris,
to be in a position to crush both heresy and usurpation."

"They are everywhere where they are not wanted," said
Bussy. "Where is Madame de Montpensier, for instance?"

"She entered Paris this morning."

"No one has seen her."

"Yes, monsieur."

"Who was it?"

"Salcède."

"Then, how did she pass?"

"In her own fashion. Something took place at the gates of
Paris this morning, gentlemen, of which you appear to be
ignorant. The orders were to open only to those who brought
a card of admission—signed by whom I know not. Immediately before us five or six men, some of whom were poorly
clothed, passed with these cards, before our eyes. Now, who
were those men? What were the cards? Reply, gentlemen
of Paris, who promised to learn everything concerning your
city."

Thus Mayneville, from the accused, became the accuser,
which is the great art of an orator.

"Were they soldiers?"

"There were but two swords among the six; I think they
were Gascons. This concerns you, M. Poulain, to find out.
But to return to the League. Salcède, who had betrayed us,
and would have done so again, not only did not speak, but
retracted on the scaffold—thanks to the duchess, who, in the
suite of one of these card-bearers, had the courage to penetrate the crowd even to the place of execution, and made
herself known to Salcède, at the risk of being pointed out.
At this sight Salcède stopped his confession, and an instant
after, the executioner stopped his repentance. Thus, gentlemen, you have nothing to fear as to our enterprise in
Flanders; this secret is buried in the tomb."

It was this last speech which had so pleased all the conspirators. Their joy seemed to annoy Briquet; he slipped
down from his place, and returning to the court, said to the
porter: "Parma and Lorraine." The gate was opened, and
he left.

## CHAPTER XII

### THE CHAMBER OF HIS MAJESTY HENRI III

In a great room at the Louvre sat Henri, pale and unquiet. Since his favourites, Schomberg, Quelus and Maugiron had been killed in a duel, St. Mégrin had been assassinated by M. de Mayenne, and the wounds left by their deaths were still fresh and bleeding. The affection he bore his new favourites was very different from what he had felt for the old. He had overwhelmed d'Epernon with benefits, but he only loved him by fits and starts, and at certain times he even hated him, and accused him of cowardice and avarice.

The king knew his men well, for he was remarkably clear-sighted; and though often betrayed, was never deceived. But ennui was the curse of his life; he was ennuyé now, and was wondering if anyone would come and amuse him, when M. le Duc d'Epernon was announced. Henri was delighted.

"Ah! good evening, duke; I am enchanted to see you. Why were you not present at the execution of Salcède?—I told you there would be room in my box."

"Sire, I was unable to avail myself of your majesty's kindness."

"Unable?"

"Yes, sire; I was busy."

"Well, duke, do not look gloomy; I am sad enough already. Do be gay."

"Gaiety cannot be forced, sire."

The king struck the table angrily. "You are a bad friend," said he; "I lost all, when I lost my former ones."

The king looked at him with an expression which he well understood.

"Ah! your majesty reproaches me with your benefits," said he, "but I do not reproach you with my devotion."

"Lavalette," cried Henri, "you make me sad; you who are so clever, and could so easily make me joyful. It is not your nature to fight continually, like my old favourites; but you are facetious and amusing, and give good counsel. You know all my affairs, like that other humble friend, with whom I never experienced a moment's ennui."

"Of whom does your majesty speak?"

"Of my poor jester, Chicot. Alas! where is he?"

D'Epernon rose, piqued. "Your majesty's souvenirs, to-day, are not very amusing for other people," said he.

"Why so?"

" Your majesty, without intending it, perhaps, compared me to Chicot, which is not very flattering."

" You are wrong, d'Epernon; I could only compare to Chicot a man who loves me, and whom I love."

" It was not to resemble Chicot, I suppose, that your majesty made me a duke?"

" Chicot loved me, and I miss him; that is all I can say. Oh! when I think that in the same place where you now are have been all those young men, handsome, brave, and faithful —that there, on that very chair on which you have placed your hat, Chicot has slept more than a hundred times——"

" Perhaps that was very amusing," interrupted the duke, " but certainly not very respectful."

" Alas! he has now neither mind nor body."

" What became of him?"

" He died, like all who loved me."

" Well, sire, I think he did well to die; he was growing old, and I have heard that sobriety was not one of his virtues. Of what did he die—indigestion?"

" Of grief."

" Oh! he told you so, to make you laugh once more."

" I beg, duke, that you will not laugh at those who loved me, and whom I loved."

" Oh! sire, I do not desire to laugh, but just now you reproached me with want of gaiety, parfandious!"

" Well, now I am in the mood to hear bad news, if you have any to tell. Luckily I have strength to bear it, or I should be dead ten times a day."

" Which would not displease certain people we know."

" Oh! against them I have the arms of my Swiss."

" I could find you a better guard than that."

" What is it?"

" Will your majesty be so good as to accompany me to the old buildings of the Louvre?"

" What shall I see there?"

" Oh! come first."

" It is a long way, duke."

" We can go in five minutes through the galleries."

" D'Epernon——"

" Well, sire?"

" If what you are about to show me be not worth seeing, take care."

" I answer for it, sire."

" Come, then," said the king, rising.

The duke took his cloak, presented the king's sword to him, then, taking a light, preceded his majesty.

## CHAPTER XIII

### THE DORMITORY

In less than five minutes they arrived at their destination.
The duke took out a key, and, after crossing a court, opened
an arched door, the bottom of which was overgrown with
long grass. They went along a dark corridor, and then up a
staircase to a room, of which d'Epernon had also the key.
He opened the door, and showed the king forty-five beds,
and in each of them a sleeper.

The king looked at all this with a troubled curiosity.
" Well," said he, " who are these people?"

" People who sleep to-night, but will not do so to-morrow
night."

" Explain yourself. Are these your friends?"

" Chosen by me, sire; intrepid guards, who will not quit
your majesty, and who, gentlemen all, will be able to go
wherever your majesty goes, and will let no one approach
you."

" And you thought of this, d'Epernon?"

" I, alone, sire."

" We shall be laughed at."

" No, we shall be feared."

" But they will ruin me?"

" How can a king be ruined?"

" I cannot pay my Swiss!"

" Look at these men, sire; do you think they would be very
expensive to keep?"

" Stay, there is one speaking in his sleep; let us listen."

Indeed, one of the gentlemen called out: " If you are a
woman, fly!"

The king approached him softly. " Ah! ah!" said he, " he
is a gallant."

" What do you think of him, sire?"

" His face pleases me, and he has white hands and a well-
kept beard."

" It is Ernanton de Carmainges, a fine fellow, who is
capable of much."

" He has left behind him some love, I suppose, poor fellow.
But what a queer figure his next neighbour is."

" Ah! that is M. de Chalabre. If he ruins your majesty, it
will not be without enriching himself, I answer for it."

" And that one, with such a sombre air; he does not seem
as though he dreamed of love."

" What number, sire?"

" Number 12."

" M. de St. Maline, a brave fellow, with a heart of bronze."

" Well, Lavalette, you have had a good idea."

" Then your majesty accepts?"

" There is only one difficulty, duke."

" What is it?"

" Want of money."

" Sire, I have found a method.   Six months ago a tax was levied on shooting and fishing."

" Well?"

" The first payment produced 65,000 crowns, which have not yet been disposed of."

" I destined it for the war, duke."

" The first interest of the kingdom is the safety of the king."

" Well; there still would remain 20,000 crowns for the army."

" Pardon, sire, but I had disposed of them, also."

" Ah!"

" Yes, sire; your majesty had promised me money."

" Ah! and you give me a guard to obtain it."

" Oh! sire.   But look at them; will they not have a good effect?"

" Yes, when dressed, they will not look bad.   Well, so be it."

" Well, then, sire, I have a favour to ask."

" What is it, then?"

" I desire the command of these forty-five gentlemen."

" What! you wish to march at their head?"

" No; I should have a deputy; only I desire that they should know me as their head."

" Well, you shall have it.   But who is to be your deputy?"

" M. de Loignac, sire."

" Ah! that is well."

" Then it is decided?"

" Yes; let it be as you wish."

" Then I will go at once to the treasurer, and get my forty-five purses."

" Good; then I will return."

" Content, sire?"

" Tolerably."

" Well guarded, at all events."

" By men who sleep."

" They will not sleep to-morrow, sire."

## CHAPTER XIV

### THE SHADE OF CHICOT

The king, as we have said, was never deceived as to the character of his friends; he knew perfectly well that d'Epernon was working for his own advantage, but as he expected to have had to give and receive nothing in return, whereas he had got forty-five guards, he had thought it a good idea.

"These men are doubtless brave, and will be perhaps very devoted," thought he; "and forty-five swords always ready to leap from their scabbards are a grand thing."

This thought brought to his mind the other devoted swords that he regretted so bitterly. He became sad again, and inquired for Joyeuse. They replied that he had not returned.

"Alas! he is always late; but whatever be the hour, bring him here."

The servants extinguished the candles and lighted a lamp of essences, which gave a pale blue flame, that the king liked. Henri was tired and soon slept, but not for long; he awoke, thinking he heard a noise in the room.

"Joyeuse," he asked; "is it you?"

No one replied. The light burned dim, and only threw faint circles on the ceiling of carved oak.

"Alone, still!" murmured the king. "Mon Dieu! I am alone all my life, as I shall be after death."

"'Alone after death;' that is not certain," said a powerful voice near the bed.

The king started up and looked round him in terror. "I know that voice," cried he.

"Ah! that is lucky," replied the voice.

"It is like the voice of Chicot."

"You burn, Henri; you burn."

Then the king, getting half out of bed, saw a man sitting in the very chair which he had pointed out to d'Epernon.

"Heaven protect me!" cried he; "it is the shade of Chicot."

"Ah! my poor Henriquet, are you still so foolish?"

"Then you are Chicot, himself," cried the king, joyfully.

"Do not be too sure."

"Then you are not dead, my poor Chicot?"

"Dead to some—alive to others."

"And to me?"

"Dead."

"Why dead to me?"

"It is easy to comprehend that you are not the master here."

"Chicot!"

"Do not be angry, or I shall be so, also."

"Speak then, my friend," said the king, fearful that Chicot would vanish.

"Well, I had a little affair to settle with M. de Mayenne, you remember?"

"Perfectly."

"I settled it; I beat this valiant captain without mercy. He sought for me to hang me; and you who, I thought, would protect me, abandoned me, and made peace with him. Then I declared myself dead and buried by the aid of my friend Gorenflot, so that M. de Mayenne had ceased to search for me."

"What a frightful courage you had, Chicot; did you not know the grief your death would cause me?"

"I have never lived so tranquilly as since the world thought me dead."

"Chicot, my head turns; you frighten me—I know not what to think."

"Well! settle something."

"I think that you are dead and——"

"Come, come," cried Chicot; "'you have only to touch me to be convinced."

"But how did you come?"

"Why, I have still the key that you gave me, and which I hung round my neck to enrage your gentlemen, and with this I entered."

"By the secret door, then?"

"Certainly."

"Well, Chicot, I take you now under my protection, and wish that you should be resuscitated and appear openly."

"What folly!"

"I will protect you, on my royal word."

"Bah! I have better than that."

"What?"

"My hole, where I remain."

"I forbid it," cried the king, jumping out of bed.

"Henri, you will catch cold; go back to bed, I pray."

"You are right, but you exasperated me. How, when I have enough guards, Swiss, Scotch, and French, for my owr defence, should I not have enough for yours?"

"Well, I have more troops than you."

"You have troops?"

"Why not?"

" What are they?"

" You shall hear. First, all the army that MM. de Guise are raising in Lorraine."

" Are you mad?"

" No; a real army—at least six thousand men."

" But how can you, who fear M. de Mayenne so much, be defended by the soldiers of M. de Guise?"

" Because I am dead."

" Again this joke!"

" No; I have changed my name and position."

" What are you then?"

" I am Robert Briquet, merchant and leaguer."

" You a leaguer?"

" A devoted one, so that I keep away from M. de Mayenne. I have, then, for me, first, the army of Lorraine—6,000 men; remember that number."

" I listen."

" Then, at least one hundred thousand Parisians."

" Famous soldiers!"

" Sufficiently so to annoy you much: 6,000 and 100,000 are 106,000; then there is the Pope, the Spaniards, M. de Bourbon, the Flemings, Henri of Navarre, the Duc d'Anjou——"

" Have you done?" interrupted Henri, impatiently.

" There still remain three classes of people."

" What are they?"

" First the Catholics, who hate you because you only three parts exterminated the Huguenots; then the Huguenots, who hate you because you have three parts exterminated them; and the third party is that which desires neither you, nor your brother, nor M. de Guise, but your brother-in-law, Henri of Navarre."

" Provided that he abjure. But these people of whom you speak are all France."

" Just so. These are my troops as a leaguer; now add, and compare."

" You are joking, are you not, Chicot?"

" Is it a time to joke, when you are alone, against all the world?"

Henri assumed an air of royal dignity. " Alone I am," said he, " but at the same time I alone command. You show me an army, but where is the chief? You will say, M. de Guise; but do I not keep him at Nancy? M. de Mayenne, you say yourself, is at Soissons, the Duc d'Anjou is at Brussels, and the King of Navarre at Pau; so that if I am alone, I am free. I am like a hunter in the midst of a plain, waiting to see his prey come within his reach."

" On the contrary; you are the game whom the hunters track to his lair."

" Chicot!"

" Well! let me hear whom you have seen come."

" A woman."

" My sister Margot?"

" No; the Duchesse de Montpensier."

" She! at Paris?"

" Mon Dieu! yes."

" Well, if she be; I do not fear women."

" True; but she comes as the avant courier to announce the arrival of her brother."

" Of M. de Guise?"

" Yes."

" And you think that embarrasses me?  Give me ink and paper."

" What for?  To sign an order for M. de Guise to remain at Nancy?"

" Exactly; the idea must be good, since you had it also."

" Execrable, on the contrary."

" Why?"

" As soon as he receives it he will know he is wanted at Paris, and he will come."

The king grew angry.  " If you only returned to talk like this," said he, " you had better have stayed away."

" What would you have?  Phantoms never flatter.  But be reasonable; why do you think M. de Guise remains at Nancy?"

" To organise an army."

" Well; and for what purpose does he destine this army?"

" Ah, Chicot! you fatigue me with all these questions."

" You will sleep better after it.  He destines this army——"

" To attack the Huguenots in the north——"

" Or rather, to thwart your brother of Anjou, who has called himself Duke of Brabant, and wishes to build himself a throne in Flanders, for which he solicits your aid——"

" Which I never sent."

" To the great joy of the Duc de Guise.  Well, if you were to feign to send this aid—if they only went half way——"

" Ah! yes, I understand; M. de Guise would not leave the frontier."

" And the promise of Madame de Montpensier that her brother would be here in a week——"

" Would be broken."

" You see, then?"

" So far, good; but in the south——"

" Ah, yes; the Béarnais——"

" Do you know what he is at?"

" No."

" He claims the towns which were his wife's dowry," said the king.

" Insolent! to claim what belongs to him."

" Cahors, for example; as if it would be good policy to give up such a town to an enemy."

" No; but it would be like an honest man."

" But to return to Flanders. I will send some one to my brother—but whom can I trust? Oh! now I think of it, you shall go, Chicot."

" I, a dead man?"

" No; you shall go as Robert Briquet."

" As a bagman?"

" Do you refuse?"

" Certainly."

Henri was about to reply, when the door opened and the Duc de Joyeuse was announced.

" Ah! there is your man," said Chicot; " who could make a better ambassador?"

Chicot then buried himself in the great chair, so as to be quite invisible in the dim light. M. de Joyeuse did not see him. The king uttered a cry of joy on seeing his favourite, and held out his hand.

" Sit down, Joyeuse, my child," said he; " how late you are."

" Your majesty is very good," answered Joyeuse, approaching the bed, on which he sat down.

## CHAPTER XV

### THE DIFFICULTY OF FINDING A GOOD AMBASSADOR

Chicot was hidden in his great chair, and Joyeuse was half lying on the foot of the bed in which the king was bolstered up, when the conversation commenced.

" Well, Joyeuse, I want your brother."

" He, like myself, is at your majesty's service."

" I wish to send him a little mission."

" Out of Paris?"

" Yes."

" In that case, it is impossible."

" How so?"

" Du Bouchage cannot go away just now."

The king looked astonished. "What do you mean?" said he.

"Sire," said Joyeuse quietly, "it is the simplest thing possible. Du Bouchage is in love, but he had carried on his negotiations badly, and everything was going wrong; the poor boy was growing thinner and thinner."

"Indeed," said the king, "I have remarked it."

"You understand, sire, that no sooner had he made me his confidant, than I undertook to save him."

"So that——"

"So that already the cure commences."

"What, is he less in love?"

"No; but he has more hope of making her so. For the future, instead of sighing with the lady, we mean to amuse her in every possible way. To-night I stationed thirty Italian musicians under her balcony."

"Ah! ma foi! music would not have amused me when I was in love with Madame de Condé."

"Imagine that this evening, after having given my lesson to Du Bouchage, I went to see her, with my head full of his love story, and, believing myself almost as much in love as he, I found a trembling frightened woman, and thinking I had disturbed her somehow, I tried to reassure her, but it was useless. I interrogated her, but she did not reply. I tried to embrace her, and she turned her head away. I grew angry, and we quarrelled; and she told me she should never be at home to me any more."

"Poor Joyeuse; what did you do?"

"Pardieu, sire! I took my hat and cloak, bowed, and went out, without once looking back."

"Bravo, Joyeuse! it was courageous."

A second noise came from the chair; one might have thought the dog was laughing at the words of Joyeuse.

Joyeuse bowed stiffly, and said: "Your orders, sire?"

The king began to melt. "Go," said he, "to Rouen, where I wish you to embark, unless you prefer going by land to Brussels."

Joyeuse did not answer, but only bowed.

"Do you prefer the land route, duke?" asked Henri.

"I have no preference when I have an order to execute, sire."

"Monsieur," replied the king, angry again, "you will go then to Rouen; you will go on board your ship, and will take the garrisons of Caudebec, Harfleur, and Dieppe, which I will replace afterwards. You will put them on board six transports, and place them at the service of my brother, who expects aid from me."

"My commission, if you please, sire."

"And since when have you been unable to act by virtue of your rank as admiral?"

"I only obey, sire; and, as much as possible, avoid responsibility."

Joyeuse bowed and turned to the door. The king's heart misgave him. "What!" cried he, "not even the courtesy of an adieu? You are not polite, but that is a common reproach to naval people."

"Pardon me, sire, but I am a still worse courtier than I am a seaman;" and, shutting the door violently, he went out.

"See how those love me, for whom I have done so much," cried the king; "ungrateful Joyeuse!"

"Well, are you going to recall him?" said Chicot, advancing. "Because, for once in your life, you have been firm, you repent it."

"Then if I wish to send you somewhere you will not object to go?"

"Not only I do not object, but I request it."

"Will you go to Navarre?"

"I would go to the devil."

"You are joking."

"No; since my death I joke no more."

"But you refused just now to quit Paris."

"I was wrong, and I repent. I will go to Navarre, if you will send me."

"Doubtless; I wish it."

"I wait your orders, gracious prince," said Chicot, assuming the same attitude as Joyeuse.

"But you do not know if the mission will suit you. I have certain projects of embroiling Margot with her husband."

"Divide to reign was the A B C of politics one hundred years ago."

"Then you have no repugnance?"

"It does not concern me; do as you wish. I am ambassador; that is all; and as long as I am inviolable, that is all I care for."

"Well, I will give you a letter."

"Give it me, then."

"But you must know my intentions concerning Margot and her husband. My letter will make a noise, and they will question you; you must be able to reply."

"Mon Dieu!" said Chicot, shrugging his shoulders, "how obtuse you are, great king. Do you think I am going to

carry a letter a hundred and fifty leagues without knowing
what is in it? Be easy, the first halt I make I shall open your
letter and read it. What! have you sent ambassadors for ten
years to all parts of the world, and know no better than
that? Come, rest in peace, and I will return to my solitude."

Henri looked at him in astonishment again.

"Ah! you did not expect that," said Chicot. "Well, till
to-morrow, when I or my messenger will come——"

"How shall I know your messenger when he arrives?"

"He will say he comes from the shade." And Chicot
disappeared as rapidly as almost to reawaken the king's
fears as to whether he were a shade or not.


## CHAPTER XVI

### THE SERENADE

From the Louvre Chicot had not far to go to his home.
He went to the bank of the Seine and got into a little boat
which he had left there.

He soon arrived at the opposite bank, where he fastened
his boat. On entering the Rue Des Augustins, he was struck
by the sound of instruments and voices in the street at that
late hour.

"Is there a wedding here?" thought he, "I have not long
to sleep, and now this will keep me awake."

As he advanced, he saw a dozen flambeaux carried by
pages, while thirty musicians were playing on different
instruments. The band was stationed before a house, that
Chicot, with surprise, recognised as his own.

"Pardon me, my friend," said he, addressing himself to a
torch-bearer, "but can you tell me, if you please, whom all
this music is for?"

"For the bourgeois who lives there," replied he, pointing
out to Chicot his own house.

"Decidedly it is for me!" thought he. "Whom do you
belong to?" he asked.

"To the bourgeois who lives there."

"Ah! they not only come for me, but they belong to me—
still better. Well! we shall see," and piercing through the
crowd, he opened his door, went upstairs, and appeared at
his balcony, in which he placed a chair and sat down.

"Gentlemen," said he, "are you sure there is no mistake?"
is all this really for me?"

"Are you M. Robert Briquet?"

" Himself."

" Then we are at your service, monsieur," said the leader of the band, giving the sign to recommence.

" Certainly it is unintelligible," thought Chicot. He looked around; all the inhabitants of the street were at their windows, excepting those of the opposite house, which, as we have said, remained dark and quiet. But on glancing downwards, he saw a man wrapped in a dark cloak, and who wore a black hat with a red feather, leaning against the portico of his own door, and looking earnestly at the opposite house.

The leader of the band just then quitted his post and spoke softly to this man, and Chicot instantly guessed that here lay all the real interest in the scene. Soon after, a gentleman on horseback, followed by two squires, appeared at the corner of the street, and pushed his way through the crowd, while the music stopped.

" M. de Joyeuse," murmured Chicot, who recognised him at once.

The cavalier approached the gentleman under the balcony.

" Well! Henri," said he, " what news?"

" Nothing, brother."

" Nothing?"

" No; she has not even appeared."

" They have not made noise enough."

" They have roused all the neighbourhood."

" They did not cry as I told them, that it was all in honour of this bourgeois."

" They cried it so loud, that there he is, sitting in his balcony, listening."

." And she has not appeared?"

" Neither she, nor anyone."

" The idea was ingenious, however, for she might, like the rest of the people, have profited by the music given to her neighbour."

" Ah! you do not know her, brother."

" Yes, I do; or at all events I know women, and as she is but a woman, we will not despair."

" Ah! you say that in a discouraged tone, brother."

" Not at all; only give the bourgeois his serenade every night."

" But she will go away."

" Not if you do not speak to her, or seem to be doing it on her account, and remain concealed. Has the bourgeois spoken?"

" Yes, and he is now speaking again."

" Hold your tongue up there, and go in," cried Joyeuse, out

of humour. "Diable! you have had your serenade, so keep quiet."

"My serenade! that is just what I want to know the meaning of; to whom is it addressed?"

"To your daughter."

"I have none."

"To your wife, then."

"Thank God, I am not married."

"Then to yourself—and if you do not go in——" cried Joyeuse, advancing with a menacing air.

"Ventre de biche! but if the music be for me——"

"Old fool!" growled Joyeuse. "If you do not go in and hide your ugly face, they shall break their instruments over your head."

"Let the man alone, brother," said Henri, "the fact is, he must be very much astonished."

"Oh! but if we get up a quarrel, perhaps she will look to see what is the matter; we will burn this house down, if necessary."

"No, for pity's sake, brother, do not let us force her attention; we are beaten, and must submit."

Chicot, who heard all, was mentally preparing the means of defence, but Joyeuse yielded to his brother's request, and dismissed the pages and musicians.

Then he said to his brother: "I am in despair; all conspires against us."

"What do you mean?"

"I have no longer time to aid you."

"I see now that you are in travelling dress; I did not remark it before."

"I set off to-night for Antwerp, by desire of the king."

"Mon Dieu!"

"Come with me, I entreat."

"Do you order me, brother?" said Henri, turning pale at the thought.

"No; I only beg you."

"Thank you, brother. If I were forced to give up passing my nights under this window."

"Well?"

"I should die."

"You are mad."

"My heart is here, brother; my life is here."

Joyeuse crossed his arms with a mixture of anger and pity. "If our father," he said, "begged you to let yourself be attended by Miron, who is at once a philosopher and a doctor?"

"I should reply to my father that I am well and that my brain is sound, and that Miron cannot cure love sickness."

"Well, then, Henri, I must make the best of it. She is but a woman, and at my return I hope to see you more joyous than myself."

"Yes, yes, my good brother, I shall be cured—I shall be happy, thanks to your friendship, which is my most precious possession."

"After your love."

"Before my life."

Joyeuse, much touched, interrupted him.

"Let us go, brother," said he.

"Yes, brother, I follow you," said Du Bouchage, sighing.

"Yes, I understand; the last adieux to the window; but you have also one for me, brother."

Henri passed his arms round the neck of his brother, who leaned down to embrace him.

"No!" cried he. "I will accompany you to the gates," and with a last look towards the window, he followed his brother.

Chicot continued to watch. Gradually everyone disappeared, and the street was deserted. Then one of the windows of the opposite house was opened, and a man looked out.

"There is no longer anyone, madame," said he; "you may leave your hiding-place and go down to your own room," and lighting a lamp, he gave it into a hand stretched out to receive it.

Chicot looked earnestly, but as he caught sight of her pale but sublime face, he shuddered and sat down, entirely subjugated, in his turn, by the melancholy influence of the house.

## CHAPTER XVII

### CHICOT'S PURSE

Chicot passed the remainder of the night dreaming in his armchair, for the face of that woman brought before him a number of illustrious shades connected with many happy or terrible souvenirs, and he who had regretted his sleep on first arriving, now thought no more of it.

When morning dawned he got up, threw a cloak over his shoulders, and with the firmness of a sage, examined the bottom of his purse and his shoes. Chicot, a man of lively imagination, had made in the principal beam which ran through his house a cavity, a foot and a half long and six inches wide, which he used as a strong box, to contain 1,000 crowns in gold. He had made the following calculation: "I spend the twentieth part of one of these crowns every day; therefore I have enough to last me for 20,000 days. I cannot live so long as that, but I may live half as long, and as I grow older my wants and expenses will increase, and this will give me twenty-five or thirty good years to live, and that is enough." He was therefore tranquil as to the future.

This morning on opening his store, "Ventre de biche!" he cried: "Times are hard, and I need not be delicate with Henri. This money did not come from him, but from an old uncle. If it were still night, I would go and get 100 crowns from the king; but now I have no resource but in myself or in Gorenflot."

This idea of drawing money from Gorenflot made him smile. "It would be odd," thought he, "if Gorenflot should refuse 100 crowns to the friend through whom he was appointed prior to the Jacobins. But this letter of the king's. I must go and fetch it. But the Joyeuses are in truth capable of burning my house down some night, to attract the lady to her window, and my 1,000 crowns! really, I think it would be better to hide them in the ground. However, if they burn my house the king shall pay me for it."

Thus reassured he left the house, and at that moment saw at the window of the opposite house the servant of the unknown lady. This man, as we have said, was completely disfigured by a scar extending from the left temple to the cheek; but although bald and with a grey beard, he had a quick, active appearance, and a fresh and young-looking complexion. On seeing Chicot, he drew his hood over his head, and was going in, but Chicot called out to him:

"Neighbour! the noise here last night quite disgusted me, and I am going for some weeks to my farm; will you be so obliging as to look after my house a little?"

"Willingly, monsieur."

"And if you see robbers?"

"Be easy, monsieur, I have a good arquebuse."

"I have still one more favour to ask."

"What is it?"

"I hardly like to call it out."

"I will come down to you."

He came down accordingly, with his hood drawn closely round his face, saying, as a sort of apology: "It is very cold this morning."

"Yes," said Chicot, "there is a bitter wind. Well, monsieur, I am going away."

"You told me that before!"

"Yes, I know; but I leave a good deal of money behind me."

"So much the worse; why not take it with you?"

"I cannot; but I leave it well hidden—so well, that I have nothing to fear but fire. If that should happen, will you try and look after that great beam you see on the right."

"Really, monsieur, you embarrass me. This confidence would have been far better made to a friend than to a stranger of whom you know nothing."

"It is true, monsieur, that I do not know you; but I believe in faces, and I think yours that of an honest man."

"But, monsieur, it is possible that this music may annoy my mistress also, and then she might move."

"Well, that cannot be helped, and I must take my chance."

"Thanks, monsieur, for your confidence in a poor unknown; I will try to be worthy of it;" and bowing, he went into the house.

Chicot murmured to himself: "Poor young man, what a wreck; and I have seen him so gay and so handsome."


## CHAPTER XVIII

### THE PRIORY OF THE JACOBINS

The priory which the king had bestowed upon Gorenflot was situated near the Porte St. Antoine. This was at that time a very favourite quarter, for the king frequently visited the Château of Vincennes, and different noblemen had built charming residences in its neighbourhood.

The priory was built on four sides of an immense court, planted with trees; it had a kitchen-garden behind, and a number of out-houses, which made it look like a small village. Two hundred monks occupied the dormitories situated at the end of the courtyard, while in the front, four large windows, with a balcony before them, gave to these apartments air and light.

Half-past seven in the morning had just struck. The prior had profited by the rule which gave to him an hour's more sleep than to the other monks, and now, although he had risen, he was quietly continuing his sleep in a large armchair as soft as eider-down. The furniture of the room was more mundane than religious; a carved table, covered with a rich cloth, books of religious gallantry—that singular mixture of love and devotion, which we only meet with at that epoch of art—expensive vases, and curtains of rich damask, were some of the luxuries of which Dom Modeste Gorenflot had become possessed by the grace of God, of the king, and of Chicot.

Gorenflot slept, as we have said, in his chair, when the door opened softly, and two men entered. The first was about thirty-five years of age, thin and pale, and with a look which commanded, even before he spoke; lightnings seemed to dart from his eyes when they were open, although the expression was generally softened by a careful lowering of the white eyelids. This was Brother Borromée, who had been for the last three weeks treasurer of the convent. The other was a young man about seventeen or eighteen, with piercing black eyes, a bold look, and whose turned-up sleeves displayed two strong arms quick in gesticulation.

"The prior sleeps still, Father Borromée," said he; "shall we wake him?"

"On no account, Brother Jacques."

"Really, it is a pity to have a prior who sleeps so long, for we might have tried the arms this morning. Did you notice what beautiful cuirasses and arquebuses there were among them?"

"Silence! brother; you will be heard."

"How unlucky," cried the young man, impatiently, stamping his feet, "it is so fine to-day, and the court is so dry."

At the sound, Gorenflot looked up and said, sleepily: "Who is there?

"Pardon me," said Borromée, "if we interrupt your pious meditations, but I have come to take your orders."

"Ah! good morning, Brother Borromée; what orders do you want?"

"About the arms?"

"What arms?"

"Your reverence said to me: 'Brother Borromée, it would be wise to procure arms for the use of the brethren; gymnastic exercises develop the bodily force, as pious exhortations do those of the soul '."

"I said that?"

"Yes, reverend prior; and I, an unworthy but obedient brother, hastened to obey."

"It is strange, but I remember nothing about it."

"You even added this text: "Militat spiritu, militat gladio '."

"Well, if I said so, of course I had my reasons for it. Indeed, that has always been my opinion."

"Then I will finish executing your orders, reverend prior," said Borromée, retiring with Jacques.

"Go," said Gorenflot, majestically.

"Ah!" said Borromée, "I had forgotten; there is a friend in the parlour who asks to see your reverence."

"What is his name?"

"M. Robert Briquet."

"Oh! he is not a friend; only an acquaintance."

"Then your reverence will not see him?"

"Oh, yes! let him come up; he amuses me."

## CHAPTER XIX

### THE TWO FRIENDS

When Chicot entered, the prior did not rise, but merely bent his head.

"Good morning," said Chicot.

"Ah! there you are; you appear to have come to life again."

"Did you think me dead?"

"Diable! I never saw you."

Chicot knew that before being warmed by two or three bottles of old Burgandy, Gorenflot was sparing of his words; and so, considering the time of the morning, it was probable that he was still fasting, Chicot sat down to wait.

"Will you breakfast with me, M. Briquet?" asked Gorenflot.

"Perhaps."

"You must not be angry with me, if it has become impossible for me to give as much time as I could wish."

Chicot laughed. "I angry!" said he, "at what? Because you are impudent, ignorant, and rude? Oh! my dear monsieur, I have known you too long to be angry at these little imperfections."

Gorenflot remained stupefied.

"Adieu," said Chicot.

"Oh! do not go."

"My journey will not wait."

"You travel?"

"I have a mission."

"From whom?"

"From the King."

"A mission from the king! then you have seen him again?"

"Certainly."

"And how did he receive you?"

"With enthusiasm; he has a memory, king as he is."

Gorenflot rose, and seized him by the hand. "Come! let us explain ourselves," said he.

"On what?"

"On your susceptibility to-day."

"I! I am the same to-day as on all other days."

"No."

"A simple mirror of the people I am with. You laugh, and I laugh; you are rude, so am I."

"Can you not be indulgent to a man who has so much work on his shoulders? Governing this priory is like governing a province; remember, I command two hundred men."

"Ah! it is too much indeed for a servant of God."

"I will humble myself."

"From your idleness."

"Well! from to-morrow I will join my monks in their exercises."

"What exercises?"

"Of arms."

"Arms! '

"Yes; but it will be fatiguing to command."

"Who had this idea?"

"I, it seems."

"You! impossible!"

"No. I gave the order to Brother Borromée."

"Who is he?"

"The new treasurer."

"Where does he come from?"

"M. le Cardinal de Guise recommended him."

"In person?"

"No, by letter."

"And it is with him you decided on this?"

"Yes, my friend."

"That is to say, he proposed it and you agreed."

"No, my dear M. Chicot; the idea was entirely mine."

"And for what end?"

"To arm them."

"Oh! pride, pride! Confess that the idea was his."

"Oh! I do not know. And yet it must have been mine, for it seems that I pronounced a very good Latin text on the occasion."

"You! Latin! Do you remember it?"

"Militat spiritu——"

"Militat gladio."

"Yes, yes; that was it."

"Well, you have excused yourself so well that I pardon you. You are still my true friend."

Gorenflot wiped away a tear.

" Now let us breakfast, and I promise to be indulgent."

" Listen! I will tell the cook that if the fare be not regal, he shall be placed in confinement; and we will try some of the wine of my penitent."

" I will aid you with my judgment."

# CHAPTER XX

## THE BREAKFAST

Gorenflot was not long in giving his orders. The cook was summoned.

Chicot favoured him with a questioning glance.

" Brother Eusebius," said Gorenflot, in a severe voice, " listen to what my friend M. Briquet is about to tell you. It seems that you are negligent, and I hear of grave faults in your last soup, and a fatal mistake in the cooking of your ears. Take care, brother, take care; a single step in a wrong direction may be irremediable."

The monk grew red and pale by turns, and stammered out an excuse.

" Enough," said Gorenflot, " what can we have for break-fast to-day?"

" Eggs fried with cock's combs."

" After?"

" Mushrooms."

" Well?"

" Crabs cooked with Madeira."

" Those are all trifles; tell us of something solid."

" A ham, boiled with pistachios."

Chicot looked contemptuous.

" Pardon!" cried Eusebius, " it is cooked in sherry wine."

Gorenflot hazarded an approving glance toward Chicot.

" Good! is it not, M. Briquet?" said he.

Chicot made a gesture of half-satisfaction.

" And what have you besides?"

" You can have some eels."

" Oh! we will dispense with the eels," said Chicot.

" I think, M. Briquet," replied the cook, " that you would regret it if you had not tasted my eels."

" What! are they rarities?"

" I nourish them in a particular manner."

"Oh, oh!"

"Yes," added Gorenflot; "it appears that the Romans or the Greeks—I forget which—nourished their lampreys as Eusebius does his eels. He read of it in an old author called Suetonius."

"Yes, monsieur, I mince the intestines and livers of fowls and game with a little pork, and make a kind of sausage meat, which I throw to my eels, and they are kept in soft water, often renewed, in which they become large and fat. The one which I shall offer you to-day weighs nine pounds."

"It must be a serpent!" said Chicot.

"It swallowed a chicken at a meal."

"And how will it be dressed?"

"Skinned and fried in anchovy paste, and done with bread crumbs; and I shall have the honour of serving it up with a sauce flavoured with garlic and allspice, lemons and mustard."

"Perfect!" cried Chicot.

Brother Eusebius breathed again.

"Then we shall want sweets," said Gorenflot.

"I will invent something that shall please you."

"Well, then, I trust to you; be worthy of my confidence."

Eusebius bowed and retired. Ten minutes after, they sat down, and the programme was faithfully carried out. They began like famished men, drank Rhine wine, Burgundy, and Hermitage.

They ate as long as they could, and then sat drinking and talking, when suddenly a great noise was heard.

"What is that?" asked Chicot.

"It is the exercise which commences."

"Without the chief? Your soldiers are badly disciplined, I fear."

"Without me! never!" cried Gorenflot, who had become excited with wine. "That cannot be, since it is I who command—I who instruct—and stay, here is Brother Borromée, who comes to take my orders."

Indeed, as he spoke, Borromée entered, throwing on Chicot a sharp and oblique glance.

"Reverend prior," said he, "we only wait for you to examine the arms and cuirasses."

"Cuirasses!" thought Chicot, "I must see this," and he rose quietly.

"You will be present at our manœuvres?" said Gorenflot, rising in his turn, like a block of marble on legs. "Your arm, my friend; you shall see some good instruction."

## CHAPTER XXI

### BROTHER BORROMEE

When Chicot, sustaining the reverend prior, arrived in the courtyard, he found there two bands of one hundred men each, waiting for their commander. About fifty among the strongest and most zealous had helmets on their heads and long swords hanging to belts from their waists. Others displayed with pride bucklers, on which they loved to rattle an iron gauntlet.

Brother Borromée took a helmet from the hands of a novice, and placed it on his head. While he did so, Chicot looked at it and smiled.

"You have a handsome helmet there, Brother Borromée," said he; "where did you buy it, my dear prior?"

Gorenflot could not reply, for at that moment they were fastening a magnificent cuirass upon him, which, although spacious enough to have covered Hercules Farnese, constrained woefully the undulations of the flesh of the worthy prior, who was crying:

"Not so tight! I shall stifle; stop!"

But Borromée replied: "It made part of a lot of armour that the reverend prior bought yesterday to arm the convent."

"I!" said Gorenflot.

"Yes; do you not remember that they brought several cuirasses and casques here, according to your reverence's orders?"

"It is true," said Gorenflot.

"Ventre de biche!" thought Chicot; "my helmet is much attached to me, for, after having taken it myself to the Hôtel Guise, it comes here to meet me again."

At a sign from Borromée, the monks now formed into lines, while Chicot sat down on a bench to look on.

Gorenflot stood up. "Attention," whispered Borromée to him.

Gorenflot drew a gigantic sword from the scabbard, and waving it in the air, cried in the voice of a stentor: "Attention!"

"Your reverence will fatigue yourself, perhaps, in giving the orders," said Borromée, softly; "if it please you to spare your precious health, I will command to-day."

"I should wish it, I am stifling."

Borromée bowed and placed himself at the head of the troop.

"What a complaisant servant," said Chicot.

"He is charming, I told you so."

"I am sure he does the same for you every day."

"Oh! every day. He is as submissive as a slave."

"So that you have really nothing to do here—Brother Borromée acts for you?"

"Oh! mon Dieu, yes."

While the monks went through their exercises, Gorenflot said: "You shall see my little Jacques."

"Who is Jacques?"

"A nice lad, calm-looking, but strong, and quick as lightning. Look, there he is with a musket in his hand, about to fire."

While they spoke, Jacques loaded a heavy musket, and placing himself at one hundred yards from the mark, fired, and the ball lodged in the centre, amidst the applause of the monks.

"That was well done!" cried Chicot.

"Thank you, monsieur," said Jacques, whose cheeks coloured with pleasure.

"You manage your arms well," added Chicot.

"I study, monsieur."

"But he is best at the sword," said Gorenflot; "those who understand it, say so, and he is practising from morning till night."

"Ah! let us see," said Chicot.

"No one here, except perhaps myself, is capable of fencing with him; but will you try him yourself, monsieur?" said Borromée.

"I am but a poor bourgeois," said Chicot; "formerly I have used my sword like others, but now my legs tremble and my arm is weak."

"But you practise still?"

"A little," replied Chicot, with a smile.

"However, you, Brother Borromée, who are all muscle and tendon, give a lesson to Brother Jacques, I beg, if the prior will permit it."

"I shall be delighted," cried Gorenflot.

The two combatants prepared for the trial. Borromée had the advantage in height and experience. The blood mounted to the cheeks of Jacques and animated them with a feverish colour. Borromée gradually dropped all appearance of a monk, and was completely the maître d'armes: he accompanied each thrust with a counsel or a reproach, but often the vigour and quickness of Jacques triumphed over the skill of his teacher, who was several times touched.

When they paused, Chicot said :" Jacques touched six times and Borromée nine; that is well for the scholar, but not so well for the master."

The flash of Borromée's eyes showed Chicot that he was proud.

" Monsieur," replied he, in a tone which he endeavoured to render calm, " the exercise of arms is a difficult one, especially for poor monks."

" Nevertheless," said Chicot, " the master ought to be at least half as good again as his pupil, and if Jacques were calmer, I am certain he would fence as well as you."

" I do not think so," replied Borromée, biting his lips with anger.

" Well! I am sure of it."

" M. Briquet, who is so clever, had better try Jacques himself," replied Borromée, in a bitter tone.

" Oh! I am old."

" Yes, but learned."

" Ah! you mock," thought Chicot, " but wait. " Then he said: " I am certain, however, that Brother Borromée, like a wise master, often lets Jacques touch him out of complaisance."

" Ah!" cried Jacques, frowning in his turn.

" No," replied Borromée, " I love Jacques, certainly, but I do not spoil him in that manner. But try yourself, M. Briquet."

" Oh, no."

" Come on, only one pass."

" Try," said Gorenflot.

" I will not hurt you, monsieur," said Jacques, " I have a very light hand."

" Dear child," murmured Chicot, with a strange glance. " Well!" said he, " since everyone wishes it, I will try," and he rose slowly, and prepared himself with about the agility of a tortoise.

## CHAPTER XXII

### THE LESSON

Fencing was not at that time the science that it is now. It was common to see the fencer throw himself forward, draw back again, or jump to the right or left, so that agility, not only of the hand, but of the whole body, was necessary. Chicot did not appear to have learned in this school, but seemed to have forestalled the modern style, of which the superiority and grace is in the agility of the hands and immovability of the body. He stood erect and firm, with a wrist at once strong and supple, and with a sword which seemed a flexible reed from the point to the middle of the blade, and an inflexible steel from thence to the guard.

At the very first commencement, Jacques, seeing before him this man of bronze, whose wrist alone seemed alive, gave some impatient passes, which merely made Chicot extend his arm, and at every opening left by the young man, strike him full on the chest. Jacques, red with anger and emulation as this was repeated, bounded back, and for ten minutes displayed all the resources of his wonderful agility—he flew like a tiger, twisted like a serpent, and bounded from right to left; but Chicot, with his calm air and his long arm, seized his time, and putting aside his adversary's sword, still sent his own to the same place, while Borromée grew pale with anger. At last, Jacques rushed a last time on Chicot, who, parrying his thrust with force, threw the poor fellow off his equilibrium, and he fell, while Chicot himself remained firm as a rock.

" You did not tell us you were a pillar," said Borromée, biting his nails with vexation.

" I, a poor bourgeois!" said Chicot.

" But monsieur, to manage a sword as you do, you must have practised enormously."

" Oh! mon Dieu! yes, monsieur, I have often held the sword, and have always found one thing."

" What is that?"

" That for him who holds it, pride is a bad counsellor and anger a bad assistant. Now, listen, Jacques," added he: " you have a good wrist, but neither legs nor head; you are quick, but you do not reason. There are three essential things in arms—first the head, then the hands and legs: with the one you can defend yourself, with the others you may conquer, but with all three you can always conquer."

" Ah! monsieur," said Jacques, " try Brother Borromée; I should like to see it."

" No," said the treasurer; " I should be beaten, and I would rather confess it than prove it."

" How modest and amiable he is!" said Gorenflot.

" On the contrary," whispered Chicot, " he is stupid with vanity. At his age I would have given anything for such a lesson," and he sat down again.

Jacques approached him, and admiration triumphing over the shame of defeat:

"Will you give me some lessons, M. Briquet?" said he; "the prior will permit it, will you not, your reverence?"

"With pleasure, my child."

"I do not wish to interfere with your master," said Chicot, bowing to Borromée.

"Oh! I am not his only master," said he. "Neither all the honour nor the defeat are wholly due to me."

"Who is the other, then?"

"Oh! no one!" cried Borromée, fearing he had committed an imprudence.

"Who is he, Jacques?" asked Chicot.

"I remember," said Gorenflot, "he is a little fat man who comes here sometimes and drinks well."

"I forget his name," said Borromée.

"I know it," said a monk who was standing by. "It is Bussy Leclerc."

"Ah! a good sword," said Chicot.

Jacques reiterated his request.

"I cannot teach you," said Chicot. "I taught myself by reflection and practice; and I advise you to do the same."

Gorenflot and Chicot now returned to the house.

"I hope," said Gorenflot, with pride, "that this is a house worth something, and well managed."

"Wonderful! my friend; and when I return from my mission——"

"Ah! true, dear M. Chicot; let us speak of your mission."

"So much the more willingly, that I have a message to send to the king before I go."

"To the king, my dear friend! You correspond with the king?"

"Directly."

"And you want a messenger?"

"Yes."

"Will you have one of our monks? It would be an honour to the priory."

"Willingly."

"Then you are restored to favour?"

"More than ever."

"Then," said Gorenflot, "you can tell the king all that we are doing here in his favour."

"I shall not fail to do so."

"Ah! my dear Chicot," cried Gorenflot, who already believed himself a bishop.

"But first I have two requests to make."

"Speak."

"First, money, which the king will restore to you."

"Money! I have my coffers full."

"Ma foi! you are lucky."

"Will you have 1,000 crowns?"

"No, that is far too much; I am modest in my tastes, humble in my desires, and my title of ambassador does not make me proud; therefore 100 crowns will suffice."

"Here they are; and the second thing?"

"An attendant."

"An attendant!"

"Yes, to accompany me; I love society."

"Ah! my friend, if I were but free, as formerly."

"But you are not."

"Greatness enslaves me," murmured Gorenflot.

"Alas!" said Chicot, "one cannot do everything at once. But not being able to have your honourable company, my dear prior, I will content myself with that of the little Jacques; he pleases me."

"You are right, Chicot, he is a rare lad."

"I am going to take him 250 leagues, if you will permit it."

"He is yours, my friend."

The prior struck a bell, and when the servant appeared said: "Let Brother Jacques come here, and also our messenger.

Ten minutes after both appeared at the door.

"Jacques," said Gorenflot, "I give you a special mission."

"Me?" cried the young man, astonished.

"Yes, you are to accompany M. Robert Briquet on a long journey."

"Oh!" cried he, enthusiastically, "that will be delightful. We shall fight every day—shall we not, monsieur?"

"Yes, my child."

"And I may take my arquebuse?"

"Certainly."

Jacques bounded joyfully from the room.

"As to the message, I beg you to give your orders Advance, Brother Panurge."

# CHAPTER XXIII

## THE PENITENT

Panurge advanced. He looked intelligent, but like a fox.

"Do you know the Louvre?" said Chicot.

"Yes, monsieur."

" And in the Louvre a certain Henri de Valois?"

" The king."

" Just so. You will ask to speak to him."

" Will they let me?"

" Yes, till you come to his valet de chambre. Your frock is a passport, for the king is very religious."

" And what shall I say to the valet de chambre?"

" Say you are sent by the shade."

" What shade?"

" Curiosity is a vice, my brother."

" Pardon!"

" Say then that you want the letter."

" What letter?"

" Again!"

" Ah! true."

" You will add that the shade will wait for it, going slowly along the road to Charenton."

" It is on that road, then, that I am to join you?"

" Exactly."

As Panurge went out, Chicot thought he saw someone listening at the door, but could not be sure. He fancied it was Borromée.

" Where do you go?" asked Gorenflot.

" Towards Spain."

" How do you travel?"

" Oh! anyhow; on foot, on horseback, in a carriage—just as it happens."

" Jacques will be good company for you."

" Thanks, my good friend, I have now, I think, only to make my adieux."

" Adieu; I will give you my benediction."

" Bah; it is useless between us."

" You are right; but it does for strangers," and they embraced.

" Jacques!" call the prior, " Jacques!"

Borromée appeared.

" Brother Jacques," repeated the prior.

" Jacques is gone."

" What! gone," cried Chicot.

" Did you not wish someone to go to the Louvre?"

" Yes; but it was Panurge."

" Oh! stupid that I am," cried Borromée, " I understood it to be Jacques."

Chicot frowned, but Borromée appeared so sorry that it was impossible to say much.

" I will wait then," said he, " till Jacques returns."

Borromée bowed, frowning in his turn. "Apropos," said he, "I forgot to announce to your reverence that the unknown lady has arrived and desires to speak to you."

"Is she alone?" asked Gorenflot.

"No; she has a squire with her."

"Is she young?"

Borromée lowered his eyes. "She seems so," said he.

"I will leave you," said Chicot, "and wait in a neighbouring room."

"It is far from here to the Louvre, monsieur, and Jacques may be long, or they may hesitate to confide an important letter to a child."

"You make these reflections rather late," replied Chicot, "however, I will go on the road to Charenton and you can send him after me." And he turned to the staircase.

"Not that way, if you please," said Borromée, "the lady is coming up, and she does not wish to meet anyone."

"You are right," said Chicot, smiling, "I will take the little staircase."

"Do you know the way?"

"Perfectly." And Chicot went out through a cabinet which led to another room, from which led the secret staircase. The room was full of armour, swords, muskets, and pistols.

"They hide Jacques from me," thought Chicot, "and they hide the lady, therefore of course I ought to do exactly the opposite of what they want me to do. I will wait for the return of Jacques, and I will watch the mysterious lady. Oh! here is a fine shirt of mail thrown into a corner; it is much too small for the prior, and would fit me admirably. I will borrow it from Gorenflot, and give it to him again, when I return." And he quietly put it on under his doublet. He had just finished when Borromée entered.

Chicot pretended to be admiring the arms.

"Is monsieur seeking some arms to suit him?" asked Borromée.

"I! mon Dieu! what do I want with arms?"

"You use them so well."

"Theory, all theory; I may use my arms well, but the heart of a soldier is always wanting in a poor bourgeois like me. But time passes, and Jacques cannot be long; I will go and wait for him at the Croix Faubin."

"I think that will be best."

"Then you will tell him as soon as he comes?"

"Yes."

"And send him after me?"

"I will not fail."

"Thanks, Brother Borromée; I am enchanted to have made your acquaintance."

He went out by the little staircase, and Borromée locked the door behind him.

"I must see the lady," thought Chicot.

He went out of the priory and went on the road he had named; then, when out of sight, he turned back, crept along a ditch and gained, unseen, a thick hedge which extended before the priory. Here he waited to see Jacques return or the lady go out.

## CHAPTER XXIV

### THE AMBUSH

Chicot made a slight opening through the hedge, that he might see those who came and went. The road was almost deserted as far as he could see; there was no one but a man poorly clothed measuring the ground with a long, pointed stick. Chicot had nothing to do, and therefore was preparing to watch this man, when a more important object attracted his attention.

The window of Gorenflot's room opened with folding-doors on to a balcony, and Chicot saw them open, and Gorenflot come out, with his most gallant manner and winning smile, leading a lady almost hidden under a mantle of velvet and fur.

"Oh!" thought Chicot, "here is the penitent. She looks young; it is very odd, but I find resemblances in everyone I see. And here comes the squire; as for him, there is no mistake; I know him, and if he be Mayneville—ventre de biche!—why should not the lady be Madame de Montpensier? And, morbleu! that woman *is* the duchess!"

After a moment, he saw the pale head of Borromée behind them.

"What are they about?" thought Chicot; "does the duchess want to board with Gorenflot?"

At this moment Chicot saw M. de Mayneville make a sign to someone outside. Chicot looked round, but there was no one to be seen but the man measuring. It was to him, however, that the sign was addressed, for he had ceased measuring, and was looking towards the balcony. Borromée began also to gesticulate behind Mayneville, in a manner unintelligible to Chicot, but apparently clear to this man, for he went further off, and stationed himself in another place, where he stopped at a fresh sign. Then he began to run quickly towards the gate of the priory, while M. de Mayneville held his watch in his hand.

"Diable!" said Chicot, "this is all very odd."

As the man passed him, he recognised Nicholas Poulain, the man to whom he had sold his armour the day before. Shortly after, they all re-entered the room and shut the window, and then the duchess and her squire came out of the priory and went towards the litter which waited for them. Gorenflot accompanied them to the door, exhausting himself in bows and salutations. The curtains of the litter were still open, when a monk, in whom Chicot recognised Jacques, advanced from the Porte St. Antoine, approached, and looked earnestly into it. The duchess then went away, and Nicholas Poulain was following, when Chicot called out from his hiding-place:—

"Come here, if you please."

Poulain started, and turned his head.

"Do not seem to notice, M. Nicholas Poulain," said Chicot.

The lieutenant started again. "Who are you, and what do you want?" asked he.

"I am a friend, new, but intimate; what I want will take long to explain; come here to me."

"What for?"

"You shall know when you come."

"But——"

"Come and sit down here, without appearing to notice me."

"Monsieur!"

"Oh! M. Robert Briquet has the right to be exacting."

"Robert Briquet!" cried Poulain, doing as he was desired.

"That is right; it seems you were taking measures in the road."

"I?"

"Yes, there is nothing surprising that you should be a surveyor, especially as you acted under the eyes of such great people."

"Great people! I do not understand."

"What! you did not know?"

"What do you mean?"

"You did not know who that lady and gentlemen on the balcony were?"

"I declare——"

"Oh! how fortunate I am to be able to enlighten you. Only imagine, M. Poulain; you had for admirers Madame de Montpensier and M. de Mayneville. Do not go away. If a still more illustrious person—the king—saw you——"

" Ah! M. Briquet——"

" Never mind; I am only anxious for your good."

" But what harm have I done to the king, or to you, or anybody?"

" Dear M. Poulain, my ideas may be wrong, but it seems to me that the king would not approve of his lieutenant of the Provostry acting as surveyor for M. de Mayneville; and that he might also take it ill that you should omit in your daily report the entrance of Madame de Montpensier and M. de Mayneville, yesterday, into his good city of Paris."

" M. Briquet, an omission is not an offence, and his majesty is too good——"

" M. Poulain, I see clearer than you, and I see——"

" What?"

" A gallows."

" M. Briquet!"

" And more—a new cord, four soldiers at the four cardinal points, a number of Parisians around, and a certain lieutenant of my acquaintance at the end of the cord."

Nicholas Poulain trembled so that he shook the hedge. " Monsieur!" cried he, clasping his hands.

" But I am your friend, dear M. Poulain, and I will give you a counsel."

" A counsel?"

" Yes; and very easy to follow. Go at once, you understand, to——"

" Whom?"

" Let me think. To M. d'Epernon."

" M. d'Epernon, the king's friend?"

" Take him aside, and tell him all about this."

" This is folly."

" No, it is wisdom. It is clear that if I denounce you as the man of the cuirasses and measures, they will hang you; but if, on the contrary, you disclose all, with a good grace, they will reward you. You do not appear convinced, however. Well! that will give me the trouble of returning to the Louvre, but I do not mind doing that for you," and he began to rise.

" No, no; stay here, I will go."

" Good! But you understand, no subterfuges, or to-morrow I shall send a little note to the king, whose intimate friend I have the honour to be, so that if you are not hung till the day after to-morrow, you will only be hung the higher."

" I will go; but you abuse your position."

" Oh! M. Poulain, you were a traitor five minutes ago,

and I make you the saviour of your country. Now, go quickly, for I am in a hurry. The Hôtel d'Epernon—do not forget."

Nicholas Poulain ran off, with a despairing look.

"Ah! it was time," said Chicot, "for someone is leaving the priory. But it is not Jacques; that fellow is half as tall again."

Chicot then hastened to the Croix Faubin, where he had given the rendezvous. The monk, who was there to meet him, was a giant in height; his monk's robe, hastily thrown on, did not hide his muscular limbs, and his face bore anything but a religious expression. His arms were as long as Chicot's own, and he had a knife in his belt.

As Chicot approached, he turned and said: :" Are you M. Robert Briquet?"

"I am."

"Then I have a letter for you from the reverend prior." Chicot took the letter, and read as follows:—

"My dear friend, I have reflected since we parted; it is impossible for me to let the lamb confided to me go amongst the wolves of the world. I mean, you understand, our little Jacques, who has fulfilled your message to the king. Instead of him, who is too young, I send you a good and worthy brother of our order; his manners are good, and his humour innocent, and I am sure you will like him. I send you my benediction. Adieu, dear friend."

"What fine writing," said Chicot; "I will wager it is the treasurer's."

"It was Brother Borromée who wrote it," said the Goliath.

"In that case you will return to the priory, my friend."

"I?"

"Yes; and tell his reverence that I have changed my mind, and intend to travel alone."

"What! you will not take me, monsieur?" said the man, with astonishment, mixed with menace.

"No, my friend."

"And why, if you please?"

"Because I must be economical, and you would eat too much."

"Jacques eats as much as I do."

"Yes, but Jacques was a monk."

"And what am I?"

"You, my friend, are a gendarme, or a foot soldier."

"What do you mean? Do you not see my monk's robe?"
"The dress does not make the monk, my friend; tell Brother Borromée that, if you please."

The giant disappeared, grumbling, like a beaten hound.


## CHAPTER XXV

### THE GUISES

On the evening of the same day on which Chicot set off for Navarre, we shall find again, in a large room at the Hôtel Guise, the person who, disguised as a page, had entered Paris behind Carmainges, and who was also, as we know, the penitent of Gorenflot. On this occasion her sex was disclosed, and, elegantly dressed, with her hair glittering with precious stones, she was waiting impatiently for someone.

At last a horse's step was heard, and the usher almost immediately announced M. le Duc de Mayenne. Madame de Montpensier ran to her brother so hastily, that she forgot to proceed on the point of the right foot, as was her habit, in order to conceal her lameness.

"Are you alone, brother?" asked she.

"Yes, my sister."

"But Henri; where is Henri? Do you know that everyone expects him here?"

"Henri has nothing to do here, and plenty to do in Flanders and Picardy. We have work to do there, and why should we leave it to come here, where our work is done?"

"But where it will be quickly undone, if you do not hasten."

"Bah!"

"Bah! if you like. I tell you the citizens will be put off no longer; they insist upon seeing their Duke Henri."

"They shall see him at the right time. And Salcède——?"

"Is dead."

"Without speaking?"

"Without uttering a word."

"Good! and the arming?"

"Finished."

"And Paris?"

"Is divided into sixteen quarters."

"And each quarter has the chief pointed out?"

"Yes."

"Then let us live in peace, and so I shall say to our good bourgeoisie."

"They will not listen to you."

"Bah!"

"I tell you they are furious."

"My sister, you judge others by your own impatience. What Henri says must be done; and he says we are to remain quiet."

"What is to be done, then?" asked the duchess impatiently.

"What do you wish to do?"

"Firstly, to take the king."

"That is your fixed idea; I do not say it is bad, if it could be done; but think how often we have failed already."

"Times are changed, the king has no longer defenders."

"No; except the Swiss, Scotch, and French guards."

"My brother, when you wish it, I will show you the king on the road with only two lacqueys."

"I have heard that a hundred times, and never seen it once."

"You will see it if you stay here only three days."

"Another project: tell me what it is."

"You will laugh at a woman's idea."

At this moment, M. de Mayneville was announced. "My accomplice," said she: "let him enter."

"One word, monseigneur," said he to M. de Mayenne as he entered; "they suspect your arrival at the Louvre."

"How so?"

"I was conversing with the captain of the guard at St. Germain-l'Auxerrois, when two Gascons passed——"

"Do you know them?"

"No; they were quite newly dressed. 'Cap de Bious!' said one, 'you have a magnificent doublet, but it will not render you so much service as your cuirass of yesterday.' 'Bah!' said the other; 'however heavy the sword of M. de Mayenne may be, it will do no more harm to this satin than to my cuirass,' and then he went on in a series of bravadoes, which showed that they knew you were near."

"And do whom did these men belong?"

"I do not know; they talked so loudly, that some passers-by approached, and asked if you were really coming. They were about to reply, when a man approached, who I think was De Loignac, and touched them on the shoulder. He said some words in a low voice, and they looked submissive, and accompanied him, so that I know no more; but be on your guard."

"You did not follow them?"

"Yes, but from afar. They went towards the Louvre, and disappeared behind the Hôtel des Meubles."

"I have a very simple method of reply," said the duke.

"What?"

"To go and pay my respects to the king to-night."

"To the king?"

"Certainly; I have come to Paris—he can have nothing to say against that."

"The idea is good," said Mayneville.

"It is imprudent," said the duchess.

"It is indispensable, sister, if they indeed suspect my arrival. Besides, it was the advice of Henri to go at once and present to the king the respects of the family; that once done, I am free, and can receive whom I please."

"The members of the committee, for example, who expect you."

"I will receive them at the Hôtel St. Denis on my return from the Louvre. You will wait for us, if you please, my sister."

"Here?"

"No; at the Hôtel St. Denis, where I have left my equipages. I shall be there in two hours."

## CHAPTER XXVI

### THE LOUVRE

That same day, about noon, the king came out of his cabinet and called for M. d'Epernon. The duke, when he came, found the king attentively examining a young monk.

The king took D'Epernon aside: "Look, what an odd-looking monk," said he.

"Does your majesty think so?—I think him very ordinary."

"Really!" Then to the monk, the king said: "What is your name?"

"Brother Jacques, sire."

Your family name?"

"Clement."

"Good. You have performed your commission very well."

"What commission, sire?" said the duke, with his wonted familiarity.

"Nothing!" said Henri. "It is a little secret between me and someone you do not know."

"How strangely you look at the lad, sire! you embarrass him."

"It is true; I know not why, but it seems to me that I have seen him before; perhaps it was in a dream. Go, my child; I will send the letter to him who asks for it; be easy. D'Epernon give him ten crowns."

When he was gone, the king said to D'Epernon: "Duke, have you among your Forty-five two or three men who can ride?"

"Twelve, at least, sire; and in a month all will be good horsemen."

"Then choose two, and let them come to me at once."

The duke went out, and calling De Loignac, said to him: "Choose me two good horsemen, to execute a commission for his majesty."

De Loignac went to the gallery where they were lodged, and called M. de Carmainges and M. de St. Maline. They soon appeared, and were conducted to the duke, who presented them to the king, who dismissed the duke.

"You are of my Forty-five, then?" said he to the young men. "Good! Then mount your horses, and take the road to Tours—do you know it?"

"We will inquire."

"Go by Charenton."

"Yes, sire."

"And proceed till you overtake a man travelling alone."

"Will your majesty describe him?" said St. Maline.

"He has long arms and legs, and has a large sword by his side."

"May we know his name, sire?" asked Carmainges.

"He is called 'the Shade'."

"We will ask the name of every traveller we see, sire."

"And we will search the hotels."

"When you find him, give him this letter."

Both the young men held out their hands.

"M. de Carmainges, you shall carry the letter, and you, M. de St. Maline, shall deliver it."

Ernanton took the precious deposit, and was going to place it in his doublet, when St. Maline stopped him, kissed the letter, and then returned it to Ernanton.

This made Henri smile. "Come, gentlemen," said he, "I see I shall be well served."

"Is this all, sire?"

"Yes, gentlemen; only our last recommendation. This letter is more precious than the life of a man—for your heads, do not lose it; give it secretly to the Shade, who will give you a receipt for it, which you will bring back to me; and, above all, travel as though it were on your own affairs. Go."

The two young men went out—Ernanton full of joy, and St. Maline filled with jealousy. M. d'Epernon waited for them, and wished to question them, but Ernanton replied:

"M. le Duc, the king did not authorise us to speak."

They went to the stables, when the king's huntsman gave them two strong horses. M. d'Epernon would have followed them, but at that moment he was told that a man much wished to speak to him at once.

The duke turned. Near him was a man, bowing perpetually.

"Who are you?" asked the duke.

"Nicholas Poulain, monsieur."

"And you wish to speak to me?"

"This concerns the life of his majesty," said Poulain, in a low voice.

"Oh! oh! then come into my cabinet."


## CHAPTER XXVII

### THE REVELATION

Nicholas Poulain followed the duke into his cabinet.

"Now let us hear your conspiracy," said the duke.

"It is the king. They wish to carry him off."

"Oh! again that old story," replied the duke, disdainfully.

"This time the thing is serious, M. le Duc."

"On what day do they intend to do it?"

"The first time that his majesty goes to Vincennes in his litter."

"How will they do it?"

"By killing his two attendants."

"And who will do it?"

"Madame de Montpensier."

D'Epernon began to laugh.

"And she occupies herself with that at Soissons?"

"No; she is in Paris."

"In Paris!"

"I can answer for it."

"Have you seen her?"

"Yes."

"You thought you did?"

"I have had the honour of speaking to her."

" The honour!"

" I am wrong; the misfortune."

" But, my dear lieutenant, the duchess cannot carry off the king."

" With her associates, of course."

" And where will she be when this takes place?"

" At a window of the Jacobin Friary, which is, as you know, on the road to Vincennes."

" What the devil do you tell me?"

" The truth, monsieur; all is prepared to stop the litter at the gate of the priory."

" And who made the preparations?"

" Alas!——"

" Finish quickly."

" I did, monsieur."

D'Epernon started back. " You, who denounce them!"

" Monsieur, a good servant should risk all in the service of the king."

The duke looked fixedly at Poulain. " There must be more in it," said he; " resolute as the duchess is, she would not attempt such an enterprise alone."

" She expects her brother."

" The Duke Henri?"

" No, monsieur, only the Duc de Mayenne."

" Ah! good," said D'Epernon; " now I must set to work to counteract these fine projects."

" Doubtless, monsieur; it was for that I came."

" If you have spoken the truth you shall be rewarded; and, first, here are a thousand crowns for you, and you shall keep this secret between you and me."

The duke approached a coffer. Poulain thought it was for the money, and held out his hand, but he only drew out a little book and wrote: " Three thousand livres to M. Nicholas Poulain."—" It is as if you had them," said he.

Nicholas bowed, and looked puzzled.

" Then it is agreed?" said the duke.

" What, monsieur?"

" That you will continue to instruct me?"

Nicholas hesitated.

" What! has your noble devotion vanished already?"

" No, monsieur."

" Then I may count on you?"

" You may."

" And I alone know this?"

" You alone."

"Now you may go, my friend; and, parfandious, let M. de Mayenne look to himself."

When D'Epernon returned to the king he found him playing at cup and ball. D'Epernon assumed a thoughtful air, but the king did not remark it. However, as the duke remained perfectly silent, the king raised his head and said: "Well, Lavalette, what is the matter, are you dead?"

"Your most cruel enemies surround you at this moment."

"Bah! who are they?"

"First, the Duchesse de Montpensier."

"Yes; that is true; she came to see Salcède; but what is that to me?"

"You knew it, then?"

"You see I did."

"But that M. de Mayenne was here?"

"Yes, since yesterday evening."

"What! this secret?" cried D'Epernon, with a disagreeable surprise.

"Are there, then, any secrets from the king? You are zealous, dear Lavalette, but you are slow. This news would have been good at four o'clock yesterday, but to-day——"

"Well, sire, to-day?"

"It comes too late, you will agree?"

"Still too soon, sire, it seems, since you will not listen to me."

"I have been listening for half-an-hour."

"You are menaced—they lay ambushes for you."

"Well, yesterday you gave me a guard, and assured me that my immortality was secured. Are your Forty-five no longer worth anything?"

"Your majesty shall see."

"I should not be sorry, duke; when shall I see?"

"Sooner perhaps than you think."

"Ah! you want to frighten me."

"You shall see, sire. Apropos, when do you go to Vincennes?"

"On Saturday."

"That is enough, sire." D'Epernon bowed and withdrew.

## CHAPTER XXVIII

### TWO FRIENDS

We will now follow the two young men sent by the king. Scarcely on horseback, Ernanton and St. Maline, determined that one should not get before the other, nearly crushed each other in the gateway. The face of St. Maline became purple, and that of Ernanton pale.

" You hurt me, monsieur," cried the former; " do you wish to crush me?"

" You also hurt me, only I did not complain."

" You wish to give a lesson, I believe?"

" I wish to give you nothing."

" Ah!" cried St. Maline, " pray repeat that."

" My dear monsieur, when the king gives me a letter to carry, I carry it."

" I will tear it from you by force."

" You will not force me, I hope, to shoot you like a dog."

" You!"

" Yes; I have a pistol, and you have not."

" You shall pay for this."

" I trust so, after my commission is over; but, meanwhile, I beg you to observe that as we belong to the king, it is setting a bad example to quarrel.

St. Maline was furious, he bit his fingers with rage. As they crossed the Rue St. Antoine, Ernanton saw a litter with a lady in it. " My page!" cried he, and he rode towards it; but she did not seem to recognise him, and passed on.

The young men now rode on without speaking. St. Maline soon discovered, to his chagrin, that his horse was not as good as Ernanton's, and could hardly keep pace with him. This annoyed him so much that he began to quarrel with his horse, and to fret him so perpetually with the spur, that at last the animal started off and made for the River Bievre, where he got rid of his rider by throwing him in. One might have heard half a mile off the imprecations of St. Maline, although he was half stifled by the water. By the time he scrambled out his horse had got some little way off. He himself was wet and muddy, and his face bleeding with scratches, and he felt sure that it was useless to try and catch it; and to complete his vexation, he saw Ernanton going down a cross-road which he judged to be a short cut.

He climbed up the banks of the river, but now could see neither Ernanton nor his own horse. But while he stood there, full of sinister thoughts towards Ernanton, he saw him reappear from the cross-road, leading the runaway horse, which he had made a détour to catch. At this sight St. Maline was full of joy and even of gratitude; but gradually his face clouded again as he thought of the superiority of Ernanton over himself, for he knew that in the same situation he should not even have thought of acting in a similar manner.

He stammered out thanks, to which Ernanton paid no attention, then furiously seized the reins of his horse and mounted again. They rode on silently till about half-past two, when they saw a man walking with a dog by his side.

Ernanton said: "There is he whom we seek waiting for us."

## CHAPTER XXIX

### ST. MALINE

Ernanton was not deceived; the man he saw was really Chicot. He on his side had seen the cavaliers coming, and suspecting that it was for him that they came, waited for them.

Ernanton and St. Maline looked at each other.

"Speak, monsieur, if you wish," said Ernanton to his adversary.

St. Maline was suffocated by this courtesy, he could not speak, he could only bend his head; then Ernanton, advancing, said to Chicot:

"Monsieur, would it be indiscreet to inquire your name?"

"I am called 'The Shade.'"

"Do you expect anything?"

"Yes, monsieur."

"Will you be good enough to tell us what?"

"A letter."

"From where?"

"From the Louvre."

"Sealed with what seal?"

"The royal seal"

Ernanton put his hand into the breast of his doublet and drew out a letter.

"That is it," said Chicot, "and for greater certainty, I was to give you something in exchange, was I not?"

"A receipt."

"Yes."

"Monsieur," continued Ernanton, "I was told to carry it, but this gentleman was to deliver it." And he handed the letter to St. Maline, who gave it to Chicot.

"You see," said Ernanton, "that we have faithfully fulfilled our mission. There is no one here, and no one has seen us give you the letter."

"It is true, gentlemen; but to whom am I to give the receipt?"

" The king did not say," said St. Maline, with a meaning air.

" Write two, monsieur, and give one to each of us. It is far from this to the Louvre, and some misfortune may happen to one of us on the road," and as he spoke, Ernanton's eyes flashed in their turn.

" You are wise," said Chicot, drawing his tablets from his pocket, from which he tore out two pages and wrote on each: " Received from the hands of M. de St. Maline the letter brought by M. Ernanton de Carmainges.—THE SHADE."

" Adieu, monsieur," said St. Maline, taking his.

" Adieu, monsieur, and a pleasant journey to you," added Ernanton. " Have you anything else to send to the Louvre?"

" Nothing, I thank you."

Then the young men set off towards Paris; and Chicot in the opposite direction. When he was out of sight:

" Now, monsieur," said Ernanton to St. Maline, " dismount if you please."

" And why so?"

" Our task is accomplished; we have now to converse, and this place appears excellent for an explanation of this sort."

" As you please, monsieur;" and they got off their horses.

Then Ernanton said: "You know, monsieur, that without any cause on my part, you have during the whole journey insulted me grievously. You wished to make me fight at an inopportune time, and I refused; but now the time is good and I am your man."

But St. Maline was angry no longer, and did not wish to fight.

" Monsieur," replied he, " when I insulted you, you responded by rendering me a service. I can no longer hold the language I did just now."

" No; but you think the same."

" How do you know?"

" Because your words were dictated by hatred and envy, and they cannot already be extinct in your heart."

St. Maline coloured, but did not reply.

Ernanton continued: "If the king preferred me to you, it was because I pleased him best. If I was not thrown into the Bievre like you, it was because I ride better; if I did not accept your challenge before, it was because I was wiser than you; if I now summon you to draw your sword, it is because I have more honour; and if you hesitate, I shall say more courage."

St. Maline looked like a demon, and drew his sword furiously.

"I have fought eleven times," said he, "and two of my adversaries are dead. Are you aware of that, monsieur?"

"And I, monsieur, have never fought, for I have never had occasion, and I did not seek it now. I wait your pleasure, monsieur."

"Oh!" said St. Maline, "we are compatriots, and we are both in the king's service; do not let us quarrel. You are a brave man, and I would give you my hand if I could. What would you have? I am envious—it is my nature. M. de Chalabre, or M. de Montcrabeau, would not have made me angry; it was your superior merit. Console yourself, therefore, for I can do nothing against you, and unluckily your merit remains. I should not like anyone to know the cause of our quarrel."

Ernanton was calmed; St. Maline was no longer an object of anger but of pity.

"Good fortune should cure you," said he; "when you succeed, you should hate less."

"However high I should rise, others would be higher."

They rode on silently for some time. At last Ernanton held out his hand to St. Maline, and said: "Shall I try to cure you?"

"No, do not try that; you would fail. Hate me, on the contrary, and I shall admire you."

An hour after they entered the Louvre; the king had gone out, and would not return until evening.


# CHAPTER XXX

### DE LOIGNAC'S INTERVIEW WITH THE FORTY-FIVE

Each of the young men placed himself at a window to watch for the return of the king. Ernanton, however, soon forgot his present situation, and became abstracted in thinking who the woman could be who had entered Paris as his page, and whom he had since seen in such a splendid litter; and with a heart more disposed to love adventure than to make ambitious calculations, he forgot why he was sitting there, till, suddenly raising his head, he saw that St. Maline was no longer there. He understood at once that he had seen the king arrive, and had gone to him. He rose quickly, traversed the gallery, and arrived at the king's room just as St. Maline was coming out.

"Look!" cried he joyfully, "what the king has given me," and he showed a gold chain.

"I congratulate you, monsieur," said Ernanton, quietly, and he entered in his turn.

St. Maline waited impatiently until he came out again, which he did in about ten minutes, although it appeared an hour to St. Maline.

When Ernanton came out, he looked all over him, and seeing nothing, he cried joyfully: "And you, monsieur, what has he given to you?"

"His hand to kiss," replied Ernanton.

St. Maline crushed his chain impatiently in his hands, and they both returned in silence. As they entered the hall, the trumpet sounded, and at this signal all the Forty-five came out of their rooms, wondering what was the matter; while they profited by this reunion to examine each other. Most of them were richly dressed, though generally in bad taste. They all had a military tournour, and long swords, boots and gloves of buckskin or buffalo, all well gilded or well greased, were almost universal.

All the gentlemen were there admiring each other, when M. de Loignac entered frowning, and placed himself in front of them, with a countenance anything but agreeable.

"Gentlemen," said he, "are you all here?"

"All!" they replied.

"Well, gentlemen, this very day a measure of his majesty's has been betrayed, and a step which he wished to take rendered, perhaps, impossible."

Terror began to replace pride in the minds of the Forty-five, and they looked at each other with suspicion and disquietude.

"Two of you, gentlemen," continued De Loignac, "have been heard in the open street chattering like a couple of old women, and that about grave things."

St. Maline advanced. "Monsieur," said he, "pray explain at once, that suspicion may not rest on us all."

"That is easy. The king heard to-day that one of his enemies—precisely one of those whom we have been enrolled to guard him against—had arrived in Paris to conspire against him. This name was pronounced quietly, but was overheard by a soldier on guard, that is to say, by a man who should be regarded as a wall—deaf, dumb and immovable. However, that man repeated this name in the street with a noise and boasting, which attracted the attention of the passers-by and raised quite an emotion; I know it, for I was there, and heard and saw all, and had I not placed my hand on his shoulder to stop him, he would have compromised such grave interests, that, had he not been quiet at

my touch, I should have been compelled to poniard him on
the spot."

Pertinax de Montcrabeau and Perducas de Pincornay
turned deadly pale, and Montcrabeau tried to stammer out
some excuses. All eyes were turned towards them.

"Nothing can excuse you," said De Loignac; "even if you
were drunk you should be punished for that; and you shall be
punished."

Montcrabeau nearly fainted, and Pertinax grew paler than
ever.

"I shall have," De Loignac continued, "for smaller offences
lighter punishments, as imprisonment, for instance. For this
time, I spare the lives of M. de Montcrabeau and M. de
Pincornay, because they probably acted in ignorance, and
shall only enforce against them my third method of punishment—a fine. You have received one thousand livres apiece,
gentlemen; you will each return one hundred."

They all retired except Ernanton, who lingered behind.

"Do you wish anything?" asked De Loignac.

"Yes, monsieur," said Ernanton, bowing; "it seems to me
that you have forgotten to point out to us our duties. To be
in the king's service has a glorious sound, doubtless, but I
should wish to know in what this service consists?"

"That, monsieur, is a question to which I cannot reply."

"May I ask why, monsieur?"

"Because I, myself, am often ignorant in the morning of
what I shall have to do in the evening."

"Monsieur, you are placed in such a high position that you
must know much of which we are ignorant."

"You love the king, I suppose?"

"I do; and I ought to do so, as a subject and a gentleman."

"Well! that is the cardinal point by which to regulate your
conduct."

"Very well, monsieur; but there is one point which disquiets me."

"What is it?"

"Passive obedience."

"It is an essential condition."

"So I understand; but it is sometimes difficult for persons
who are delicate on points of honour."

"That does not concern me, M. de Carmainges."

"But, monsieur, when an order displeases you——"

"I read the signature of M. d'Epernon, and that consoles
me."

"And M. d'Epernon?"

"He reads the signature of his majesty, and consoles himself as I do."

"You are right, monsieur, and I am your humble servant;" and Ernanton was about to retire, when De Loignac stopped him.

"I will say to you," said he, "what I have not said to the others, for no one else has had the courage to speak to me thus."

Ernanton bowed.

"Perhaps," continued De Loignac, "a great personage will come to the Louvre this evening; if so, do not lose sight of him, and follow him when he leaves."

"Pardon me, monsieur; but that seems the work of a spy."

"Do you think so? It is possible; but look here"—and he drew out a paper which he presented to Ernanton, who read:—

"'Have M. de Mayenne followed this evening, if he presents himself at the Louvre.—D'EPERNON.'"

"Well, monsieur?"

"I will follow M. de Mayenne," said Ernanton, bowing.


# CHAPTER XXXI

### THE BOURGEOIS OF PARIS

M. de Mayenne, with whom they were so much occupied at the Louvre, set out from the Hôtel Guise, booted and on horseback, as though he had just arrived. He was received by the king affectionately.

"Well, cousin," said he, "you have, then, come to visit Paris?"

"Yes, sire; but we have our business at Soissons."

"What business, duke?"

"Your majesty's, sire."

"Ah! true; continue, Mayenne, to do as you have done; I know how to appreciate the conduct of my subjects."

The duke retired, smiling. The king rubbed his hands, and De Loignac made a sign to Ernanton, who spoke to his valet, and then followed M. de Mayenne. There was no fear of missing him, for the news of his arrival had spread, and some hundred leaguers had assembled to greet him.

As the duke reached his hotel, Ernanton saw a litter pierce

through the crowd. De Mayenne approached it, and the curtains were opened, and Ernanton thought he recognised his former page. The litter disappeared under the gateway, and Mayenne followed; an instant after, M. de Mayneville appeared on the balcony, and thanked the Parisians in the duke's name, but begged them to disperse and go home.

All went away accordingly, except ten men, who had entered after the duke. These were the deputies of the League, who were sent to thank M. de Mayenne for his visit, and to beg that his brothers would come also. They had a number of plans, which only wanted the sanction and support of the chiefs. Bussy Leclerc came to announce that he had instructed the monks of three monasteries in the use of arms, and had enrolled 500 bourgeois in a regiment.

Lachapelle-Marteau had worked on the magistrates and had 200 black robes ready for councillors. Brigard had gained the merchants of the Rue Lombards and the Rue St. Denis. Crucé could answer for the University of Paris, and Delbar promised for all the sailors in the port, a dangerous body of 500 men. Each of the others had something to offer, even Nicholas Poulain, the friend of Chicot.

When Mayenne had heard them all, he said: " I admire your strength, but I do not see the end you propose to yourselves."

Bussy Leclerc answered: " We want a change, and as we are the strongest——"

" But how will you arrive at this change?"

" It seems to me," replied Bussy, boldly, " that as the idea of the Union came from our chiefs, it is for them to point out its aim."

" You are perfectly right," said Mayenne, " but it is also for them to judge of the proper time for action. The troops of M. de Guise may be ready, but he does not give the signal until he thinks fit."

" But, monseigneur, we are impatient."

" For what?"

" To arrive at our end. We also have our plan."

" Ah! that is different; if you have your own plan, I say no more."

" Yes, monseigneur; but may we count on your aid?"

" Doubtless, if this plan be approved by my brother and myself."

" We believe it will."

" Let me hear it then."

The leaguers looked at each other, then Marteau advanced.

" Monseigneur," said he, " we think the success of our plan certain. There are particular points where all the strength of the city lies—the great and the little Châtelet, the Hôtel de Ville, the arsenal and the Louvre."

" It is true."

" All these are guarded, but could easily be surprised."

" I admit this also."

" The town itself, however, is defended outside, firstly, by the chevalier of the watch with his archers. We thought of seizing him in his house, which could be easily done, as it is a lonely place."

Mayenne shook his head. " However lonely," said he, " you cannot force a door and fire twenty shots without attracting attention."

" We have foreseen this objection, but one of the archers of the watch is on our side. In the middle of the night, two or three of us will go and knock at the door; the archer will open, and tell his chief that the king wishes to speak to him, which would not appear strange, as he is often sent for in this manner. Once the door is open we will introduce ten men— sailors who lodge near—who will soon finish him."

" Murder him?"

" Yes, monseigneur. At the same time we will force the doors of the other functionaries who might take his place, such as M. d'O, M. de Chiverny, and M. le Procureur Laguesle. St. Bartholomew has taught us how to manage."

" This is all well, gentlemen; but you have not told me if you mean, at the same time, to force the doors of the Louvre —that strong and well-guarded fortress. Believe me, the king is not so easily taken as the chevalier of the watch."

" We have chosen four thousand men, who hate the king, for this undertaking."

" Very good; but supposing all this accomplished, the watch disarmed, the authorities disappeared, and all obstacles removed, what do you mean to do?"

" Form a new government of honest people. As for ourselves, so long as our commerce is successful, and we have enough for our wives and children, we care for little else. Some amongst us might desire a command, and they should have it. We are not difficult to satisfy."

" Oh!" murmured Nicholas Poulain, " I wish I were out of all this."

## CHAPTER XXXII

### BROTHER BORROMEE

It was about ten o'clock in the evening when the deputies returned home. Nicholas Poulain remained behind the others, reflecting on the perplexing situation in which he found himself, and considering whether he should report all that he had heard to M. d'Epernon, when, in the middle of the Rue de la Pierre-au-Réal, he ran right against a Jacobin monk. They both began to swear, but, looking up, recognised each other.

"Brother Borromée!" cried Poulain.

"Nicholas Poulain!" exclaimed the monk.

"How are you?" asked Nicholas, cautiously. "Where in the world were you running to in such a hurry at this time of night? Is the priory on fire?"

"No; I was going to the Duchesse de Montpensier's hôtel, to speak to M. de Mayneville."

"And what for?"

"Oh! it is very simple," said Borromée, seeking for a specious answer; "the reverend prior was solicited by the duchess to become her confessor; he accepted at the time, but since then he has had scruples, and has sent me to tell her not to rely upon him."

"Very good, but you are going away from the Hôtel Guise."

"Exactly so; for I hear she is at the Hôtel St. Denis, with her brother."

"Quite true; but why do you deceive me? It is not the treasurer who is sent with these sort of messages."

"But to a princess! Now do not detain me, or I shall miss her."

"She will return, you might have waited for her."

"True; but I shall not be sorry to see M. le Duc also."

"Oh! that is more like the truth, so go on. There is something new going on," thought Nicholas; "but why should I try to discover what it is?"

Meanwhile the brother and sister had been conversing together, and had settled that the king had no suspicions, and was therefore easy to attack. They also agreed that the first thing to be done was to organise the League more generally in the provinces, while the king abandoned his brother, who was the only enemy they had to fear, so long as Henri of Navarre occupied himself only with love affairs.

"Paris is all ready, but must wait," said Mayenne.

At this moment M. de Mayneville entered, and announced Borromée.

"Borromée! who is he?" cried the duke.

"The man whom you sent me from Nancy, when I asked for a man of action and mind."

"I remember; I told you he was both. But he was called Borroville."

"Yes, monseigneur; but now he is a monk, and called Borromée."

"Borroville a monk! and why so?"

"That is our secret, monseigneur; you shall know hereafter, but now let us see him, for his visit disquiets me."

"Why, Borroville," cried the duke, laughing, as he entered; "what a disguise!"

"Yes, monseigneur, I am not much at my ease in this devil of a dress, I confess; but, as it is worn in the service of her highness, I do not complain."

"Well! now speak."

"M. le Duc, the king is sending succours to the Duc d'Anjou."

"Bah! we have heard that the last three years."

"Yes; but this time it is certain. At two o'clock this morning, M. de Joyeuse set out for Rouen; he is to take ship to Dieppe, and convey three thousand men to Antwerp."

"Oh! who told you that, Borroville?"

"I heard it from a man who is going to Navarre."

"To Navarre! to Henri?"

"Yes, monseigneur."

"And who sends him?"

"The king, with a letter."

"What is his name?"

"Robert Briquet; he is a great friend of Gorenflot's."

"We must have this letter."

"Certainly," said the duchess.

"How was it that this did not occur to you?" said Mayneville.

"I did think of it, and wished to send one of my men, who is a perfect Hercules, with M. Briquet, but he suspected, and dismissed him."

"You must go yourself."

"Impossible!"

"And why?"

"Because he knows me."

"As a monk, but not as captain, I hope."

"Ma foi! I do not know; he seems to know everything."

"What is he like?"

"He is tall—all nerves, muscles and bones; silent, but mocking."

"Ah! ah! and clever with his sword?"

"Marvellously."

"A long face?"

"Yes."

"And an old friend of the prior's?"

"Yes."

"Oh! I have a suspicion which I must have cleared up. Borroville, you must go to Soissons, to my brother——"

"But the priory?"

"Oh! you can invent some excuse to Gorenflot; he believes all you say," said Mayneville.

"You will tell my brother all you know about the mission of M. de Joyeuse."

"Yes, monseigneur."

"And Navarre——" said the duchess.

"Oh! I charge myself with that," said Mayenne. "Let them saddle me a fresh horse, Mayneville." Then he murmured to himself: "Can he be still alive?"

## CHAPTER XXXIII

### CHICOT, LATINIST

After the departure of the young men, Chicot went on quietly; but as soon as they had disappeared in the valley, he stopped at the top of a hill and looked all round him; then, seeing no one, he seated himself, and commenced an examination. He had now two purses, for he perceived that the packet he had received contained money, besides the letter. It was quite a royal purse, embroidered with an " H " at each end.

"It is pretty," said Chicot, "no one could be more generous or more stupid. Decidedly I shall never make anything of the king. All that astonishes me is that he did not have the letter embroidered outside also. Now let me see how much money he has sent. One hundred crowns; just the sum I borrowed from Gorenflot. Ah! pardon, Henri, this is good. But the purse annoys me; if I were to keep it I should feel as if the very birds, as they flew over my head, would denounce me as a royal messenger."

So saying, he drew from his pocket Gorenflot's bag, emptied the king's money into it, then placed a stone in the purse, and threw it into the Orge, which flowed under the bridge at his feet.

" So much for myself—now for Henri," said Chicot; and he took up the letter, broke the seal with the utmost tranquillity, and sent the envelope into the river after the purse. " Now," said he, " let us read."

> " ' Dear brother, the deep love which you felt for our late dear brother and king, Charles IX., still clings to the Louvre and to my heart; it grieves me, therefore, to have to write to you about vexatious things. You are strong, however, against ill fortune, so that I do not hesitate to communicate these things to you—things which can only be told to a tried friend. Besides, I have an interest in warning you—the honour of my name and of your own, my brother. We resemble each other in one thing, that we are each surrounded with enemies. Chicot will explain to you.
>
> " ' M. de Turenne, your servant, causes daily scandal at your court; God forbid that I should interfere in your affairs, except where your honour is concerned, but your wife, whom to my regret I call my sister, should be more careful than she is of your honour. I advise you, there-fore, to watch the communications of Margot with Turenne, that she does not bring shame on the house of Bourbon. Act as soon as you shall be sure of the fact, into which I pray you to inquire as soon as Chicot shall have explained to you my letter.
>
> " ' Those whom as brother and king I denounce to you, generally meet at a little château called Loignac, the pretext being generally the chase. This château is, besides, the focus for intrigues to which the Guises are not strangers, and you know the strange love with which my sister pursued Henri de Guise. I embrace you, and am ever ready to aid you in all, and for all; meanwhile aid yourself by the advice of Chicot, whom I send to you. Your affectionate,' etc.

" *Age auctore Chicot*," said Chicot, " here am I, installed counsellor of the king of Navarre! This seems to me a bad commission, and in flying one ill, I have fallen into a worse one. Really, I should almost prefer Mayenne. But the letter is clever, and if Henriot be like other husbands, it will embroil him at once with his wife, Turenne, the Guises, and even with Spain. But if Henri de Valois is so well informed of all that passes in Navarre, he must have some spy there."

" Then, again," continued he, " this letter will lead me

into mischief if I meet a Spaniard, a Lorraine, a Béarnais, or a Fleming curious enough to wish to know what brings me here, and I should be very foolish not to remember that there is a chance of that. M. Borromée, above all, I suspect may play me some trick. Besides, what did I seek in asking the king for this mission? Tranquillity. And now I am going to embroil the King of Navarre with his wife. However, that is not my affair, except that I shall make mortal enemies, who will prevent me from ever reaching the happy age of eighty.

" Ma foi! but that is not much, for it is only worth living when you are young. But then I might as well have waited for the knife of M. de Mayenne. However, I will take precautions, and will translate this fine letter into Latin, and engrave it on my memory; then I will buy a horse, because from Juvisy to Pau I should have too often to put the right foot before the left if I walked—but first I will destroy this letter."

This he proceeded to do; tearing it into an infinite number of little pieces, sending some into the river, others into the air, and burying the rest in holes in the ground.

" Now, let me think of my Latin theme," said he; and this study occupied him until he arrived at Corbeil, where he bestowed a glance at the Cathedral, but fixed an earnest look at a traiteur's, whence came an appetising smell of dinner. We will not describe either the dinner he made or the horse he bought; suffice it to say that the dinner was long and the horse was bad.


## CHAPTER XXXIV

### THE FOUR WINDS

Chicot, with his little horse, which ought to have been a big one to have carried him, after having slept at Fontainebleau, made a détour to the right, and proceeded towards the little village of Orgeval. He would have gone further that day, but his horse failed him. He put up, therefore, at a good hotel, and went through the rooms to select one where the doors closed well, and chose an apartment which had just been repaired, and the door of which was furnished with a formidable lock.

Before going to bed, although the hotel had appeared almost empty, he locked the door and placed a heavy table and a chest of drawers against it. He then put his purse under his pillow, and repeated to himself three times over the translation of the king's letter. There was an extremely high wind blowing, and as it howled in the neighbouring trees, it was with a feeling of great satisfaction that Chicot plunged into a very comfortable bed.

He had a lamp by his bedside, and he occupied himself for some time in reading a book which he had brought with him; but, although he liked the book, in reading the third chapter he fell asleep. The wind moaned about the house, sometimes like a child crying, and sometimes like a husband scolding his wife; and as Chicot slept, it seemed to him, in his dreams, that the tempest came nearer and nearer. All at once a sudden squall of invincible force broke locks and bolts— pushed the chest of drawers, which fell on the lamp, which it extinguished, and on the table, which it smashed.

Chicot had the faculty of waking quickly, and with all his senses about him, so he jumped out of bed and got hold in an instant of his purse and his sword. It was quite dark, but it seemed to him that the whole room was being torn to pieces by the four winds of heaven; for the chairs were fall-ing, and the table breaking more and more under the weight of the drawers. As he could do nothing against the gods of Olympus, he contented himself with standing in one corner, with his sword held out before him, so that if any of these mythological personages approached, they would spit them-selves upon it.

At last he profited by a momentary cessation in the uproar to cry loudly: " Help! help!"

He made so much noise that it seemed to quiet the elements, as if Neptune had pronounced the famous *Quos ego,* and, after six or seven minutes, during which Eurus, Notus, Boreas and Aquilo seemed to beat a retreat, the host appeared with a lantern and enlightened the scene, which looked deplorably like a field of battle. The great chest of drawers was overturned on the broken table; the door was held only by one of its hinges, and the bolts were broken; three or four chairs were on the floor with their legs in the air, and, to crown all, the crockery, which had been on the table, lay in bits on the floor.

" This is a regular pandemonium," cried Chicot, recognising his host.

" Oh! monsieur," cried the host, clasping his hands, " what has happened?"

" Are there demons lodging here?" asked Chicot.

" Oh! what weather," replied the host pathetically.

" But the bolts do not hold; this house must be made of cardboard. I would rather go away—I prefer the road."

"Oh! my poor furniture," sighed the host.

"But my clothes! where are they? They were on this chair."

"If they were there, they ought to be there still," replied the host.

"What! 'if they were there.' Do you think I came here yesterday in this costume?"

The host drew back towards the door. "You call me thief!" said he.

"You are responsible for my clothes, and they are gone—you will not deny that?"

"You insult me."

Chicot made a menacing gesture.

"Hola!" cried the host; "hola! help!"

Four men armed with sticks immediately appeared.

"Ah! here are the four winds," cried Chicot, making a thrust with his sword at one of them; but they all rapidly disappeared, not, however, before one of them had whispered something to the host.

"Your clothes shall be found," growled he.

"Well! that is all I ask."

They soon made their appearance, but visibly deteriorated.

"Ah! there are nails in your staircase; what a devil of a wind it was," said Chicot.

"Now you will go to bed again?" said the host.

"No, I thank you, I have slept enough; leave me your lantern and I will read."

Chicot replaced the chest of drawers against the door, dressed himself, got into bed again, and read till daybreak, when he asked for his horse, paid his bill, and went away, saying to himself:—

"We shall see, to-night."


## CHAPTER XXXV

### HOW CHICOT CONTINUED HIS JOURNEY, AND WHAT HAPPENED TO HIM

Chicot passed his morning in congratulating himself on the sang-froid and patience he had displayed through his night of trials.

Every tree, rising ground, or wall, served him for a point of observation. He also concluded on the road alliances, if not offensive, at least defensive. Four grocers from Paris, who were going to Orleans to order preserves, and to Limoges for dried fruits, allowed Chicot, who called himself a hosier from Bordeaux, returning home, to join their company, which was rendered more formidable by four clerks, who were following their masters. It was quite a little army, and scarcely less formidable in mind than in number, so warlike a spirit had the League introduced among the Parisian shop-keepers. At all events, three cowards together have less fear than one brave man alone. At least they reached Etampes, the town fixed on for supper and sleeping. They supped, and each went to his room.

Chicot, who had not been sparing during the repast, either of his fun, which amused his companions, or of the Muscat and Burgundy, went to bed, after having settled to travel again with the grocers on the morrow. Chicot, therefore, thought himself guarded like a prince by the four travellers, whose rooms were in the same corridor and close to his own.

About half-past nine a blow was struck on the door of the room where the clerks all slept. One of them opened in a very bad humour, and found himself face to face with the host.

"Gentlemen," said he, "I see with pleasure that you are sleeping all ready dressed, for I wish to render you a great service. Your masters grew very warm over politics at supper-time, and it seems that a sheriff of the town heard them and reported it. Now, as we are very loyal here, the mayor sent down the watch, and they have arrested your masters and carried them off. The prison is near the Hôtel de Ville; go, my lads, your mules are ready for you, your masters will join you on the road."

The four clerks shook like hares, ran downstairs, jumped on their mules, and took the road back to Paris, telling the host to let their masters know, if they should return to the hotel.

Having seen them disappear, the host went to knock very gently at one of the doors in the corridor.

One of the merchants cried out in a loud voice: "Who is there?"

"Why, it seems you talked rather too freely at table, and the mayor has been informed by some spy, and has sent to arrest you. Luckily, I thought of showing them your clerks' room instead of yours, so that they are busy upstairs arresting them."

"Can this be true?"

"Pure and simple truth. Make haste, and escape while you can."

Of course Chicot had received no warning. While the

merchants were flying, he was sleeping peacefully.

The host now descended into the hall, where stood six armed men, one of whom seemed to command the others.

"Well?" said this one.

"I have obeyed your orders, monsieur."

"Your inn is deserted?"

"Absolutely."

"The person is not awakened."

"No."

Then the officer ordered two men to place themselves under Chicot's window, while he himself, with the three others, mounted to his room.

"You know the order," said the officer. "If he opens and lets us search, and we find what we seek, we will not do him the least harm; but if the contrary happens, a good blow with dagger; no pistol, you understand—besides, it is useless, being four against one."

The officer knocked.

"Who is there?" cried Chicot.

"Your friends the grocers, who have something important to tell you."

"Ventre de biche! I do not smell the grocery."

"Ah! you will not open?" cried the officer, impatiently. "Break open the door."

Chicot ran to the window, but saw below two naked swords shining.

"I am caught," said he.

"Ah! ah!" cried the officer, who had heard the noise of the window opening; "you fear the perilous leap, and you are right. Come, open!"

Chicot heard three blows struck on the door.

"They have three muskets," said he; "and below there are only two swords, and only fifteen feet to jump; I prefer the swords to the muskets."

And tying his bag to his belt, he got on the window-sill with his drawn sword. The two men below stood ready with their drawn swords, but, as Chicot guessed, on seeing him jump sword in hand, they drew back, intending to strike him as he came to the ground. Chicot alighted on his feet, and one of the men gave him a thrust immediately. Thanks, however, to Gorenflot's coat of mail, the blade broke like glass.

"He has armour!" cried the soldier.

"Pardieu!" said Chicot, cutting open his head with a blow of his sword.

The other began to cry out, thinking now only of defending

himself, but, at the second pass, Chicot laid him by his comrade; so that when the door was burst open, the officer saw through the window his two sentinels lying in their blood, and Chicot running quietly away.

" He is a demon; he is steel-proof!" cried he.

## CHAPTER XXXVI

### THE THIRD DAY OF THE JOURNEY

Chicot knew he was safe in the city of Etampes, where he was under the protection of the magistrates who would have arrested the officer immediately on his complaint.

At break of day he started again, but a prey to anxiety, for although two attempts had failed, the third might be successful. He determined when he reached Orleans to send to the king to ask for an escort.

But as the road to Orleans was passed without accident, Chicot began to think again that it was needless, and that the king would lose his good opinion of him, and also that an escort would be a great trouble. He went on, therefore, but his fears began to return as evening advanced. All at once he heard behind him the galloping of horses, and turning round he counted seven cavaliers, of whom four had muskets on their shoulders. They gained rapidly on Chicot, who, seeing flight was hopeless, contented himself with making his horse move in zig-zags, so as to escape the balls which he expected every moment. He was right, for when they came about fifty feet from him, they fired, but thanks to his manœuvre, all the balls missed him. He immediately abandoned the reins and let himself slip to the ground, taking the precaution to have his sword in one hand and a dagger in the other.

He came to the ground in such a position that his head was protected by the breast of his horse.

A cry of joy came from the troop, who, seeing him fall, believed him dead.

" I told you so," said a man, riding up, with a mask on his face; " you failed because you did not follow my orders. This time, here he is; search him, and if he moves, finish him."

Chicot was not a pious man, but at such a moment he remembered his God and murmured a fervent prayer.

Two men approached him sword in hand, and as he did not stir, came fearlessly forward; but instantly Chicot's dagger

was in the throat of one, and his sword half buried in the side
of the other.

"Ah! treason!" cried the chief, "he is not dead; charge
your muskets."

"Be firm, and I will aid you," cried a voice, which seemed
to Chicot to come from Heaven.

It was that of a fine young man, on a black horse. He had
a pistol in each hand, and cried again to Chicot: "Stoop!
morbleu, stoop!"

Chicot obeyed.

One pistol was fired, and a man rolled at Chicot's feet;
then the second, and another man fell.

"Now we are two to two," cried Chicot; "generous young
man, you take one, here is mine," and he rushed on the
masked man, who defended himself as if used to arms.

The young man seized his opponent by the body, threw
him down, and bound him with his belt. Chicot soon
wounded his adversary, who was very corpulent, between
the ribs; he fell, and Chicot, putting his foot on his sword
to prevent him from using it, cut the strings of his mask.

"M. de Mayenne! ventre de biche, I thought so," said he.

The duke did not reply; he had fainted from loss of blood
and the weight of his fall. Chicot drew his dagger, and was
about coolly to cut off his head, when his arm was seized by a
grasp of iron, and a voice said:—

"Stay, monsieur; one does not kill a fallen enemy."

"Bah! do you know this wretch?"

"That wretch is M. le Duc de Mayenne, a prince equal in
rank to many kings."

"All the more reason. And who are you?"

"He who has saved your life, monsieur."

"And who, if I do not deceive myself, brought me a letter
from the king three days ago."

"Precisely."

"Then you are in the king's service?"

"I have that honour."

"And yet you save M. de Mayenne? Permit me to tell
you, monsieur, that that is not being a good servant."

"I think differently."

"Well, perhaps you are right. What is your name?"

"Ernanton de Carmainges."

"Well, M. Ernanton, what are we to do with this great
carcass?"

"I will watch over M. de Mayenne, monsieur."

Chicot made no more compliments, but got on Ernanton's
horse and disappeared.

D

## CHAPTER XXXVII

### ERNANTON DE CARMAINGES

Ernanton remained on the field of battle, much embarrassed what to do with the two men, who would shortly open their eyes. As he deliberated, he saw a waggon coming along, drawn by two oxen, and driven by a peasant. Ernanton went to the man and told him that a combat had taken place between the Huguenots and Catholics, that four had been killed, but that two were still living. The peasant although desperately frightened, aided Ernanton to place first M. de Mayenne and then the soldier in the waggon. The four bodies remained.

It was in the stable, on a bed of straw, that M. de Mayenne recovered his consciousness. Ernanton immediately dismissed the peasant.

" Who are you, monsieur?" asked Mayenne.

Ernanton smiled.

" Do you not recognise me?" said he.

" Yes, I do now; you are he who came to the assistance of my enemy."

" Yes, but I am he who prevented your enemy from killing you."

" You know me, then?" said Mayenne, with a scrutinising glance.

" I had no need to know you, monsieur; you were a wounded man, that was enough."

" Be frank; you knew me?"

" It is strange, monsieur, that you will not understand me. It seems to me that it is equally ignoble to kill a defenceless man, as six men to attack one."

" Do you think me dangerously wounded?"

" I have examined your wound, monsieur, and I think that although it is serious, you are in no danger of death. believe the sword slipped along the ribs, and did not penetrate the breast. Breathe, and I think you will find no pain in the lungs."

" Ah!" said Mayenne, with evident satisfaction. " But the living man; where is he?"

" In the barn, close by."

" Bring him to me, monsieur; and if you are a man of honour, promise me to ask him no questions."

" I am not curious, monsieur; and I wish to know no more of this affair than I know already."

The duke looked at him uneasily.

"Monsieur," said Ernanton, "will you charge someone else with the commission you have just given me?"

"I was wrong, monsieur, I acknowledge it; have the kindness to render me the service I ask of you."

Five minutes after, the soldier entered the stable. He uttered a cry on seeing the duke, but he put his finger on his lip, and the man was silent.

"Monsieur," said Mayenne to Ernanton, "my gratitude to you will be eternal; and, doubtless, some day we shall meet under more favourable circumstances. May I ask to whom I have the honour of speaking?"

"I am the Vicomte Ernanton de Carmainges, monsieur."

"You were going to Beaugency?"

"Yes, monsieur."

"Then I have delayed you, and you cannot go on to-night."

"On the contrary, monsieur, I am about to start at once."

"For Beaugency?"

"No, for Paris," said Ernanton; "somewhat unwillingly."

The duke appeared astonished.

"Pardon," said he, "but it is strange that going to Beaugency, and being stopped by an unforeseen circumstance, you should return without fulfilling the end of your journey."

"Nothing is more simple, monsieur; I was going to a rendezvous for a particular time, which I have lost by coming here with you; therefore I return."

"M. de Carmainges, give me your word of honour that if I entrust you with a letter it shall be given to the person to whom it is addressed."

"I give it, monsieur."

"I believe you; I am sure I may trust you. I must tell you a part of my secret. I belong to the guards of Madame de Montpensier."

"Well?"

"Will you therefore put into her own hands the letter I am about to write?"

"I will seek for ink and paper."

"It is needless, my soldier will get my tablets."

He instructed the soldier to take them from his pocket, opened them by a spring, wrote some lines in pencil, and shut them again. It was impossible for anyone who did not know the secret to open them without breaking them.

"Monsieur," said Ernanton, "in three days these tablets shall be delivered."

"Into her own hands?"

"Yes, monsieur."

The duke, exhausted by talking, and by the effort of writing the letter, sank back on his straw.


# CHAPTER XXXVIII

### THE STABLE-YARD

Ernanton arrived at Paris on the third day. At three in the afternoon he entered the Louvre, among his comrades. The Gascons called out in surprise at seeing him, and M. de Loignac looked gloomy, and signed to him to enter a little room, where he always gave his private audiences.

"This is nice behaviour, monsieur," said he; "five days and five nights absent; and you whom I thought so well of."

"Monsieur, I did what I was told to do."

"What were you told to do?"

"To follow M. de Mayenne, and I have followed him."

"For five days and nights?"

"Yes, monsieur."

"Then he has left Paris?"

"He left that same evening, and that seemed to me suspicious."

"You are right, monsieur, go on."

Ernanton related clearly and energetically all that had taken place. When Ernanton mentioned the letter:

"You have it, monsieur?" asked De Loignac.

"Yes, monsieur."

"Diable! that deserves attention; come with me, I beg of you."

Ernanton followed De Loignac to the court-yard of the Louvre. All was preparing for the king's going out, and M. d'Epernon was seeing two new horses tried, which had been sent from England, as a present from Elizabeth to Henri, and which were that day to be harnessed to the king's carriage for the first time.

De Loignac approached D'Epernon.

"Great news, M. le Duc," said he.

"What is it?" said D'Epernon, drawing to one side.

"M. de Carmainges has seen M. de Mayenne lying wounded in a village beyond Orleans."

"Wounded!"

"Yes, and more, he has written a letter to Madame de Montpensier, which M. de Carmainges has in his pocket."

"Oh! oh! send M. de Carmainges to me."

"Here he is," said De Loignac, signing to Ernanton to advance.

"Well, monsieur, it seems you have a letter from M. de Mayenne."

"Yes, monsieur."

"Addressed to Madame de Montpensier?"

"Yes, monsieur."

"Give it to me," and the duke extended his hand.

"No one shall touch it," cried Ernanton, starting back and drawing from his breast the tablet of M. de Mayenne, "for I will break it to pieces, since I can save it no other way; M. de Mayenne will approve my conduct, and the king will pardon me."

The young man was about to execute his threat, when a touch arrested his arm. He turned and saw the king, who, coming down the staircase behind them, had heard the end of the discussion.

"What is the matter, gentlemen?" said he.

"Sire," cried D'Epernon, furiously, "this man, one of your Forty-five Guardsmen, of which he shall soon cease to form part, being sent by me to watch M. de Mayenne, in Paris, followed him to Orleans, and received from him a letter for Madame de Montpensier."

"You have received this letter?" asked the king of Ernanton.

"Yes, sire, but M. d'Epernon does not you tell under what circumstances."

"Well, where is this letter?"

"That is just the cause of the quarrel, sire. M. de Carmainges resolutely refuses to give it to me, and determines to carry it to its address."

Carmainges bent one knee before the king. "Sire," said he, "I am a poor gentleman, but a man of honour. I saved the life of your messenger, who was about to be assassinated by M. de Mayenne and six of his followers, for I arrived just in turn to the fortune of the combat."

"And M. de Mayenne?"

"Was dangerously wounded."

"Well, after?"

"M. de Mayenne, reduced to one companion, for the four others were killed, did not wish to separate from him, and, ignorant that I belonged to your majesty, confided to me a letter to his sister. I have this letter, sire, and here it is; I offer it to your majesty who has the right to dispose of it and of me. My honour is dear to me, sire, but I place it fearlessly in your hands."

Ernanton, so saying, held out the tablets to the king, who gently put them back.

"What did you say, D'Epernon?" said he; "M. de Carmainges is an honest man and a faithful servant."

"But, sire," said D'Epernon, "think of what that letter may contain. Do not play at delicacy, when, perhaps, your majesty's life is concerned."

"You will deliver your letter, M. de Carmainges," said the king.

"I will deliver my letter."

"Just so. M. de Carmainges, have you promised anything else to M. de Mayenne than to deliver that letter to his sister?"

"No, sire."

"No secrecy as to the place where you find her?"

"No, sire."

"Then I will impose only one condition on you."

"I am your majesty's servant."

"Deliver your letter, and then come to me at Vincennes, where I shall be this evening."

"Yes, sire."

"And you will tell me where you found the duchess?"

"I will, sire."

"I ask no other confidences; remember."


## CHAPTER XXXIX

### THE SEVEN SINS OF MAGDALENE

The king, however, on seeing his horses, did not wish to be alone in the carriage, but desired D'Epernon to sit by him. De Loignac and St. Maline rode on each side, and an outrider in front. The king was, as usual, surrounded by dogs, and there was also a table in the carriage, covered with illuminated pictures, which the king cut out with wonderful s'ill, in spite of the movement of the carriage. He was just then occupied with the life of Magdalene, the sinner. The different pictures were labelled "Magdalene gives way to the sin of anger,"—"Magdalene gives way to the sin of gluttony," and so on through the seven cardinal sins. The one that the king was occupied with, as they passed through the Porte St. Antoine, represented Magdalene giving way to anger.

Fully occupied with this important work, the king merely raised his eyes as they passed by the convent of the Jacobins, from which vespers were sounding on every bell, and of which every window and door was closed.

But a hundred steps farther on, an attentive observer would have seen him throw a more curious glance on a fine-looking house on his left, which, built in the midst of a charming garden, opened on the road. This house was called Bel-Esbat, and, unlike the convent, had every window open with the exception of one, before which hung a blind. As the king passed, this blind moved perceptibly; Henri smiled at D'Epernon, and then fell to work on another picture. This was the sin of luxury. The artist had represented this in such glowing colours, and had painted the sin with so much courage and minuteness, that we can only describe a small part of it, viz:—that Magdalene's guardian angel was flying back to heaven affrighted, and hiding his face in his hands. All this occupied the king so much, that he never noticed an image of vanity who rode by his carriage. It was a pity; for St. Maline was very happy and proud on his horse, as he rode so near that the could hear the king say to his dog: " Gently, M. Love, you get in my way;" or to M. le Duc d'Epernon: " Duc, I believe these horses will break my neck." At last they arrived at Vincennes, and as the king had still three sins to cut out, he went at once to his own room to finish them. It was a bitterly cold day, therefore St. Maline sat down in a chimney corner to warm himself, and was nearly falling asleep, when De Loignac put his hand on his shoulder.

" You must work to-day," said he; " you shall sleep some other day; so get up, M. de St. Maline."

" I will not sleep for a fortnight, if necessary, monsieur."

" Oh! we shall not be so exacting as that."

" What must I do, monsieur?"

" Get on your horse and return to Paris."

" I am ready; my horse is standing saddled."

" Good; go then straight to the room of the Forty-five, and awaken everyone; but excepting three, whom I will name to you, no one must know where he is going, nor what he is about to do."

" I will obey these instructions implicitly."

" Here then are some more; leave fourteen of these gentlemen at the Port St. Antoine, fifteen others half way, and bring the rest here."

" Yes, monsieur; but at what hour must we leave Paris?"

" When night falls."

" On horseback or on foot?"

" On horseback."

" Armed?"

" Fully; with daggers, pistols, and swords."

" With armour?"

" Yes."

" What else?"

" Here are three letters; one for M. de Chalabre, one for M. de Biron, and one for yourself. M. de Chalabre will command the first party, M. de Biron the second, and yourself the third."

" Good, monsieur."

" These letters are only to be opened at six o'clock. M. de Chalabre will open his at the Porte St. Antoine, M. de Biron his at the Croix Faubin, and you yours on your return."

" Must we come quickly?"

" As quickly as possible, without creating suspicion. Let each troop come out of Paris by a different gate; M. de Chalabre by the Porte Bourdelle; M. de Biron by the Porte du Temple, and you through the Porte St. Antoine. All other instructions are in the letters. Go quickly from here to the Croix Faubin, but then slowly; you have still two hours before dark, which is more than necessary. Now do you well understand your orders?"

" Perfectly, monsieur."

" Fourteen in the first troop, fifteen in the second, and fifteen in the third; it is evident that they do not count Ernanton, and that he no longer forms part of the Forty-five," said St. Maline to himself when De Loignac was gone.

He fulfilled all his directions punctually. When he arrived among the Forty-five, the greater number of them were already preparing for their supper. But with one word he put an end to all this: " To horse, gentlemen," said he; and leaving them without another word, went to explain his orders to MM. de Biron and Chalabre. Some, while buckling on their belts and grasping their cuirasses, ate great mouthfuls, washed down by a draught of wine; and others, whose supper was less advanced, armed themselves with resignation. They called over the names, and only forty-four, including St. Maline, answered.

" M. Ernanton de Carmainges is missing," said De Chalabre, whose turn it was to exercise these functions. A profound joy filled the heart of St. Maline, and a smile played on his lips, a rare thing with this sombre and envious man.

The forty-four therefore set off on their different routes.

# CHAPTER XL

## BEL-ESBAT

It is needless to say that Ernanton, whom St. Maline thought ruined, was, on the contrary, pursuing the course of his unexpected and ascending fortunes. He had, of course, gone first to the Hôtel Guise. There, after having knocked at the great door and had it opened, he was only laughed at when he asked for an interview with the duchess. Then, as he insisted, they told him that he ought to know that her highness lived at Soissons and not at Paris. Ernanton was prepared for this reception, so it did not discourage him.

"I am grieved at her highness's absence," said he, "for I had a communication of great importance to deliver to her from the Duc de Mayenne."

"From the Duc de Mayenne! Who charged you to deliver it?"

"The duke himself."

"Will you let me see it?"

"Willingly." And Ernanton drew out the letter.

"What singular ink!" said the man.

"It is blood," said Ernanton, calmly.

The porter grew pale at these words, and at the idea that this blood belonged to M. de Mayenne.

"Monsieur," said the servant, "I do not know if you will find Madame de Montpensier in Paris or its environs; but go to a house in the Faubourg St. Antoine, called Bel-Esbat, which belongs to the duchess; it is the first on the left-hand going to Vincennes, after the convent of the Jacobins. You will be sure to find someone there in the service of the duchess sufficiently in her confidence to be able to tell you where Madame la Duchesse is just now."

"Thank you," said Ernanton, who saw that the man either could or would say no more.

He found Bel-Esbat easily, and without more inquiries, rang, and the door opened.

"Enter," said a man, who then seemed to wait for some password, but as Ernanton did not give any, he asked him what he wanted.

"I wish to speak to Madame la Duchesse de Montpensier."

"And why do you come here for her?"

"Because the porter at the Hôtel Guise sent me here."

" Madame la Duchesse is not here."

"That is unlucky, as it will prevent me from fulfilling the mission with which M. de Mayenne charged me."

" For Madame la Duchesse?"

"Yes."

"From M. le Duc de Mayenne?"

"Yes."

Ernanton followed the valet, and was shown into a little room, where a simply though elegantly dressed lady was seated at an embroidery frame.

"Here is the gentleman from M. de Mayenne, madame," said the servant.

She turned, and Ernanton uttered a cry of surprise.

"You, madame!" cried he, recognising at once his page and the lady of the litter.

"You!" cried the lady in her turn, letting her work drop, and looking at Ernanton.

"Leave us," said she to the valet.

"You are of the household of Madame de Montpensier, madame?" said Ernanton.

"Yes; but you, monsieur, how do you bring here a message from the Duc de Mayenne?"

"Madame, all my mission consists in delivering a letter to her highness."

"Well, then, give me the letter," said the lady, holding out her hand.

"Madame, I believed I had had the honour of telling you that this letter was addressed to the duchess."

"But, as the duchess is absent, and I represent her here, you may——"

"I cannot, madame."

"You distrust me, monsieur?"

"I ought to do so, madame; but," said the young man with an expression there was no mistaking, "in spite of the mystery of your conduct, you have inspired me, I confess, with very different sentiments."

"Really," said the lady, colouring a little under Ernanton's ardent gaze.

Ernanton bowed.

"Take care, monsieur," said she, laughing, "you are making a declaration of love."

"Yes, madame; I do not know if I may ever see you again, and the opportunity is too precious for me to let it slip."

"Thank you, monsieur. And now that we know each other, and that everything is explained, give me the letter, since it does exist."

"Impossible, madame."

The unknown seemed trying not to grow angry. "Impossible?" repeated she.

"Yes, impossible, for I swore to M. de Mayenne to deliver it only to the duchess herself."

"Say, rather," cried the lady, giving way to her irritation, "that you have no letter; that, in spite of your pretended scruples, it was a mere pretext for getting in here; that you wished to see me again, and that was all. Well, monsieur, you are satisfied; not only you have effected your entrance, but you have seen me, and have told me you adore me."

"In that, as in all the rest, I have told you truth, madame."

"Well, so be it, you adore me; you wished to see me, and you have seen me. I have procured you a pleasure in return for a service. We are quits. Adieu!"

"It seems to me, madame, that you are very hard on what would have been, after all, only a trick of love, if it had not been, as I have already told you, an affair of the greatest importance. I put aside all your injurious expressions, and I will forget all I might have said, affectionate or tender, since you are so badly disposed towards me. But I will not go out from here under the weight of your unworthy suspicions. I have a letter from the duke for Madame de Montpensier, and here it is; you can see the handwriting and the address."

Ernanton held out the letter to the lady, but without leaving go of it.

She cast her eyes on it, and cried: "His writing! Blood!"

Without replying, Ernanton put the letter back in his pocket, bowed low, and, very pale and bitterly hurt, turned to go. But she ran after him, and caught him by the skirt of his cloak.

"Ah! obstinate and stupid that you are," cried the duchess, with a fury mingled with majesty; "do you not recognise me? —or rather, could you not divine that I was the mistress?— and are these the eyes of a servant? I am the Duchesse de Montpensier; give me the letter."

"You are the duchess!" cried Ernanton, starting back.

"Yes, I am. Give it to me; I want to know what has happened to my brother."

But instead of obeying, as the duchess expected, the young man, recovering from his first surprise, crossed his arms.

"How can I believe you, when you have already lied to me twice?" said he.

She darted towards the bell, and rang it furiously; a valet appeared.

"What does madame want?" said he.

She stamped her foot with rage. "Mayneville!" cried she, "I want Mayneville. Is he not here?"

"Yes, madame."

"Let him come here."

The valet went, and a minute after, Mayneville entered.

"Did you send for me, madame?" said he.

"Madame! And since when am I simply madame?" cried she angrily.

"Your highness!" said Mayneville, in surprise.

"Good!" said Ernanton, "I have now a gentleman before me, and if he has lied, I shall know what to do."

"You believe then, at last?" said the duchess.

"Yes, madame, I believe, and here is the letter," and, bowing, the young man gave to Madame de Montpensier the letter so long disputed.


## CHAPTER XLI

### THE LETTER OF M. DE MAYENNE

The duchess seized the letter, opened it, and read it eagerly, while various expressions passed over her face, like clouds over the sky. When she had finished, she gave it to Mayneville to read. It was as follows:—

"MY SISTER,

"I tried to do myself the work I should have left to others, and I have been punished for it. I have received a sword wound from the fellow whom you know. The worst of it is, that he has killed five of my men, and among them Boularon and Desnôises, who are my best, after which he fled. I must tell you that he was aided by the bearer of this letter, a charming young man, as you may see. I recommend him to you; he is discretion itself.

"One merit which he will have, I presume, in your eyes, my dear sister, is having prevented my conqueror from killing me, as he much wished, having pulled off my mask when I had fainted, and recognised me.

"I recommend you, sister, to discover the name and profession of this discreet cavalier; for I suspect him, while he interests me. To my offers of service, he replied that the master whom he served let him want for nothing.

"I can tell you no more about him, but that he pre-

tends not to know me. I suffer much, but believe my
life is not in danger. Send me my surgeon at once; I am
lying like a horse upon straw, the bearer will tell you
where.

> "Your affectionate brother,
> "MAYENNE."

When they had finished reading, the duchess and Mayneville looked at each other in astonishment. The duchess
broke the silence first.

"To whom," said she, "do we owe the signal service that
you have rendered us, monsieur?"

"To a man who, whenever he can, helps the weak against
the strong."

"Will you give me some details, monsieur?"

Ernanton told all he had seen, and named the duke's place
of retreat.

Madame de Montpensier and Mayneville listened with
interest. When he had finished, the duchess said:

"May I hope, monsieur, that you will continue the work so
well begun, and attach yourself to our house?"

"Madame," said he, "I have already had the honour of
telling M. de Mayenne that I serve a good master, who treats
me too well for me to desire to seek another."

"Then, monsieur, that is all you have to tell me?" asked the
duchess.

"I have executed my commission, and it only remains for
me to present my humble respects to your highness."

The duchess let him go, but when the door shut behind
him, she stamped her foot impatiently.

"Mayneville," said she, "have that young man followed."

"Impossible, madame; all our household are out, I myself
am waiting for the event. It is a bad day on which to do
anything else than what we have decided to do."

"You are right, Mayneville; but afterwards——"

"Oh! afterwards, if you please, madame."

"Yes; for I suspect him, as my brother does."

"He is a brave fellow, at all events; and really we are
lucky, a stranger coming to render us such a service."

"Nevertheless, Mayneville, have him watched. But night
is falling, and Valois must be returning from Vincennes."

"Oh! we have time before us; it is not eight o'clock, and
our men have not arrived."

"All have the word, have they not?"

"All."

"How many do you expect?"

"Fifty; it is more than necessary, for besides them we have two hundred monks, as good as soldiers, if not better."

"As soon as our men have arrived, range your monks on the road."

"They are all ready, madame; they will intercept the way, our men will push the carriage towards them, the gates of the convent will be open, and will have but to close behind the carriage."

"The monks will be armed under their robes?"

"Yes."

"Mind you kill those two fellows whom we saw pass, riding at the sides of the carriage, then we can describe what passes as pleases us best."

## CHAPTER XLII

### HOW DOM GORENFLOT BLESSED THE KING AS HE PASSED BEFORE THE PRIORY OF THE JACOBINS

Ernanton went away with a full heart but a quiet conscience. He set off at full gallop as soon as he left Bel-Esbat, but he had scarcely gone a hundred yards when he came on a body of cavaliers who stretched right across the road. He was surrounded in a minute, and half-a-dozen swords and pistols presented at him.

"Oh!" said Ernanton, "robbers on the road, a league from Paris——"

"Silence, if you please," said a voice that Ernanton thought he recognised. "Your sword, your arms; quick."

And one man seized the bridle of the horse, while another stripped him of his arms.

"Peste! what clever thieves!" said Ernanton. "At least, gentlemen, do me the favour to tell me——"

"Why, it is M. de Carmainges!" said the man who had seized his sword.

"M. de Pincornay!" cried Ernanton. "Oh, fie; what a bad trade you have taken up."

"I said silence," cried the voice of the chief; "and take this man to the dépôt."

"But, M. de St. Maline, it is our companion, Ernanton de Carmainges."

"Ernanton here!" cried St. Maline, angrily; "what is he doing here?"

"Good evening, gentlemen," said Carmainges; "I did not, I confess, expect to find so much good company."

Ernanton was then conducted by his companions to the court-yard of Vincennes. Here he found fifty disarmed cavaliers, who, looking pale and dispirited, and surrounded by fifty light horse, were deploring their bad fortune, and anticipating a disastrous ending to an enterprise so well planned. The Forty-five had taken all these men, either by force or cunning, as they had, for precaution, come to the rendezvous either singly, or two or three together at most  Now all this would have rejoiced Ernanton had he understood it, but he saw without understanding.

"Monsieur," said he to St. Maline, "I see that you were told of the importance of my mission, and that, fearing some accident for me, you were good enough to take the trouble to escort me here; now I will tell you that you were right; the king expects me, and I have important things to say to him. I will tell the king what you have done for his service."

St. Maline grew red and then pale; but he understood, being clever when not blinded by passion, that Ernanton spoke the truth, and that he was expected. There was no joking with MM. de Loignac and d'Épernon; therefore he said: "You are free, M. Ernanton; I am delighted to have been agreeable to you."

Ernanton waited for no more, but began to mount the staircase which led to the king's room. St. Maline followed him with his eyes, and saw De Loignac meet him on the stairs, and sign to him to come on. De Loignac then descended to see the captives with his own eyes, and pronounced the road perfectly safe and free for the king's return.   He knew nothing of the Jacobin convent, and the artillery and musketry of the fathers. But D'Épernon did, being perfectly informed by Nicholas Poulain.  Therefore, when De Loignac came and said to his chief: "Monsieur, the roads are free," D'Épernon replied:

"Very well, the king orders that the Forty-five guards form themselves into three compact bodies, one to go before and one on each side of the carriage, so that if there be any firing it may not reach the carriage."

"Very good!" said De Loignac, "only I do not see where firing is to come from."

"At the priory of the Jacobins, monsieur, they must draw close."

This dialogue was interrupted by the king, who descended the staircase, followed by several gentlemen, among whom St. Maline, with rage in his heart, recognised Ernanton.

The light horse were left in charge of the prisoners, and forbidden to address a word to them. The king got into his carriage with his naked sword by his side, and, as nine o'clock struck, they set off.

M. de Mayneville was still at his window, only he was infinitely less tranquil and hopeful, for none of his soldiers had appeared, and the only sound heard along the silent black road was now and then horses' feet on the road to Vincennes. When this occurred, Mayneville and the duchess vainly tried to see what was going on. At last Mayneville became so anxious that he sent off a man on horseback, telling him to inquire of the first body of cavaliers they met. The messenger did not return, so the duchess sent another, but neither reappeared.

"Nine o'clock!" replied Mayneville, rather to himself than to the duchess. "Well! here are the Jacobins coming out of their convent, and ranging themselves along the walls."

"Listen!" cried the duchess. They began to hear from afar a noise like thunder.

"It is cavalry!" cried the duchess; "they are bringing him, we have him at last;" and she clapped her hands in the wildest joy.

"Yes," said Mayneville, "I hear a carriage and the gallop of horses."

And he cried out loudly: "Outside the walls, my brothers, outside!"

Immediately the gates of the priory opened, and a hundred armed monks marched out, with Borromée at their head, and they heard Gorenflot's voice crying: "Wait for me, wait for me; I must be at the head to receive his majesty."

"Go to the balcony, prior," cried Borromée, "and overlook us all."

"Ah! true; I forgot that I had chosen that place, but luckily you are here to remind me."

Borromée despatched four monks to stand behind the prior, on the pretence of doing him honour.

Soon the road was illumined by a number of torches, thanks to which the duchess and Mayneville could see cuirasses and swords shining. Incapable of moderation, she cried:

"Go down, Mayneville, and bring him to me."

"Yes, madame, but one thing disquiets me."

"What is it?"

"I do not hear the signal agreed on."

But at that moment De Loignac, at the head of the first body of guards, cried, brandishing his large sword: "Vive le Roi!"

"Vive le Roi!" replied enthusiastically all the Forty-five,

with their Gascon accent. The duchess grew pale and sank down almost fainting. Mayneville, sombre, but resolute, drew his sword, not knowing but what the house was to be attacked. The cortège advanced, and had reached Bel-Esbat. Borromée came a little forward, and as De Loignac rode straight up to him, he immediately saw that all was lost, and determined on his part.

"Room for the king!" cried De Loignac. Gorenflot, delighted with the scene, extended his powerful arm and blessed the king from his balcony. Henri saw him, and bowed smilingly, and at this remark of favour Gorenflot gave out a "Vive le Roi!" with his stentorian voice. The rest, however, remained mute; they expected a different result from their two months' training. But Borromée, feeling certain from the absence of the duchess's troops of the fate of the enterprise, knew that to hesitate a moment was to be ruined, and he answered with a "Vive le Roi!" almost as sonorous as Gorenflot's. Then all the rest took it up.

"Thanks, reverend father, thanks," cried Henri; and then he passed the convent, where his course was to have terminated, like a whirlwind of fire, noise, and glory, leaving behind him Bel-Esbat in obscurity.

From her balcony hidden by the golden scutcheon, behind which she was kneeling, the duchess saw and examined each face on which the light of the torches fell.

"Oh!" cried she, "look, Mayneville! That young man, my brother's messenger, is in the king's service. We are lost!"

"We must fly immediately, madame, now the Valois is conqueror."

"We have been betrayed; it must have been by that young man, he must have known all."

The king had already, with all his escort, entered the Porte St. Antoine, which had opened before him and shut behind him.

## CHAPTER XLIII

### HOW CHICOT BLESSED KING LOUIS II. FOR HAVING INVENTED POSTING, AND RESOLVED TO PROFIT BY IT

Chicot, to whom our readers will now permit us to return, after his last adventure, went on as rapidly as possible. Once within the limits of the little principality of Navarre, a country whose poverty was proverbial in France,

Chicot, to his great astonishment, ceased to see the impress of that misery which showed itself in every house and on every face in the finest provinces of that fertile France which he had just left. The wood-cutter who passed along, with his arm leaning on the yoke of his favourite ox, the girl with short petticoats and quiet steps, carrying water on her head, the old man humming a song of his youthful days, the tame bird who warbled in his cage, or pecked at his plentiful supply of food, the brown, thin, but healthy children playing about the roads, all said in a language clear and intelligible to Chicot: "See, we are happy here."

Often he heard the sound of heavy wheels, and then saw coming along the waggon of the vintages, full of casks and of children with red faces.

"Ventre de biche!" said Chicot; "I have never seen Gascony so rich. I confess the letter weighs on my mind, although I have translated it into Latin. However, I have never heard that Henriot, as Charles IX. called him, knew Latin; so I will give him a free French translation."

Chicot inquired, and was told that the king was at Nérac. He turned to the left to reach this place, and found the road full of people returning from the market at Condom. He learned, for Chicot, careful in answering the questions of others, was a great questioner himself, that the King of Navarre led a very joyous life, and was always changing from one love to another.

Chicot knew Queen Marguerite well, and he knew that if she was blind to these love affairs, it was when she had some motive for placing a bandage over her eyes.

Chicot entered Nérac in the evening. Chicot could see the simplicity of the royal manners by the ease with which he obtained an audience. A valet opened the door of a rustic-looking apartment bordered with flowers, above which was the king's ante-chamber and sitting-room. An officer or page ran to find the king, wherever he might be when anyone wished for an audience, and he always came at the first invitation. Chicot was pleased with this; he judged the king to be open and candid, and he thought so still more when he saw the king coming up a winding walk bordered with laurels and roses, an old hat on his head, and dressed in a dark green doublet and grey boots, and with a cup and ball in his hand. He looked gay and happy, as though care never came near him.

"Who wants me?" said he to the page.

"A man who looks to me half courtier, half soldier."

Chicot heard these words, and advanced.

"It is I, sire."

"What! M. Chicot in Navarre! Ventre St. Gris! welcome, dear M. Chicot!"

"A thousand thanks, sire."

"Page, take wine up to my room. Come, Chicot, I will conduct you."

Chicot followed the king, thinking: "How disagreeable! to come and trouble this honest man in his peace and his ignorance. Bah! he will be philosophical."

## CHAPTER XLIV

### HOW THE KING OF NAVARRE GUESSES THAT " TURENNIUS " MEANS TURENNE, AND " MARGOTA " MARGOT

The King of Navarre's room was not very sumptuous, for he was not rich, and did not waste the little he had.

The king seated himself, with his constant smile, in a great armchair of leather with gilt nails, and Chicot, at his command, sat down on a stool similar in material. Henri looked at him smilingly, but with curiosity.

"You will think I am very curious, dear M. Chicot," began the king, "but I cannot help it. I have so long looked on you as dead, that in spite of the pleasure your resurrection causes me, I can hardly realise the idea. Why did you so suddenly disappear from this world?"

"Oh, sire!" said Chicot, "you disappeared from Vincennes. Everyone eclipses himself according to his need."

"I recognise by your ready wit that it is not to your ghost I am speaking." Then, more seriously: "But now we must leave wit and speak of business."

"I am ready, your Majesty."

"First, your letters of credit. I know it is needless, since you are the ambassador; but I must do my duty as king."

"Sire, I ask your majesty's pardon; but all the letters of credit that I had I have drowned in rivers, or scattered in the air."

"And why so?"

"I had one, sire, but I was forced to destroy it, for M. de Mayenne ran after me to steal it from me."

"Bravo! your journey is interesting; you must tell me the details. But one thing disquiets me—if the letter was destroyed for M. de Mayenne, it is also destroyed for me. How, then, shall I know what my brother Henri wrote?"

" Sire, it exists in my memory."

" How so?"

"Sire, before destroying it I learnt it by heart."

" An excellent idea, M. Chicot. You will recite it to me, will you not?"

" Willingly, sire."

" Word for word."

" Yes, sire, although I do not know the language, I have a good memory."

" What language?"

" Latin."

" I do not understand you; was my brother Henri's letter written in Latin?"

" Yes, sire."

" And why?"

" Ah! sire, doubtless because Latin is an audacious language—a language which may say anything, and in which Persius and Juvenal have immortalised the follies and errors of kings."

" Kings?"

" And of queens, sire."

The king began to frown.

" Then let us try. I know a little Italian, and my Gascon patois is something like Spanish; perhaps I may understand Latin without ever having learned it."

" Your majesty orders me to repeat it, then?"

" I beg you, dear M. Chicot."

Chicot began.

" Frater carissime,

" Sincerus amo quo te prosequebatur germanus noster Carolus Nonus, functus nuper, colet usque regiam nostram et pectori meo pertinaciter adhœret."

" If I am not mistaken," said Henri, interrupting, " they speak in this phrase of love, obstinacy, and of my brother, Charles IX."

" Very likely," said Chicot; " Latin is such a beautiful language, that all that might go in one sentence."

" Go on," said the king.

Chicot began again, and Henri listened with the utmost calm to all the passages about Turenne and his wife, only at the word " Turennius," he said.

" Does not ' Turennius ' mean Turenne?"

" I think so, sire."

" And 'Margota ' must be the pet name which my brothers gave to their sister Marguerite, my beloved wife."

"It is possible," said Chicot; and he continued his letter to the end without the king's face changing in the least.

"Is it finished?" asked Henri, when he stopped.

"Yes, sire."

"How unlucky that I only understood two words: 'Turennius' and 'Margota.'"

"An irreparable misfortune, sire, unless your majesty decides on having it translated by someone."

"Well, I have an idea. Go and find my wife. She is learned, and will understand it if you recite it to her; then she can explain it to me."

"That is an excellent plan."

"Is it not? Go."

"I will, sire."

"Mind not to alter a word of the letter."

"That would be impossible, sire. To do that I must know Latin."

"Go, then, my friend."

'Chicot took leave and went, more puzzled with the king than ever.

## CHAPTER XLV

### THE AVENUE THREE THOUSAND FEET LONG

The queen inhabited the other wing of the castle. The famous avenue began at her very window, and her eyes rested only on grass and flowers. A native poet (Marguerite, in the provinces as in Paris, was always the star of the poets) had composed a sonnet about her.

Full of hatred for her enemies, but patient that she might avenge herself better—feeling instinctively that under the mask of carelessness and long-suffering worn by Henri of Navarre he had a bad feeling towards her—she had accustomed herself to replace by poetry, and by the semblance of love, relations, husbands, and friends.

When Chicot arrived at the place indicated to him by Henri, he found no one, Marguerite, they said, was at the end of the famous avenue. When he had gone about two-thirds down it, he saw at the end, in an arbour covered with jasmine, clematis, and broom, a group covered with ribands, feathers, velvets, and swords.

A sudden flush passed over Marguerite's face, and she turned quickly. Chicot was standing near; Marguerite quitted the circle, and, waving an adieu to the company, advanced towards the Gascon.

"M. Chicot!" cried she, in astonishment.

"Here I am, at your majesty's feet," said he, "and find you ever good and beautiful, and queen here, as at the Louvre."

"It is a miracle to see you here, monsieur; they said you were dead."

"I pretended to be so."

"And what do you want with us, M. Chicot? Am I happy enough to be still remembered in France?"

"Oh, madame," said Chicot, smiling, "we do not forget queens of your age and your beauty. The King of France even writes on this subject to the King of Navarre."

Marguerite coloured. "He writes?"

"Yes, madame."

"And you have brought the letter?"

"I have not brought it, madame, for reasons that the King of Navarre will explain to you, but learned it by heart and repeated it."

"I understand. This letter was important, and you feared to lose it, or have it stolen."

"That is the truth, madame; but the letter was written in Latin."

"Oh, very well; you know I know Latin."

"And the King of Navarre, does he know it?"

"Dear M. Chicot, it is very difficult to find out what he does or does not know. If one can believe appearances, he knows very little of it, for he never seems to understand when I speak to anyone in that language. Then you told him the purport of the letter?"

"It was to him it was addressed?"

"And did he seem to understand?"

"Only two words."

"What were they?"

"Turennius et Margota."

"Turennius et Margota?"

"Yes; those two words were in the letter."

"Then what did he do?"

"He sent me to you, madame."

"To me?"

"Yes, saying that the letter contained things of too much importance to be confided to a stranger, and that it was better to take it to you, who were the most beautiful of learned ladies, and the most learned of beautiful ones."

"I will listen to you, M. Chicot, since such are the king's orders."

"Thank you, madame; where would you please it to be?"

"Come to my room."

Marguerite looked earnestly at Chicot, who, through pity for her, had let her have a glimpse of the truth. Perhaps she felt the need of a support, for she turned towards a gentleman in the group, and said:

"M. de Turenne, your arm to the castle. Precede us, M. Chicot."

## CHAPTER XLVI

### MARGUERITE'S ROOM

Marguerite's room was fashionably furnished; and tapestries, enamels, china, books and manuscripts in Greek, Latin and French covered all the tables; while birds in their cages, dogs on the carpets, formed a living world round Marguerite.

Chicot was invited to sit down in a beautiful armchair of tapestry, representing a Cupid scattering a cloud of flowers; and a page, handsome and richly dressed, offered to him refreshment. He did not accept it, but as soon as the Vicomte de Turenne had left them, began to recite his letter. We already know this letter, having read it in French with Chicot, and therefore think it useless to follow the Latin translation. Chicot spoke with the worst accent possible, but Marguerite understood it perfectly, and could not hide her rage and indignation. She knew her brother's dislike to her, and her mind was divided between anger and fear.

"But do you not understand it, M. Chicot? I thought you were a good Latin scholar."

"Madame, I have forgotten it; all that I remember is that Latin has no article, that it has a vocative, and that the head belongs to the neuter gender."

"Really!" said someone, entering noiselessly and merrily. It was the King of Navarre. "The head is of the neuter gender, M. Chicot? Why is it not masculine?"

"Ah, sire, I do not know; it astonishes me as much as it does your majesty."

"It must be because it is sometimes the man, sometimes the woman that rules, according to their temperaments."

"That is an excellent reason, sire."

"I am glad to be a more profound philosopher than I thought—but to return to the letter. Madame, I burn to hear news from the court of France, and M. Chicot brings them to me in an unknown tongue."

" Do you not fear, sire, that the Latin is a bad prognostic?" said Chicot.

" M. Chicot is right, sire," said the queen.

" What!" said Henri, " does the letter contain anything disagreeable, and from your brother, who is so clever and polite?"

" Even when he had me insulted in my litter, as happened near Sens, when I left Paris to rejoin you, sire."

" When one has a brother whose own conduct is irreproachable," said Henri, in an indefinable tone between jest and earnest, " a brother a king, and very punctilious——"

" He ought to care for the true honour of his sister and of his house. I do not suppose, sire, that if your sister, Catherine d'Albret, occasioned some scandal, you would have it published by a captain of the guards."

" Oh! I am like a good-natured bourgeois, and not a king; but the letter, the letter; since it was addressed to me, I wish to know what it contains."

" It is a perfidious letter, sire."

" Bah!"

" Oh! yes, and which contains more calumnies than are necessary to embroil a husband with his wife, and a friend with his friends."

" Oh! oh! embroil a husband with his wife; you and me then?"

" Yes, sire."

Chicot was on thorns; he would have given much, hungry as he was, to be in bed without supper.

" The storm is about to burst," thought he.

" Sire," said Marguerite, " I much regret that your majesty has forgotten your Latin."

" Come, ma mie, you have understood badly; let me hear if all this be in the letter."

Marguerite looked defiant.

" Do you want your followers or not, sire?" said she.

" Do I want them? what a question! What should I do without them, and reduced to my own resources?"

" Well, sire, the king wishes to detach your best servants from you."

" I defy him."

" Bravo, sire!" said Chicot.

" Dear M. Chicot," said Henri, " pray wait for me in my room, the queen has something particular to say to me."

## CHAPTER XLVII

### THE EXPLANATION

To get rid of a witness whom Marguerite believed to know more of Latin than he allowed, was already a triumph, or at least a pledge of security for her; for alone with her husband she could give whatever translation of the Latin that she pleased.

Henri and his wife were then left tête-à-tête. He had on his face no appearance of disquietude or menace; decidedly he could not understand Latin.

"Monsieur," said Marguerite, "I wait for you to interrogate me."

"Listen to me, madame; I am uneasy."

"About what, sire?"

"About a current report."

"A report; your majesty uneasy about a report?"

"It is then your opinion, madame, that one should despise reports?"

"Absolutely, sire; particularly kings and queens."

"Why so, madame?"

"Because, as everyone talks of us, we should have enough to do to listen to them all."

"Well, I believe you are right, ma mie, and I am about to furnish you with an excellent opportunity of exercising your philosophy."

Marguerite believed that the decisive moment had come, and rallied all her courage.

"So be it, sire," said she.

Henri began in the tone of a penitent who has some great sin to acknowledge.

"You know the great interest I take in Fosseuse?"

"Ah!" cried Marguerite triumphantly, seeing he was not about to accuse her; "yes, yes; the little Fosseuse, your friend."

"She is ill, ma mie, and the doctors do not understand her malady."

"That is strange, sire. Fosseuse, who you say is a pearl of purity, ought to allow the doctors to penetrate into the secret of her illness."

"Alas! it is not so."

"What!" cried the queen; "is she not a pearl of purity?"

"I mean that she persists in hiding the cause of her illness from the doctors."

"But, to you, sire, her confidant, her father."

"I know nothing, or at least wish to know nothing."

"Then, sire," said Marguerite, who now believed that she had to confer instead of asking a pardon; "then, sire, I do not know what you want; and wait for you to explain."

"Well, then ma mie, I will tell you. I wish you—but it is asking a great deal."

"Speak on, sire."

"To have the goodness to go to Fosseuse."

"But what is the object of this visit?"

"It is very simple, madame."

"Still, you must tell me, for I am not clever enough to guess it."

"Well! you will find Fosseuse among the ladies of honour sleeping in their room; and they, you know, are so curious and indiscreet that one cannot tell to what extremity Fosseuse may be reduced."

"If she wishes to hide, let her not count on me. I may shut my eyes to certain things, but I will never be an accomplice," said Marguerite.

Henri seemed not to have heard, but he stood for a minute in a thoughtful attitude, and then said: "Margota cum Turennio. Ah! those were the names, madame—'Margota cum Turennio.'"

Marguerite grew crimson.

"Guilty is 'nocens,' is it not?"

"Yes."

"Well, there was that word in the letter—'Margota cum Turennio, ambo nocentes, conveniunt in castello nomine Loignac.' Mon Dieu; how I regret that my knowledge is not as great as my memory is good."

"Ambo nocentes," repeated Marguerite, in a low voice, and turning very pale, "he understood it all."

And Henri kissed the cold hand of Marguerite. Then turning on the threshold of the door, he said:

"Say everything kind from me to Fosseuse, and do for her as you have promised me. I set off for the chase; perhaps I shall not see you till my return, perhaps never—these wolves are wicked beasts. Come, and let me embrace you, ma mie."

Then he embraced Marguerite, almost affectionately, and went out, leaving her stupefied with all she had heard.

## CHAPTER XLVIII

### THE SPANISH AMBASSADOR

The king rejoined Chicot, who was still agitated with fears as to the explanation. " Well, Chicot," said Henri, " do you know what the queen says?"

" No."

" She pretends that your cursed Latin will disturb our peace."

" Oh, sire, forget it, and all will be at an end. It is not with a piece of spoken Latin as though it were written; the wind carries away the one, fire cannot sometimes destroy the other."

" I! I think of it no more."

At this moment the door of the room opened, and D'Aubiac announced: " The ambassador from Spain."

" Ma foi!" said Henri. " And what the devil can he want here?"

" Yes," said Chicot, " What the devil does he want here?"

" We shall soon know; perhaps our Spanish neighbour has some frontier dispute to settle with us."

" I will retire," said Chicot. " This is doubtless a real ambassador from his majesty Philippe II., while I——"

" Open the library door, Chicot, and go in there——"

" But from there I shall hear all, in spite of myself."

" Oh! never mind; I have nothing to hide. Apropos; have you nothing more to say to me from your king?"

" Nothing at all, sire."

Chicot hastened to his place of concealment, and drew the tapestry close.

When the first preliminaries of etiquette were over, the ambassador said:

" Can I speak freely to your majesty?"

" You may, monsieur."

" Sire, I bring the answer from his Catholic majesty."

" An answer," thought Chicot; " then there was a question."

" An answer to what?" said Henri.

" To your proposals of last month."

" Ma foi! I am very forgetful! please to recall to me what they were."

" About the invasions of the Lorraine princes?"

" Yes, I remember, particularly those of M. de Guise; go on, monsieur?"

" Sire, the king, my master, although much begged to sign a

treaty of alliance with Lorraine, prefers one with Navarre. I know my master's intentions with regard to you."

" May I also know them?"

" Sire, my master will refuse nothing to Navarre."

Chicot bit his fingers to convince himself that he was not dreaming.

" What can I ask then?" said Henri.

" Whatever your majesty pleases."

" Diable!"

" If your majesty will speak openly and frankly?"

" Ventre St. Gris, it is embarrassing."

" Shall I tell you his majesty the King of Spain's proposals?"

" I listen."

" The King of France treats the Queen of Navarre as an enemy, he repudiates her as a sister, and covers her with opprobrium. All this, but I beg your majesty's pardon for touching on so delicate a subject—"

" Go on."

" All this, then, is public."

" Well! monsieur, and what of all this?"

" It is consequently easy for your majesty to repudiate as a wife her whom her brother disclaims as a sister. This once done, the alliance between the King of Navarre and the King of Spain is concluded, and the King of Spain will give the infanta, his daughter, to your majesty, and he himself will marry Madame Catherine de Navarre, your majesty's sister."

A movement of pride shook Henri, while Chicot shuddered with terror. The one saw his star rising, radiant like the morning sun; the other saw the sceptre of the Valois ready to decline and fall.

For an instant there was profound silence, and then Henri said:

" The proposal, monsieur, is magnificent, and crowns me with honour."

" His majesty," said the negotiator, who already calculated on an enthusiastic acceptance, " proposes only one condition."

" Ah! a condition; that is but just; let me hear it."

" In aiding your majesty against the Lorraine princes, that is to say, in opening to your majesty a way to the throne, my master desires to facilitate by your alliance the safety of Flanders, which the Duc d'Anjou is already attacking; your majesty will understand that it is pure preference on my master's part for you over the Lorraine princes, since MM. de Guise, his natural allies, as Catholic princes, make of themselves a party against the Duc d'Anjou in Flanders. Now, this is the only condition, which you must think reasonable. His majesty the King of Spain, allied to you by a double marriage, will help you to——" the ambassador seemed to seek for the right word, " to succeed to the King of France, and you will guarantee Flanders to him. I may then, now, knowing your majesty's wisdom, regard the negotiation as happily terminated."

Henri took two or three turns up and down the room.

"This, then," said he at last, " is the answer you were charged to bring me?"

"Yes, sire."

"Nothing else?"

"Nothing else, sire."

"Well! I refuse the offer of the King of Spain."

"You refuse the hand of the infanta!" cried the Spaniard, with a start, as though he had received a sudden wound.

"It would be a great honour, but I cannot think it a greater one than that of having married a daughter of France."

"Take care, sire," said the ambassador; "the good understanding between two neighbours may be destroyed by a hasty word."

"Monsieur, my crown is so light, that I should scarcely feel the difference if it slipped off; besides, I believe I can guard it. Therefore, once more adieu, monsieur, and tell the king your master that I have greater ambitions than he dreams of." And the Béarnais, becoming once more, not himself, but what he generally seemed to be, conducted the ambassador, with a courteous smile, to the door.


## CHAPTER XLIX

### THE POOR OF HENRI OF NAVARRE

Chicot remained plunged in profound surprise. Henri lifted the tapestry, and, striking him on the shoulder, said:

"Well, M. Chicot, how do you think I managed?"

"I confess to you, sire, that I am not so penetrating as you are."

"Doubtless Henri would be delighted if I repudiated his sister."

"How so? Pray explain to me."

"You know they forgot to pay me my wife's dowry."

"I guessed as much, sire."

"This dowry was to consist of 300,000 golden crowns and some towns, among others, Cahors."

"A pretty town, mordieu!"

"I have claimed, not the money, but Cahors."

"Ventre de biche! sire, in your place, I should have done the same."

"And that is why—do you understand now?"

"No, indeed, sire."

"Why they wish me to quarrel with my wife and repudiate her. No wife, no dowry, no more 300,000 crowns, no Cahors. It is one way of eluding a promise, and Henri is clever in laying snares."

"You would much like to hold Cahors, sire?"

"Doubtless; for after all, what is my principality of Béarn? A poor little place, clipped by the avarice of my mother-in-law and brother-in-law."

"While Cahors——"

"Cahors would be my rampart, the safeguard of my religion."

"Well, sire, go into mourning for Cahors; for, whether you break with Madame Marguerite or not, the King of France will never give it to you, and unless you take it——"

"Oh, I would soon take it, if it was not so strong, and, above all, if I did not hate war."

"Cahors is impregnable, sire."

"Oh! impregnable! But if I had an army, which I have not——"

"Listen, sire. We are not here to flatter each other. To take Cahors, which is held by M. de Vesin, one must be a Hannibal or a Cæsar; and your majesty——"

"Well?" said Henri, with a smile.

"Has just said, you do not like war."

Henri sighed, and his eyes flashed for a minute; then he said:

"Oh, I do not pretend to make others tremble, so long as I do not tremble myself. But if I cannot get Cahors, then, and you think I cannot——"

"I think so, sire, for three reasons."

"Tell them to me, Chicot."

"Willingly. The first is that Cahors is a town of good produce, which Henri III. will like to keep for himself."

"That is not very honest."

"It is very royal, sire."

"I shall remember your lesson, Chicot. Now, your second reason."

"Madame Catherine——"

"Oh! does my good mother still mix in politics?"

"Always; and she would rather see her daughter at Paris than at Nérac—near her than near you."

"You think so? Yet she does not love her daughter to distraction."

"No; but Madame Marguerite serves you as a hostage, sire."

"You are cunning, Chicot. Devil take me, if I thought of that! But you may be right; a daughter of France would be a hostage in case of need. Well, the third?"

"Between the Duc d'Anjou, who seeks to make a throne for himself in Flanders, between MM. de Guise, who wish for a crown, and shake that of France, and his majesty the King of Spain, who wishes for universal monarchy, you hold the balance and maintain a certain equilibrium."

"I, without weight?"

"Just so. If you became powerful, that is to say, heavy, you would turn the scale, and would be no longer a counterpoise, but a weight."

"Ah! I like that reason, and it is admirably argued. This is the explanation of my situation?"

"Complete."

"And I, who did not see all this, and went on hoping."

"Well, sire, I counsel you to cease to hope."

"Then I must do for this debt what I do for those of my farmers who cannot pay their rent; I put a P against their names."

"Which means paid."

"Just so."

"Put two P's, sire, and give a sigh."

"So be it, Chicot; you see I can live in Béarn, even without Cahors."

"I see that, and also that you are a wise and philosophical king. But what is that noise?"

"Noise, where?"

"In the courtyard, I think."

"Look out of window."

"Sire, there are below a dozen of poorly-clothed people."

"Ah! they are my poor," said the king, rising.

"Your majesty has poor?"

"Doubtless; does not God recommend charity? If I am not a Catholic, Chicot, I am a Christian."

They went down, but Henri seemed thoughtful and preoccupied. Chicot looked at him, and thought: "What the devil made me talk politics to this brave prince, and make him sad? Fool that I was!"

Once in the court, Henri approached the group of mendicants. There were a dozen men in different costumes. Henri took the purse from the hands of Chicot and made a sign, and then each man came forward and saluted Henri with an air of humility, which did not preclude a glance full of intelligence at the king. Henri replied by a motion of the head; then, putting his fingers into the purse, which Chicot held open, he took out a piece.

"Do you know that it is gold, sire?" said Chicot.

"Yes, my friend, I know."

"Peste! you are rich."

"Do you not see that each of these pieces serves for two? On the contrary, I am so poor that I am forced to cut my gold in two."

"It is true," said Chicot, with surprise; "they are half-pieces, with fantastic designs."

"Oh, I am like my brother Henri, who amuses himself in cutting out images; I amuse myself with clipping my ducats."

"Nevertheless, sire, it is an odd method of giving charity," said Chicot, who divined some hidden mystery.

"What would you do?"

"Instead of cutting the gold, I would give one piece between two."

"They would fight, and I should do harm instead of good."

Henri then took one of the pieces, and, placing himself before the first beggar, looked at him inquiringly.

"Agen," said the man.

"How many?" asked Henri.

"Five hundred."

"Cahors;" and he gave him the piece and took a second. The man bowed and withdrew.

The next advanced and said: "Auch."

"How many?"

"Three hundred and fifty."

"Cahors;" and he gave him his piece.

"Narbonne," said the third.

"How many?"

"Eight hundred."

"Cahors;" and he gave him his piece.

"Montauban," said the fourth.

"How many?"

"Six hundred."

"Cahors."

Each one in this way pronounced a name and a number and received a piece of gold, and to each Henri replied "Cahors."

This over, there were no pieces left in the purse.

"That is all, sire," said Chicot.

" Yes; I have finished.

" Sire, am I permitted to be curious?"

" Why not?   Curiosity is natural."

" What did these beggars say, and what did you reply?"
Henri smiled.

" Indeed," continued Chicot, " all is mysterious here."

" Do you think so?"

" Sure, sire!"

" Come and sup, my friend, nothing enlightens the mind
ike eating and drinking.  Let us go to table, and you shall
ee that if my pistoles are cut, my bottles are full."

Then, passing his arm familiarly through Chicot's, the king
vent back to his room, where supper was served.  Passing by
he queen's room, he glanced at it, and saw no light.

" Page," said he, " is not her majesty at home?"

" Her majesty is gone to see Mademoiselle de Mont-
morency, who is ill."

" Ah! poor Fosseuse!" said Henri, " it is true, the queen
has such a good heart.  Come to supper, Chicot."


## CHAPTER L

### THE TRUE MISTRESS OF THE KING OF NAVARRE

The repast was joyous.  Henri seemed no longer to have
any weight either on his heart or his mind, and he was an
xcellent companion.   As for Chicot, he dissembled the
uneasiness he had felt since the coming of the Spanish ambas-
ador and the scene with the mendicants.  He endeavoured to
drink little and keep cool to observe everything; but this Henri
vould not allow.  However, Chicot had a head of iron, and as
or Henri, he said he could drink these wines of the country
ike milk.

" I envy you," said Chicot to the king; " your court is
delightful, and your life pleasant."

" If my wife were here, Chicot, I would not say what I am
bout to say, but in her absence I will tell you that the best
art of my life is that which you do not see."

" Ah! sire, they tell, indeed, fine tales of you."
Henri leaned back in his chair to laugh.

" They say I reign more over my female than my male
ubjects, do they not?" said he.

" Yes, sire, and it astonishes me."

" Why so?"

E

"Because, sire, you have much of that restless spirit which makes great kings."

"Here is a man determined to make me want something," cried Henri.

"God forbid, sire; I desire with all my heart, on the contrary, that your majesty should want nothing."

"Nothing calls you back to Paris, does it, Chicot?"

"No, sire."

"Then you will pass some days with me?"

"If your majesty does me the honour to wish for my company, I ask no better than to give you a week."

"So be it; in a week you will know me like a brother. Drink, Chicot."

"Sire, I am no longer thirsty," said Chicot, who had given up all hopes of seeing the king take too much.

"Then I will leave you; a man should not stay at table when he does nothing. Drink, I tell you."

"Why, sire?"

"To sleep better. Do you like the chase, Chicot?"

"Not much, sire; and you?"

"Passionately; since I lived at the court of Charles IX."

"Why did your majesty do me the honour to ask me?"

"Because I hunt to-morrow, and thought to take you with me."

"Sire, it would be a great honour, but——"

"Oh! this chase will rejoice all eyes; besides, I am a good hunter, and I wish you to see me to advantage."

"Sire, I am at your orders."

"Good! then it is settled. Ah! here is a page to disturb us."

"Some important business, sire?"

"You are a gentleman, Chicot. Now go quickly."

"Adieu, sire; a good night to you."

"Adieu! and sleep well. You will find the page in the gallery, who will show you your room."

Chicot went out; but, after taking a few steps, returned just in time to see Henri let in—not a woman, but a man. Chicot put his eye to the large keyhole.

The man took off his hat, and Chicot saw the noble but severe face of Duplessis-Mornay, the rigid and vigilant counsellor of Henri of Navarre.

But Henri's face showed only joy; and after locking the door, he sat down eagerly to examine some maps, plans, and letters, which his minister had brought him. The king then began to write and to mark the maps.

"Oh! this is the way Henri of Navarre makes love," thought Chicot.

At this moment he heard steps behind him, and fearful of being surprised, he turned hastily away, and, seeing the page, asked for his room.

"Come with me, if you please, monsieur," said D'Aubiac, "and I will conduct you."

Chicot began to understand the King of Navarre. Therefore, instead of going to sleep, he sat sombre and thoughtful on his bed, while the moon shed its silver light over stream and meadows.

"Henri is a real king, and he conspires," thought Chicot. "All this palace, park, town—the whole province—is a focus of conspiracy. All the women make love, but it is political love, and all the men live in the hope of a future. Henri is clever, his talent borders on genius, and he is in communication with Spain, the land of deceit. Who knows if even his noble answer to the ambassador was not a farce, and if he did not warn the ambassador of it by some sign unknown to me? Henri has spies; those beggars were nothing more nor less than gentlemen in disguise. Those pieces of gold, so artistically cut, were pledges of recognition—rallying signs.

"The Duc de Guise has both arm and head, but he has the disadvantage of being known as brave and skilful, so that everyone is on their guard against him, while no one fears the Béarnais. I alone have seen through him. Well, having seen through him, I have no more to do here; so while he works or sleeps, I will go quietly out of the ctiy. There are not many ambassadors, I think, who can boast of having fulfilled their mission in one day, as I have. So I will leave Nérac, and gallop till I am in France." And he began to put on his spurs.

## CHAPTER LI

### CHICOT'S ASTONISHMENT AT FINDING HIMSELF SO POPULAR AT NERAC

Chicot, having taken his resolution, began to prepare his little packet. "How much time will it take me," thought he, as he did so, "to carry to the king news of what I have seen and fear? Two days to arrive at a city whence the governor can send couriers; Cahors, for example, of which Henri of Navarre thinks so much. Once there, I can rest, for after all a man must rest some time. Come, then, Chicot, speed and sang froid. You thought you had accomplished your mission, and you are but half-way through it."

Chicot now extinguished the light, opened his door softly, and began to creep downstairs on tip-toe.

He went into an ante-chamber, but he had hardly gone four steps before he kicked against something. This something was D'Aubiac lying on a mat.

"Ah! good evening, M. d'Aubiac," said Chicot, "but get out of the way a little, I beg; I want to go for a walk."

"Ah; but it is forbidden to walk by night near the castle."

"My little friend, you are very vigilant for your age. Have you nothing to occupy yourself with?"

"No."

"You neither gamble nor fall in love."

"To gamble one must have money, M. Chicot, and to be in love, one must find a lady."

"Assuredly," said Chicot, and feeling in his pocket he drew out ten pistoles and slipped them into the page's hand, saying: "Seek well in your memory, and I bet you will find some charming woman, to whom I beg you to make some presents with this."

"Oh, M. Chicot!" said the page, "it is easy to see that you come from the court of France; you have manners to which one can refuse nothing; go then, but make no noise."

Chicot went on, glided like a shadow into the corridor, and down the staircase, but at the bottom he found an officer sleeping on a chair, placed right against the door, so that it was impossible to pass.

"Ah! little wretch of a page," murmured Chicot, "you knew this."

Chicot looked round him to see if he could find no other way by which he could escape with the assistance of his long legs. At last he saw what he wanted: it was an arched window, of which the glass was broken. Chicot climbed up the wall with his accustomed skill, and without making more noise than a dry leaf in the autumn wind; but unluckily, the opening was not big enough, so when he had got his head and one shoulder through, and had taken away his foot from its resting place on the wall, he found himself hanging between heaven and earth, without being able either to advance or retreat.

He began then a series of efforts, of which the first result was to tear his doublet and scratch his skin. What rendered his position more difficult was his sword, of which the handle would not pass, making a hook by which Chicot hung on to the sash. He exerted all his strength, patience, and industry, to unfasten the clasp of his shoulder-belt; but it was just on this clasp that his body leaned, therefore he was obliged to change his manœuvre, and at last he succeeded in drawing his sword from its sheath and pushing it through one of the interstices; the sword therefore fell first on the flagstones, and Chicot now managed to get through after it. All this, however, was not done without noise, therefore Chicot, on rising, found himself face to face with a soldier.

"Ah! mon Dieu! have you hurt yourself, M. Chicot?" said he.

Chicot was surprised, but said: "No, my friend, not at all."

"You must go back, M. Chicot."

"Not by that way, at all events; it is too troublesome."

"If I were an officer instead of a soldier, I would ask you why you come out so; but that is not my business, which is only that you should go back again. Go in, therefore, M. Chicot, I beg you."

And the soldier said this in such a persuasive tone, that Chicot was touched. Consequently he put his hand in his pocket and drew out another ten pistoles.

"Go quickly then, M. Chicot," said the man.

Chicot was in the street at last. The night was not favourable for flight, being bright and cloudless, and he regretted the foggy nights of Paris, where people might pass close to each other unseen. The unfortunate fugitive had no sooner turned the corner of the street than he met a patrol. He stopped of himself, thinking it would look suspicious to try and pass unseen.

"Oh, good evening, M. Chicot!" said the chief; "shall we reconduct you to the palace? You seem as though you had lost your way."

"It is very strange," murmured Chicot, "everyone knows me here." Then aloud, and as carelessly as he could: "No, cornet, I am not going to the palace."

"Where are you going then?"

"I cannot sleep well at night, and then I always walk. Nérac is a charming city, and I wish to see it."

"My men shall conduct you where you please."

"Oh, monsieur, I would rather go alone."

"You will be assassinated."

"I have my sword."

"Ah, true; then you will be arrested for bearing arms."

Chicot, driven to despair, drew the officer aside, and said:

"Come, monsieur, you are young; you know what love is— an imperious tyrant."

"Doubtless, M. Chicot."

"You are a gallant man, cornet. But how did you know me?"

"I saw you at the palace with the king. Apropos, which way are you going?"

"Towards the Porte of Agen. Am I not in the right road?"

"Yes; go straight on; I wish you success."

"Thank you;" and Chicot went on. But before he had taken a hundred steps he met the watch.

"Peste! this town is well guarded," thought Chicot.

"You cannot pass!" cried the provost, in a voice of thunder.

"But monsieur, I want——"

"Ah, M. Chicot, is it you? In the streets in this cold?" asked the officer.

"The king has given me a commission for the lieutenant of the Porte of Agen."

"Ah!"

"That astonishes you?"

"Yes."

"It ought not, since you know me."

"I know you from having seen you at the palace with the king."

He arrived at the gate, which was guarded by a sentinel walking up and down, his musket on his shoulder.

"My friend, will you open the gate for me?" said Chicot.

"I would with pleasure, but I have not the keys."

"And who has them?"

"The officer for the night."

Chicot sighed.

"And where is he?"

The soldier rang a bell to wake his officer.

"What is it?" said he, passing his head through a window.

"Lieutenant, it is a gentleman who wants the gate opened."

"Ah! M. Chicot," cried the officer, "I will be down in a moment."

"What! does everyone know me?" cried Chicot. "Nérac seems a lantern, and I the candle."

"Excuse me, monsieur," said the officer, approaching, "but I was asleep."

"Of course!" growled Chicot. "Well! the king has sent me on a commission to Agen; this is the right gate, is it not?"

"Yes, M. Chicot."

Chicot began to breathe; the door creaked on its hinges and opened, and Chicot saw liberty through it.

"Adieu! monsieur," said he advancing.

"Adieu, M. Chicot, a pleasant journey. But stay, one

moment; I have forgotten to ask for your pass," cried he, seizing Chicot by the sleeve to stop him..

"How! my pass?"

"Certainly, M. Chicot; you know what a pass is? You understand that no one can leave a town like Nérac without a pass, particularly when the king is in it."

"And who must sign this pass?"

"The king himself; so if he sent you he cannot have forgotten to give you a pass."

"Ah! you doubt that the king sent me?" cried Chicot, with flashing eyes, for he saw himself on the point of failing, and had a great mind to kill the officer and sentinel, and rush through the gate.

"I doubt nothing you tell me, but reflect that if the king gave you this commission——"

"In person, monsieur."

"All the more reason, then: if he knows you are going out, I shall have to give up your pass to-morrow morning to the governor."

"And who is he?"

"M. de Mornay, who does not jest with disobedience, M. Chicot."

Chicot put his hand to his sword, but another look showed him that the outside of the gate was defended by a guard who would have prevented his passing if he had killed the officer and sentinel.

"Well!" said Chicot to himself, with a sigh; "I have lost my game," and he turned back.

"Shall I give you an escort, M. Chicot?" said the officer.

"No, thank you."

Chicot returned to his room in a rage.


## CHAPTER LII

### HOW THEY HUNTED THE WOLF IN NAVARRE

When Marguerite left the king, she went at once to the apartments of the maids of honour, and performed her promise with regard to Fosseuse. When she returned, the king thanked her warmly, and then went up to Chicot's room, where he found him still asleep. Henri shook him to wake him. "Come, compère," said he, "get up, it is two in the morning."

"Sire, you seem very gay this morning; what is it?"

"I am always gay when I am setting off for the chase. Come, out of bed, compère."

"You want me, sire?"

"Yes; you shall be my historian."

"To count the shots?"

"Just so."

Chicot dressed murmuringly, while the king remained in the ante-chamber.

"My horse," cried Henri; "and tell M. de Mornay that I am ready."

Chicot found the preparations much less sumptuous than those of Henri III. A dozen or fifteen gentlemen only, among whom he recognised the Vicomte de Turenne, formed the whole suite. And as they were none of them rich, they all wore, instead of the usual hunting dress, their helmets and cuirasses, which made Chicot ask if the wolves in Gascony used muskets and artillery.

"No," said Henri; "but they are fierce beasts, who have claws and teeth, and draw hunters into places where they are likely to tear their clothes on the thorns, if they wear silk and velvet, or even cloth and buff, but not if they wear cuirasses."

"That is a reason, but not a good one, sire."

"What would you have? I have no other."

When they had ridden about haf-an-hour:

"Look," said Henri to Chicot, "are not those cavaliers that I see there?"

Chicot looked and said: "Yes, sire, cavaliers, but not huntsmen.

"Why not?"

"Because they are armed like Amadis or Rolando," replied Chicot.

"Ah! what matters the dress, my dear Chicot? you see we are not particular as to that."

"But I see at least 200 men there."

"Ah! that is a good number."

Chicot began to feel very curious. He had really named too low a number, for the group before them consisted of 200 men, who came silently and joined their party; each man was well armed and mounted, and they were led by a gentleman who came and kissed Henri's hand with much devotion.

They passed the River Gers, and then came on a second troop of 100 men; the chief approached, and seemed to be making excuses for not bringing more men. Henri gave him his hand. They went on till they came to the Garonne; this they also passed, and about half a league on the other side, 300 cavaliers, hidden in a pine forest, suddenly came in sight.

The day finished at Muroy, where the gentlemen of the country gave a grand supper to the king, of which Chicot took his part enthusiastically, as it had not been deemed necessary to stop on the road for anything so unimportant as dinner, and he had eaten nothing since he had left Nérac.

Henri had the best house in the town, half the troops slept within doors, the other half in the street where the king was.

"When are we to begin the hunt?" asked Chicot of Henri, as he was undressing.

"You will know to-morrow; meanwhile, lie down there on those cushions on my left; here is Mornay snoring already at my right."

"Peste!" said Chicot, "he makes more noise asleep than awake."

"It is true he is not very talkative; but see him at the chase."

Day had partly appeared, when a great noise of horses awoke Chicot. They dressed, drank some spiced wine, and took other refreshment, and then Henri cried:

"To horse! gentlemen, we have a long day's work before us."

Chicot saw with astonishment that 500 cavaliers had swelled the train during the night.

"Sire!" cried he, "you have an army."

"Wait!" replied Henri.

At Lauzerte, 600 more men came and ranged themselves behind the cavaliers.

"Foot soldiers!" cried Chicot.

"Nothing but beaters," said the king.

Chicot frowned and spoke no more. Twenty times his eyes turned towards the country, and the idea of flight presented itself to him. But Chicot had his guard of honour, doubtless as ambassador of the King of France, and so well was he recommended to this guard, that he could not make a movement that was not repeated by ten men.

This annoyed him, and he said so to the king.

"Diable!" said Henri, "it is your own fault; you tried to run away from Nérac, and I am afraid you will try it again."

"Sire, if I give my word as a gentleman not to do so?"

"That will do."

At this moment they were going through the town of Mont-cuq, and four field-pieces took their place in the army.

"I return to my first idea," said Chicot, "that the wolves in this country are different from others, and are differently treated; with artillery, for instance."

"Ah!" said Henri, "it is a mania of the people of Montcuq. Since I gave them these four pieces they take them about everywhere."

"Well, sire, shall we arrive to-day?"

"No, to-morrow."

"To-morrow morning or evening?"

"Morning."

"Then," said Chicot, "it is at Cahors we are to hunt, is it not, sire?"

"On that side," replied Henri.

The next morning, by eight o'clock, they were before Cahors, with 1,000 foot soldiers and 2,000 horse.

They found the city in a state of defence, M. de Vezin having heard rumours of the advance.

"Ah!" said the king, "he is warned; that is very annoying."

"We must lay siege in due form, sire," said Mornay; "we expect still about 2,000 men, and that is enough."

"Let us assemble the council and begin the trenches."

Chicot listened to all this in amazement. The pensive air of Henri alone reassured him, for it confirmed his suspicions that he was no warrior. He let everyone speak, and said nothing. All at once he raised his head, and said in a commanding tone:

"Gentlemen, this is what we must do. We have 3,000 men, and you say you expect 2,000 more, Mornay?"

"Yes, sire."

"That will make 5,000. In a regular siege we should lose 1,000 or 1,500 men in two months, their death would discourage the others, and we should lose 1,000 more in retreating. Let us sacrifice 500 men at once, and take Cahors by assault."

"What do you mean, sire?" said Mornay.

"My dear friend, we will go straight to the nearest gate. We shall find a fosse in our way, which we will cover with fascines; we may leave 200 men on the road, but we shall reach the gate.

"After, sire?"

"Then we will break it down with petards and go in. It will not be difficult."

Chicot looked at Henri, astonished.


## CHAPTER LIII

### HOW HENRI OF NAVARRE BEHAVED IN BATTLE

The little army advanced near the town, then they breakfasted. The repast over, two hours were given for the officers and men to rest. Henri was very pale, and his hands trembled visibly, when at three o'clock in the afternoon the officers appeared under his tent.

"Gentlemen," said he, "we are here to take Cahors; therefore we must take it—by force. Do you understand? M. de Biron, who has sworn to hang every Huguenot, is only forty-five leagues from here, and doubtless a messenger is already despatched to him by M. de Vezin. In four or five days he will be on us, and as he has 10,000 men with him, we should be taken between the city and him. Let us, then, take Cahors before he comes, that we may receive him well. Come, gentlemen, I will put myself at your head, and let the blows fall as thick as hail."

The men replied to this speech by enthusiastic cries.

"Well said," said Chicot to himself. "It was lucky he had not to speak with his hands, though, or he would have stammered finely. Let us see him at the work."

As they were setting off, the king said to Chicot:

"Pardon me, friend Chicot, I deceived you by talking of wolves, hunting, and such things, but you see Henri will not pay me his sister's dowry, and Margot cries out for her dear Cahors. One must do what one's wife wants, for peace sake; therefore I am going to try and take Cahors."

At this moment the noise of cannon and a furious fire of musketry was heard; it was M. de Vezin's reply to the summons to surrender given by Mornay.

"Hem!" said Chicot, "what do you think of this music, sire?"

"It makes me cold in the marrow of my bones," replied Henri. "Here, my horse! my horse!" cried he.

Chicot looked and listened, unable to understand him. Henri mounted, and then said:

"Come, Chicot, get on horseback, too; you are not a warrior, either, are you?"

"No, sire."

"Well, come, we will be afraid together; come and see, my friend. A good horse here, for M. Chicot."

Henri set off at full gallop, and Chicot followed him. On arriving in front of his little army, Henri raised his visor, and cried:

"Out with the banner; out with the new banner!"

They drew forth banner, which had the double scutcheon of Navarre and Bourbon; it was white, and had chains of gold on one side, and fleur-de-lis on the other.

Again the cannon from Cahors were fired, and the balls tore through a file of infantry near the king.

" Ventre St. Gris! did you see, Chicot?" said the king, whose teeth chattered.

" He will be ill," thought Chicot.

" Cursed body," murmured Henri, " ah! you fear, you tremble; wait till you have something to tremble for." And striking his spurs into his horse, he rushed onwards before cavalry, infantry, and artillery, and arrived at a hundred feet from the place, red with the fire of the batteries which thundered from above  There, he kept his horse immovable for ten minutes, his face turned towards the gate of the city, and crying: " The fascines! ventre St. Gris! the fascines!"

Mornay had followed him, sword in hand, and then came Chicot; behind them the young Huguenot gentlemen, crying: " Vive Navarre!" and each with a fascine, which he threw in, and the fosse was soon filled. Then came the artillery, and with the loss of thirty men succeeded in placing their petards under the gate. The shot whistled like a wirlwind of iron round Henri's head, and twenty men fell in an instant before his eyes. " Forward!" cried he, and rushed on through the midst of the fire, and arrived just as the soldiers had fired the first petard. The gate was broken in two places; the second petard was lighted, and a new opening was made in the wood; but twenty arquebuses immediately passed through, vomiting balls on the soldiers and officers, and the men fell like mowed grass.

" Sire," cried Chicot, " in Heaven's name retire!"

Mornay said nothing; he was proud of his pupil, but from time to time he tried to place himself before him. Once Henri felt the damp on his brow, and a cloud pass over his eyes.

" Ah, cursed nature," cried he, " you shall not conquer me!" Then, jumping off his horse: " An axe!" cried he, and with a vigorous arm he struck down wood and iron. At last a beam gave way, and a part of the gate and a portion of the wall fell, and one hundred men rushed to the breach, crying: " Navarre! Navarre! Cahors is ours!"

Chicot had not quitted the king; he was with him under the gate when he entered, one of the first, but at each discharge he saw him shudder and lower his head.

" Ventre St. Gris! did you ever see such a coward, Chicot?" said he.

" No, sire, I have never seen a coward like you."

M. de Vezin defended himself during five days and nights from street to street and from house to house. Luckily for the rising fortunes of Henri of Navarre, he had counted too much on the walls and garrison of Cahors, and had neglected to send to M. de Biron.

During these five days and nights, Henri commanded like a captain and fought like a soldier, slept with his head on a stone, and awoke sword in hand. Each day they conquered a street or a square, which each night the garrison tried to retake. On the fourth night the enemy seemed willing to give some rest to the Protestant army. Then it was Henri who attacked in his turn. He forced an intrenched position, but it cost him seven hundred men. M. de Turenne and nearly all the officers were wounded, but the king remained untouched. To the fear that he had felt at first, and which he had so heroically vanquished, succeeded a feverish restlessness, a rash audacity. All the fastenings of his armour were broken, as much by his own efforts as by the blows of the enemy. He struck so vigorously that he always killed his man. When this last post was forced, the king entered into the enclosure, followed by the eternal Chicot, who, silent and sad, had for five days seen growing at his sides the phantom of a monarchy destined to destroy that of the Valois.

"Well, Chicot, of what are you thinking?" said Henri to him.

"Sire, that you are a real king."

The siege was soon over after this. M. de Vezin was taken, and the garrison surrendered.

Then Henri dictated to Mornay a letter, which Chicot was to carry to the King of France. It was written in bad Latin, and finished with these words:

"Quod mihi dixisti profuit multum. Cognosco meos devotos; nosce tuos. Chicotos cætera expedit."

Which means: "What you told me was very useful. I know my faithful followers; know yours. Chicot will tell you the rest."

"And now, friend Chicot," said Henri, "embrace me; but take care not to soil yourself, for, mordieu, I am as bloody as a butcher. Take my ring, and adieu, Chicot; I keep you no longer, gallop to France, and tell all you have seen."

## CHAPTER LIV

### WHAT WAS PASSING AT THE LOUVRE ABOUT THE TIME CHICOT ENTERED NERAC

The necessity of following Chicot to the end of his mission has kept us a long time away from the Louvre. The king, after having passed so bravely through his adventurous return from Vincennes, experienced that retrospective emotion which sometimes is felt by the bravest heart after the danger is over. .

At two o'clock everyone slept in the Louvre. The next day, Henri took four bouillons in bed instead of two, and then sent for MM. de Villeguie and D'O to come to his room, to speak about a new financial edict. The queen received the order to dine alone, but it was added that in the evening the king would receive. He asked for lunch, and, while he ate, had an edifying discourse read to him, which he interrupted by saying to the reader: "Was it not Plutarch who wrote the life of Sylla?"

"Yes, sire," said the reader, much astonished at being interrupted in his pious reading by this profane question.

"Do you remember that passage where the historian recounts how the dictator avoided death?"

The reader hesitated.

At this moment, the Cardinal de Joyeuse was announced.

"Ah! here is a learned man, he will tell me at once!" cried the king.

"Your majesty asked, I think, in what manner, and when, Sylla narrowly escaped death?"

"Just so—can you answer me, cardinal?"

"Nothing more easy, sire."

"So much the better."

"Sylla, who had killed so many men, never risked his life but in combats; did your majesty mean in one of those?"

"You are so learned, my dear cardinal."

"Your majesty is too good."

"Now, explain to me how this Roman lion, who was so cruel, was never annoyed by his enemies."

"Carbon, the enemy of Sylla, said often: ' I have to fight at once a lion and a fox who inhabit the soul of Sylla, but it is the fox who gives me most trouble."

"Ah! it was the fox?"

"Plutarch says so, sire."

"And he is right, cardinal. But apropos of combats, have you any news of your brother?"

"Of which brother, sire? I have two."

"Of the Duc d'Arques, my friend."

"Not yet, sire."

"If M. d'Anjou, who always plays the fox, will only play the lion a little for once."

The cardinal did not reply, so Henri, signing to him to remain, dressed himself sumptuously, and passed into the room where the court waited for him. He entered, looking full of good humour, kissed the hands of his wife and mother, paid all sorts of compliments to the ladies, and even offered them sweetmeats.

"We were unquiet about your health, my son," said Catherine.

"You were wrong, madame; I have never been better."

"And to what happy influence do you owe this amelioration, my son?"

"To having laughed much, madame."

Everyone looked astonished.

"Laughed! you can laugh much, my son; then you are very happy?"

"It is true, madame."

"And about what were you so much amused?"

"I must tell you, mother, that yesterday I went to Vincennes."

"I knew it."

"Oh! you knew it; well, my people told me, before my return of an enemy's army whose muskets shone on the road."

"An enemy's army on the road to Vincennes?"

"Yes, mother."

"And where?"

"In front of the Jacobins, near the house of our good cousin."

"Near Madame de Montpensier's?"

"Precisely so, near Bel-Esbat. I approached, bravely to give battle, and I perceived——"

"What, sire?" cried the queen, in alarm.

"Reassure yourself, madame. I perceived an entire priory of good monks, who presented arms to me with acclamations"

Everyone laughed, and the king continued:

"Yes, your are right to laugh; I have in France more than ten thousand monks, of whom I can make, if necessary, ten thousand musquetaires; then I will create a Grand-Master of the Tonsured Musketeers, and give the place to you, cardinal."

"Sire, I accept."

The ladies now, according to etiquette, rose, and, bowing to the king, retired. The queen followed with her ladies of honour. The queen-mother remained; the king's gaiety was a mystery that she wished to fathom.

"Cardinal," said the king, "what has become of your brother, Du Bouchage?"

"I do not know, sire."

"How! you do not know?"

"No; I never see him now."

A grave, sad voice from the end of the room said: " Here I
am, sire."

" Ah! it is he," cried Henri.  " Approach, comte; approach."

The young man obeyed.

" Mon Dieu!" cried the king, " he is no longer a man, but a
shade."

" Sire, he works hard," said the cardinal, stupefied himself
at the change in his brother during the last week.  He was as
pale as wax, and looked thin and wan.

" Come here, young man," said the king.    " Thanks,
cardinal, for your quotation from Plutarch; in a similar case I
shall apply to you again."

The cardinal saw that Henri wished to be left alone with his
brother, and took his leave.

There only remained the queen-mother, D'Epernon, and Du
Bouchage.  The king beckoned to the latter, and said :

" Why do you hide thus behind the ladies; do you not know
it gives me pleasure to see you?"

" Your kind words do me honour, sire," said the young
man, bowing.

" Then how is it that we never see you here now?"

" If your majesty has not seen me, it is because you have
not deigned to cast an eye on the corner of the room.  I am
here every day regularly; I never have failed, and never will,
as long as I can stand upright; it is a sacred duty to me."

" And is it that that makes you so sad?"

" Oh! your majesty cannot think so?"

" No, for you and your brother love me, and I love you.
Apropos, do you know that poor Anne has written to me from
Dieppe?"

" I did not, sire."

" Yes; but you know he did not like going?"

" He confided to me his regrets at leaving Paris."

" Yes; but do you know what he said?  That there existed
a man who would have regretted Paris much more; and that if
I gave you this order you would die."

" Perhaps, sire."

" He said yet more, for your brother talks fast when he is
not sulky; he said that if I had given such an order you would
have disobeyed it."

" Your majesty was right to place my death before my disobedience; it would have been a greater grief to me to disobey
than to die, and yet I should have disobeyed."

" Du Bouchage, you are mad; you will kill yourself with
fancies."

" I know it well, sire."

"But," cried the king, impatiently, "is it a marriage you wish for?"

"Sire, my wish is to inspire love. You see that the whole world is powerless to aid me in this; I alone can obtain it for myself."

"Then why despair?"

"Because I feel that I shall never inspire it."

"Try, try, my child; you are young and rich. Where is the woman that can resist at once beauty, youth and wealth? There are none, Du Bouchage."

"Sire, your goodness is great."

"If you wish to be discreet, and tell me nothing, do so; I will find out, and then act. You know what I have done for your brother, I will do as much for you; a hundred thousand crowns shall not stop me."

Du Bouchage seized the king's hand, and pressed his lips to it.

"May your majesty ask one day for my blood, and I will shed it to the last drop to show you how grateful I am for the protection that I refuse."

Henri III. turned on his heel angrily.

"Really," said he, "these Joyeuses are more obstinate than a Valois. Here is one who will bring me every day his long face and eyes circled with black; that will be delightful."

"Oh! sire, I will smile so, when I am here, that everyone shall think me the happiest of men."

"Yes, but I shall know the contrary, and that will sadden me."

"Does your majesty permit me to retire?" asked Du Bouchage.

"Go, my child, and try to be a man."

When he was gone the king approached D'Epernon, and said:

"Lavalette, have money distributed this evening to the Forty-five, and give them holiday for a night and a day to amuse themselves. By the mass! they saved me like Sylla's white horse."

"Saved?" said Catherine.

"Yes, mother."

"From what?"

"Ah! ask D'Epernon."

"I ask you, my son."

"Well, madame, our dear cousin, the sister of your good friend M. de Guise—oh! do not deny it; you know he is your good friend—laid an ambush for me."

"An ambush!"

"Yes, madame, and I narrowly escaped imprisonment or assassination."

"By M. de Guise?"

"You do not believe it?"

"I confess I do not."

"D'Epernon, my friend, relate the adventure to my mother. If I go on speaking, and she goes on shrugging her shoulders, I shall get angry, and that does not suit my health. Adieu, madame; cherish M. de Guise as much as you please, but I would advise them not to forget Salcède."


## CHAPTER LV

### RED PLUME AND WHITE PLUME

It was eight in the evening, and the house of Robert Briquet, solitary and sad-looking, formed a worthy companion to that mysterious house of which we have already spoken to our readers. One might have thought that these two houses were yawning in each other's face. Not far from there the noise of brass was heard, mingled with confused voices, vague murmurs, and squeaks.

It was probably this noise that attracted a young and handsome cavalier, with a violet cap, red plume, and grey mantle, who, after stopping for some minutes to hear this noise, went on slowly and pensively towards the house of Robert Briquet. Now this noise of brass was that of saucepans; these vague murmurs, those of pots boiling on fires and spits turned by dogs; those cries, those of M. Fournichon, host of the "Brave Chevalier," and of Madame Fournichon, who was preparing her rooms. When the young man with the violet hat had well looked at the fire, inhaled the smell of the fowls, and peeped through the curtains, he went away, then returned to recommence his examinations. He continued to walk up and down, but never passed Robert Briquet's house, which seemed to be the limit of his walk. Each time that he arrived at this limit he found there, like a sentinel, a young man about his own age, with a black cap, a white plume, and a violet cloak, who, with frowning brow and his hand on his sword, seemed to say: "Thou shalt go no further." This continued for about five minutes, until, as they once again came face to face, the young man in the white plume walked straight up against the other, who, taken unawares, with difficulty saved himself from falling.

"Monsieur," cried he, "are you mad, or do you mean to insult me?"

"Monsieur, I wish to make you understand that you annoy me much. It seems to me that you might have seen that without my telling you."

"Not at all, monsieur; I never see what I do not wish to see."

"There are, however, certain things which would attract your attention, I hope, if they shone before your eyes;" and he drew his sword as he spoke, which glittered in the moonlight.

The red plume said quietly: "One would think, monsieur, that you had never drawn a sword before, you are in such a hurry to attack one who does not attack you."

"But who will defend himself, I hope."

"Monsieur, I have particular business here. Now, if you will have it, I will cross swords with you, but I will not go away."

"Monsieur, I am Comte Henri de Bouchage, brother of the Duc de Joyeuse. Once more, will you yield me the place, and go away?"

"Monsieur," replied the other, "I am the Vicomte Ernanton de Carmainges. You do not annoy me at all, and I do not ask you to go away."

Du Bouchage reflected a moment, and then put his sword back in its sheath.

"Excuse me, monsieur," said he; "I am half mad, being in love."

"And I also am in love, but I do not think myself mad for that."

Henri grew pale.

"It is true; pardon, M. de Carmainges; but, in truth, there is no one so unhappy as I am under Heaven."

There was so much real grief and eloquent despair in these words, that Ernanton was profoundly touched.

"Oh! mon Dieu; I understand," said he; "you fear that we are rivals."

"I do."

"Well, monsieur, I will be frank."

Joyeuse grew pale again.

"I," continued Ernanton, "have a rendezvous."

"In this street?"

"Yes."

"Written?"

"Yes; in very good writing."

"A woman's?"

" No; a man's."

" What do you mean?"

" I cannot refuse you, monsieur. I will tell you the tenor of the note."

" I listen."

" You will see if it is like yours."

" Oh, monsieur, I have no rendezvous—no note."

" This is it, then: ' M. Ernanton, my secretary, is charged by me to tell you that I have a great desire to talk with you for an hour; your merit has touched me.' I pass over another phrase still more flattering."

" Then you are waited for?"

" No; I wait, as you see."

" Are they to open the door to you?"

" No; to whistle three times from the window."

Henri, trembling all over, placed one hand on Ernanton's arm, and with the other pointed to the opposite house.

" From there?" said he.

" Oh! no; from there," said Ernanton, pointing to the " Brave Chevalier."

Henri uttered a cry of joy.

" M. de Carmainges, for three months I have loved like a madman, and I have not yet had the happiness of hearing the sound of her voice."

" Diable! you are not far advanced. But stay."

" What is it?"

" Did not someone whistle?"

" Indeed, I think I heard something."

A second whistle was now distinctly heard.

" M. le Comte," said Ernanton, " you will excuse me for taking leave, but I believe that is my signal."

A third whistle sounded.

" Go, monsieur," said Joyeuse; " and good luck to you."

Ernanton made off quickly, while Joyeuse began to walk back more gloomily than ever.

" Now for my accustomed task," said he; " let me knock as usual at this cursed door which never opens to me."


## CHAPTER LVI

### THE DOOR OPENS

On arriving at the door of the house, poor Henri was seized by his usual hesitation.

" Courage," said he to himself.

Ten o'clock struck. Henri lifted the knocker, and struck once, then again.

And he turned to go; but scarcely had he taken two steps, when the key turned in the lock, and, to his profound surprise, the door opened, and a man stood bowing on the threshold. It was the same whom he had seen before.

"Good-evening, monsieur," said he, in a harsh voice, but whose sound appeared to Du Bouchage sweeter than the song of birds.

Henri joined his hands and trembled so, that the servant put out a hand to save him falling, with a visible expression of respectful pity.

"Speak then, monsieur, and tell me what you desire."

"My friend, you already know. Many times, you know, I have waited for you and surprised you at the turn of a street, and have offered you gold enough to enrich you, had you been the greediest of men; at other times I have threatened you, but you have never listened to me, and have always seen me suffer without seeming to pity me. To-day you tell me to speak—to express my wishes; what then has happened, mon Dieu?"

The servant sighed. He had evidently a pitying heart under a rough covering. Henri heard this sigh, and it encouraged him.

"You know," continued he, "that I love, and how I love; you have seen me pursue a woman and discover her, in spite of her efforts to fly me; but never in my greatest grief has a bitter word escaped me, or have I given heed to those violent thoughts which are born of despair and the fire of youth."

"M. le Comte," replied the man, "the lady whom you accuse is, believe me, far from having the hard, insensible heart you think; she has seen you, and understood what you suffer, and feels for you the warmest sympathy."

Henri uttered a doleful cry.

"She loves!" cried he. "Ah! mon Dieu!"

"Yes, she loves; but be not jealous of the man she loves, M. le Comte, for he is no more of this world. My mistress is a widow."

These words restored hope and life to the young man.

The servant shook his head.

"This lady, M. le Comte, has also sworn eternal fidelity to death; but I know her, and she will keep her word."

"I will wait ten years, if necessary; since she lives, I may hope."

"Oh! young man, do not reckon thus. She has lived, you say; yes, so she has, not a month, or a year, but seven years.

You hope that she will console herself; never, M. le Comte, never. I swear it to you—I, who was but the servant of him who is dead, and yet I shall never be consoled."

"My friend," cried Joyeuse, "intercede for me."

"I! Listen, M. le Comte. Had I believed you capable of using violence towards my mistress, I would have killed you long ago with my own hand. If, on the contrary, I could have believed that she would love you, I think I should have killed her. Now, M. le Comte, I have said what I wished to say; do not seek to make me say more, for, on my honour—and although not a nobleman, my honour is worth something—I have told you all I can."

Henri rose.

"I thank you," said he, "for having had compassion on my misfortunes; now I have decided."

"Then you will be calmer for the future. M. le Comte, you will go away; and leave us to ourselves?"

"Yes, be easy; I will go away, and for ever."

And he went away rapidly, throwing a heavy purse of gold at the feet of the servant.


## CHAPTER LVII

### HOW A GREAT LADY LOVED IN THE YEAR 1586

The whistles which Ernanton had heard were really his signal. Thus, when the young man reached the door, he found Dame Fournichon on the threshold waiting for her customers with a smile.

When the young man entered the ante-chamber, he smelt a strong aromatic odour, the work, doubtless, of some susceptible person, who had thus tried to overcome the smell of cooking exhaled from the kitchen.

Ernanton, after opening the door, stopped for an instant to contemplate one of those elegant female figures which must always command attention, if not love. Reposing on cushions enveloped in silk and velvet, this lady was occupied in burning in the candle the end of a little stick of aloes, over which she bent so as to inhale the full perfume. By the manner in which she threw the branch in the fire, and pulled her hood over her masked face, Ernanton perceived that she had heard him enter, but she did not turn.

"Madame," said the young man, "you sent for your humble servant—here he is."

"Ah! very well," said the lady; "sit down, I beg, M Ernanton."

"Pardon, madame, but before anything I must thank you for the honour that you do me."

"Ah! that is civil, and you are right; but I presume you do not know whom you are thanking, M. de Carmainges."

"Madame, you have your face hidden by a mask and your hands by gloves; I cannot then recognise you—I can but guess."

"And you guess who I am?"

"Her whom my heart desires, whom my imagination paints, young, beautiful, powerful, and rich; too rich and too powerful for me to be able to believe that what has happened to me is real, and that I am not dreaming."

"By what do you recognise me?"

"By your voice, your grace, and your beauty."

"Then, on the receipt of my letter, you guessed that it came from me?"

"Oh! no, madame, not for a moment; I believed I was the subject of some joke, or the victim of some error, and it is only during the last few minutes that, seeing you, touching you——" and he tried to take her hand, but she withdrew it.

"Enough!" said the lady.

"Alas! madame, I am in love."

"And you are convinced that I reciprocate this love?" Ernanton rose piqued.

"No, madame," replied he.

"Then what do you believe?"

"I believe that you have something important to say to me, and that, not wishing to receive me at your Hôtel, or at Bel-Esbat, you preferred this isolated spot."

"You thought that?"

"Yes."

"And what do you think I could have to say to you?" asked the lady, rather anxiously.

"How can I tell? Perhaps something about M. de Mayenne."

"Had you not already told me all you knew of him?"

"Perhaps, then, some question about last night's event."

"What event? of what do you speak?" asked the lady, visibly agitated.

"Of the panic experienced by M. d'Epernon and the arrest of the Lorraine gentlemen."

"They arrested them?"

"Yes, those who were found on the road to Vincennes."

"Which is also the road to Soissons, where M. de Guise holds his garrison. Ah! M. Ernanton, you, who belong to the court, can tell me why they arrested these gentlemen."

" I belong to the court?"

" Certainly."

" You know that, madame?"

" Ah! to find out your address, we were forced to make inquiries. But what resulted from all this?"

" Nothing, madame, to my knowledge."

" Then why did you think I should wish to speak of it?"

" I am wrong again, madame."

" From what place are you, monsieur?"

" From Agen."

" What, you are a Gascon! and yet are not vain enough to suppose that when I saw you at the Porte St. Antoine, on the day of Salcède's execution, I liked your looks."

Ernanton reddened, and looked confused

The lady went on.   " That I met you in the street, and found you handsome."

Ernanton grew scarlet.

" That, afterwards, when you brought me a message from my brother, I liked you."

" Madame, I never thought so, I protest."

" Then you were wrong," said the lady, turning on him two eyes which flashed through her mask.

Ernanton clasped his hands.

" Madame, are you mocking me?" cried he.

" Ma foi! no.  The truth is, that you pleased me."

Ernanton fell on his knees.

" Speak, madame, speak, that I may be sure this is not all a dream, and perhaps I shall dare to answer."

" Monsieur," said she, " it appears you have heard, but not understood me.  No familiarity, if you please; let us each remain in our places.  Some day I shall give you the right to call me yours; but this right you have not yet."

Ernanton rose, pale and angry.

" Ah! you are angry, I believe," said the duchess, haughtily.

" I am, madame, but it is against myself; for I have for you, madame, not a passing caprice, but a real love.  It is your heart I seek to obtain, and therefore I am angry with myself for having compromised the respect that I owe you, and which I will only change into love when you command me.  From this moment, madame, I await your orders."

" Come, come, do not exaggerate, M. de Carmainges; now you are all ice, after being all flame."

At these words she rose.

It was time, for the young man seized her in his arms, and his lips touched her mask; but through this mask her eyes darted such a flaming glance that he drew back.

"Well," said she, "we shall meet again. Decidedly you please me, M. de Carmainges."

Ernanton bowed.

"When are you free?" asked she.

"Alas! very rarely, madame."

"Ah! your service is fatiguing, is it not?"

"What service?"

"That which you perform near the king. Are you not some kind of guard to his majesty?"

"I form part of a body of gentlemen, madame."

"That is what I mean. They're all Gascons, are they not?"

"Yes, madame."

"How many are there? I forget."

"Forty-five."

"What a singular number."

"I believe it was chance."

"And these forty-five gentlemen never quit the king, you say?"

"I did not say so, madame."

"Ah! I thought you did; at least, you said you had very little liberty."

"It is true, I have very little; because by day we are on service near the king, and at night we stay at the Louvre."

"But you have not explained to me," said the duchess, with her insinuating smile, "how you happened to be free this evening, and how you came."

"This evening, madame, I was thinking of asking permission of De Loignac, our captain, who is very kind to me, when the order came to give a night's holiday to the Forty-five."

"And on what account was this leave given?"

"As recompense, I believe, madame, for a somewhat fatiguing service yesterday at Vincennes."

"Well! listen, Carmainges," said the duchess, with a gentle familiarity which filled the heart of the young man with joy; "this is what you must do, whenever you think you shall be at liberty—send a note here to the hostess, and every day I will send a man to inquire."

"Oh, mon Dieu; madame, you are too good!"

"What is that noise?" said the duchess, laying her hand on his arm.

"Indeed, a noise of spurs, of voices, of doors shutting, and joyous exclamations, came from the room below, like the echo of an invasion. Ernanton looked out.

"It is my companions," said he, "who have come here to spend their holiday."

"But by what chance? just where we are."

"Because it is just here, madame, that we each had a rendezvous on our arrival, and on the happy day of their entry in Paris my friends conceived an affection for the wine and the cooking of M. Fournichon. But you, how did you come to choose this place?"

"I chose, and you will easily understand that, the most deserted part of Paris, a place near the river, where no one was likely to recognise me, or suspect that I could come; but, mon Dieu! how noisy your companions are."

Indeed, the noise was becoming a perfect storm, but all at once they heard a sound of footsteps on the little staircase which led to their room, and Madame Fournichon's voice, crying, from below: "M. de St. Maline, M. de St. Maline!"

"Mon Dieu! M. de Carmainges," cried the duchess, "will those people dare to enter here?"

"I am here, madame; have no fear."

"Oh! they are forcing the doors," cried she.

Indeed, St. Maline rushed so furiously against the door, that, being very slight, it was at once broken open.

## CHAPTER LVIII

### HOW ST. MALINE ENTERED INTO THE TURRET, AND WHAT FOLLOWED

Ernanton's first thought when he saw the door of the ante-chamber fly open was to blow out the light.

"M. de St. Maline," cried the hostess, "I warn you that the persons whom you are troubling are your friends."

"Well! all the more reason to present our compliments to them," cried Perducas de Pincornay, in a tipsy voice.

"And what friends are they? We will see!" cried St. Maline.

The good hostess, hoping to prevent a collision, glided among them, and whispered Ernanton's name in St. Maline's ear.

"Ernanton!" cried St. Maline, aloud, for whom this revelation was oil instead of water thrown on the fire, "that is not possible."

Ernanton appeared on the threshold, with a face which did not announce that patience was one of the virtues which, according to St. Maline, he possessed.

"By what right has M. de St. Maline broken down the door, and intends to break a second?" said he.

"Ah! it is he, really; it is Ernanton!" cried St. Maline. "I recognise his voice; but as to his person, devil take me if I can see it in this darkness."

"You do not reply to my question, monsieur," said Ernanton

St. Maline began to laugh noisily, which reassured some of his comrades, who were thinking of retiring.

Montcrabeau descended, and returned with a light, which he offered to St. Maline.

"No, no," said he; "keep it; I may, perhaps, want both hands."

And he made a step forward.

"I take you all to witness," cried Ernanton, "that I am insulted without reason, and that in consequence"—and he drew his sword—"I will bury this sword in the breast of the first man who advances."

St. Maline, furious, was about to draw his sword also; but before he had time to do so, the point of Ernanton's was on his breast, and as he advanced a step, without Ernanton's moving his arm, St. Maline felt the iron on his flesh, and drew back furious, but Ernanton followed him, keeping the sword against his breast. St. Maline grew pale; if Ernanton had wished it, he could have pinned him to the wall, but he slowly withdrew his sword.

"You merit two deaths for your insolence," said he, "but I will touch you no more; let me pass. Come, madame, I answer for your free passage."

Then appeared a woman, whose head was covered by a hood, and her face by a mask, and who took Ernanton's arm, tremblingly. St. Maline stood by, stifling with rage at his merited punishment. He drew his dagger as Ernanton passed by him. Did he mean to strike Ernanton, or only to do what he did? No one knew, but as they passed, his dagger cut through the silken hood of the duchess and severed the string of her mask, which fell to the ground. This movement was so rapid that in the half light no one saw or could prevent it. The duchess uttered a cry; St. Maline picked up the mask and returned it to her, looking now full in her uncovered face.

"Ah!" cried he, in an insolent tone, "it is the beautiful lady of the litter. Ernanton, you get on fast."

Ernanton stopped and half-drew his sword again; but the duchess drew him on, saying: "Come on, I beg you, M. Ernanton."

"We shall meet again, M. de St. Maline," said Ernanton, "and you shall pay for this, with the rest."

And he went on without meeting with any further opposition, and conducted the duchess to her litter, which was guarded by two servants.

When they arrived at the Pont Neuf, which then merited the name, as it was scarcely seven years since Ducerceau had built it, the duchess gave her hand to Ernanton, saying: " Now go, monsieur."

" May I dare to ask when I shall see you again, madame?"

" That depends on the length of time which you take in executing my commission, and your haste will be a proof to me of your desire to see me again."

" Oh, madame, I shall not be idle."

" Well, then go, Ernanton."

" It is strange," thought the young man, as he retraced his steps; " I cannot doubt that she likes me, and yet she does not seem the least anxious as to whether or not I get killed by that brute of a St. Maline. But, poor woman, she was in great trouble, and the fear of being compromised is, particularly with princesses, the strongest of all sentiments."

Ernanton, however, could not forget the insult he had received, and he returned straight to the hotel. He was naturally decided to infringe all orders and oaths, and to finish with St. Maline; he felt in the humour to fight ten men, if necessary. This resolution sparkled in his eyes when he reached the door of the " Brave Chevalier."

At this sight, several voices cried: " Come here, Ernanton; come this side, Carmainges; there is room here."

" Thank you," replied the young man; " but it is near M. de St. Maline that I wish to sit."

St. Maline rose, and all eyes were fixed on him. But as he rose, his face changed its expression.

" I will make room for you, monsieur," said he, gently; " and in doing so address to you my frank and sincere apologies for my stupid aggression just now; I was drunk; forgive me."

This declaration did not satisfy Ernanton; but the cries of joy that proceeded from all the rest decided him to say no more, although a glance at St. Maline showed him that he was not to be trusted. St. Maline's glass was full, and he filled Ernanton's.

" Peace! peace!" cried all the voices.

Carmainges profited by the noise, and leaning towards St. Maline, with a smile on his lips, so that no one might suspect the sense of what he was saying, whispered:

" M. de St. Maline, this is the second time that you have

insulted me without giving me satisfaction; take care, for at the third offence I will kill you like a dog."

And the two mortal enemies touched glasses as though they had been the best friends.

## CHAPTER LIX

### WHAT WAS HAPPENING IN THE MYSTERIOUS HOUSE

While the hotel of the "Brave Chevalier," the abode, apparently, of the most perfect concord, with closed doors and open cellars, showed through the openings of the shutters the light of its candles and the mirth of its guests, an unaccustomed movement took place in that mysterious house of which our readers have as yet only seen the outside.

The servant was going from one room to another, carrying packages which he placed in a trunk. These preparations over, he loaded a pistol, examined his poniard, then suspended it, by the aid of a ring, to the chain which served him for a belt, to which he attached besides a bunch of keys and a book of prayers bound in black leather.

While he was thus occupied, a step, light as that of a shadow, came up the staircase, and a woman, pale and phantomlike under the folds of her white veil, appeared at the door, and a voice, sad and sweet as the song of a bird in the wood, said:

"Remy, are you ready?"

"Yes, madame, I only wait for your box."

"At what hour have you ordered the horses?" said the lady, at last.

"At two o'clock."

"And one has just struck."

"Yes, madame."

"No one is watching outside?"

"No one."

"Not even that unhappy young man?"

"But listen! is that not the trot of a horse that I hear?"

"Yes, I think so."

"Can it be ours?"

"It is possible; but it is an hour too soon."

"It stops at the door, Remy."

Remy ran down and arrived just as three hurried blows were struck on the door.

"Who is there?" said he.

"I!" replied a trembling voice, "I, Grandchamp, the baron's valet."

"Ah! mon Dieu! Grandchamp, you at Paris! speak low! Whence do you come?"

"From Méridor. Alas, dear M. Remy!"

"Well," cried the lady from the top of the stairs, "are they our horses, Remy?"

"No, madame, it is not them. What is it, Grandchamp?"

"You do not guess?"

"Alas! I do; what will she do, poor lady?"

"Remy," cried she again, "you are talking to someone?"

"Yes, madame."

"I thought I knew the voice."

"Indeed, madame."

She now descended, saying:

"Who is there? Grandchamp?"

"Yes, madame, it is I," replied the old man sadly, uncovering his white head.

"Grandchamp! you! Oh! mon Dieu! my presentiments were right; my father is dead?"

"Indeed, madame, Méridor has no longer a master."

Pale, but motionless and firmly, the lady listened; Remy went to her and took her hand softly.

"How did he die; tell me, my friend?" said she.

"Madame, M. le Baron, who could no longer leave his arm-chair, was struck a week ago by an attack of apoplexy. He muttered your name for the last time, then ceased to speak, and soon was no more."

Diana went up again without another word. Her room was on the first story, and looked only into a court-yard. The furniture was sombre, but rich, the hangings, in Arras tapestry, represented the death of our Saviour, a prie-dieu and stool in carved oak, a bed with twisted columns, and tapestries like the walls were the sole ornaments of the room. Not a flower, no gilding, but in a frame of black was contained a portrait of a man, before which the lady now knelt down, with dry eyes, but a sad heart.

"I had begged thee to wait, although thy soul must have thirsted for vengeance; and as the dead see all, thou hast seen, my love, that I lived only not to kill my father, else I would have died after you; and then, you know, on your bleeding corpse I uttered a vow to give death for death, blood for blood, but I would not do it while the old man called me his innocent child. Thou hast waited, beloved, and now I am free; the last tie which bound me to earth is broken. I am all yours, and now I am free to come to you."

She rose on one knee, kissed the hand, and then went on: "I can weep no more—my tears have dried up in weeping over your tomb. In a few months I shall rejoin you, and you will then reply to me, dear shade, to whom I have spoken so often without reply." Diana then rose, and seating herself in her chair, muttered: "Poor father!" and then fell into a profound reverie. At last she called Remy.

The faithful servant soon appeared.

"Here I am, madame."

"My worthy friend, my brother—you, the last person who knows me on this earth—say adieu to me."

"Why so, madame?"

"Because the time has come for us to separate."

"Separate!" cried the young man. "What do you mean, madame?"

"Yes, Remy. My project of vengeance seemed to me noble and pure while there remained an obstacle between me and it, and I only contemplated it from afar off; but now that I approach the execution of it—now that the obstacle has disappeared—I do not draw back, but I do not wish to drag with me into crime a generous and pure soul like yours; therefore you must quit me, my friend."

Remy listened to the words of Diana with a sombre look.

"Madame," replied he, "do you think you are speaking to a trembling old man? Madame, I am but twenty-six; and snatched as I was from the tomb, if I still live, it is for the accomplishment of some terrible action—to play an active part in the work of Providence. Never, then, separate your thoughts from mine, since we both have the same thoughts, sinister as they may be. Where you go, I will go; what you do, I will aid in; or if, in spite of my prayers, you persist in dismissing me——"

"Oh!" murmured she, "dismiss you! What a word, Remy!"

"If you persist in that resolution," continued the young man, "I know what I have to do, and all for me will end with two blows from a poniard—one in the heart of him whom you know, and the other in your own."

"Remy! Remy!" cried Diana, "do not say that. The life of him you threaten does not belong to you—it is mine—I have paid for it dearly enough. I swear to you, Remy, that on the day on which I knelt beside the dead body of him"—and she pointed to the portrait—"on that day I approached my lips to that open wound, and the trembling lips seemed to say to me: 'Avenge me, Diana!—avenge me!'"

"Madame——"

"Therefore, I repeat, vengeance is for me, and not for you;

besides, for whom and through whom did he die? By me and through me."

" I must obey you, madame, for I also was left for dead. Who carried me away from the middle of the corpses with which that room was filled?—You. Who cured me of my wounds?—You. Who concealed me?—You always. Order, then, and I will obey, provided that you do not order me to leave you."

" So be it, Remy; you are right; nothing ought to separate us more.

Remy pointed to the portrait.

" Now, madame," said he, " he was killed by treason—it is by treason that he must be revenged. Ah! you do not know one thing—the hand of God is with us, for to-night I have found the secret of the 'Aqua tofana,' that poison of the Medicis and of René the Florentine."

" Really?"

" Come and see, madame."

" But where is Grandchamp?"

" The poor old man has come sixty leagues on horseback; he is tired out, and has fallen asleep on my bed."

" Come, then," said Diana; and she followed Remy.


# CHAPTER LX

### THE LABORATORY

Remy led the lady into a neighbouring room; and pushing a spring which was hidden under a board in the floor, and which opening disclosed a straight dark staircase, gave his hand to Diana to help her to descend. Twenty steps of this staircase, or rather ladder, led into a dark and circular cave, whose only furniture was a stove with an immense hearth, a square table, two rush chairs, and a quantity of phials and iron boxes. In the stove a dying fire still gleamed, while a thick black smoke escaped through a pipe fastened into the wall. From a still placed on the hearth a few drops of a liquid, yellow as gold, was dropping into a thick white phial. Diana looked round her without astonishment or terror; the ordinary feelings of life seemed to be unknown to her who lived only in the tomb. Remy lighted a lamp, and then approached a well hollowed out in the cave, attached a bucket to a long cord, let it down into the well, and then drew it up full of a water as cold as ice and as clear as crystal.

" Approach, madame," said he.

Diana drew near. In the bucket he let fall a single drop of the liquid contained in the phial, and the entire mass of the water became instantaneously yellow; then the colour evaporated, and the water in ten minutes became as clear as before.

Remy looked at her.

"Well?" said she.

"Well, madame," said he, "now dip in that water, which has neither smell nor colour, a glove or a handkerchief; soak it in scented soap, pour some of it into the basin where you are about to wash your hands or face, and you will see, as was seen at the court of Charles IX., the flower kill by its perfume, the glove poison by its contact, the soap kill by its introduction into the pores of the skin. Pour a single drop of this pure oil on the wick of a lamp or candle, and for an hour the candle or lamp will exhale death, and burn at the same time like any other."

"Can I see this phial, Remy?"

"Yes, madame, presently."

Remy then separated it from the still with infinite care, then corked it with soft wax, tied the top up in cloth, and then presented it to Diana.

She took it, held it up to the light, and, after looking at it, said:

"It will do; when the time arrives we will choose gloves, lamp, soap, or flowers, as convenient. Will the liquor keep in metal?"

"It eats it away."

"But then, perhaps, the bottle will break?"

"I think not—see the thickness of the crystal; besides, we can shut it up in a covering of gold."

"Listen, Remy! I hear horses; I think ours have arrived."

"Probably, madame, it is about the time; but I will go and send them away."

"Why so?"

"Are they not useless?"

"Instead of going to Méridor, we will go into Flanders. Keep the horses."

"Ah! I understand!" and Remy's eyes gave forth a flash of sinister joy.

At this moment they heard knocking.

"Here are our horses, madame," said Remy; "go up quickly and I will close the trap-door."

Diana obeyed, and found Grandchamp, whom the noise had wakened, at the door.

The old man was not a little surprised to hear of his

F

mistress's intended departure, who informed him of it without telling him where she was going.

"Grandchamp, my friend," said she, "Remy and I are going to accomplish a pilgrimage on which we have long determined; speak of this journey to none, and do not mention my name to anyone."

"Oh! I promise you, madame," replied the old servant; "but we shall see you again?"

"Doubtless, Grandchamp; if not in this world, in the next. But, apropos, Grandchamp, this house is now useless to us."

Diana drew from a drawer a bundle of papers.

"Here are the title-deeds; let or sell this house; but if, in the course of a month, you do not find a purchaser, abandon it and return to Méridor."

"But if I find someone, how much am I to ask?"

"What you please, Grandchamp."

"Shall I take the money to Méridor?"

"Keep it for yourself, my good Grandchamp."

"What, madame, such a sum?"

"Yes, I owe it to you for your services; and I have my father's debts to pay as well as my own. Now, adieu."

Then Diana went upstairs, cut the picture from the frame, rolled it up, and placed it in her trunk.

## CHAPTER LXI

### WHAT MONSEIGNEUR FRANCOIS, DUC D'ANJOU, DUC DE BRABANT AND COMTE DE FLANDERS, WAS DOING IN FLANDERS

Our readers must now permit us to leave the king at the Louvre, Henri of Navarre at Cahors, Chicot on the road, and Diana in the street, to go to Flanders to find M. le Duc d'Anjou, recently named Duc de Brabant, and to whose aid we have seen sent the great admiral of France—Anne, Duc de Joyeuse. The camp of the new Duke of Brabant was situated on the banks of the Scheldt, and the army, although we disciplined, was agitated by a spirit easy to understand.

Indeed, many Calvinists assisted the duke, not from sympathy for him, but in order to be as disagreeable as possible to Spain and to the Catholics of France and England; they fought rather from self-love than from conviction or devotion, and it was certain that, the campaign once over, they would abandon their leader or impose conditions on him. With regard to these conditions, the duke always gave them to understand that when the time came he should be ready, and was constantly saying: " Henry of Navarre made himself a Catholic, why should not I become a Huguenot? On the opposite side, on the contrary, there existed a perfect unity of feeling. Antwerp had intended to give entrance to him, at her own time and on her own conditions. However, all these different opinions interfered sadly with the discipline of the duke's army. Joyeuse, who we know had never liked the mission, was annoyed to find among these men such antagonistic opinions, and felt instinctively that the time for success was past, and both as an idle courtier and as a captain, grumbled at having come so far only to meet with defeat. He declared loudly that the Duc d'Anjou had been wrong in laying siege to Antwerp, and argued that to possess a great city with its own consent was a real advantage; but that to take by assault the second capital of his future states was to expose himself to the dislike of the Flemings; and Joyeuse knew the Flemings too well not to feel sure that if the duke did take Antwerp, sooner or later they would revenge themselves with usury. This opinion Joyeuse did not hesitate to declare in the duke's tent.

While the council was held among his captains, the duke was lying on a couch and listening, not to the advice of the admiral, but to the whispers of Aurilly. This man, by his cowardly compliances, his base flatteries, and his continual assiduities, had secured the favour of the prince. With his lute, his love messages, and his exact information about all the persons and all the intrigues of the court—with his skilful manœuvres for drawing into the prince's net whatever prey he might wish for, he had made a large fortune, while he remained to all appearance the poor luteplayer. His influence was immense, because it was secret.

Joyeuse, seeing the duke talking to Aurilly, stopped short. The duke, who had, after all, been paying more attention than he seemed to do, asked him what was the matter.

" Nothing, monseigneur; I am only waiting until your highness is at liberty to listen to me."

" Oh! but I do listen, M. de Joyeuse. Do you think I cannot listen to two people at once, when Cæsar dictated seven letters at a time?"

" Monseigneur," said Joyeuse, with a glance at the musician, " I am no singer to need an accompaniment when I speak."

" Very good, duke; be quiet, Aurilly. Then you disapprove of a coup de main on Antwerp?"

" Yes, monseigneur."

" Then you fear a repulse?"

" Yes, monseigneur, I do."

"You will not be there, M. de Joyeuse."

"Why not?"

"Because you can hardly have such doubts of your own bravery as already to see yourself flying before the Flemings. In any case, reassure yourself, these prudent merchants have the habit, when they march to battle, of cumbering themselves with such heavy armour that they would never catch you if you did run."

"Monseigneur, I do not doubt my own courage. I shall be in the front, but I shall be beaten there, as the others who are behind will be."

"But your reasoning is not logical, M. de Joyeuse; you approve of my taking the lesser places."

"I approve of your taking those that do not defend themselves."

"And then I am to draw back from the great city because she talks of defending herself?"

"Better than to march on to destruction."

"Well, I will not retreat."

"Your highness must do as you like; and we are here to obey."

"Prove to me that I am wrong."

"Monseigneur, see the army of the Prince of Orange. It was yours, was it not? Well, instead of sitting down before Antwerp with you, it is in Antwerp, which is very different. William, you say, was your friend and counsellor; and now you not only do not know where he is, but you believe him to be changed into an enemy. See the Flemings—when you arrived they were pleased to see you; now they shut their gates at your sight, and prepare their cannon at your approach, not less than if you were the Duc d'Alva. Well! I tell you, Flemings and Dutch, Antwerp and Orange, only wait for an opportunity to unite against you, and that opportunity will be when you order your artillery to fire."

"Well, we will fight at once Flemings and Dutch, Antwerp and Orange."

"No, monseigneur, we have but just men enough to attack Antwerp, supposing we have only the inhabitants to deal with; and whilst we are engaged in the assault, William will fall on us with his eternal eight or ten thousand men, always destroyed and always reappearing, by the aid of which he has kept in check during ten or twelve years the Duc d'Alva, Requesens, and the Duc de Parma."

"Then you persist in thinking that we shall be beaten?"

"I do."

"Well, it is easy for you to avoid it, M. de Joyeuse," said

he prince angrily; " my brother sent you here to aid me, but
may dismiss you, saying that I do not need aid."

" When your highness speaks thus," said Joyeuse, " I will
ay no more. I am here to obey you, and will do so with all
ny heart, whether you lead me to death or victory; and yet
——but I will say no more."

" Speak."

" No, I have said enough."

" No, I wish to hear."

" In private then, if it pleases your highness."

All rose and retired to the other end of the spacious tent.

" Speak," said François.

" Monseigneur may care little for a check from Spain, a
heck which will render triumphant those drinkers of Flemish
eer, or this double-faced Prince of Orange; but will you bear
o patiently the laughter of M. de Guise?"

François frowned.

" What has M. de Guise to do with it?" said he.

" M. de Guise tried to have you assassinated, monseigneur;
alcède confessed it at the torture, and, if I mistake not, he
lays a great part in all this, and he will be delighted to see
ou receive a check before Antwerp, or even perhaps to
btain, for nothing, that death of a son of France, for which
e had promised to pay so dearly to Salcède. Read the his-
ory of Flanders, monseigneur, and you will see that the
lemings are in the habit of enriching their soil with the blood
f princes, and of the best French warriors."

The duke shook his head.

" Well, Joyeuse," said he, " I will give, if it must be, the
ursed joy to the Lorraines of seeing me dead, but not that of
eeing me flying. I thirst for glory, Joyeuse; for alone of all
ny name, I have still my battles to win."

" You forget Cateau Cambresis, monseigneur."

" Compare that with Jarnac and Moncontour, Joyeuse."
hen, turning to the others, who were standing far off, he
aid: " Gentlemen, the assault is still resolved on; the rain has
eased, the ground is good, we will make the attack this night."

Joyeuse bowed.

" Will your highness give full directions? we wait for them,"
aid he.

" You have eight vessels, without counting the admiral's
hip, have you not, M. de Joyeuse?"

" Yes, monseigneur."

" You will force the line; the thing will be easy, the Antwer-
ans having only merchant vessels in the port; then you will
ing them to bear upon the fort. Then, if the quay is

defended, you will attempt a landing with your 1,500 men
Of the rest of the army I will make two columns; one com
manded by M. de St. Aignan, the other by myself. Both wil
attempt an escalade by surprise, at the moment when the firs
cannot-shot is fired.

"The cavalry will remain in position, in case of a repulse, t
protect the retreating columns. Of these three attacks, on
must surely succeed. The first column which gains th
ramparts will fire a rocket to let the others know."

"But one must think of everything, monseigneur," sai
Joyeuse; "and supposing all three attacks should fail?"

"Then we must gain the vessels under the protection of ou
batteries"

All bowed.

## CHAPTER LXII

### MONSEIGNEUR

However, the Antwerpians did not quietly see the hostil
preparations of the Duc d'Anjou, and Joyeuse was not wron
in attributing to them all the enmity possible. Antwerp wa
like a beehive at night, calm on the exterior, but within full o
movement and murmur.

The Flemings in arms patrolled the streets, barricaded the
houses, and fraternised with the battalions of the Prince o
Orange, of whom part were already in garrison there, whil
the other part entered the city in fractions.

When all was ready for a vigorous defence, the Prince o
Orange, on a dark and moonless night, entered the cit
quietly, and went to the Hôtel de Ville, where his confidant
had everything ready for his reception. There he received a
the deputies of the bourgeoisie, passed in review the officer
of the paid troops, and communicated his plans to them, th
chief of which was to profit by this movement of the Du
d'Anjou to break with him. The duke had done just wha
William wished to bring him to, and he saw with pleasure th
new competitor for the sovereignty ruin himself, like so man
others.

William would have taken the offensive, but the governo
objected, and determined to wait for the arrival o
Monseigneur.

Nine o'clock in the evening sounded, and the uncertaint
became real anxiety, some scouts having protested that the
had seen a movement in the French camp. A little flat bo

had been seen on the Scheldt to reconnoitre, for the Antwerpians were less unquiet as to what would occur by land than by sea; but the barque had not returned. William became more and more impatient, when the door of the hall opened, and a valet appeared and announced "Monseigneur." As he spoke, a man, tall and imperious-looking, wearing with supreme grace the cloak which entirely enveloped him, entered the hall, and saluted courteously those who were there. But at the first glance, his eye, proud and piercing, sought out the prince in the midst of his officers.

He went straight up to him and offered him his hand, which the prince pressed with affection, and almost with respect.

They called each other "Monseigneur." After this the unknown took off his cloak. He was dressed in a buff doublet, and had high leather boots; he was armed with a long sword, which seemed to make part of himself, so easily it hung, and with a little dagger, which was passed through his belt. His boots were covered with mud and dust, and his spurs were red with the blood of his horse. He took his place at the table.

"Well, where are we?" asked he.

"We know by our spies," said the burgomaster, "that a movement is preparing in the French camp; they are making ready for an attack, but as we do not know on which side it will come, we have disposed the guns so that they may be equally distributed over the whole rampart."

"That is wise," replied the unknown, with a slight smile to William, who held his tongue, and let the bourgeois speak of war.

"We have done the same with our civic guards; they are spread over the whole wall, and have orders to run at once to the point of attack. However, it is the opinion of the greater number of our members that it is impossible that the French meditate anything but a feigned attack."

"Gentlemen," said the unknown, "you are in error; a regular assault is preparing against you, and your plans, however good, are incomplete."

"But, monseigneur——"

"Incomplete in this, that you expect an attack, and have prepared to meet it."

"Certainly."

"Well, it is you who will make the attack, not wait for it, if you will trust to me."

"Ah!" cried William, "that is something like speaking."

"At this moment," said the stranger, who saw that he might reckon on the prince's support, "the ships of M. de

Joyeuse are getting ready." "But," said the burgomaster,
"why does monseigneur believe that the attack is about to
commence?"

"Here are the probabilities. The infantry is Catholic; it
will fight alone; that is, on one side. The cavalry is Calvinist;
they will fight alone on another side. The navy is under M.
de Joyeuse, from Paris, who will take his share of the combat
and the glory. That is three sides."

"Then let us form three corps," said the burgomaster.

"Make only one, gentlemen, with all your best soldiers, and
leave any of whom you may be doubtful in close fight to
guard your walls. Then with this body make a vigorous sally
when François least expects it. They mean to attack; let them
be forestalled, and attacked themselves. If you wait for
their assault you are lost, for no one equals the French at an
attack, as you, gentlemen, have no equals at defending your
towns."

The Flemings looked radiant.

"What did I say, gentlemen?" said William

"It is a great honour," said the unknown, "to have been
without knowing it, of the same opinion as the greatest
captain of the age."

Both bowed courteously.

"Then," continued the unknown, "it is settled: you will
make a furious sortie on the infantry and cavalry. I trust that
your officers will so conduct it as to defeat your enemies."

"But their vessels?" cried the burgomaster. "The wind is
north-east, and they will be in our city in two hours."

"You have yourselves six old ships and thirty boats at St
Marie; that is a mile off, is it not? That is your maritime
barricade across the Scheldt."

"Yes, monseigneur, that is so. How do you know all these
details?"

Monseigneur smiled

"I know them, as you see; it is there that lies the fate of the
battle."

"Then," said the burgomaster, "we must send aid to our
brave seamen."

"On the contrary, you may dispose otherwise of the 400
men who are there; twenty brave, intelligent, and devoted men
will suffice."

The Antwerpians opened their eyes in surprise.

"Ma foi, monseigneur," said William, "you have done
wonders. It would have taken me six months to obtain what
you have done in ten minutes."

"This, then, is my plan, gentlemen," said monseigneur

"The French, with the admiral's galley at their head, will try to force a passage. Make your line long enough, and from all your boats let the men throw grappling-irons; and then, having made fast the enemy's ships, set fire to all your own boats, having previously filled them with combustible materials, and let your men escape in one reserved for the purpose."

"Oh!" cried William, "I see the whole French fleet burning."

"Yes, the whole; then no more retreat by sea and none by land, for at the same time you must open the sluices of Malines, Berchem, Lier, Duffel, and Antwerp. Repulsed by you, pursued by your open dykes, enveloped on all sides by these waters unexpectedly and rapidly rising, by this sea, which will have a flow, but no ebb, the French will be drowned—overwhelmed—destroyed."

The officers uttered a cry of joy.

"There is but one drawback," said the prince.

"What is it, monseigneur?"

"That it would take a day to send our orders to the different towns, and we have but an hour."

"And an hour is enough."

"But who will instruct the fleet?"

"It is done?"

"By whom?"

"By me. If these gentlemen had refused to give it to me, I should have bought it."

"But Malines, Lier, Duffel?"

"I passed through Malines and Lier, and sent a sure agent to Duffel. At eleven o'clock the French will be beaten; at one they will be in full retreat; at two Malines will open its dykes, Lier and Duffel their sluices, and the whole plain will become a furious ocean, which will drown houses, fields, woods and villages, it is true, but at the same time will destroy the French so utterly, that not one will return to France."

A silence of admiration and terror followed these words; then all at once the Flemings burst into applause. William stepped forward, and, holding out his hand, said:

"Then, monseigneur, all is ready on our side?"

"All; and, stay—I believe on the side of the French also." And he pointed to an officer who was entering.

"Gentlemen," cried the officer, "we have just heard that the French are marching towards the city."

"To arms!" cried the burgomaster.

"To arms!" cried all.

"One moment, gentlemen," cried monseigneur; "I have to give one direction more important than all the rest."

"Speak!" cried all.

"The French will be surprised; it will not be a combat, nor even a retreat, but a flight. To pursue them you must be lightly armed. No cuirasses, morbleu! It is your cuirasses, in which you cannot move, which have made you lose all the battles you have lost. No cuirasses, gentlemen. We will meet again in the combat. Meanwhile, go to the place of the Hôtel de Ville, where you will find your men in battle array."

"Thanks, monseigneur," said William; "you have saved Belgium and Holland."

"Prince, you overwhelm me."

"Will your highness consent to draw the sword against the French?" asked the prince.

"I will arrange so as to fight against the Huguenots," replied the unknown, with a smile which his more sombre companion might have envied.

## CHAPTER LXIII

### FRENCH AND FLEMINGS

At the moment when the members of the council left the Hôtel de Ville, the officers went to put themselves at the head of their troops, and execute the orders they had received. At the same time the artillery sounded. This artillery surprised the French in their nocturnal march, by which they had hoped to surprise the town; but instead of stopping their advance, it only hastened it. If they could not take the city by surprise, they might, as we have seen the King of Navarre do at Cahors, fill up the moats with fascines and burst open the gates with petards.

The cannon from the ramparts continued to fire, but in the darkness took scarcely any effect, and after having replied to the cries of their adversaries, the French advanced silently towards the ramparts with that fiery intrepidity which they always show in attack.

But all at once, doors and posterns opened, and from all sides poured out armed men, if not with the fierce impetuosity of the French, with a firmness which rendered them massive as a rolling wall.

It was the Flemings, who advanced in close ranks, and compact masses, above which the cannon continued to thunder, although with more noise than effect. Then the combat began hand to hand, foot to foot, sword to sword, and the flash of pistols lighted up faces red with blood.

But not a cry—not a murmur—not a complaint was heard, and the Flemings and French fought with equal rage. The Flemings were furious at having to fight, for fighting was neither their profession nor their pleasure; and the French were furious at being attacked when they meant to have taken the initiative.

While the combat was raging furiously, explosions were heard near St. Marie, and a light rose over the city, like a crest of flames. It was Joyeuse attacking and trying to force the barrier across the Scheldt, and who would soon penetrate into the city, at least, so the French hoped.

But it was not so; Joyeuse had weighed anchor and sailed, and was making rapid progress, favoured by the west wind.

The seven ships advanced in silence, disposed in the form of a wedge, of which the admiral's galley formed the point. Joyeuse himself had taken his first lieutenant's place, and was leaning over the bowsprit, trying to pierce the fogs of the river and the darkness of the night. Soon, through this double obscurity, he saw the pier extending itself darkly across the stream; it appeared deserted, but, in that land of ambushes, there seemed something terrifying in this desertion.

However, they continued to advance, and soon were within sight of the barrier, scarcely ten cable lengths off; they approached nearer and nearer, and yet not a single " Qui vive!" struck their ears.

The sailors only saw in this silence a carelessness which rejoiced them; but their young admiral, more far-seeing, feared some ruse. At last the prow of the admiral's ship touched the two ships which formed the centre of the barrier, and made the whole line, which was fastened together by chains, tremble.

All at once Joyeuse heard under his feet a crackling sound, and a smell of sulphur filled the air. A thought crossed his mind, and he ran and opened a hatchway; the vessel was burning. A cry of : " To our ships!" sounded through all the line. Each climbed back again more quickly than he had come in; but Joyeuse, this time, was the last. Just as he reached his galley, the flames burst out over the whole bridge of boats, like twenty volcanoes, of which each ship or boat was the crater; the order was instantly given to cut the ropes and break the chains and grappling-irons, and the sailors worked with the rapidity of men who knew that their safety depended on their exertions.

All at once twenty explosions were heard, and each of the French ships trembled to its centre. It was the cannons that defended the port, and which, fully charged and then abandoned by the Antwerpians, exploded as the fire gained on them, breaking everything within their reach.

The flames mounted like gigantic serpents along the masts, rolled themselves round the yards, then, with their forked tongues, came to lick the sides of the French vessels.

Joyeuse had done his best to free himself, but in vain; the flames had reached the French ships, and showers of fire fell about him. The Flemish barrier was broken, and the French burning ships drifted to the shore. Joyeuse saw that he could not save his ships, and he gave orders to lower the boats, and land on the left bank. This was quickly done, and all the sailors were embarked to a man before Joyeuse quitted his galley. His sang-froid kept everyone in order, and each man landed with a sword or an axe in his hand. Before he had reached the shore, the fire reached the magazine of his ship, which blew up, lighting the whole horizon.

The Calvinist cavalry had charged, and done wonders. Before the swords of its cavaliers a pathway opened, but the wounded Flemings pierced the horses with their large cutlasses, and in spite of this brilliant charge, a little confusion showed itself in the French columns, and they only kept their ground instead of advancing, while from the gates of the city new troops continually poured out. All at once, almost under the walls of the city, a cry of " Anjou! France!" was heard behind the mass of the Antwerpians. This was Joyeuse and his 1,500 sailors, armed with hatchets and cutlasses. They had to revenge their fleet in flames and 200 of their companions burned or drowned.

No one could manage his long sword better than Joyeuse: every blow cut open a head, every thrust took effect. The group of Flemings on which he fell were destroyed like a field of corn by a legion of locusts. Delighted with their first success, they continued to push on; but the Calvinist cavalry, surrounded by troops, began to lose ground. M. de St. Aignan's infantry, however, kept their place.

But now the person that had been called monseigneur came out of the city on a beautiful black horse. He wore black armour, and was followed by 300 well-mounted cavaliers, whom the Prince of Orange had placed at his disposal.

By a parallel gate came out William himself, with a picked body of infantry who had not yet appeared.

Monseigneur hastened where he was most wanted, that is to say, where Joyeuse was fighting with his sailors.

The Flemings recognised him, and opened their ranks, crying, joyfully: " Monseigneur! monseigneur!" Joyeuse and his men saw the movement, heard the cries, and all at once found themselves opposed to a new troop. Joyeuse pushed his horse towards the black knight, and their swords met.

"Ah!" cried the young admiral, "this man is a Frenchman, and, what is more, he has studied fencing under the same master as I have."

At these words the unknown turned away, and tried to find a new antagonist.

"If you are French," cried Joyeuse, "you are a traitor, for you fight against your king, your country, and your flag."

The unknown only replied by attacking Joyeuse with fresh fury; but now Joyeuse was on his guard, and knew with what a skilful swordsman he had to deal. He parried two or three thrusts with as much skill as fury, and it was now the stranger who made a step back.

But at this moment a cavalier cried:

"Monseigneur, no more skirmishing; your presence is wanted over there."

Glancing towards the point indicated, the unknown saw the Flemings giving way before the Calvinist cavalry.

"Yes," cried he, "those are the men I wanted."

At this moment so many cavaliers pressed on the sailors, that they made their first step in retreat.

The black cavalier profited by this movement to disappear in the mêlée.

A quarter of an hour after the French began to give way, M. de St. Aignan tried to retreat in good order, but a last troop of 2,000 infantry and 500 horse came out fresh from the city, and fell on this harassed and already retreating army. It was the old band of the Prince of Orange, which had fought in turn against the Duc d'Alva, Don John, Requesens, and Alexander Farnèse. In spite of the coolness of the chiefs and the bravery of many, a frightful rout commenced.

At this moment the unknown fell again on the fugitives, and once more met Joyeuse with his now diminished band. The young admiral was mounted on his third horse, two having been killed under him; his sword was broken, and he had taken from a sailor one of their heavy hatchets, which he whirled round his head with the greatest apparent ease. From time to time he turned and faced his enemy, like the wild boar who cannot make up his mind to fly, and turns desperately on his hunter. The Flemings, who by monseigneur's advice had fought without cuirasses, were active in the pursuit, and gave no rest to the Angevin army. Something like remorse seized the unknown at the sight of this disaster.

" Enough, gentlemen," cried he, in French, " to-night they are driven from Antwerp, and in a week' will be driven from Flanders; ask no more of the God of battles."

" Ah! he is French," cried Joyeuse ;" I guessed it, traitor. Ah! be cursed, and may you die the death of a traitor."

This furious imprecation seemed to disconcert the unknown more than a thousand swords raised against him; he turned, and conqueror as he was, fled as rapidly as the conquered. But this retreat of a single man changed nothing in the state of affairs. Fear is contagious, it seized the entire army, and the soldiers began to fly like madmen. The horses went fast, in spite of fatigue, for they also felt the influence of fear; the men dispersed to seek a shelter, and in some hours the army, as an army, existed no longer. This was the time when the dykes were to be opened. From Lier to Termonde, from Haesdouk to Malines—each little river, swollen by its tributaries—each canal overflowed, and spread over the flat country its contingent of furious water.

The Duc d'Anjou, at the head of the fugitives, mounted on an excellent horse, and accompanied by a single servant, pushed forward without appearing to think of anything.

The fugitives hoped to, gain Brussels, where the duke had many partisans, although they were not free from anxiety as to their reception. At Brussels, which was about eight leagues off, they would find food for the famishing troops, and a place of security from whence to recommence the campaign at a more favourable time. M. d'Anjou breakfasted in a peasant's hut, between Hèboken and Heckhout. It was empty, but a fire still burned in the grate.

The soldiers and officers wished to imitate their chief, and spread themselves about the village, but found with a surprise mingled with terror that every house was deserted and empty.

M. de St. Aignan, who had aided them in their search, now called to the officers:

" March on, gentlemen."

" But we are tired and dying with hunger, colonel."

" Yes, but you are alive; and if you remain here another hour you will be dead. Perhaps it is already too late."

M. de St. Aignan knew nothing; but he suspected some great danger. They went on; but two or three thousand men straggled from the main body, or, worn out with fatigue, lay down on the grass, or at the foot of a tree, wearied, desolate, and despairing. Scarcely three thousand able men remained to the Duc d'Anjou.

## CHAPTER LXIV

### THE TRAVELLERS

While these disasters, the forerunners of a still greater one, were taking place, two travellers, mounted on excellent horses, left Brussels on a fine night, and rode towards Mechlin. They rode side by side, without any apparent arms but a large Flemish knife, of which the handle appeared in the belt of one of them. They were about half a league from Brussels, when the tallest of them said:

"Madame, you were quite right to set off to-night; we shall gain seven leagues by it, and shall probably arrive at Mechlin by the time the result of the attack on Antwerp is known. In two days of short marches, and you must take easy stages, we shall reach Antwerp."

The person who was called madame, in spite of her male costume, replied in a voice calm, grave and sweet:

"My friend, believe me, God will tire of protecting this wicked prince, and will strike him cruelly; let us hasten to put our projects into execution, for I am not one of those who believe in fatality, and I think that men have perfect freedom in will and deed. If we leave his punishment to God, and do not act ourselves, it was not worth while living so unhappily until now."

At this moment a blast of north wind, cold and biting, swept across the plain.

"You shiver, madame," said the other traveller; "take your cloak."

"No, thank you, Remy; I no longer feel pain of body or mind."

Remy rode on silently, only now and then stopping and looking back.

"You see no one behind us?" asked she, after one of these halts.

"No one, madame."

"That cavalier whom we met at Valenciennes, and who inquired about us, after looking at us so curiously?"

"He is not here, madame."

"But I fancied I saw him again near Mons."

"And I, madame, am sure I saw him just before we entered Brussels."

"Brussels?"

"Yes; but he must have stopped there."

Just as they were about to enter Vilvoide, Remy turned his

head, for he heard the sound of horses's feet behind them. He stopped and listened, but could see nothing. His eyes uselessly tried to pierce through the darkness of the night.

"I thought I heard a horse's feet. I am not sure, but I will stay behind a minute to find out."

The lady, without replying, went on, and Remy got off his horse and let him follow her, while he hid himself behind an immense post and waited. The lady knocked at the door of the inn, behind which, according to the hospitable custom of the country, watched, or rather slept, a maid-servant. The girl woke up and received the traveller with perfect good-humour, and then opened the stable-door for the two horses.

"I am waiting for my companion," said Diana; "let me sit by the fire; I shall not go to bed until he comes."

The servant threw some straw to the horses, shut the stable-door, then returned to the kitchen, put a chair by the fire, snuffed the candle with her fingers, and went to sleep again.

Meanwhile Remy was watching for the arrival of the traveller whose horse he had heard. He saw him enter the town and go on slowly, and seeming to listen; then, seeing the inn, he appeared to hesitate whether to go there or to continue his journey. He stopped close to Remy, who laid his hand on his knife.

"It is he again," thought Remy, "and he is following us. What can he want?"

After a minute the traveller murmured in a low voice: "They must have gone on, and so will I," and he rode forward.

"To-morrow we will change our route," thought Remy.

And he rejoined Diana, who was waiting impatiently for him.

"Well," said she softly, "are we followed?"

"There is no one, I was wrong; you may sleep in perfect safety, madame."

"I am not sleepy, Remy."

"At least have supper, madame; you have scarcely eaten anything."

"Willingly, Remy."

They awakened the poor servant, who got up as good-humouredly as before, and hearing what they wanted, took from the cupboard a piece of salt pork, a cold leveret, and some sweets, which she set before them, together with a frothing jug of Louvain beer.

"Tell me, my girl," said Remy, "is there any cross-road from here to Mechlin?"

"Yes, monsieur, but it is very bad, while the regular road is a very fine one."

"Yes, my child, I know that, but we wish to travel by the other."

"Oh! I told you, monsieur, because, as your companion is a lady, the road would not do for her."

"Why not?"

"Because to-night a great number of people will cross the country to go to Brussels."

"To Brussels?"

"Yes; it is a temporary emigration."

"For what reason?"

"I do not know; they had orders."

"From whom—the Prince or Orange?"

"No; from monseigneur."

"Who is he?"

"I do not know, monsieur."

"And who are the emigrants?"

"The inhabitants of the country and of the villages which have no dykes or ramparts."

"Danger every way," thought Remy; "however, the young man is before us." And as the horses had not been unsaddled, they mounted again, and the rising sun found them on the banks of the Dyle.


## CHAPTER LXV

### EXPLANATION

The danger that Remy braved was a real one, for the traveller, after having passed the village and gone on for a quarter of a league, and seeing no one before him, made up his mind that those whom he sought had remained behind in the village. He would not retrace his steps, but lay down in a field of clover; having made his horse descend into one of those deep ditches which in Flanders serve as divisions between the properties, he was therefore able to see without being seen. This young man, as Remy knew, and Diana suspected, was Henri du Bouchage, whom a strange fatality threw once more into the presence of the woman he had determined to fly.

Letters from Flanders announced the intended coup de main on Antwerp, and Henri hoped to arrive in time for it. He pleased himself with the idea that he should die sword in hand, in his brother's arms, under a French flag, and that his death would be talked about until the sound even reached the solitude in which the mysterious lady lived. Noble follies! glorious, yet sad dreams!

Just as—full of these thoughts—he came in sight of Valenciennes, from whose church tower eight o'clock was sounding, he perceived that they were about to close the gates. He pushed on, and nearly overturned, on the drawbridge, a man who was fastening the girths of his horse. Henri stopped to make excuses to the man, who turned at the sound of his voice, and then quickly turned away again. Henri started, but immediately thought: "I must be mad; Remy here, whom I left four days ago in the Rue de Bussy; here now, without his mistress. Really, grief must be turning my brain and making me see everything in the form of my own fancies." At the first hotel that he came to he stopped, gave his horse to a servant, and sat down on a bench before the door, while they prepared his bed and supper. But as he sat there he saw two travellers approaching, and this time he saw more clearly.

"Now," murmured he, "I do not dream, and still I think I see Remy. I cannot remain in this uncertainty; I must clear up my doubts."

He got up and ran down the road after them, but they had disappeared. Then he went to all the hotels and questioned the servants, and after much search discovered that two cavaliers had been seen going towards a small inn in the Rue de Beffroi. The landlord was just shutting the doors when Henri entered. Whilst the man offered him rooms and refreshment, he looked round, and saw on the top of the staircase Remy going up, lighted by a servant; of his companion he saw nothing. Du Bouchage had no longer any doubts and he asked himself, with a dreadful sinking of the heart why Remy had left his mistress and was travelling without her; for Henri had been so occupied in identifying Remy that he had scarcely looked at his companion. The next morning when he rose, he was much surprised to learn that the two travellers had obtained from the governor permission to go out; and that, contrary to all custom, the gates had been opened for them. Thus, as they had set out at one o'clock, they had six hours' start of him. Henri put his horse to gallop and passed the travellers at Mons. He saw Remy; but Remy must have been a sorcerer to know him for he had on a soldier's great coat and rode another horse Nevertheless, Remy's companion, at a word from him, turned away his head before Henri could see his face. But the young man did not lose courage; he watched them to their hotel and then questioning, with the aid of an irresistible auxiliary learned that Remy's companion was a very handsome, but very silent and sad-looking young man.

Henri trembled. "Can it be a woman?" asked he.

"It is possible," replied the host; "many women travel thus disguised just now, to go and rejoin their lovers in Flanders; but it is our business to see nothing, and we never do."

Henri felt heart-broken at this explanation. Was Remy, indeed, accompanying his mistress dressed as a cavalier; and was she, as the host suggested, going to rejoin her lover in Flanders?

At Brussels he gathered information as to the Duc d'Anjou's intended campaign. The Flemings were too hostile to the duke to receive well a Frenchman of distinction, and were too proud of their position to refrain from humiliating a little this gentleman who came from France and questioned them in a pure Parisian accent, which always seemed ridiculous to the Belgians. Henri began to conceive serious fears with reference to this expedition, in which his brother was to bear so prominent a part, and he resolved in consequence to push on rapidly to Antwerp. It was a constant surprise to him to see Remy and his companion, in spite of their desire not to be seen, continue to follow the same road as himself.

Henri, now hidden in the clover field, felt certain of seeing the face of the young man who accompanied Remy, and thus putting an end to all his doubts. As they passed, unsuspicious of his vicinity, Diana was occupied in braiding up her hair, which she had not dared to untie at the inn.

Henri recognised her, and nearly fainted. The travellers passed on, and then anger took, in Henri's mind, the place of the goodness and patience he had exercised while he believed Remy and the lady sincere towards him. But after the protestations of Remy, this journey seemed to him a species of treason.

When he had recovered a little from the blow, he rose, shook back his beautiful light hair, and mounted his horse, determined no longer to take those precautions that respect had made him hitherto observe, and he began to follow the travellers openly, and with his face uncovered. Remy soon perceived him, and, seeing him thus openly advance without any further attempt at concealment, grew troubled; Diana noticed it and turned also.

"Is it not that young man following us?"

Remy, still trying to reassure her, said: "I do not think so, madame. As well as I can judge by the dress, it is some young Walloon soldier, going probably to Amsterdam, and passing by the theatre of war to see adventures."

They turned to the left, taking a road hardly made, but which visibly led to Villebrock; Henri also quitted the road, and turned down the lane, still keeping his distance from them.

Remy's disquietude showed itself in his constantly turning to look behind him. At last they arrived at Villebrock. Of 200 houses which this village contained, not one was inhabited; some forgotten dogs and lost cats ran wildly about the solitude, the former calling for their masters by long howls. Remy knocked at twenty door, but found no one.

They rode on, therefore, without another word, and Henri du Bouchage followed.

## CHAPTER LXVI

### THE WATER

As the travellers advanced, the country took an equally strange aspect, for it was utterly deserted, as well as the towns and villages. The only people who animated this dreary solitude were Remy and his companion, and Henri following behind and preserving ever the same distance. The night came on dark and cold, and the north-east wind whistled in the air, and filled the solitude with its menacing sound.

The lady turned.

" Is he still there?" she said.

" Oh! I was not thinking of him; think no more of him, madame, I beg of you; we need not fear a single man. No, the danger that I fear or rather feel, or divine with a sort of instinct, is unknown to me, and therefore I dread it. Look, madame, do you see those willows bending in the wind?"

" Yes."

" By their side I see a little house; I beg you, let us go there. If it is inhabited, we will ask for hospitality; and if not, we will take possession of it. I beg you to consent, madame."

Remy's emotion and troubled voice decided Diana to yield, so she turned her horse in the direction indicated by him. Some minutes after, they knocked at the door. A stream (which ran into the Nethe, a little river about a mile off), bordered with reeds and grassy banks, bathed the feet of the willows with its murmuring waters. Behind the house, which was built of bricks, and covered with tiles, was a little garden, encircled by a quickset hedge.

All was empty, solitary, and deserted, and no one replied to

e blows struck by the travellers.  Remy did not hesitate; he
rew his knife, cut a branch of willow, with which he pushed
ack the bolt and opened the door.  The lock, the clumsy
ork of a neighbouring blacksmith, yielded almost without
esistance.  Remy entered quickly, followed by Diana, then,
osing the door again, he drew a massive bolt, and thus
trenched seemed to breathe more freely.  Feeling about, he
ound a bed, a chair, and a table in an upper room.  Here he
stalled his mistress, and then, returning to the lower room,
aced himself at the window, to watch the movements of Du
ouchage.

His reflections were as sombre as those of Remy.  "Cer-
inly," said he to himself, " some danger unknown to us, but
f which the inhabitants are not ignorant, is about to fall on
e country.  War ravages the land; perhaps the French have
ken, or are about to assault Antwerp, and the peasants,
ized with terror, have gone to take refuge in the towns."

But this reasoning, however plausible, did not quite satisfy
m.  Then he thought: " But what are Remy and his mistress
oing here?  What imperious necessity drags them towards
is danger?  Oh, I will know; the time has come to speak to
is woman, and to clear away all my doubts.  Never shall I
id a better opportunity."

He approached the house, and then suddenly stopped, with
hesitation common to hearts in love.

"I will stay here, and take these trees for a shelter, and then
can hear her voice when she speaks, and see her shadow on
e window."

He lay down, then, under the willows, listening, with a
elancholy impossible to describe, to the murmur of the
ater that flowed at his side.  All at once he started; the
ise of cannon was brought distinctly to him by the wind.
"Ah!" said he, " I shall arrive too late; they are attacking
ntwerp."

His first idea was to rise, mount his horse, and ride on as
uickly as possible; but to do this he must quit the lady, and
e in doubt, so he remained.

During two hours he lay there, listening to the reports.  He
d not guess that what he heard was his brother's ships
owing up.  At last, about two o'clock, all grew quiet.

He lay still, and had just fallen asleep, when his horse,
hich was grazing quietly near him, pricked up his ears and
ighed loudly.

The horse neighed and began to run forwards to the west,
t his master caught the bridle and jumped on his back, and
en was able to keep him quiet.  But after a minute, Henri

himself began to hear what the horse had heard. A long murmur, like the wind, but more solemn, which seemed to come from different points of the compass, from south to north.

"What is it?" said Henri; "can it be the wind? No, it is the wind which brings this sound, and I hear the two distinctly. An army in march, perhaps? But no; I should hear the sound of voices and of regular marching. Is it the crackling of a fire? No, there is no light in the horizon; the heaven seems even to grow darker."

"What do I see?" cried he. What he saw his horse had seen before him; for he had only been able to make him advance by furious spurring, and when they arrived at the top of the hill he reared so as nearly to fall backwards. They saw in the horizon an infinite body rolling over the plain, and visibly and rapidly approaching. The young man looked in wonder at this strange phenomenon, when, looking back to the place he had come from, he saw that plain beginning to be covered with water, and that the little river had overflowed and was beginning to cover the reeds which a quarter of an hour before had stood up stifly on its banks.

"Fool that I am," cried he, "I never thought of it. The water! the water! The Flemings have broken their dykes!"

Henri flew to the house, and knocked furiously at the door.

"Open! open!" cried he.

No one replied.

"Open, Remy!" cried he, furious with terror; "it is Henri du Bouchage."

"Oh! you need not name yourself, M. le Comte," answered Remy from within, "I recognised you long ago; but I warn you, that if you break in the door you will find me behind it with a pistol in each hand."

"But you do not understand," cried Henri; "the water; is the water!"

"The water!" cried Remy.

"Yes, the water; it invades us; see, at your feet, the river overflows, and in five minutes we shall be surrounded."

"Madame! madame!" cried Remy.

"Do not frighten her, Remy; get ready the horses at once."

Remy ran to the stable, and Henri flew up the staircase. At Remy's cry Diana had opened her door; Henri seized her in his arms and carried her away as he would have done a child. But she, believing in treason or violence, struggled, and clung to the staircase with all her might.

"Tell her that I am saving her, Remy!" cried Henri.

Remy heard the appeal, and cried:     •

" Yes, yes, madame, he is saving you, or rather he will save
ou.   Come, for Heaven's sake!"


## CHAPTER LXVII

### FLIGHT

Henri, without losing time in reasoning with Diana, carried
er out of the house, and wished to place her before him on
is horse; but she, with a movement of invincible repugnance,
lided from his arms, and was received by Remy, who placed
er on her own horse.

Her horse, however, as well as that of Remy, was fatigued
ith their long journey, and Henri, as he turned back each
noment, saw that they could not keep up with him.

" See, madame!" said he, " how my horse outstrips yours,
nd yet I am holding him in with all my strength; for heaven's
ake, madame, while there is yet time, if you will not ride with
ne, take my horse and leave me yours."

" No, thank you, monsieur," replied she, in her usual calm
oice.

" But, madame," cried Henri, in despair, " the water gains
n us; do you hear! do you hear?"

Indeed, a horrible crashing was now heard; it was the dyke
f a neighbouring village giving way, to swell the inundation.
oards and props had given way, a double row of stakes
roke with a noise like thunder, and the water, rushing over
ne ruins, began to invade an oak wood, of which they saw
ne tops trembling, and heard the branches cracking as
ough a flight of demons were passing under the leaves.

The uprooted trees knocking against the stakes, the wood of
uined houses floating on the waters, the distant neighings and
ries of horses and men carried away by the inundation,
ormed a concert of sounds so strange and gloomy, that the
rror which agitated Henri began to seize also Diana.  She
ourred her horse, and he, as if he understood the danger,
doubled his efforts.  But the water gained on them, and
efore ten minutes it was evident that it would reach them.
very instant Henri turned and cried: " Quicker, madame!
or pity's sake; the water comes; here it is!"

Remy's horse, exhausted, fell, and could not rise again,
espite the efforts of his rider

" Save her in spite of herself," cried Remy.

And at the same moment, as he disengaged himself from

the stirrups, the water passed over the head of the faithfu
servant. His mistress, at this sight, uttered a terrible cry, an
tried to jump off her horse to perish with him. But Henri
seeing her intention, seized her round the waist, and placin
her before him, set off like an arrow.

" Remy! Remy!" cried the lady, " I wish to die with you
I will, monsieur, I will go to him; in the name of God,
will."

She pronounced these words with so much energy an
angry authority, that the young man unfolded his arms, an
let her slip to the ground, saying:

" Well, madame, we will all three die here together; it is
joy I had not hoped for."

As he said these words he stopped his horse, and the wate
reached them almost immediately; but, by a last effort of lov
the young man kept hold of Diana's arm as she stood on th
ground. The flood rolled over them. It was a sublim
spectacle to see the sangfroid of the young man, whose entir
bust was raised above the water, while he sustained Dian
with one arm, and with the other guided the last efforts of h
expiring horse.

There was a moment of terrible struggle, during which th
lady, upheld by Henri, kept her head above water, while wit
his left hand he kept off the floating wood and the corpse
which would have struck against them.

One of the bodies floating past sighed out: " Adie
madame!"

" Heavens!" cried Henri, " it is Remy!" And without ca
culating the danger of the additional weight, he seized him b
his sleeve, drew him up, and enabled him to breathe free
But the exhausted horse now sank in the water to its nec
then to its eyes, and finally disappeared altogether.

" We must die," murmured Henri. " Madame, my life an
soul belonged to you."

As he spoke, he felt Remy slip from him, and he no long
tried to retain him—it was useless. His only care was
sustain Diana above the water, that she, at least, might die th
last, and that he might be able to say to himself, in his la
moments, that he had done his utmost to save her. All a
once, a joyful cry sounded at his side; he turned, and sa
Remy, who had found a boat, which had belonged to th
little house where they had taken shelter, and which the wat
had carried away. Remy, who had regained his strengt
thanks to Henri's assistance, had seized it as it floated pa
The oars were tied to it, and an iron hook lay in the botto
He held out the hook to Henri, who seized it, and drawin

Diana with him, raised her over his shoulders, and passed her to Remy, and then climbed in himself. The first rays of the rising sun showed them the plains inundated, and the boat swimming like an atom on that ocean covered with wrecks. Towards the left rose a little hill, completely surrounded by water, looking like an island in the midst of the sea. Henri took the oars and rowed towards it.

Remy had a wound in his shoulder, where a floating beam had struck against him; but Diana, thanks to Henri's protection, was free from all injury, although she was cold and wet. At last they noticed in the horizon, on the eastern side, something like fires burning on a height which the water could not reach.

"Well, M. le Comte," said Remy, "what do you think of those fires?"

"Those fires, which seem to you to announce a hospitable shelter, appear to me to be full of danger."

"And why so?"

"Remy," said Henri, lowering his voice, "look at these corpses; they are all French—there is not one Fleming; they announce to us a great disaster. The dykes have been broken to finish the destruction of the French army, if it has been conquered—to nullify the victory, if they have been victors. Those fires are as likely to have been lighted by enemies as by friends, and may be simply a ruse to draw fugitives to destruction."

"Nevertheless, we cannot stay here; my mistress will die of cold and hunger."

"You are right, Remy; remain here with madame, and I will go to the jetty, and return to you with news."

"No, monsieur," said Diana, "you shall not expose yourself alone; we have been saved together; we will live or die together. Remy, your arm. I am ready."

Each word which she pronounced had so irresistible an accent of authority that no one thought of disputing it. Henri bowed, and walked first.

It was more calm; the jetty formed, with the hill, a kind of bay, where the water slept. All three got into the little boat, which was once more launched among the wrecks and floating bodies. A quarter of an hour after, they touched the jetty. They tied the chain of the boat to a tree, landed once more. walked along the jetty for nearly an hour, and then arrived at a number of Flemish huts, among which, in a place planted with lime trees, were two or three hundred soldiers sitting round a fire, above whom floated the French flag. Suddenly a sentinel, placed about one hundred feet from the bivouac, cried: " Qui vive?"

" France," replied Du Bouchage. Then, turning to Diana, he said: " Now, madame, you are saved. I recognise the standard of the gendarmes of Aunis, a corps in which I have many friends."

The gendarmes of Aunis, of whom our fugitives were claiming hospitality, had retired in good order after the defeat and the sauve qui peut of the chiefs. Wherever there is similarity of position and sentiment, and the habit of living together, it is common to find unanimity in execution as well as in thought. It had been so that night with the gendarmes of Aunis; for seeing their chiefs abandon them, they agreed together to draw their ranks closer, instead of breaking them. They therefore put their horses to the gallop, and, under the conduct of one of the ensigns, whom they loved for his bravery and respected for his birth, they took the road to Brussels.

Like all the actors in this terrible scene, they saw the progress of the inundation, and were pursued by the furious waters; but by good luck found in this spot a position strong both against men and water.

Such was the recital which Henri received from them.

" And the rest of the army?" asked he.

" Look," replied the ensign; " the corpses which pass each moment answer your question."

" But—my brother," said Henri, in a choking voice.

" Alas! M. le Comte, we do not know. He fought like a lion, but he survived the battle; as to the inundation I cannot say."

Henri shook his head sadly; then, after a minute's pause, said: " And the duke?"

" Comte, the duke fled one of the first. He was mounted on a white horse, with no spot but a black star on the forehead. Well, just now we saw the horse pass among a mass of wrecks, the foot of a rider was caught in the stirrup and was floating on the water."

" Great God!"

" Good heavens!" echoed Remy, who had drawn near and heard the tale.

" Dead! he also? the heir to the crown! What a misfortune!"

Remy turned to his mistress, and with an expression impossible to describe, said:

" He is dead  madame, you see."

"I praise the Lord, who has spared us a crime," said she, raising her eyes to Heaven.

"Yes, but it prevents our vengeance."

"Vengeance only belongs to a man when God forgets."

"But you, yourself, comte," said the ensign to Henri, "what are you about to do?"

The comte started. "I?" said he.

"Yes."

"I will wait here till my brother's body passes," replied he, gloomily, "then I will try to draw him to land. You may be sure that if once I hold him, I shall not let go."

Remy looked pityingly at the young man; but Diana heard nothing—she was praying.


## CHAPTER LXVIII

### TRANSFIGURATION

After her prayer Diana rose so beautiful and radiant that the comte uttered a cry of surprise and admiration.

"Madame, you live! Oh! let me tell you all the joy which overflows my heart when I see you here in safety, after having seen you on the threshold of the tomb."

"M. le Comte," replied Diana, with majestic solemnity, "do not say to me things fit only to be said to a woman; I belong to another world, and do not live for this."

"What do you mean, madame? do you also wish to die?"

Remy, awakened by the cry of the young comte, began to listen.

"You saw me pray, did you not?" said Diana.

"Yes," answered Henri.

"This prayer was my adieu to earth; the joy that you remarked on my face—the joy that fills me even now, is the same you would see in me if the angel of death were to come and say to me: 'Rise, Diana, and follow me.'"

"Diana! Diana! now I know your name; Diana, cherished name!" murmured the young man.

"Oh, silence!" cried she, "forget this name which escaped me; no living person has the right to pierce my heart by pronouncing it."

"Oh! madame, do not tell me you are going to die."

"I do not say that," replied she, in her grave voice; "I say that I am about to quit this world of tears—of hatreds—of bad passions—of vile interests and desires. I say that I have nothing left to do among the creatures whom God created my fellow mortals; I have no more tears, no more blood in my heart; no more thoughts—they are dead. I am a worthless offering, for in renouncing the world I sacrifice nothing, neither desires nor hopes; but such as I am I offer myself to my God, and he will accept me—he who has made me suffer so much, and yet kept me from sinking under it."

Henri knelt. "Thanks, madame," said he, "I bow to my destiny. You belong to God; I cannot be jealous."

As he rose, they heard the sound of trumpets on the plain, from which the water was rapidly disappearing. The gendarmes seized their arms and were on horseback at once.

Henri listened. "Gentlemen," cried he, "those are the admiral's trumpets; I know them. Oh, God! may they announce my brother!"

"You see that you still wish something, and still love something; why, then, should you choose despair, like those who desire nothing—like those who love no one?"

"A horse!" cried Henri; "who will lend me a horse?"

"But the water is still all around us," said the ensign.

"But you see that the plain is practicable; they must be advancing, since we hear their trumpets."

"Mount to the top of the bank, M. le Comte. The sky is clear, perhaps you will see."

Henri climbed up; the trumpets continued to sound at intervals, but were seemingly stationary. A quarter of an hour after, Henri returned; he had seen a considerable detachment of French troops entrenched on a hill at some distance. Excepting a large ditch, which surrounded the place occupied by the gendarmes of Aunis, the water had begun to disappear from the plain, the natural slope of the ground in the immediate neighbourhood making the waters run towards the sea, and several points of earth, higher than the rest, began to reappear. The slimy mud brought by the rolling waters had covered the whole country, and it was a sad spectacle to see, as the wind cleared the mist, a number of cavaliers stuck in the mud, and trying vainly to reach either of the hills. From the other hill, on which the flag of France waved, their cries of distress had been heard, and that was why the trumpets had sounded.

"France!" cried one who came from the opposite hill, at the same time raising his hat, which had a white plume in it.

"Oh! it is you!" cried Henri, with a burst of joy.

"You, Henri! you, my brother!" cried the other.

And they set off as quickly as their horses could manage to go, and soon, among the frantic acclamations of the spectators on each side, embraced long and tenderly. Soon,

ll—gendarmes and light horse—Huguenots and Catholics—
ushed along the road, pioneered by the two brothers. Soon
he two camps were joined, and there, where they had thought
o find death, nearly 3,000 Frenchmen cried: "Thank God!"
and "Vive la France!"

"Gentlemen," said a Huguenot officer, "it is 'Long live the
admiral,' you should cry, for it is to M. de Joyeuse alone
hat we now owe the happiness of embracing our countrymen."

Immense acclamations followed this speech. The two
rothers talked for some time, and then Joyeuse asked Henri
f he had heard news of the duke.

"It appears he is dead," replied Henri.

"Is that certain?"

"The gendarmes saw his horse drowned, and a rider, whose
ead was under water, dragged by the stirrup."

"It has been a sad day for France," said Joyeuse. Then
urning to his men he said: "Come, gentlemen, let us not lose
me. Once the waters have retired we shall probably be
ttacked. Let us intrench ourselves until the arrival of news
nd food."

Henri went back.

"We are now in the midst of an army," said he to Remy;
hide yourselves in the lodging I will show you, and do not
t madame be seen by anyone."

Remy installed himself with Diana in the lodging pointed
ut. About two o'clock the Duc de Joyeuse entered, with his
umpets blowing, lodged his troops, and gave strict injunc-
ons to prevent disorder. He distributed barley to the men,
nd hay to the horses, and to the wounded some wine and
eer, which had been found in the cellars, and himself, in
ght of all, dined on a piece of black bread and a glass of
ater. Everywhere he was received as a deliverer with cries
f gratitude.

"Now," said he to his brother, when they were alone, "let
e Flemings come, and I will beat them, and even, if this goes
n, eat them, for in truth I am very hungry, and this is
iserable stuff," added he, throwing into a corner the piece of
read, which in public he had eaten so enthusiastically.

"I cannot leave here until I have certain news of the army
-for the position is good, and I could defend myself against
ve times our number; but I may send out a body of scouts,
nd they will bring news and provisions also, for Flanders is a
ne country."

"Not very, brother."

"I speak of it as God made it, and not men, who eternally

spoil the works of God. Do you know, Henri, what folly this prince committed—what this unlucky François has lost through pride and precipitation? His soul is gone to God, so let us be silent; but in truth he might have acquired immortal glory and one of the most beautiful kingdoms in Europe, while he has, on the contrary, aided no one but William of Orange. But do you know, Henri, that the Antwerpians fought well?"

"And you also; so they say, brother."

"Yes, it was one of my good days; and besides there was something that excited me."

"What was it?"

"I met on the field of battle a sword that I knew."

"French?"

"Yes, French."

"In the ranks of the Flemings?"

"At their head, Henri; this is a secret which forms a sequel to Salcède's business."

"However, dear brother, here you are, safe and sound, to my great joy; I, who have done nothing yet, must do something, also."

"And what will you do?"

"Give me the command of your scouts, I beg."

"No, it is too dangerous, Henri; I would not say so before strangers, but I do not wish you to die an obscure death. The scouts may meet with some of those horrid Flemings who fight with flails and scythes; you kill one thousand of them, and the last cuts you in two or disfigures you. No, Henri; if you will die, let it be a more glorious death than that."

"My brother, grant me what I ask, I beg; I promise you to be prudent, and to return here."

"Well, I understand."

"What?"

"You wish to try if the fame of a brave action will not soften the heart of this ferocious tigress. Confess that that is what makes you insist on it."

"I will confess it, if you wish, brother."

"Very well; now, what men would you like to take?"

"Let me take one hundred of the gendarmes of Aunis; I have plenty of friends there, and can choose whom I like."

"That will do."

"When shall I set out?"

"At once. Take one day's rations for the men and two for the horses. Remember, I want speedy and certain news."

"I go, brother; are there any other orders?"

"Do not spread the news of the duke's death; let it be

believed he is here. Exaggerate my strength, and if you find the duke's body, although he was a bad man and a poor general, yet, as he belonged to the royal house of France, have it put in an oak coffin and brought back by your men, that he may be buried at St. Denis."

And the young men, once more embracing each other, separated with smiles.

## CHAPTER LXIX

### THE EXPEDITION

Henri, full of joy, hastened to Diana and Remy.

"Get ready; in a quarter of an hour we set out," said he. "You will find two horses saddled at the door of the little wooden staircase leading to this corridor; join my suite and say nothing."

Then, going out on the balcony, he cried:

"Trumpet of the gendarmes, sound the call."

The call was quickly heard, and all the gendarmes ranged themselves round the house.

"Gendarmes," said Henri, "my brother has given me, for the time, the command of your company, and has ordered me to set out to-night to obtain provisions and information as to the movements of the enemy, and one hundred of you are to accompany me; the mission is dangerous, but necessary for the safety of all. Who are willing to go?"

The whole three hundred offered themselves.

"Gentlemen," said Henri, "I thank you all; you have rightly been called the example to the army, but I can but take one hundred; and as I do not wish to choose, let chance decide. Monsieur," continued he, to the ensign, "draw lots, if you please."

While this was being done, Joyeuse gave his last instructions to his brother. "Listen, Henri," said he; "the country is drying, and there is a communication between Courteig and Rupelmonde; you will march between a river and a stream—the Scheldt and the Rupel. I trust that there will be no necessity for you to go as far as Rupelmonde to find provisions. My men took three peasants prisoners; I give one of them to you for a guide—but no false pity! at the least appearance of treason shoot him without mercy."

They traversed two leagues in three hours, which brought the adventurous band to the banks of the Rupel, along which a stony road ran; but here danger succeeded to difficulty, and two or three horses lost their footing on the slimy stones, and rolled with their riders into the still rapid waters of the river. More than once also, from some boat on the opposite bank, shots were fired, and one man was killed at Diana's side. She manifested regret for the man, but no fear for herself. Henri, in these different circumstances, showed himself to be a worthy captain and true friend; he rode first, telling all the men to follow in his steps, trusting less to his own sagacity than to that of the horse his brother had given him.

At last they arrived on the banks of the Scheldt; the night was dark, and the gendarmes found two men who were trying, in bad Flemish, to obtain from a boatman a passage to the other side, which he refused. The ensign, who understood Dutch, advanced softly, and heard the boatman say: "You are French, and shall die here; you shall not cross."

"It is you who shall die, if you do not take us over at once," replied one of the men, drawing his dagger.

"Keep firm, monsieur," cried the ensign, "we will come to your aid."

But as the two men turned at these words, the boatman loosened the rope, and pushed rapidly from the shore. One of the gendarmes, however, knowing how useful this boat would be, went into the stream on his horse and fired at the boatman, who fell. The boat was left without a guide, but the current brought it back again towards the bank. The two strangers seized it at once and got in. This astonished the ensign.

"Gentlemen," said he, "who are you, if you please?"

"Gentlemen, we are marine officers, and you are gendarmes of Aunis, apparently."

"Yes, gentlemen, and very happy to have served you; will you not accompany us?"

"Willingly."

"Get into the waggons, then, if you are too tired to ride."

"May we ask where are you going?" said one.

"Monsieur, our orders are to push on to Rupelmonde."

"Take care," answered he. "We did not pass the stream sooner, because this morning a detachment of Spaniards passed, coming from Antwerp. At sunset we thought we might venture, for two men inspire no disquietude; but you a whole troop——"

"It is true; I will call our chief."

Henri approached, and asked what was the matter.

"These gentlemen met this morning a detachment of Spaniards following the same road as ourselves."

" How many were they?"

" About fifty."

" And does that stop you?"

" No, but I think it would be well to secure the boat, in case we should wish to pass the stream; it will hold twenty men."

" Good! let us keep the boat. There should be some houses at the junction of the Scheldt and Rupel?"

" There is a village," said a voice.

An hour after they arrived at the village, which was occupied by the fifty Spaniards, but they, taken by surprise when they least expected it, made little resistance. Henri had them disarmed, shut up in the strongest house in the village, and left ten men to guard them. Ten more were sent to guard the boat, and ten others placed as sentinels, with the promise of being relieved in an hour. Twenty of the others then sat down in the house opposite to that in which the prisoners were, to the supper which had been prepared for them. Henri chose a separate room for Remy and Diana; he then placed the ensign at table with the others, telling them to invite the two naval officers when they arrived. He next went out to look for accommodation for the rest of the men, and when he returned in half-an-hour he found them waiting supper for him. Some had fallen asleep on their chairs, but his entrance roused them. The table, covered with cheese, pork, and bread, with a pot of beer by each man, looked almost tempting. Henri sat down and told them to begin.

" Apropos!" said he, " have the strangers arrived?"

" Yes, there they are at the end of the table."

Henri looked and saw them in the darkest corner of the room.

" Gentlemen," said he, " you are badly placed, and I think you are not eating."

" Thanks, M. le Comte," said one, " we are very tired, and more in need of rest than food; we told your officers so, but they insisted, saying that it was your orders that we should sup with you. We feel the honour, but if, nevertheless, instead of keeping us longer you would give us a room——"

" Is that also the wish of your companion?" said Henri, and he looked at this companion, whose hat was pushed down over his eyes, and who had not yet spoken.

" Yes, comte," replied he, in a scarcely audible voice.

Henri rose, walked straight to the end of the table, while everyone watched his movements and astonished look.

G

"Monsieur," said he, to the one who had spoken first, "do me a favour?"

"What is it, M. le Comte?"

"Tell me if you are not Aurilly's brother, or Aurilly himself?"

"Aurilly!" cried all.

"And let your companion," continued Henri, "raise his hat a little and let me see his face, or else I shall call him monseigneur, and bow before him." And as he spoke he bowed respectfully, hat in hand. The officer took off his hat.

"Monseigneur le Duc d'Anjou!" cried all. "The duke, living!"

"Ma foi, gentlemen," replied he, "since you will recognise your conquered and fugitive prince, I shall not deny myself to you any longer. I am the Duc d'Anjou."

"Vive monseigneur!" cried all.

## CHAPTER LXX

### PAUL-EMILE

"Oh! silence, gentlemen," said the prince, "do not be more content than I am at my good fortune. I am enchanted not be dead, you may well believe; and yet, if you had not recognised me, I should not have been the first to boast of being alive."

"What! monseigneur," cried Henri, "you recognise me—you found yourself among a troop of Frenchmen, and would have left us to mourn your loss, without deceiving us?"

"Gentlemen, besides a number of reasons which made me wish to preserve my incognito, I confess that I should not have been sorry, since I was believed to be dead, to hear what funeral oration would have been pronounced over me.'

"Monseigneur!"

"How many men have you, Du Bouchage?" asked he.

"One hundred, monseigneur."

"Ah! a hundred out of ten thousand; that is like the defeat of Cannes. Gentlemen, they will send a bushel o your rings to Antwerp, but I doubt if the Flemish beautie could wear them, unless they had their fingers pared by thei husbands' knives, which, I must say, cut well."

"Monseigneur," replied Henri, "if your battle was lik the battle of Cannes, at least we are more lucky than th Romans, for we have preserved our Paulus-Emilius!"

"On my life, gentlemen, the Paulus-Emilius of Antwerp was Joyeuse; and doubtless, to preserve the resemblance with his heroic model to the end, your brother is dead, is he not, Du Bouchage?"

Henri felt wounded at this cold question.

"No, monseigneur, he lives," replied he.

"Ah! so much the better," said the duke, with his icy smile. "What! our brave Joyeuse lives! Where is he, that I may embrace him?"

"He is not here, monseigneur."

"Ah! wounded?"

"No, monseigneur, he is safe and sound."

"But a fugitive like me, wandering, famished, and ashamed. Alas! the proverb is right—' For glory, the sword; after the sword, blood; after blood, tears.'"

"Monseigneur, I am happy to tell your highness that my brother has been happy enough to save three thousand men, with whom he occupies a large village about seven leagues from here, and I am acting as scout for him."

The duke grew pale.

"Three thousand men! he has saved three thousand men! he is a perfect Xenophon, and it is very lucky for me that my brother sent him to me. It is not the Valois who can take for their motto ' Hilariter.'"

"Oh! monseigneur," said Henri, sadly, seeing that this gaiety hid a sombre jealousy.

"It is true, is it not, Aurilly?" continued the duke; "I return to France like François after the battle of Pavia; all is lost but honour. Ah! ah!"

A sad silence received these laughs, more terrible than sobs.

"Meanwhile, monseigneur," said Henri, "will your highness take the command of my men? It is not fit that I should continue to do so when you are here."

"So be it; and, first, I order everyone to sup, particularly you, Du Bouchage—you have eaten nothing."

"Monseigneur, I am not hungry."

"In that case, return to visit the posts. Tell the chiefs that I live, but beg them not to rejoice too openly until we gain a better citadel, or rejoin the army of our invincible Joyeuse, for I confess I do not wish to be taken now, after having escaped from fire and water."

"Monseigneur, you shall be strictly obeyed, and no one shall know excepting ourselves that we have the honour of your company among us."

"And these gentlemen will keep the secret?" said the duke, looking round.

All bowed, and Du Bouchage went out.

It only required an hour for this fugitive, this conquered runaway, to become again proud, careless, and imperious. To command 100 men or 100,000 men, was still to command.

While Du Bouchage executed his orders with the best grace he could, François asked questions. He was astonished that a man of the rank of Du Bouchage had consented to take the command of this handful of men, and of such a perilous expedition. The duke was always suspicious, and asked, therefore, and learned that the admiral had only yielded to his brother's earnest request. It was the ensign who gave this information—he who had been superseded in his command by Henri himself, as Henri had been by the duke.

The prince fancied he detected a slight irritation in this man's mind against Du Bouchage; therefore he continued to interrogate him.

"But," said he, "what was the comte's reason for soliciting so earnestly such a poor command?"

"First, zeal for the service, no doubt."

"First!—what else?"

"Ah! monseigneur, I do not know."

"You deceive me—you do know."

"Monseigneur, I can give only, even to your highness, public reasons."

"You see," said the duke, turning to the others, "I was quite right to hide myself, gentlemen, since there are in my army secrets from which I am excluded."

"Ah! monseigneur," said the ensign, "you misunderstand me; there are no secrets but those which concern M. du Bouchage. Might it not be, for example, that, while serving the general interests, he might have wished to render a service to some friend or relation by escorting him?"

"Who here is a friend or relation of the comte? Tell me, that I may embrace him."

"Monseigneur," said Aurilly, mixing in the conversation "I have discovered a part of the secret. This relation whom M. de Bouchage wished to escort is—a lady."

"Ah! ah! why did they not tell me so frankly? That dear Henri—it is quite natural. Let us shut our eyes to the relation, and speak of her no more."

"You had better not, monseigneur, for there seems a great mystery."

" How so?"

" Yes, the lady, like the celebrated Bradamante, about whom I have so often sung to your highness, disguises herself in the dress of a man."

" Oh! monseigneur," cried the ensign, " M. du Bouchage seems to me to have a great respect for this lady, and probably would be very angry at any indiscretion."

" Doubtless, monsieur; we will be mute as sepulchres—as mute as poor St. Aignan; only, if we see the lady, we will try not to make grimaces at her.    Where is this lady, Aurilly?"

" Upstairs."

" Upstairs! what, in this house?"

" Yes, monseigneur; but hush! here is M. du Bouchage."

" Hush!" said the prince, laughing.


## CHAPTER LXXI

### ONE OF THE SOUVENIRS OF THE DUC D'ANJOU

Henri, as he entered, could hear the hateful laugh of the prince, but he had not lived enough with him to know the danger that always lurked in his laughs.  Besides, he could not suspect the subject of conversation, and no one dared to tell him in the duke's presence.  Besides, the duke, who had already settled his plan, kept Henri near him until all the other officers were gone. He then changed the distribution of the posts. Henri had established his quarters in that house, and had intended to send the ensign to a post near the river, but the duke now took Henri's place, and sent him where the ensign was to have been.  Henri was not astonished, for the river was an important point.  Before going, however, he wished to speak to the ensign, and recommend to his care the two people under his protection, and whom he was forced for the time to abandon.  But at the first word that Henri began to speak to him the duke interposed.  " Secrets?" said he, with his peculiar smile.

The ensign had understood, when too late, the fault he had been guilty of.

" No, monseigneur," replied he, " M. le Comte was only asking me how much powder we had left fit to use."

" Ah!" said the duke, forced to seem to believe what he was told.  And as he turned to the door the ensign whispered to Henri: "The prince knows you are escorting someone."

Henri started, but it was too late. The duke remarked the start, and, as if to assure himself that his orders were executed, proposed to Henri to accompany him to his post, which he was forced to accede to.

Henri wished to warn Remy to be on his guard, but it was impossible; all he could do was to say to the ensign:

"Watch well over the powder; watch it as I would myself, will you not?"

"Yes, M. le Comte," replied the young man.

On the way the duke said to Du Bouchage: "Where is this powder that you speak of?"

"In the house we have just left, your highness."

"Oh! be easy, then, Du Bouchage; I know too well the importance of such an article, in our situation, to neglect it. I will watch over it myself."

They said no more until they arrived, when the duke, after giving Henri many charges not to quit his post, returned. He found Aurilly wrapped in an officer's cloak, sleeping on one of the seats in the dining-room. The duke woke him. "Come," said he.

"Yes, monseigneur."

"Do you know what I mean?"

"You wish to know who is the brave creature who has followed the MM. de Joyeuse through fire and water?"

"You have just hit it, 'per mille pericula Martis!' as Margot would say. Apropos, have you written to her, Aurilly?"

"To whom, monseigneur?"

"To my sister Margot?"

"Had I to write to her?"

"Certainly."

"About what?"

"To tell her that we are beaten—ruined, and that she must look out for herself; for that Spain, disembarrassed of me in the north, will fall on her in the south."

"Ah! true."

"You have not written?"

"No, monseigneur."

"You slept?"

"Yes, I confess it; but even if I had thought of it, with what could I have written? I have here neither pen, paper nor ink."

"Well, seek. 'Quare et invenies,' as it is written."

"How in the devil's name am I to find it in the hut of a peasant, who probably did not know how to write?"

"Seek, stupid! if you do not find that, you will find——

"What?"

"Something else."

"Oh! fool that I was," cried Aurilly. "Your highness is right; I am stupid; but I am very sleepy, you see."

Aurilly rose, and, with a step light as a bird, went up the staircase. In five minutes he returned to his master.

"Well?" asked he.

"Well! before this door lies a man, wrapped in a grey cloak."

"What kind of a man?"

"Monseigneur, it was impossible to see his face; but I could perfectly see a large Flemish knife in his belt, and his hand on it."

"It is amusing; go and waken the fellow."

"Oh, no, monseigneur."

"Why not?"

"Why, without counting the knife, I do not wish to amuse myself with making a mortal enemy of MM. de Joyeuse, who stands so well at court. If you had been king of this country, it might have passed; but now you must be gracious, above all with those who saved you, and Joyeuse did save you. They will say so, whether you do or not."

"You are right, Aurilly, and yet—and yet——"

"I understand. Your highness has not seen a woman's face for fifteen mortal days. I do not speak of the kind of animals who live here; they are males and females, but do not deserve to be called men and women."

"I must see this lady, Aurilly."

"Well, monseigneur, you may see her; but not through the door."

"So be it; then I will see her through the window."

"Ah! that is a good idea, and I will go and look for a ladder for you."

Aurilly glided into the courtyard, and under a shed found what he wanted. He manœuvred it amongst horses and men so skilfully as to wake no one, and placed it in the street against the outer wall.

The duke mounted the ladder, Aurilly standing at the foot.

The room in which Henri had placed Diana was matted, and had a large oaken bed with serge curtains, a table, and a few chairs.

Diana, whose heart seemed relieved from an enormous weight since she had heard the false news of the duke's death, had, almost for the first time since her father's death, eaten something more substantial than bread, and drunk a

little wine. After this she grew sleepy, and Remy had left
her, and was sleeping outside her door, not from any
suspicion, but because such had been his habit ever since
they had left Paris.

Diana herself slept with her elbow on the table and her
head leaning on her hand. A little lamp burned on the
table, and all looked peaceful here, where such tempestuous
emotions had raged and would soon again. In the glass
sparkled the Rhine wine, scarcely touched by Diana. She,
with her eyes closed, her eyelids veined with azure, her
mouth slightly opened, her hair thrown back, looked like a
sublime vision to the eyes that were violating the sanctity
of her retreat. The duke, on perceiving her, could hardly
repress his admiration, and leaned over to examine every
detail of her ideal beauty. But all at once he frowned, and
came down two or three steps with a kind of nervous
precipitation, and leaning back against the wall, crossed his
arms and appeared to reflect. Aurilly watched him as he
stood there, with a dreamy air, like a man trying to recall
some old souvenir. After a few minutes he remounted and
looked in again, but Aurilly called out: "Quick! quick!
monseigneur, come down; I hear steps."

The duke came down, but slowly.

"It was time," said Aurilly.

"Whence comes the sound?"

"From there," said Aurilly, pointing to a dark street.
"But the sound has ceased; it must have been some spy
watching us."

"Remove the ladder."

Aurilly obeyed; however, no one appeared, and they heard
no more noise.

"Well, monseigneur, is she beautiful?" said Aurilly.

"Very beautiful," said the prince, abstractedly.

"What makes you sad then? Did she see you?"

"No, she was asleep."

"Then what is the matter?"

"Aurilly, it is strange, but I have seen that woman somewhere."

"You recognised her, then?"

"No, I could not think of her name; but her face gave me
a fearful shock. I cannot tell how it is; but I believe I did
wrong to look."

"However, just on account of the impression she has
made on you, we must find out who she is."

"Certainly we must."

A hasty step was heard, and Henri's voice crying: "Monseigneur!"

"You here!" said the duke, while Aurilly bounded back to his side; "you here, comte?—on what pretext have you quitted your post?"

"Monseigneur," replied Henri, firmly, "your highness can punish me, if you think proper: meanwhile, my duty was to come here, and I came."

The duke glanced towards the window. "Your duty, comte? Explain that to me," said he.

"Monseigneur, horsemen have been seen on the Spanish side of the river, and we do not know if they are friends or enemies."

"Numerous?" asked the duke, anxiously.

"Very numerous, monseigneur."

"Well, comte, no false bravery; you will do well to return. Awake the gendarmes and let us decamp; it will be the most prudent plan."

"Doubtless, monseigneur; but it will be urgent, I think, to warn my brother."

"Two men will do."

"Then I will go with a gendarme."

"No, no, Du Bouchage; you must come with us. Peste! it is not at such a moment that I can separate from a defender like you."

"When does your highness set out?" said Henri, bowing.

"At once, comte."

"Hola! some one," cried Henri.

The young ensign came out immediately from the dark street. Henri gave his orders, and soon the place was filled with gendarmes preparing for departure. Among them the duke talked with his officers.

"Gentlemen," said he, "the Prince of Orange is pursuing me, it seems; but it is not proper that a son of France should be taken prisoner. Let us, therefore, yield to numbers, and fall back upon Brussels. I shall be sure of life and liberty whilst I remain amongst you."

Then, turning to Aurilly: "You remain," said he. "This woman cannot follow us. Joyeuse will not dare to bring her with him in my presence. Besides, we are not going to a ball, and the race we shall run would fatigue a lady."

"Where are you going, monseigneur?"

"To France. I think my business is over here."

"But to what part of France? Does monseigneur think it prudent to return to court?"

"No; I shall stop at one of my castles, Château-Thierry, for example."

"Has your highness decided on that?"

"Yes; Château-Thierry suits me in all respects; it is a good distance from Paris, about twenty-eight leagues, and I can watch from thence MM. de Guise, who are half the year at Soissons. So bring the beautiful unknown to Château-Thierry."

"But, monsieur, perhaps she will not be brought."

"Nonsense; since Du Bouchage accompanies me, and she follows him, it will be quite natural."

"But she may wish to go somewhere else, if she sees that I wish to bring her to you."

"But I repeat that it is not to me that you are to bring her, but to the comte. Really, one would think it was the first time you had aided me in such circumstances. Have you money?"

"I have the two rouleaux of gold that you gave me when you left the camp."

"Well, by any and every method, bring me the lady to Château-Thierry; perhaps when I see her nearer I shall recognise her."

"And the man also?"

"Yes; if he is not troublesome."

"But if he is?"

"Do with him what you would do with a stone which is in your way—throw it away."

"Good, monseigneur."

While the two conspirators formed their plans, Henri went up and woke Remy. He knocked at the door in a peculiar fashion, and it was almost immediately opened by Diana. Behind Remy she perceived Henri.

"Good evening, monsieur," said she, with a smile which had long been foreign to her face.

"Oh! pardon me, madame," said Henri, "for intruding on you; but I come to make my adieux."

"Your adieux, comte; you are going?"

"To France, madame."

"And you leave us?"

"I am forced to do so, my duty is to obey the prince."

"The prince; is there a prince here?" asked Remy.

"Yes, M. le Duc d'Anjou, who was believed dead, and who has been miraculously saved, has joined us."

Diana uttered a terrible cry, and Remy turned as pale as though he had been suddenly struck with death.

"The Duc d'Anjou living!" cried Diana. "The Duc d'Anjou here?"

"Yes; I believe that he knows there is a lady here, and he thinks that she is a friend of mine."

"And what makes you think so?"

"Our young ensign saw him place a ladder against this window, and look in."

"No, no!" cried Diana, wildly, "no, God cannot have done this! He cannot have brought this man to life again; no, monsieur, you must be wrong, he is dead."

At this moment, as if in reply, the duke's voice was heard calling from below:

"Comte, we are waiting for you."

"You hear him, madame," said Henri. "For the last time, adieu."

"Oh! he lives; the demon lives!" murmured she; "and we must live also. He is setting out for France; so be it, Remy, we also must go to France."

## CHAPTER LXXII

### HOW AURILLY EXECUTED THE COMMISSION OF THE DUC D'ANJOU

To the confusion occasioned by the departure of the troops a profound silence succeeded. When Remy believed the house to be empty, he went down to prepare for his departure and that of Diana; but on opening the door of the room below, he was much surprised to see a man sitting by the fire, evidently watching him, although he pretended to look careless. Remy approached, according to his custom, with a slow, halting step, and uncovering his head, bald like that of an old man. He could not, however, see the features of the man by the fire.

"Pardon, monsieur," said he, "I thought myself alone here."

"I also thought so," replied the man, "but I see with pleasure that I shall have companions."

"Oh! very sad companions, monsieur; for except an invalid young man whom I am taking back to France——"

"Ah!" said Aurilly, "I know whom you mean."

"Really."

"Yes; you mean the young lady."

"What young lady?"

"Oh! do not be angry, my good friend; I am the steward

of the house of Joyeuse, and I rejoined my young master by his brother's order, and at his departure the comte recommended to my good offices a young lady and an old servant, who were returning to France."

As he thus spoke, he approached Remy with a smiling and affectionate look. But Remy stepped back, and a look of horror was painted for an instant on his face.

"You quit me," said Aurilly.

"I must consult my mistress; I can decide nothing, you understand."

"Oh! that is natural; but permit me to present myself. I will explain my directions in all their details."

"No, no, thank you; madame is perhaps asleep, and her sleep is sacred to me."

"As you wish. Besides, I have told you what my master told me to say."

"To me?"

"To you and the young lady."

"Your master, M. le Comte du Bouchage, you mean?"

"Yes."

"Thank you, monsieur."

When he had shut the door, all the appearance of age vanished, except the bald head, and Remy mounted the staircase with an agility more like a young man of twenty-five, than the old man he had appeared to be a few minutes before.

"Madame! madame!" cried he, in an agitated voice.

"Well, what is it, Remy; is not the duke gone?"

"Yes, madame, but there is a worse demon here; a demon on whom, during six years, I have daily called down heaven's vengeance, as you have on his master."

"Aurilly?"

"Yes, Aurilly; the wretch is below, forgotten by his infernal accomplice."

"Does he know me?"

"I do not think so."

"And did he recognise you?"

"Oh! madame," said Remy, with a sad smile, "no one recognises me."

"One moment, Remy! I do not ask the life of that wretch of you, but before you kill him, let us find out what he wants of us; perhaps he may make his evil intentions useful. How did he represent himself to you, Remy?"

"As the steward of M. du Bouchage, madame."

"You see he lies; therefore, he has some reason for lying. Let us find out his intentions, and conceal our own."

" I will act as you wish, madame."

" What does he ask now?"

" To accompany us."

" In what character?"

" As the count's steward."

" Tell him I accept."

" Oh! madame."

" Add that I am thinking of going to England, where I have relations, but have not quite decided; lie like him, Remy; to conquer we must fight with equal arms."

" But he will see you?"

" I will wear my mask. Besides, I suspect he knows me."

" Well, madame, then, so be it."

And Remy went down, but still hesitating.

Aurilly waited for him impatiently. Remy advanced armed with an unshakable resolution, but his words were quiet and calm.

" Monsieur," said he, " my mistress cannot accept your proposal."

" And why not?"

" Because you are not the steward of M. du Bouchage."

Aurilly grew pale. " Who told you so?" said he.

" No one; but M. du Bouchage, when he left, recommended to my care the person whom I accompany, and never spoke of you."

Remy smiled, but did not reply.

" Well, you have guessed rightly, my good man; I do not belong to the Comte du Bouchage."

" Ah! and to whom do you belong?"

" To a more powerful lord."

" Take care; you are lying again."

" Why so?"

" There are not many people above the house of Joyeuse."

" Not that of France?"

" Oh! oh!"

" And see how they pay," said Aurilly, sliding into Remy's hand one of the rouleaux of gold.

Remy shuddered and took a step back, but controlling himself, said:

" You serve the king?"

" No, but his brother, the Duc d'Anjou."

" Oh! very well! I am the duke's most humble servant."

" That is excellent."

" But what does monseigneur want?"

" Monseigneur," said Aurilly, trying again to slip the gold into Remy's hand, " is in love with your mistress."

"He knows her, then?"

"He has seen her.

"Seen her! when?"

"This evening."

"Impossible; she has not left her room."

"No, but the prince, by his conduct, has shown that he is really in love."

"Why, what did he do?"

"Took a ladder and climbed to the balcony."

"Ah! he did that?"

"He wants her to come to Château-Thierry, where he is going at his utmost speed."

"That is, upon my word, a passion very quickly conceived."

"My good man," said Aurilly, "you have trivial ideas, and I fear we shall never understand each other; I have preferred kindness to violence, but if you force me to change my plans, well! I will change them."

"What will you do?"

"I told you I had full powers from the duke to kill you and carry off the lady."

"And you believe you could do it with impunity?"

"I believe all my master tells me to believe. Come, will you persuade your mistress to come to France?"

"I will try, but I can answer for nothing."

While Remy went up, Aurilly proceeded to the stables without feeling any doubt as to the result.

"Well!" said Diana, on seeing Remy.

"Well, madame, the duke has seen you."

"And——"

"And he says he loves you."

"Loves me! but you are mad, Remy."

"No; I tell you that he—that man—that wretch, Aurilly, told me so."

"But, then, he recognised me?"

"If he had, do you think that Aurilly would have dared to present himself and talk to you of love in the prince's name? No, he did not recognise you."

"Yes, you must be right, Remy. So many things have passed during six years through that infernal brain, that he has forgotten me. Let us follow this man."

"But this man will recognise you."

"Remy, I thought I told you I had a mask, and that you told me you had a knife."

"It is true, madame; and I begin to think that God is

assisting us to punish the wicked." Then, calling Aurilly from the top of the staircase: "Monsieur!" said he.

"Well!" replied Aurilly.

"My mistress thanks M. du Bouchage for having provided thus for her safety, and accepts with gratitude your obliging offer."

"It is well," said Aurilly, "the horses are ready."

"Come, madame, come," said Remy, offering his arm to Diana.

Aurilly waited at the bottom of the staircase, lantern in hand, all anxiety to see the lady.

"Diable!" murmured he, "she has a mask. But between this and Château-Thierry the silk cords will be worn out or cut."


## CHAPTER LXXIII

### THE JOURNEY

They set off. Aurilly affected the most perfect equality with Remy, and showed to Diana the greatest respect. But this respect was very interested. Indeed, to hold the stirrup of a woman when she mounts or dismounts, to watch each of her movements with solicitude, to let slip no occasion of picking up her glove, is the rôle either of a lover, a servant, or a spy. In touching Diana's glove Aurilly saw her hand, in clasping her cloak he peeped under her mask, and always did his utmost to see that face which the duke had not been able to recognise, but which he doubted not he should be able to. But Aurilly had to deal with one as skilful as himself; Remy claimed to perform his ordinary services to Diana, and seemed jealous of Aurilly, while Diana herself, without appearing to have any suspicions, begged Aurilly not to interfere with the services which her old attendant was accustomed to render to her. Aurilly was then reduced to hoping for rain or sun to make her remove her mask; but neither rain nor sun had any effect, and whenever they stopped Diana took her meals in her own room. Aurilly tried to look through the keyholes, but Diana always sat with her back to the door. He tried to peep through the windows, but there were always thick curtains drawn, or if none were there, cloaks were hung up to supply their place. Neither questions, nor attempts at corruption, succeeded with Remy, who always declared that his mistress's will was his.

Aurilly began to lose patience, and the bad passions of his nature to gain the ascendant. He began to suspect some secret under all this mystery. One day he remained a little behind with Remy, and renewed his attempts at seduction, which Remy repulsed as usual.

" But," said Aurilly, " some day or other I must see your mistress."

" Doubtless," said Remy; " but that will be when she likes, and not when you like."

" But if I employ force."

" Try," said Remy, while a lightning glance, which he could not repress, shot from his eyes.

Remy rejoined Diana.

" What was he saying?" asked she.

" He expressed his constant desire——"

" To see me?"

" Yes."

Diana smiled.

" He is furious," continued Remy.

" He shall not see me; of that I am determined."

" But once we are at Château-Thierry, must he not see your face?"

" What matter, if the discovery come too late? Besides, the duke did not recognise me."

The next day they started early, and at noon were forced to stop to rest the horses. At two o'clock they set off again, and went on without stopping until four. A great forest, that of La Fère, was visible in the distance; it had the sombre and mysterious aspect of our northern forests, so imposing to southern natures, to whom, beyond all things, heat and sunshine are necessary; but it was nothing to Remy and Diana, who were accustomed to the thick woods of Anjou and Sologne. It might have been about six o'clock in the evening when they entered the forest, and after half an hour's journey the sun began to go down. A high wind whirled about the leaves and carried them towards a lake, along the shore of which the travellers were journeying. Diana rode in the middle, Aurilly on the right, and Remy on the left. No other human being was visible under the sombre arches of the trees.

From the long extent of the road, one might have thought it one of those enchanted forests, under whose shade nothing can live, had it not been for the hoarse howling of the wolves waking up at the approach of night. All at once Diana felt that her saddle, which had been put on by Aurilly, was slipping. She called Remy, who jumped down, and began to tighten the girths. At this moment Aurilly approached Diana, and while she was occupied, cut the strings of silk which fastened her mask. Before she had divined the movement, or had time to put up her hand, Aurilly seized the mask, and looked full at her. The eyes of these two people met with a look so terrible, that no one could have said which looked most pale and menacing. Aurilly let the mask and his dagger fall, and clasping his hands, cried, "Heavens and earth! Madame de Monsoreau!"

"It is a name which you shall repeat no more," cried Remy, seizing him by the girdle, and dragging him from his horse. Both rolled on the ground together, and Aurilly stretched out his hand to reach his dagger.

"No, Aurilly, no," said Remy, placing his knee on his breast.

"Le Haudoin!" cried Aurilly; "oh, I am a dead man!"

"That is not yet true, but will be in a moment," cried Remy; and drawing his knife, he plunged the whole blade into the throat of the musician.

Remy did not occupy himself with Diana at that terrible moment, but searched Aurilly, took from him the two rouleaux of gold, then tied a stone to the neck of the corpse, and threw it into the lake.

When Diana recovered herself, she and Remy, without exchanging a single word, continued their route towards Château-Thierry.

## CHAPTER LXXIV

### HOW KING HENRI III. DID NOT INVITE CRILLON TO BREAKFAST, AND HOW CHICOT INVITED HIMSELF

The day after the events that we have just related had taken place in the forest of La Fère, the King of France left his bath at about nine in the morning. His valet-de-chambre, after having rolled him in a blanket of fine wool, and sponged him with that thick Persian wadding which looks like the fleece of a sheep, had given him over to the barbers and dressers, who in their turn gave place to the perfumers and courtiers.

When Crillon, Colonel of the French guards, entered to take his majesty's orders, Henri did not invite him to breakfast but told him to go.

When he was gone, the breakfast was laid at once. The maitre d'hôtel had surpassed himself.

A certain partridge soup, with a purée of truffles and

chestnuts, attracted the king's attention, after he had eaten some fine oysters. Thus the ordinary broth, that faithful old friend of the king's, implored vainly from its golden basin; it attracted no attention. The king began to attack the partridge soup, and was at his fourth mouthful, when a light step near him made the floor creak, and a well-known voice behind him said sharply: "A plate!"

The king turned. "Chicot!" cried he.

"Himself."

And Chicot, falling at once into his old habits, sat down in a chair, took a plate and a fork and began on the oysters, picking out the finest, without saying a word.

"You here! you returned!" cried Henri.

"Hush!" said Chicot, with his mouth full; and he drew the soup towards him.

"Tell me about your journey! that will amuse me."

"Willingly; that is what I came for. Where shall I begin?"

"At the beginning. How did you make your journey?"

"Oh! delightfully."

"And met with no disagreeable adventures—no bad company?"

"Oh! who would dream of annoying an ambassador of his most Christian majesty? You calumniate your subjects, my son."

"I asked," said the king, flattered by the tranquillity that reigned in his kingdom, "because you had no official character, and might have run some risk."

"I tell you, Henriquet, that you have the most charming kingdom in the world. Travellers are nourished gratis; they are sheltered for the love of God; they walk on flowers; and as for the wheel ruts, they are carpeted with velvet and fringed with gold. It is incredible, but true."

"Then you are content?"

"Enchanted."

"Yes, yes; my police is well organised."

"Marvellously; I must do them justice."

And Chicot, drawing out a letter, gave it to the king. It was the one Henri had written after taking Cahors, and it finished with these words: "Quod mihi dixisti profuit multum, cognosco meos devotos; nosce tuos; Chicotus cætera expediet."

Which meant: "What you told me was very useful; I know my friends; know yours. Chicot will tell you the rest"

## CHAPTER LXXV

### HOW, AFTER RECEIVING NEWS FROM THE SOUTH, HENRI RECEIVED NEWS FROM THE NORTH

The king, highly exasperated, could hardly read the letter which Chicot gave to him. While he deciphered the Latin with every sign of impatience, Chicot, before a great Venetian mirror, which hung over a gilt table, was admiring the infinite grace of his own person under his military dress.

" Oh! I am betrayed." cried Henri, when he had finished the letter; " the Béarnais had a plan, and I never suspected it."

" My son," said Chicot, " you know the proverb: ' Still waters run deepest '?"

" Go to the devil with your proverbs."

Chicot went to the door as if to obey.

" No, remain."

Chicot stopped.

" Cahors taken!" continued Henri.

" Yes, and very well done too."

" Then he has generals and engineers?"

" No, he is too poor for that; he could not pay them; he does it all himself."

" He fight!" said Henri, disdainfully.

" I do not say that he rushes into it with enthusiasm; no, he resembles those people who try the water before they bathe; he just dips the ends of his fingers with a little shudder, which augurs badly, then his breast; all this takes him about ten minutes, and then he rushes into action, and through fire, like a salamander."

" Diable!"

" And I assure you, Henri, the fire was hot there."

The king rose and walked up and down the room.

" Here is a misfortune for me," cried he; " they will laugh at it: they will sing about it. Mordieu! it is lucky I thought of sending the promised aid to Antwerp; Antwerp will compensate for Cahors; the north will blot out the south."

" Amen!" said Chicot, plunging his hands into the king's sweetmeat-box to finish his dessert.

At this moment the door opened, and the usher announced: " M. le Comte du Bouchage."

" Ah!" cried Henri, " I told you so; here is news. Enter, comte, enter."

The usher opened the door, and Henri du Bouchage entered slowly and bent a knee to the king.

" Still pale and sad," said the king. " Come, friend, take a holiday air for a little while, and do not tell me good news with a doleful face: speak quickly, Du Bouchage, for I want to hear. You come from Flanders?"

" Yes, sire."

" And quickly?"

" As quickly, sire, as a man can ride."

" You are welcome. And now, what of Antwerp?"

" Antwerp belongs to the Prince of Orange."

" To the Prince of Orange!"

" Yes, to William."

" But did not my brother attack Antwerp?"

" Yes, sire; but now he is travelling to Château-Thierry."

" He has left the army?"

" Sire, there is no longer an army."

" Oh!" cried the king, sinking back in his arm-chair, " but Joyeuse——"

" Sire, my brother after having done wonders with his sailors, after having conducted the whole of the retreat, rallied the few men who escaped the disaster, and sent me home with an escort for M. le Duc d'Anjou."

" A defeat!" murmured the king. But all at once, with a strange look: " Then Flanders is lost to my brother?"

" Absolutely, sire."

" Without hope?"

" I fear so, sire."

The clouds gradually cleared from the king's brow.

" That poor François," said he, smiling; " he is unlucky in his search for a crown. He missed that of Navarre, he has stretched out his hand for that of England, and has touched that of Flanders; I would wage, Du Bouchage, that he will never reign, although he desires it so much. And how many prisoners were taken?"

The comte then gave the king a description of the battle, and of the inundations. Henri listened silently. When the recital was over, he rose, and kneeling down on his prie-dieu, said some prayers and then returned with a perfectly calm face.

" Well," said he, " I trust I bear things like a king; and you, comte, since your brother is saved, like mine, thank God, and smile a little."

" Sire, I am at your orders."

" What do you ask as payment for your services, Du Bouchage?"

"Sire, I have rendered no service."

"Come, Du Bouchage, what will you have—what would you like?"

"Since your majesty does me the honour to speak to me so kindly, I will dare to profit by your goodness. I am tired of life, sire, and yet have a repugnance to shorten it myself, for God forbids it, and all the subterfuges that a man of honour employs in such a case are mortal sins. To get one's self killed in battle or to let one's self die of hunger are only different forms of suicide. I renounce the idea, therefore, of dying before the term which God has fixed for my life, and yet the world fatigues me, and I must leave it."

"My friend!" said the king.

Chicot looked with interest at the young man, so beautiful, so brave, so rich, and yet speaking in this desponding tone.

The king was moved at this doleful request.

"Ah! I understand," said he; "you wish to become a monk, but you fear the probation."

"I do not fear the austerities, sire, but the time they leave one in indecision. It is not to soften my life, nor to spare my body any physical suffering, or my mind any moral privation, but it is to pass at once from this world to the grating which separates me from it, and which one generally attains so slowly."

The king rose smiling, and taking the comte's hand, said:

"I will do what you ask, my son. You wish to serve God, and you are right; he is a better master than I am. You have my promise, dear comte."

"Your majesty overwhelms me with joy," cried the young man, kissing Henri's hand as though he had made him duke, peer, or marshal of France. "Then it is settled?"

"On my word as a king and a gentleman."

Something like a smile passed over the lips of Du Bouchage; he bowed respectfully to the king and took leave.

"What a happy young man," said Henri.

"Oh!" said Chicot, "you need not envy him; he is not more doleful than yourself."

"But, Chicot, he is going to give himself up to religion."

"And who the devil prevents you from doing the same? I know a cardinal who will give all necessary aid, and he has more interest at Rome than you have; do you not know him? I mean the Cardinal de Guise."

"Chicot!"

"And if the tonsure disquiets you, for it is rather a delicate operation, the prettiest hands and the prettiest scissors—golden scissors, ma foi!—will give you this precious symbol, which would raise to three the number of crowns you have worn, and will justify the device: ' Manet ultima cœlo.' "

" Pretty hands, do you say?"

" Yes, do you mean to abuse the hands of Madame de Montpensier? How severe you are upon your subjects."

The king frowned, and passed over his eyes a hand as white as those spoken of, but more trembling.

" Well!" said Chicot, " let us leave that, for I see that the conversation does not please you, and let us return to subjects that interest me personally."

The king made a gesture, half indifferent, half approving.

" Well, my son, I will tell you what to do; divorce the queen and marry Madame de Montpensier; was she not once in love with you?"

" Yes, and that is the source of all her menaces, Chicot; she has a woman's spite against me, and she provokes me now and then, but luckily I am a man, and can laugh at it."

As Henri finished these words, the usher cried at the door: " A messenger from M. le Duc de Guise for his majesty."

" Is it a courier or a gentleman?" asked the king.

" It is a captain, sire."

" Let him enter; he is welcome."


## CHAPTER LXXVI

### THE TWO COMPANIONS

Chicot, at this announcement, sat down, and turned his back to the door; but the first words pronounced by the duke's messenger made him start. He opened his eyes. The messenger could see nothing but the eye of Chicot peering from behind the chair, while Chicot could see him altogether.

" You come from Lorraine?" asked the king of the new-comer, who had a fine and warlike appearance.

" Not so, sire; I come from Soissons, where M. le Duc who has been a month in that city, gave me this letter to deliver to your majesty."

The messenger then opened his buff coat, which was fastened by silver clasps, and drew from a leather pouch lined with silk not one letter, but two; for they had stuck together by the wax, and as the captain advanced to give the king one letter, the other fell on the carpet. Chicot' eyes followed the messenger, and saw the colour spread over his cheeks as he stooped to pick up the letter he had let fall. But Henri saw nothing, he opened his own letter and read, while the messenger watched him closely.

"Ah! M. Borromée," thought Chicot, "so you are a captain, are you?"

"Good," said the king, after reading the duke's letter with evident satisfaction. "Go, captain, and tell M. de Guise that I am grateful for his offer."

"Your majesty will not honour me with a written answer?"

"No, I shall see the duke in a month or six weeks, and can thank him myself."

The captain bowed and went out.

"You see, Chicot," then said the king, "that M. de Guise is free from all machinations. This grave duke has learned the Navarre business, and he fears that the Huguenots will raise up their heads, for he has also ascertained that the Germans are about to send reinforcements to Henri. Now, guess what he is about to do."

As Chicot did not reply, Henri went on.

"Well! he offers me the army that he has just raised in Lorraine to watch Flanders, and says that in six weeks it will be at my command, with its general. What do you say to that, Chicot?"

No answer.

"Really, my dear Chicot," continued the king, "you are as absurdly obstinate as a Spanish mule; and if I happen to convince you of some error, you sulk; yes, sulk."

Not a sound came to contradict Henri in this frank opinion of his friend. Now silence displeased Henri more than contradiction.

"I believe," said he, "that the fellow has had the impertinence to go to sleep. Chicot!" continued he, advancing to the arm-chair; "reply when your king speaks."

But Chicot did not reply, for he was not there; and Henri found the arm-chair empty.

He looked all round the room, but Chicot was not to be seen. The king gave a superstitious shudder; it sometimes came into his mind that Chicot was a supernatural being— a diabolic incarnation, of a good kind, it was true, but still diabolical.

He called Nambu, the usher, and questioned him, and he assured his majesty that he had seen Chicot go out five minutes before the duke's messenger left.

"Decidedly," thought Henri, "Chicot was vexed at being in the wrong. How ill-natured men are, even the best of them."

Nambu was right; Chicot had traversed the ante-chambers silently, but still he was not able to keep his spurs from sounding, which made several people turn, and bow when they saw who it was.

The captain came out five minutes after Chicot, went down the steps across the court proudly and with a satisfied air; proud of his person, and pleased that the king had received him so well, and without any suspicions of M. de Guise. As he crossed the drawbridge, he heard behind him steps which seemed to be the echo of his own. He turned, thinking that the king had sent some message to him, and great was his stupefaction to see behind him the demure face of Robert Briquet. It may be remembered that the first feeling of these two men about one another had not been exactly sympathetical.

Borromée opened his mouth, and paused; and in an instant was joined by Chicot.

"Corbœuf!" said Borromée.

"Ventre de biche!" cried Chicot.

"The bourgeois!"

"The reverend father!"

"With that helmet!"

"With that buff coat!"

"I am surprised to see you."

"I am delighted to meet you again."

And they looked fiercely at each other, but Borromée, quickly assuming an air of amiable urbanity, said: "Vive Dieu, you are cunning, M. Robert Briquet."

"I, reverend father; and why do you say so?"

"When you were at the convent of the Jacobins, you made me believe you were only a simple bourgeois."

"Ah!" replied Chicot, "and what must we say of you, M. Borromée?"

"Let us chat about it."

"I am quite ready."

"Do you like wine?"

"Yes, when it is good."

"Well! I know a little inn, which I think has no rival in Paris."

"And I know one also; what is yours called?"

"The 'Corne d'Abondance.'"

"Where is it?"

" Near the Porte Bourdelle. The host appreciates well the difference between palates like yours and mine, and those of every thirsty passer-by."

" Can we talk there?"

" Perfectly at our ease."

" Oh! I see you are well known there."

" Ma foi, no; this time you are wrong. M. Bonhomet sells me wine when I want it, and I pay when I can; that is all."

" Bonhomet! that is a name that promises well."

" And keeps its promise. Come, compère."

" Oh! oh!" said Chicot to himself; " now I must choose among my best grimaces; for if Bonhomet recognises me at once, it is all over."


## CHAPTER LXXVII

### THE CORNE D'ABONDANCE

The way along which Borromée led Chicot, never suspecting that he knew it as well as himself, recalled to our Gascon the happy days of his youth. How many times had he in those days, under the rays of the winter sun, or in the cool shade in summer, sought out this house, towards which a stranger was now conducting him. However, as Borromée walked first, it was to him that Bonhomet spoke, and he scarcely looked at Chicot, who stood behind. Time had left its traces on the face of Bonhomet, as well as on his house. Besides the wrinkles which seem to correspond on the human face to the cracks made by time on the front of buildings, M. Bonhomet had assumed airs of great importance since Chicot had seen him last. These, however, he never showed much to men of a warlike appearance, for whom he had always a great respect.

It seemed to Chicot that nothing was changed excepting the tint of the ceiling, which from grey had turned to black.

" Come, friend," said Borromée, " I know a little nook where two men may talk at their ease while they drink. Is it empty?" continued he, turning to Bonhomet.

Bonhomet answered that it was, and Borromée then led Chicot to the little room already so well known to all readers of " Chicot the Jester."

" Now," said Borromée, " wait here for me while I avail myself of a privilege granted to the habitués of this house."

" What is that?"

"To go to the cellar and fetch one's own wine."

"Ah, a jolly privilege. Go, then."

Borromée went out. Chicot watched him disappear, and then went to the wall and raised a picture, representing Credit killed by bad paymasters, behind which was a hole, through which you could see into the public room. Chicot knew this hole well, for it was his own making.

On looking through, he perceived Borromée, after placing his fingers on his lips, as a sign of caution, say something to Bonhomet, who seemed to acquiesce by a nod of the head, after which Borromée took a light, which was always kept burning in readiness, and descended to the cellar. Then Chicot knocked on the wall in a peculiar manner. On hearing this knock, which seemed to recall to him some souvenir deeply rooted in his heart, Bonhomet started, and looked round him. Chicot knocked again impatiently, like a man angry at his first call not being answered. Bonhomet ran to the little room, and found Chicot standing there upright. At this sight Bonhomet, who, like the rest of the world, had believed Chicot dead, uttered a cry, for he believed he was a ghost.

"Since when," said Chicot, "has a person like me been obliged to call twice?"

"Oh! dear M. Chicot, is it you or your shade?" cried Bonhomet.

"Whichever it be, since you recognise me, I hope you will obey me."

"Oh! certainly, dear M. Chicot."

"Then whatever noise you hear in this room, and whatever takes place here, do not come until I call you."

"Your directions will be easier to obey, since they are exactly the same as your companion has just given to me."

"Yes, but if he calls, do not come—wait until I call."

"I will, M. Chicot."

"Good! now send away everyone else from your inn, and in ten minutes let us be as free and as solitary here as if we came to fast on Good Friday."

"In ten minutes, M. Chicot, there shall not be a soul in the hotel excepting your humble servant."

"Go, Bonhomet; you are not changed, I see."

"Oh! mon Dieu! mon Dieu!" said Bonhomet, as he retired, "what is about to take place in my poor house?"

As he went, he met Borromée returning from the cellar with his bottles.

We do not know how Bonhomet managed, but when the

ten minutes had expired, the last customer was crossing the
threshold of the door, muttering:

"Oh! oh! the weather is stormy here to-day; we must
avoid the storm."


## CHAPTER LXXVIII

### WHAT HAPPENED IN THE LITTLE ROOM

When the captain re-entered the room with a basket in his
hand containing a dozen bottles, he was received by Chicot
with smiles. Borromée was in haste to uncork his bottles,
but his haste was nothing to Chicot's; thus the preparations
did not take long, and the two companions began to drink.
At first, as though their occupation was too important to
be interrupted, they drank in silence. Chicot uttered only
these words:

"Par ma foi! this is good Burgundy."

They drank two bottles in this way; at the third, Chicot
raised his eyes to Heaven, and said:

"Really, we are drinking as though we wished to
intoxicate ourselves."

"Ah!" said Borromée to himself, "you chatter; then you
are getting tipsy." Then he asked Chicot: "How many
bottles does it take you?"

"About four."

"And to get tipsy?"

"About six."

"And dead drunk?"

"Double!"

"Boaster!" thought Borromée, "he stammers already, and
has only drunk four. Come, then, we can go on," said he,
and he drew out a fifth for Chicot and one for himself.

But Chicot remarked that of the five bottles ranged beside
Borromée some were half full, and others two thirds; none
were empty. This confirmed him in his suspicions that the
captain had bad intentions with regard to him. He rose as
if to fetch his fifth bottle, and staggered as he did so.

"Well, then, my dear captain, tell me, since there is no
effect without a cause, as you say, what was the cause of
your disguise?"

"What disguise?"

"That which you wore when you came to visit Dom
Modeste."

"How was I disguised?"

" As a bourgeois."

" Ah! true."

" Will you tell me?"

" Willingly, if you tell me why you were disguised as a monk. Confidence for confidence."

" Agreed," said Borromée.

" You wish to know, then, why I was disguised," said Chicot, with an utterance which seemed to grow thicker and thicker.

" Yes, it puzzles me."

" And then you will tell me?"

" Yes, that was agreed."

" Ah! true; I forgot.  Well, the thing is very simple; I was a spy for the king."

" A spy?"

" Yes."

" Is that, then, your profession?"

" No, I am an amateur."

" What were you spying there?"

" Everyone.  Dom  Modeste  himself,  then  Brother Borromée, little Jacques, and the whole convent."

" And what did you discover, my friend?"

" I discovered that Brother Borromée was not a monk but a captain."

" Ah! you discovered that?"

" At once."

" Anything else?"

" I discovered that Jacques was practising with the foils before he began with the sword."

" Ah! you discovered that also.  Anything else."

" Give me more to drink, or I shall remember nothing."

" Remember that you are beginning your sixth bottle." Chicot held out his glass for more wine.

" Well, now do you remember?"

" Oh, yes, I should think so."

" Well, what else?"

" I saw that there was a plot."

" A plot!" cried Borromée, turning pale.

" Yes, a plot."

" Against whom?"

" Against the king."

" Of what nature?"

" To try and carry him off."

" When?"

" When he was returning from Vincennes."

" Sacré!"

"Bah! I have seen more than that; pass me one of your bottles, and I will tell you what I have seen."

Borromée hastened to comply with Chicot's desire.

"Let me hear," said he.

"Firstly, I have seen M. de Mayenne wounded."

"Bah!"

"No wonder, he was on my route. And then I have seen the taking of Cahors."

"How? the taking of Cahors?"

"Certainly. Ah! captain, it was a grand thing to see, and a brave man like you would have been delighted."

"I do not doubt it. You were, then, near the King of Navarre?"

"Side by side, my friend, as we are now."

"And you left him?"

"To announce this news to the King of France."

"Then you have been at the Louvre?"

"Yes, just before you."

"Then, as we have not quitted each other since, I need not ask you what you have done."

"On the contrary, ask; for that is the most curious of all."

"Tell me, then."

"Tell! oh, it is very easy to say tell."

"Try."

"One more glass of wine, then, to loosen my tongue. Quite full; that will do. Well, I saw, comrade, that when you gave the king the Duc de Guise's letter, you let another fall."

"Another!" cried Borromée, starting up.

"Yes, it is there."

And having tried two or three times, with an unsteady hand, he put his finger on the buff doublet of Borromée, just where the letter was. Borromée started, as though Chicot's finger had been a hot iron, and had touched his skin instead of his doublet.

"Oh, oh," said he, "there is but one thing wanting."

"What is that?"

"That you should know to whom the letter is addressed."

"Oh, I know quite well; it is addressed to the Duchesse de Montpensier."

"Good heavens! I hope you have not told that to the king."

"No; but I will tell him."

"When?"

"When I have had a nap." And he let his arms fall on the table, and his head on them.

"Then as soon as you can walk you will go to th
Louvre?"

"I will."

"You will denounce me."

"I will denounce you."

"Is it not a joke?"

"What?"

"That you will tell the king after your nap."

"Not at all. You see, my dear friend," said Chicot, hal
raising his head, "you are a conspirator, and I am a spy
you have a plot, and I denounce you; we each follow ou
business."

And Chicot laid his head down again, so that his face wa
completely hidden by his hands, while the back of his hea
was protected by his helmet.

"Ah!" cried Borromée, "you will denounce me when yo
wake!" and, rising, he made a furious blow with his dagge
on the back of his companion, thinking to pierce hin
through and nail him to the table. But he had not reckone
on the shirt of mail which Chicot had carried away from th
priory. The dagger broke upon it like glass, and for th
second time Chicot owed his life to it.

Before Borromée had time to recover from his astonish
ment, Chicot's right fist struck him a heavy blow in the face
and sent him bleeding and stunned against the wall.

In a minute, however, he was up, and sword in hand; bu
this minute had sufficed for Chicot to draw his sword also
and prepare himself. He seemed to shake off, as if b
enchantment, all the fumes of the wine, and stood with
steady hand to receive his adversary. The table, like
field of battle, covered with empty bottles, lay betwee
them, but the blood, flowing down his face infuriate
Borromée, who lunged at his adversary as fiercely as th
intervening table permitted.

"Dolt!" cried Chicot, "you see that it is decidedly yo
who are drunk, for you cannot reach me across the tabl
while my arm is six inches longer than yours, and m
sword as much longer than your sword; and here is th
proof."

As he spoke, he stretched out his arm and wounde
Borromée in the forehead. Borromée uttered a cry, stil
more of rage than of pain, and as he was brave enough
attacked with double fury.

Chicot, however, still on the other side of the table, too
a chair and sat down, saying: "Mon Dieu! how stupid thes
soldiers are; they pretend to know how to manage thei

words, and any bourgeois, if he liked, could kill them like ies. Ah! now you want to put out my eye. And now you mount on the table, but ventre de biche! take care, donkey." And he pricked him with his sword in the stomach, as he ad already done in the forehead.

Borromée roared with anger, and leaped from the table o the floor.

"That is as it should be," said Chicot; "now we are on he same level, and we can talk while we are fencing. Ah! aptain, captain, and so we sometimes try our hand a little t assassination in our spare moments, do we?"

"I do for my cause what you do for yours," said Borromée, now brought back to the seriousness of his position, nd terrified, in spite of himself, at the smothered fire which eemed gleaming in Chicot's eyes.

"So much for talking," said Chicot; "and yet, my friend, t is with no little pleasure I find that I am a better hand han you are. Ah! that was not bad."

Borromée had just made a lunge at Chicot which had lightly touched his breast.

"Not bad, but I know the thrust—it is the very same you howed little Jacques. I was just saying, then, that I have he advantage of you, for I did not begin this quarrel, owever anxiously disposed I might have been to do so. More than that, even, I have allowed you to carry out your roject by giving you every latitude you required, and yet at his very moment even, I have only been acting on the efensive, and this, because I have something to propose to ou."

"Nothing," cried Borromée, exasperated at Chicot's mperturbability, "nothing."

And he gave a thrust which would have run the Gascon ompletely through the body, if the latter had not, with his ong legs, sprung back a step, which placed him out of his dversary's reach.

"I am going to tell you what this arrangement is, all the ame, so that I shall have nothing left to reproach myself or."

"Hold your tongue," said Borromée; "hold your tongue; t will be useless."

"Listen," said Chicot; "it is to satisfy my own conscience. have no wish to shed your blood, you understand, and I on't want to kill you until I am driven to extremes."

"Kill me, kill me, I say, if you can!" exclaimed Borromée, xasperated.

"No, no; I have already once in my life killed another

such swordsman as you are; I will even say a better swordsman than you. Pardieu! you know him; he, too, was one c
De Guise's retainers—a lawyer, too."

"Ah! Nicholas David!" said Borromée, terrified at th
incident, and again placing himself on the defensive.

"Exactly so."

"It was you who killed him?"

"Oh! yes, with a pretty little thrust which I will presentl
show you, if you decline the arrangement I propose."

"Well, let me hear what the arrangement is."

"You will pass from the Duc de Guise's service to that c
the king, without, however, quitting that of the Duc."

"In other words, that I should become a spy like you
self?"

"No, for there will be a difference; I am not paid, but yo
will be. You will begin by showing me the Duc de Guise
letter to Madame la Duchesse de Montpensier; you will l
me take a copy of it, and I will leave you quiet until anothe
occasion. Well, am I not considerate?"

"Here," said Borromée, "is my answer."

Borromée's reply was: "un coupé sur les armes," s
rapidly dealt that the point of his sword slightly touche
Chicot's shoulder.

"Well, well," said Chicot, "I see I must positively sho
you Nicholas David's thrust. It is very simple and pretty

And Chicot, who had up to that moment been acting c
the defensive, made one step forward, and attacked in h
turn.

"This is the thrust," said Chicot; "I make a feint
quatre-basse."

And he did so; Borromée parried by giving way; bu
after this first step backwards he was obliged to stop, as h
found that he was close to the partition.

"Good! precisely so; you parry in a circle; that's wron
for my wrist is stronger than yours. I catch your sword
mine, thus. I return to the attack by a tierce haute, I fa
upon you, so, and you are hit, or, rather, you are a dea
man!"

In fact, the thrust had followed, or rather had accom
panied, the demonstration, and the slender rapier, penetratir
Borromée's chest, had glided like a needle complete
through him, penetrating deeply, and with a dull, heav
sound, the wooden partition behind him.

Borromée flung out his arms, letting his sword fall to th
ground; his eyes became fixed and injected with blood, h
mouth opened wide, his lips were stained with a red coloure

am, his head fell on his shoulder with a sigh, which
ounded like a death-rattle; then his limbs refused their
upport, and his body as it sunk forward enlarged the aper-
ure of the wound, but could not free itself from the partition,
upported as it was by Chicot's terrible wrist, so that the
iserable wretch, like a gigantic insect, remained fastened to
e wall, which his feet kicked convulsively.

Chicot, cold and impassable as he always was in positions
f great difficulty, especially when he had a conviction at the
ottom of his heart that he had done everything his con-
ience could require of him—Chicot, we say, took his hand
om his sword, which remained in a horizontal position,
nfastened the captain's belt, searched his doublet, took the
tter, and read the address:

" Duchesse de Montpensier."

All this time the blood was welling copiously from the
ound, and the agony of death was depicted on the features
f the wounded man.

Chicot then went and opened the door of communication,
id called Bonhomet.

He had no occasion to call twice, for the innkeeper had
een listening at the door, and had successively heard the
oise of tables and stools, the clashing of swords, and the
ll of a heavy body; besides, the worthy M. Bonhomet had
articularly, after the confidence which had been reposed in
m, too extensive an experience of the character of gentle-
en of the sword in general, and of that of Chicot in
articular, not to have guessed, step by step, what had taken
ace.

The only thing of which he was ignorant was, which of the
vo adversaries had fallen.

It must, however, be said in praise of Maître Bonhomet
at his face assumed an expression of real satisfaction when
e heard Chicot's voice, and when he saw that it was the
ascon, who, safe and sound, opened the door.

Chicot, whom nothing escaped, remarked the expression of
s countenance, and was inwardly pleased at it.

Bonhomet, trembling, entered the apartment.

" Good Heavens!" he exclaimed.

" Would you sooner have seen Chicot lying there, and
orromée alive?"

" Oh, oh no!" cried the host, from the bottom of his heart.

" Only for a miracle that would have happened."

" But dear M. Chicot, what am I to do with this body?"

" That is not your affair."

" What! not my affair?"

H

" No.  Give me some ink, a pen, and a sheet of paper."

" Immediately, dear Monsieur Chicot," said Bonhomet, a he darted out of the room.

Meanwhile Chicot, who probably had no time to los heated at the lamp the point of a small dagger, and cut in th middle of the wax the seal of the letter.  This being don and as there was nothing else to retain the despatch, Chic drew it from its envelope, and read it with the livelie marks of satisfaction.

Just as he had finished reading it, Maître Bonhomet r turned with the paper and the pen.

Chicot arranged the pen, ink, and paper before him, s himself down at the table.

Chicot copied the letter from the Duc de Guise to h sister, and made his comments thereon at every word.

" DEAR SISTER:

" The expedition from Anvers has succeeded for ever body, but has failed as far as we are concerned.  Y will be told that the Duc d'Anjou is dead; do not belie it—he is alive.

" He *lives*, you understand, and that is the who question.

" There is a complete dynasty in those words; tho two words separate the house of Lorraine from t throne of France better than the deepest abyss could b

" Do not, however, make yourself too uneasy abo that.  I have discovered that two persons, who thought were dead, are still living, and there is a gre chance of death for the prince while those two perso are alive.

" Think then only of Paris; it will be time enough f the League to act six weeks hence.  Let our Leagu know that the moment is approaching, and let them ho themselves in readiness.

" The army is on foot; we number twelve thousa sure men, all well equipped; I shall enter France with under the pretext of engaging the German Hugueno who are going to assist Henri de Navarre.  I shall defe the Huguenots, and having entered France as a friend shall act as a master."

Chicot continued:—

" P S.—I entirely approve of your plan with regard the Forty-five; only allow me to say, dear sister, th you will be conferring a greater honour on those fello than they deserve."

"Ah! diable!" murmured Chicot, "this is getting obscure." And he read it again.

"I entirely approve of your plan with regard to the Forty-five."

"What plan?" Chicot asked himself.

"Only allow me to say, dear sister, that you will be conferring a greater honour on those fellows than they deserve."

"What honour?"

Chicot resumed:—

"Than they deserve.

"Your affectionate brother,

"H. DE LORRAINE."

"At all events," said Chicot, "everything is clear, except the postscript. Very good, we will look after the postscript, then."

"Dear Monsieur Chicot," Bonhomet ventured to observe, seeing that Chicot had finished writing, if not thinking: "Dear Monsieur Chicot, you have not told me what I am to do with this corpse."

"That is a very simple affair."

"For you, who are full of imagination, it may be, but for me?"

"Well! suppose, for instance, that that unfortunate captain had been quarrelling with the Swiss Guards or the reiters, and he had been brought to your house wounded, would you have refused to receive him?"

"No, certainly, unless indeed you had forbidden me, dear M. Chicot."

"Suppose that, having been placed in that corner, he had, notwithstanding the care and attention you had bestowed upon him, departed this life while in your charge, it would have been a great misfortune, and nothing more, I suppose?"

"Certainly."

"And, instead of incurring any blame, you would deserve to be commended for your humanity. Suppose, again, that while he was dying this poor captain had mentioned the name, which you know very well, of the prior of Les Jacobins Saint Antoine?"

"Of Dom Modeste Gorenflot?" exclaimed Bonhomet, in astonishment.

"Yes, of Dom Modeste Gorenflot. Very good! You will go and inform Dom Modeste of it; Dom Modeste will hasten here with all speed, and, as the dead man's purse is found in one of his pockets—you understand it is important that the purse should be found; I mention this merely by way of advice—and as the dead man's purse is found in one of his pockets, and this letter in the other, no suspicion whatever can be entertained."

" I understand, dear Monsieur Chicot."

" In addition to which, you will receive a reward, instead of being punished."

" You are a great man, dear Monsieur Chicot; I will run at once to the Priory of St. Antoine."

" Wait a minute! did I not say there was the purse and the letter?"

" Oh! yes, and you have the letter in your hand."

" Precisely."

" I must not say that it has been read and copied?"

" Pardieu! it is precisely on account of this letter reaching its destination intact that you will receive a recompense."

" The letter contains a secret, then?"

" In such times as the present there are secrets in every thing, my dear Bonhomet."

And Chicot, with this sententious reply, again fastened the silk under the wax of the seal by making use of the same means as he had done before; he then fastened the wax so artistically that the most experienced eye would not have been able to have detected the slightest crack.

## CHAPTER LXXIX

### THE HUSBAND AND THE LOVER

It was with no inconsiderable emotion that Chicot again recognised La Rue des Augustins, so quiet and deserted, the angle formed by the block of houses which preceded his own, and lastly, his own dear house itself, with its triangular roof, its worm-eaten balcony, and its gutters ornamented with water-spouts.

It was precisely the same with regard to the furniture in the first room he came to; the same, too, with the small board which he had nailed to the joist; and lastly, the same with the thousand crowns, which were still slumbering in their oaken hiding-place.

" Ventre de biche!" murmured Chicot, sitting down in the middle of his room, after he had removed the flagstone, and with the small piece of board by his side, and his treasure under his eyes, " ventre de biche! that excellent young man is a most invaluable neighbour, for he has made other respect my money, and has himself respected it too; in sober truth, such an action is wonderful in such times as the present. Mordieux! I owe some thanks to that excellent young fellow, and he shall have them this evening."

Thereupon Chicot replaced the plank over the joist, the flagstone over the plank, approached the window, and looked towards the opposite side of the street.

The house still retained that grey and sombre aspect which the imagination bestows as their natural colour upon buildings whose character it seems to know.

"It cannot yet be their time for retiring to rest," said Chicot; "and, besides, those fellows, I am sure, are not very sound sleepers; so let us see."

He descended his staircase, crossed the road—forming, as he did so, his features into their most amiable and gracious expression—and knocked at his neighbour's door.

He remarked the creaking of the staircase, the sound of a hurried footstep, and yet he waited long enough to feel warranted in knocking again.

At this fresh summons the door opened, and the outline of a man appeared in the gloom.

"Thank you, and good evening," said Chicot, holding out his hand; "here I am back again, and I am come to return you my thanks, my dear neighbour."

"I beg your pardon," inquiringly observed a voice, in a tone of disappointment, the accent of which greatly surprised Chicot.

At the same moment the man who had opened the door drew back a step or two.

"Stay, I have made a mistake," said Chicot, "you were not my neighbour when I left, and yet I know who you are."

"And I know you too," said the young man.

"You are Monsieur le Vicomte Ernanton de Carmainges."

"And you are 'The Shade.'"

"Really," said Chicot, "I am quite bewildered."

"Well, and what do you want, monsieur?" inquired the young man, somewhat churlishly.

"Excuse me, but I am interrupting you, perhaps, my dear monsieur?"

"No, only you will allow me to ask you what you may want."

"Nothing, except that I wished to speak to the master of this house."

"Speak, then."

"What do you mean?"

"I am the master of the house, that is all."

" You? since when, allow me to ask?"

" Diable! since the last three days."

" Good! the house was for sale then?"

" So it would seem, since I have bought it."

" But the former proprietor?"

" No longer lives here, as you see."

" Where is he?"

" I don't know."

" Come, come, let us understand each other," said Chicot.

" There is nothing I should like better," replied Ernanton, with visible impatience, " only let us do so without losing any time."

" The former proprietor was a man between five-and-twenty and thirty years of age, but who looked as if he were forty."

" No; he was a man of about sixty-five or sixty-six years old, who looked his age quite."

" Bald?"

" No, on the contrary, a perfect forest of white hair."

" With an enormous scar on the left side of the head, had he not?"

" I did not observe the scar, but I did a good number of furrows."

" I cannot understand it at all," asid Chicot.

" Well," resumed Ernanton, after a moment's silence, " what did you want with that man, my dear Monsieur l'Ombre?"

Chicot was on the point of acknowledging what had just happened: suddenly, however, the mystery of the surprise which Ernanton had exhibited, reminded him of a certain prove b very dear to all discreet people.

" I wished to pay him a neighbourly visit," he said, " that is all."

In this way, Chicot did not tell a falsehood, and yet admitted nothing.

" My dear monsieur," said Ernanton politely, but reducing considerably the opening of the door which he held half-closed, " I regret I am unable to give you more precise information."

" Thank you, monsieur," said Chicot, " I must look elsewhere, then."

" But," continued Ernanton, as he gradually closed the door, " that does not interfere with my congratulating myself upon the chance which has brought me again into personal communication with you."

"You would like to see me at the devil, I believe," murmured Chicot, as he returned bow for bow.

However, as, notwithstanding this mental reply, Chicot, in his preoccupation, forgot to withdraw, Ernanton, shutting his face between the door and the doorway, said to him:

"I wish you a very good evening, monsieur."

"One moment, Monsieur de Carmainges," said Chicot.

"Monsieur, I exceedingly regret I am unable to wait," replied Ernanton, "but the fact is, I am expecting some one who will come and knock at this very door, and this person will be angry with me if I do not show the greatest possible discretion in receiving him."

"That is quite sufficient, monsieur, I understand," said Chicot; "I am sorry to have been so importunate, and I now retire."

"Adieu, dear Monsieur l'Ombre."

"Adieu, excellent Monsieur Ernanton."

And as Chicot drew back a step, he saw the door quietly shut in his face.

He listened to satisfy himself if the suspicious young man was watching his departure, but he heard Ernanton's footsteps as he ascended the staircase; Chicot could therefore return to his own house without uneasiness, and shut himself up in it, thoroughly determined not to interfere with this new neighbour's habits, but, in accordance with his usual custom, equally resolved not to lose sight of him altogether.

Chicot, accordingly, began to think, that it was strange to see Ernanton in the very house where he had seen Remy.

He considered it was strange for two reasons; the first, because of the perfect ignorance in which the two men lived with respect to each other, which led to the supposition that there must have been an intermediary between them unknown to Chicot; and the second reason, because the house must have been sold to Ernanton, who possessed no means of purchasing it.

"It is true," said Chicot, as he installed himself as comfortably as he could on his gutter, which was his usual place of observation; "it is true that the young man pretends he is expecting a visit, and that the visit is from a lady; in these days, ladies are wealthy, and allow themselves an indulgence in fancies of all kinds. Ernanton is handsome, young, and graceful; Ernanton has taken some one's fancy, a rendezvous has been arranged, and he has been directed to purchase this house; he has bought the house, and she has accepted the rendezvous.

"Ernanton," continued Chicot, "lives at Court; it must be some lady belonging to the Court, then, with whom he has this affair. Poor fellow, will he love her? Heaven preserve him from such a thing! he is going to fall headlong into that gulf of perdition. Very good! ought I not to read him a moral lecture thereupon?

"A moral lecture, which would be both useless and absurd, doubly so the former, and tenfold the latter."

Chicot had reached so far in his reasonings, his inductions, and his philosophy, which had consumed a good hour-and-a-half altogether, when he was drawn from his train of thought by the arrival of a litter proceeding from the direction of the inn of the "Brave Chevalier."

This litter stopped at the threshold of the mysterious house.

A veiled lady alighted from it, and disappeared within the door which Ernanton held half open.

And soon after a cavalier, wrapped in his cloak, made his appearance.

The cavalier drew up in the middle of the street, and seemed to be looking about him to see where he was.

The cavalier then perceived the group which was formed by the litter and its bearers.

He drove his horse against them. He was armed, for the rattling of his sword against his spurs could be distinctly heard.

The bearers of the litter seemed desirous of barring his passage, but he addressed a few words to them in a low tone of voice, and not only did they withdraw with every mark of respect, but one of them, as he sprung to the ground from his horse, even received the bridle from his hand.

The unknown advanced towards the door, and knocked loudly.

"Well," said Chicot, "I was right in remaining, after all; my presentiments, which told me that something was going to take place, have not deceived me. Here is the husband, poor Ernanton; we shall presently be witness of something serious.

"Poor Ernanton, he will be flayed alive.

"Oh! oh! I shall not suffer such a thing, however," added Chicot.

"For in fact," he resumed, "he assisted me; and consequently, when an opportunity presents itself, I ought to help him. And it seems to me that the opportunity has now arrived, or it never will do so."

Chicot was resolute and generous, and curious into the bargain; he unfastened his long sword, placed it under his arm, and hurriedly ran down the staircase.

He could open his door noiselessly, which is an indispensable piece of knowledge for anyone who may wish to listen with advantage.

Chicot glided under the balcony, then behind a pillar, and waited.

Hardly had he installed himself there, when the door opposite was opened immediately the unknown had whispered a word through the keyhole, and yet he did not venture beyond the threshold.

A moment afterwards the lady appeared within the doorway.

She took hold of the cavalier's arm, who led her to the litter, closed the door of it, and then mounted his horse.

" There is no doubt on the subject," said Chicot, " it is the husband, a good-natured fellow of a husband after all, since he does not think it worth his while to explore the house in order to be revenged on my friend Carmainges."

The litter then moved off, the cavalier walking his horse beside the door of it.

" Pardieu!" said Chicot, " I must follow those people and learn who they are, and where they are going; I shall, at all events, draw some solid counsel from my discovery for my friend Carmainges."

Chicot accordingly followed the cortège, observing the precaution, however, of keeping in the shadow of the walls, and taking care that the noise made by the footsteps of the men and of the horses should render the sound of his own inaudible.

Chicot's surprise was by no means slight when he saw the litter stop at the door of the " Brave Chevalier."

Almost immediately afterwards, as if someone had been on the watch, the door was opened.

The lady, still veiled, alighted; entered and mounted to the turret, the window of the first story of which was lighted.

The husband followed her, both being respectfully preceded by Dame Fournichon, who carried a flambeau in her hand.

" Decidedly," said Chicot, crossing his arms on his chest, " I cannot understand a single thing of the whole affair."

## CHAPTER LXXX

SHOWING HOW CHICOT BEGAN TO UNDERSTAND THE PURPORT
OF MONSIEUR DE GUISE'S LETTER

Chicot fancied that he had already certainly seen, somewhere or another, the figure of this courteous cavalier; but
his memory, having become a little confused during his
journey from Navarre, where he had met with so many
different figures, did not, with its usual facility, furnish him
with the cavalier's name on the present occasion.

While, concealed in the shade, he was interrogating himself, with his eyes fixed upon the lighted window, as to the
object of this lady and gentleman's tête-à-tête at the "Brave
Chevalier," our worthy Gascon, forgetting Ernanton in the
mysterious house, observed the door of the hostelry open,
and in the stream of light which escaped through the opening, he perceived something resembling the dark outline of a
monk's figure.

The outline in question paused for a moment to look up
at the same window at which Chicot had been gazing.

"Oh! oh!" he murmured; "if I am not mistaken, that is
the frock of a Jacobin friar. Is Maître Gorenflot so lax,
then, in his discipline as to allow his sheep to go strolling
about at such an hour of the night as this, and at such a
distance from the priory?"

Chicot kept his eye upon the Jacobin, who was making his
way along the rue des Augustins, and something seemed
instinctively to assure him that he should, through this monk,
discover the solution of the problem which he had up to that
moment been vainly endeavouring to ascertain.

Moreover, in the same way that Chicot had fancied he had
recognised the figure of the cavalier; he now fancied he could
recognise in the monk a certain movement of the shoulder,
and a peculiar military movement of the hips, which only
belong to persons in the habit of frequenting fencing rooms
and gymnastic establishments.

"May the devil seize me," he murmured, "if that frock
yonder does not cover the body of that little miscreant whom
I wished them to give me for a travelling companion, and
who handles his arquebuse and sword so cleverly."

Hardly had the idea occurred to Chicot, when, to convince
himself of its value, he stretched out his long legs, and in a
dozen strides rejoined the little fellow, who was walking

along holding up his frock above his thin and sinewy legs in order to be able to get along all the faster.

This was not very difficult, however, inasmuch as the monk paused every now and then to glance behind him, as if he was going away with great difficulty and with feelings of profound regret.

His glance was invariably directed towards the brilliantly-lighted windows of the hostelry.

Chicot had not gone many steps before he felt sure that he had not been mistaken in his conjectures.

"Hallo! my little master," he said; "hallo! my little Jacquot; hallo! my little Clément. Halt!"

And he pronounced this last word in so thoroughly military a tone, that the monk started at it.

"Who calls me?" inquired the young man rudely, with something rather antagonistic than cordial in his tone of voice.

"I!" replied Chicot, drawing himself up in front of the monk; "I! don't you recognise me?"

"Oh! Monsieur Robert Briquet!" exclaimed the monk.

"Myself, my little man. And where are you going like that, so late, darling child?"

"To the priory, Monsieur Briquet."

"Very good; but where do you come from?"

"I?"

"Of course, little libertine."

The young man started.

"I don't know what you are saying, Monsieur Briquet," he replied; "on the contrary, I have been sent with a very important commission by Dom Modeste, who will himself assure you that such is the case, if there be any occasion for it."

"Gently, gently, my little Saint Jérome; we take fire like a match, it seems."

"And not without reason, too, when one hears such things said as you were saying just now."

"Diable! when one sees a frock like yours leaving a tavern at such an hour——"

"A tavern, I!"

"Oh! of course not; the house you left just now was not the 'Brave Chevalier,' I suppose? Ah! you see I have caught you!"

"You were right in saying that I left that house, but it was not a tavern I was leaving."

"What!" said Chicot; "is not the hostelry of the sign of the 'Brave Chevalier' a tavern?"

"A tavern is a house where people drink, and as I have not been drinking in that house, that house is not a tavern for me."

"Diable! that is a subtle distinction, and I am very much mistaken if you will not some day become a very forcible theologian; but, at all events, if you did not go into that house to drink there, what did you go there for?"

Clément made no reply, and Chicot could read in his face, notwithstanding the darkness of the night, a resolute determination not to say another word.

This resolution annoyed our friend extremely, for it had almost grown a habit with him to become acquainted with everything.

It must not be supposed that Clément showed any ill-feeling in his silence; for, on the contrary, he had appeared delighted to meet, in so unexpected a manner, his learned fencing-master, Maître Robert Briquet, and had given him the warmest reception that could be expected from the close and rugged character of the youth.

The conversation had completely ceased. Chicot, for the purpose of starting it again, was on the point of pronouncing the name of Frère Borromée; but, although Chicot did not feel any remorse, or fancied he did not feel any, he could not summon up courage to pronounce that name.

His young companion, still preserving the same unbroken silence, seemed as if he were awaiting something; it seemed, too, as if he considered it a happiness to remain as long as possible in the neighbourhood of the hostelry of the "Brave Chevalier."

Robert Briquet tried to speak to him about the journey which the boy had for a moment entertained the hope of making with him.

Jacques Clément's eyes glistened at the words space and liberty.

Robert Briquet told him that in the countries through which he had just been travelling the art of fencing was held greatly in honour; he added, with an appearance of indifference, that he had even brought away with him several wonderful passes and thrusts.

This was placing Jacques upon slippery ground. He wished to know what these passes were; and Chicot, with his long arm, indicated a few of them upon the little monk's arm.

But all these delicacies and refinements on Chicot's part in no way affected little Clément's obstinate determination; and while he endeavoured to parry these unknown passes, which friend Maître Robert Briquet was showing him, he preserved an obstinate silence with respect to what had brought him into that quarter.

Thoroughly annoyed, but keeping a strong control over himself Chicot resolved to try the effect of injustice; injustice is one of the most powerful provocatives ever invented to make women, children, and inferiors speak, whatever their nature or disposition may be.

"It does not matter," he said, as if he returned to his original idea; "it does not matter, you are a delightful little monk; but that you visit hostelries is certain, and what hostelries too! Those where beautiful ladies are to be found, and you stop outside in a state of ecstasy before the window, where you can see their shadow. Oh! little one, little one, I shall tell Dom Modeste all about it."

The bolt hit its mark, more truly so even than Chicot had supposed; for when he began, he did not suspect that the wound had been so deep.

Jacques turned round like a serpent that had been trodden on.

"That is not true," he cried, crimson with shame and anger, "I don't look at women."

"Yes, yes," pursued Chicot; "on the contrary, there was an exceedingly pretty woman at the 'Brave Chevalier' when you left it, and you turned round to look at her again; and I know that you were waiting for her in the turret, and I know, too, that you spoke to her."

Chicot proceeded by the inductive process.

Jacques could not contain himself any longer.

"I certainly have spoken to her!" he exclaimed, "is it a sin to speak to women?"

"No, when one does not speak to them of one's own accord, and yielding to the temptation of Satan."

"Satan has nothing whatever to do with the matter; it was absolutely necessary that I should speak to that lady, since I was desired to hand her a letter."

"Desired by Dom Modeste!" cried Chicot.

"Yes, go and complain to him now, if you like."

Chicot, bewildered, and feeling his way as it were in the dark, perceived, at these words, a gleam of light traversing the obscurity of his brain.

"Ah!" he said, "I knew it perfectly well."

"What did you know?"

"What you did not wish to tell me."

"I do not tell my own secrets, and, for a greater reason, the secrets of others."

"Yes, but to me."

"Why should I to you?"

"You should tell them to me because I am a friend of Dom Modeste, and, for another reason, you should tell them to me because——"

"Well?"

"Because I know beforehand all you could possibly have to tell me."

Jacques looked at Chicot and shook his head with an incredulous smile.

"Very good!" said Chicot, "would you like me to tell you what you do not wish to tell me?"

"I should indeed."

Chicot made an effort.

"In the first place," he said "that poor Borromée——"

A dark expression passed across Jacques' face.

"Oh!" said the boy, "if I had been there——"

"Well! if you had been there?"

"The affair would not have turned out as it did."

"Would you have defended him against the Swiss with whom he got into a quarrel?"

"I would have defended him against everyone."

"So that he would not have been killed?"

"Either that, or I should have got myself killed along with him."

"At all events, you were not there, so that the poor devil breathed his last in an obscure tavern, and in doing so pronounced Dom Modeste's name; is not that so?"

"Yes."

"Whereupon the people there informed Dom Modeste of it?"

"A man, seemingly scared out of his wits, who threw the whole convent into consternation."

"And Dom Modeste sent for his litter, and hastened to 'La Corne d'Abondance.'"

"How do you know that?"

"Oh! you don't know me yet, my boy; I am somewhat of a sorcerer, I can tell you."

Jacques drew back a couple of steps.

"That is not all," continued Chicot, who, as he spoke, began to see clearer by the light of his own words; "a letter was found in the dead man's pocket."

"A letter—yes, precisely so."

"And Dom Modeste charged his little Jacques to carry that letter to its address."

"Yes."

"And the little Jacques ran immediately to the Hôtel de Guise."

"Oh!"

"Where he found no one."

"Bon Dieu!"

"But Monsieur de Mayneville."

"Good gracious!"

"And which same Monsieur de Mayneville conducted Jacques to the hostelry of the 'Brave Chevalier.'"

"Monsieur Briquet! Monsieur Briquet!" cried Jacques, "if you know that——"

"Eh! ventre de biche! you see very well that I do know it," exclaimed Chicot, feeling triumphant at having disentangled this secret, which was of such importance for him to learn, from the provoking intricacies in which it had been at first involved.

"In that case," returned Jacques, "you see very well, Monsieur Briquet, that I am not guilty."

"No," said Chicot, "you are not guilty in act, nor in omission, but you are guilty in thought."

"I?"

"I suppose there is no doubt you think the duchess very beautiful?"

"I!!"

"And you turned round to look at her again through the window."

"I!!!"

The young monk coloured and stammered out: "Well, it is true, she is exactly like a Virgin Mary which was placed over the head of my mother's bed."

"Oh!" muttered Chicot, "how much those people lose who are not curious!"

And thereupon he made little Clément, whom from this moment he held in his power, tell him all he had himself just told him, but this time with the details, which he could not possibly otherwise have known.

"You see," said Chicot, when he had finished, "what a poor fencing-master you had in Frère Borromée."

"Monsieur Briquet," said little Jacques, "one ought not to speak ill of the dead."

"No; but confess one thing."

"What?"

"That Borromée did not make such good use of his sword as the man who killed him."

"True."

"And now that is all I had to say to you.   Good-night,

Jacques; we shall meet again soon, and if you like——"

" What, Monsieur Briquet?"

" Why, I will give you lessons in fencing for the future."

" Oh! I shall be most thankful."

" And now off with you, my boy, for they are waiting for you impatiently at the priory."

" True, true. Thank you, Monsieur Briquet, for having reminded me of it."

And the little monk disappeared, running as fast as he could.

Chicot had a reason for dismissing his companion. He had extracted from him all he wished to know, and, on the other hand, there still remained something further for him to learn. He returned, therefore, as fast as he could to his own house. The litter, the bearers, and the horse were still at the door of the " Brave Chevalier."

He regained his gutter without making a noise.

The house opposite to his own was still lighted up, and from that moment all his attention was directed towards it.

In the first place, he observed, by a rent in the curtain, Ernanton walking up and down, apparently waiting with great impatience.

He then saw the litter return, saw Mayneville leave, and, lastly, he saw the duchess enter the room in which Ernanton, palpitating and throbbing rather than breathing, impatiently awaited her return.

Ernanton kneeled before the duchess, who gave him her white hand to kiss. She then raised the young man from the ground, and made him sit down before her at a table which was most elegantly served.

" This is very singular," said Chicot; " it began like a conspiracy, and finishes by a rendezvous."

" Yes," continued Chicot, " but who appointed this rendezvous?"

" Madame de Montpensier."

And then, as a fresh light flashed through his brain, he murmured: " I entirely approve of your plan with regard to the Forty-five; only allow me to say, dear sister, that you will be conferring a greater honour on those fellows than they deserve."

" Ventre de biche!" exclaimed Chicot, " I return to my original idea—it is not a love affair, but a conspiracy."

" Madame la Duchesse de Montpensier is in love with Monsieur Ernanton de Carmainges; let us watch over this love affair of Madame la Duchesse."

And Chicot watched until midnight had long passed, when

Ernanton hastened away, his cloak concealing his face, whilst Madame la Duchesse de Montpensier returned to her litter.

"Now," murmured Chicot, as he descended his own staircase, "what is that chance of death which is to deliver the Duc de Guise from the presumptive heir of the crown? who are those defunct persons who were thought to be dead, but are still living?"

"Mordioux! I shall trace them before long."


## CHAPTER LXXXI

### LE CARDINAL DE JOYEUSE

Youth has its obstinate resolutions, both as regards good and evil in the world, which are by no means inferior to the inflexibility of purpose of maturer years.

When directed towards good purposes, instances of this dogged obstinacy of character produce what are termed the great actions of life, and impress on the man who enters life an impulse which bears him onward, by a natural course, towards a heroism of character of some kind or another.

In this way Bayard and Du Guesclin became great captains from having been the most ill-tempered and most intractable children that ever existed; in the same way, too, the swineherd, whom nature had made the herdsman of Montalte, and whose genius had converted him into Sexte-Quinte, became a great Pope, because he had persisted in performing his duties as a swineherd in an indifferent manner.

Again, in the same way were the worst Spartan natures displayed in a heroic sense, after they had commenced life by a persistence in dissimulation and cruelty.

All we have now to sketch is the portrait of a man of an ordinary stamp, and yet, more than one biographer would have found in Henri du Bouchage, at twenty years of age, the materials for a great man.

Henri obstinately persisted in his affection and in his seclusion from the world; as his brother had begged and as the king had required him to do, he remained for some days closeted alone with his one enduring thought; and then, when that thought had become more and more fixed and unchangeable in its nature, he one morning decided to pay a visit to his brother the cardinal, an important personage, who, at the age of twenty-six, had already for two years past been a cardinal, and who, from the archbishopric of Narbonne, had passed to the highest degrees of ecclesiastical dignity, a posi-

tion to which he was indebted as much to his noble descent
as to his powerful intellect.

François de Joyeuse, whom we have already introduced
with the object of enlightening Henri de Valois respecting the
doubt he had entertained with regard to Sylla—François de
Joyeuse, young and worldly-minded, handsome and witty, was
one of the most remarkable men of the period.   Ambitious
by nature, but circumspect by calculation and position,
François de Joyeuse could assume as his device: " Nothing is
too much," and justify his device.

The only one, perhaps, of all those who belonged to the
court—and François de Joyeuse was attached to the court in
a very especial manner—he had been able to create for himself two means of support out of the religious and lay thrones
to which he in some measure approximated as a French
gentleman, and as a prince of the church; Sixtus protected
him against Henry III., Henry III. protected him against
Sixtus.   He was an Italian at Paris, a Parisian at Rome,
magnificent and able everywhere.

The sword alone of Joyeuse, the high admiral, gave the
latter more weight in the balance; but it might be noticed
from certain smiles of the cardinal, that if those temporal
arms failed him, which the hand of his brother, refined and
admired as he was, wielded so successfully, he himself knew
not only how to use, but also how to abuse, the spiritual
weapons which had been entrusted to him by the sovereign
head of the Church.

The Cardinal François de Joyeuse had very rapidly become
a wealthy man, wealthy in the first place from his own patri-
mony, and then from his different benefices.

It was to this prelate that the Comte du Bouchage betook
himself after his explanation with his brother, and after his
conversation with the King of France; but, as we have
already observed, he allowed a few days to elapse in token of
obedience to the injunction which had been imposed on him
by his elder brother, as well as by the king.

François resided in a beautiful mansion in that part of
Paris called La Cité.   The immense court-yard was never
quite free from cavaliers and litters; but the prelate, whose
garden was immediately contiguous to the bank of the river,
allowed his court-yards and his ante-chambers to become
crowded with courtiers; and as he had a mode of egress
towards the river bank, and a boat close thereto, which conveyed him without any disturbance as far and as quietly as
he chose, it not unfrequently happened that the courtier
uselessly waited to see the prelate, who availed himself of the

pretext of a serious indisposition, or a rigid penance, to postpone his reception for the day. For him it was a realisation
of Italy in the bosom of the capital of the King of France,
it was Venice embraced by the two arms of the Seine.

François was proud, but by no means vain; he loved his
friends as brothers, and his brothers nearly as much as his
friends. Five years older than Du Bouchage, he withheld
from him neither good nor evil counsel, neither his purse
nor his smile.

But as he wore his cardinal's costume with wonderful effect,
Du Bouchage thought him handsome, noble, almost formidable, and accordingly respected him more, perhaps than
he did the elder of them both. Henri, with his beautiful
cuirass, and the glittering accessories of his military costume,
tremblingly confided his love affairs to Anne, while he would
not have dared to confess himself to François.

However, when he proceeded to the cardinal's hotel, his
resolution was taken, and he accosted, frankly enough, the
confessor first, and the friend afterwards.

He entered the court-yard, which several gentlemen were at
that moment quitting, wearied at having solicited without
having obtained the favour of an audience.

He passed through the ante-chambers, saloons, and then
the more private apartments. He had been told, as others
had, that his brother was engaged in conference; but the idea
of closing any of the doors before Du Bouchage never
occurred to any of the attendants.

Du Bouchage, therefore, passed through all the apartments
until he reached the garden, a true garden of a Roman
prelate, luxurious in its shade, coolness, and perfume, such as,
at the present day, may be found at the Villa Pamphile or
the Palais Borghese.

Henri paused under a group of trees: at this moment the
gate close to the river side rolled on its hinges, and a man
shrouded in a large brown cloak passed through, followed by
a person in a page's costume. The man, perceiving Henri,
who was too absorbed in his reverie to think of him, glided
through the trees, avoiding the observation either of Du
Bouchage or of anyone else.

Henri paid no attention to this mysterious entry; and it was
only as he turned round that he saw the man entering the
apartments.

After he had waited about ten minutes, and as he was
about to enter the house, for the purpose of interrogating one
of the attendants with the view of ascertaining at what hour
precisely his brother would be visible, a servant, who seemed

to be in search of him, observed his approach, and advancing in his direction, begged him to have the goodness to pass into the library, where the cardinal awaited him.

Henri complied with this invitation, but not very readily, as he conjectured that a fresh contest would result from it; he found his brother the cardinal engaged, with the assistance of a valet-de-chambre, in trying on a prelate's costume, a little worldly-looking, perhaps, in its shape and fashion, but elegant and becoming in its style.

"Good-morning, comte," said the cardinal; "what news have you?"

"Excellent news, as far as our family is concerned," said Henri. "Anne, you know, has covered himself with glory in that retreat from Anvers, and is alive."

"Heaven be praised! and are you, too, Henri, safe and sound?"

"Yes, my brother."

"You see," said the cardinal, "that Heaven holds us in its keeping."

"I am so full of gratitude to Heaven, my brother, that I have formed the project of dedicating myself to its service. I am come to talk seriously to you upon this project, which is now well matured, and about which I have already spoken to you."

"Do you still keep to that idea, Du Bouchage?" said the cardinal, allowing a slight exclamation to escape him, which was indicative that Joyeuse would have a struggle to encounter.

"I do."

"But it is impossible, Henri," returned the cardinal; "have you not been told so already?"

"I have not listened to what others have said to me, my brother, because a voice stronger than mine, which speaks within me, prevents me from listening to anything which would turn me aside from my purpose."

"You cannot be so ignorant of the things of this world Henri," said the cardinal, in his most serious tone of voice "to believe that the voice you allude to was really that of Heaven; on the contrary—I assert it positively, too—it i altogether a feeling of a worldly nature which addresses you Heaven has nothing to do in this affair; do not abuse tha holy name, therefore, and, above all, do not confound th voice of Heaven with that of earth."

"I do not confound, my brother; I only meant to say tha something irresistible in its nature hurries me towards retrea and solitude."

"So far, so good, Henri; we are now making use of proper expressions. Well, my dear brother, I will tell you what is to be done. Taking what you say for granted, I am going to render you the happiest of men."

"Thank you, oh! thank you, my brother."

"Listen to me, Henri. You must take money, a couple of attendants, and travel through the whole of Europe, in a manner befitting a son of the house to which we belong. You will see foreign countries; Tartary, Russia, even the Laplanders, those fabulous nations whom the sun never visits; you will become absorbed in your thoughts, until the devouring germ which is at work in you becomes either extinct or satiated; and, after that, you will return to us again."

Henri, who had been seated, now rose, more serious than his brother had been.

"You have not understood me, monseigneur," he said.

"I beg your pardon, Henri; you made use of the words 'retreat and solitude.'"

"Yes, I did so; but by retreat and solitude, I meant a cloister, and not travelling; to travel is to enjoy life still. I wish almost to suffer death, and if I do not suffer it, at least to feel it."

"That is an absurd thought, allow me to say, Henri; for whoever, in point of fact, wishes to isolate himself, is alone everywhere. But the cloister, let it be. Well, then, I understand that you have come to talk to me about this project. I know some very learned Benedictines, and some very clever Augustines, whose houses are cheerful, adorned with flowers, attractive, and agreeable in every respect. Amidst the works of science and art you will pass a delightful year, in excellent society, which is of no slight importance, for one should avoid lowering one's self in this world; and if at the end of the year you persist in your project, well, then, my dear Henri, I will not oppose you any further, and will myself open the door which will peacefully conduct you to everlasting rest."

"Most certainly you still misunderstand me, my brother," replied Du Bouchage, shaking his head, "or I should rather say your generous intelligence will not comprehend me. I do not wish for a cheerful residence or a delightful retreat, but a rigorously strict seclusion, as gloomy as the grave itself. I intend to pronounce my vows, vows which will leave me no other thought or occupation than a grave to dig for myself, or constant prayer."

The cardinal frowned, and rose from his seat.

"Yes," he said, "I did perfectly understand you; and I endeavoured by opposition, without set phrases or discussion, to combat the folly of your resolutions, but you oblige me to do so; and now listen to me."

"Ah!" said Henri, despondently, "do not try to convince me; it is impossible."

"Brother, I will speak to you in the name of Heaven, in the first place; of Heaven, which you offend in saying that this wild resolution is of its inspiration. Heaven does not accept sacrifices hastily made. You are weak, since you allow yourself to be conquered by a first disappointment; how can Heaven be pleased to accept a victim as unworthy as that you offer?"

Henri started at his brother's remark.

"Oh! I shall no longer spare you. Henri, you, who never consider any of us," returned the cardinal; "you, who forget the grief which you will cause our elder brother, and will cause me, too——"

"Forgive me," interrupted Henri, whose cheeks were dyed with crimson, "forgive me, monseigneur; but is the service of Heaven then so gloomy and so dishonourable a career that all the members of a family are to be thrown into distress by it? You, for instance, my brother, whose portrait I observe suspended in this room, with all this gold, and diamonds, and purple around you, are you not both the delight and honour of our house, although you have chosen the service of Heaven, as my eldest brother has chosen that of the kings of the earth?"

"Boy, boy!" exclaimed the cardinal impatiently, "you will make me believe your brain is turned. What! will you venture to compare my residence to a cloister? my hundred attendants, my outriders, the gentlemen of my suite, and my guards, to a cell and a broom, which are the only arms and the sole wealth of a cloister? Are you mad? Did you not just now say that you repudiate these superfluities—these pictures, precious vases, pomp and distinction, which I cannot do without? Have you, as I have, the desire and hope of placing on your brow the tiara of St. Peter? That, indeed, is a career, Henri; one presses onwards towards it, struggles for it, lives in it. But as for you! it is the miner's pick, the trappist's spade, the gravedigger's tomb, that you desire; utter abandonment of life, of pleasure, of hope; and all that—I blush with shame for you, a man—all that, I say, because you love a woman who loves you not. You do foul injustice to your race, Henri, most truly."

"Brother!" exclaimed the young man, pale as death, while his eyes blazed with kindling fire, "would you sooner have me blow out my brains, or plunge in my heart the sword have the honour to wear by my side? Pardieu, monseigneur, if you, who are cardinal and prince besides, will give me absolution for so mortal a sin, the affair will be so quickly done that you shall have no time to complete your odious and unworthy thought that I am capable of dishonouring my race, which, Heaven be praised, a Joyeuse will never do."

"Come, come, Henri," said the cardinal, drawing his brother towards him, and pressing him in his arms; "come, forget what has passed, and think of those who love you. I have personal motives for entreating you. Listen to me; a rare occurrence in this world is ours, we are all happy, some from feelings of gratified ambition, the others from blessings of every kind with which Heaven has bedecked our existence. Do not, I implore you, Henri, cast the mortal poison of the retreat you speak of upon our family happiness; think how our father would be grieved at it; think, too, how all of us would bear on our countenances the dark reflection of the bitter mortification you are about to inflict upon us. I beseech you, Henri, to allow yourself to be persuaded; the cloister will not befit you. I do not say that you will die there, for, misguided man, your answer will be a smile, which alas, would be only too intelligible for me. No, believe me that the cloister is more fatal to you than the tomb. The tomb annihilates but life itself, the cloister annihilates intelligence; the cloister bows the head, instead of raising it to Heaven; the cold, humid atmosphere of the vaults passes by degrees into the blood, and penetrates the very marrow of the bones, changing the cloistered recluse into another granite statue in the convent. My brother, my dear brother, take heed; our time here below is but brief, youth visits us but once in our lives. The bright years of our earlier days will pass away, too, for you are under the influence of a deep-seated grief, but at thirty years of age you will have become a man, the vigour of maturity will have then arrived; it will hurry away with it all that remains of your worn-out sorrow, and then you will wish to live over again; but it will be too late. Then, too, you will have grown melancholy in thought, plain in person, suffering in feeling; passion will have been extinguished in your heart, the bright light of your eye will have become quenched. They whose society you seek will flee you as a whited sepulchre, whose darksome depths repel every glance. Henri, I speak as a friend, seriously, wisely; listen to me."

The young man remained unmoved and silent. The cardinal hoped that he had touched his feelings, and had shaken his resolution.

"Try some other resource, Henri. Carry this poisoned shaft, which rankles in your bosom, about with you wherever you may go, in the turmoil of life; cherish its companionship at our fêtes and banquets; imitate the wounded deer, which flees through the thickets and brakes and forests, in its efforts to draw out from its body the arrow which is rankling in the wound; sometimes the arrow falls."

"For pity's sake," said Henri, "do not persist any more; what I solicit is not the caprice of a moment, or the reflection of an hour, but is the result of a laborious and painful determination. In Heaven's name, therefore, my brother, I adjure you to accord me the favour I solicit."

"And what is the favour you ask?"

"A dispensation, monseigneur."

"For what purpose?"

"To shorten my noviciate."

"Ah! I knew it, Du Bouchage. You are worldly-minded even in your rigorousness, my poor boy. Oh! I know very well what reason you are going to give me. Yes, you are, indeed, a man of the world; you resemble those young men who offer themselves as volunteers, and are eagerly desirous for fire, balls, and blows, but care not for working in the trenches, or for sweeping out the tents. There is some resource left ye, Henri, so much the better, so much the better."

"Give me the dispensation I ask; I entreat you on my knees."

"I promise it to you; I will write to Rome for it. It will be a month before the answer arrives; but, in exchange, promise me one thing."

"Name it."

"That you will not, during this month's postponement, reject any pleasure or amusement which may be offered to you; and if, in a month hence, you still entertain the same projects, Henri, I will give you this dispensation with my own hand. Are you satisfied now, and have you nothing further to ask me?"

"No, I thank you; but a month is a long time, and the delay will kill me."

"In the meantime, and in order to change your thoughts, will you object to breakfast with me? I have some agreeable companions this morning."

And the prelate smiled in a manner which the most worldly-disposed favourites of Henri III. would have envied.

"Brother," said Du Bouchage, resisting.

"I will not accept any excuse; you have no one but myself

here, since you have just arrived from Flanders, and your own house cannot be in order just yet."

With these words the cardinal rose, and drawing aside a *portière*, which hung before a large cabinet sumptuously furnished, he said:

"Come, comtesse, let us persuade Monsieur le Comte du Bouchage to stay with us."

At the very moment, however, when the count drew aside the *portière*, Henri had observed, half reclining upon the cushions, the page who had with the gentleman entered the gate adjoining the banks of the river, and in this page, before even the prelate had announced her sex, he had recognised a woman.

An indefinable sensation, like a sudden terror, or an overwhelming feeling of dread, seized him, and while the worldly cardinal advanced to take the beautiful page by the hand, Henri du Bouchage darted from the apartment, and so quickly, too, that when François returned with the lady, smiling with the hope of winning a heart back again to the world, the room was perfectly empty.

François frowned; then, seating himself before a table covered with papers and letters, he hurriedly wrote a few lines.

"May I trouble you to ring, dear countess," he said, "since you have your hand near the bell."

And as the page obeyed, a valet-de-chambre in the confidence of the cardinal appeared.

"Let a courier start on horseback, without a moment's loss of time," said François, "and take this letter to Monsieur le Grand-amiral à Château-Thierry."

## CHAPTER LXXXII

### NEWS FROM AURILLY

On the following day the king was working at the Louvre with the superintendent of finances, when an attendant entered to inform his majesty that Monsieur de Joyeuse, the eldest son of that family, had just arrived, and was waiting for him in the large audience chamber, having come from Château-Thierry, with a message from Monsieur le Duc d'Anjou.

The king precipitately left the business which occupied him, and ran to meet a friend whom he regarded with so much affection.

A large number of officers and courtiers crowded the cabinet; the queen-mother had arrived that evening, escorted by her maids of honour, and these light-hearted girls were like suns, always attended by their satellites.

The king gave Joyeuse his hand to kiss, and glanced with a satisfied expression around the assembly.

In the angle of the entrance door, in his usual place, stood Henri du Bouchage, rigorously discharging his service and the duties which were imposed on him.

The king thanked him, and saluted him with a friendly recognition, to which Henri replied by a profound reverence.

This good intelligence which prevailed between them made Joyeuse turn his head and smilingly look at his brother, without, however, saluting him in too marked a manner, from the fear of violating etiquette.

"Sire," said Joyeuse, "I am sent to your majesty by Monsieur le Duc d'Anjou, recently returned from the expedition to Flanders."

"Is my brother well, monsieur l'amiral?" inquired the king.

"As well, sire, as the state of his mind will permit; however, I will not conceal from your majesty that he appears to be suffering greatly."

"He must need something to change the current of his thoughts after his misfortune," said the king, delighted at the opportunity of proclaiming the check which his brother had met with, while appearing to pity him.

"I believe he does, sire."

"We have been informed that the disaster has been most severe."

"Sire——"

"But that, thanks to you, a great portion of the army has been saved; thanks, monsieur l'amiral, thanks. Does poor Monsieur d'Anjou wish to see us?"

"Most anxiously so, sire."

"In that case we will see him. Are not you of that opinion, madame?" said Henri, turning towards Catherine, whose heart was wrung with feelings, the expression of which her face determinedly concealed.

"Sir," she replied, "I should have gone alone to meet my son; but since your majesty condescends to join with me in this mark of kind consideration, the journey will be a part of pleasure for me."

"You will accompany us, messieurs," said the king to the courtiers; "we shall set off to-morrow, and I shall sleep Meaux."

"Shall I at once announce this excellent news to monseigneur, sire?"

"Not so; what! leave me so soon, monsieur l'amiral? not so, indeed. I can well understand that a Joyeuse must be loved and sought after by my brother, but we have two of the same family, thank Heaven. Du Bouchage, you will start for Château-Thierry, if you please."

"Sire," said Henri, "may I be permitted, after having announced your majesty's arrival to Monseigneur le Duc d'Anjou, to return to Paris?"

"You may do as you please, Du Bouchage," said the king.

Henri bowed and advanced towards the door. Fortunately Joyeuse was watching him narrowly.

"Will you allow me to say one word to my brother?" he inquired.

"Do so; but what is it?" said the king in an undertone.

"The fact is, that he wishes to use the utmost speed to execute the commission, and to return again immediately, which happens to interfere with my projects, sire, and with those of the cardinal."

"Away with you, then, and rate this love-sick swain most roundly."

Anne hurried after his brother, and overtook him in the ante-chambers.

"Well!" said Joyeuse; "you are setting off very eagerly, Henri."

"Of course, my brother!"

"Because you wish to return here soon again?"

"That is quite true."

"You do not intend, then, to stay any time at Château-Thierry?"

"As little as possible."

"Why so?"

"Where others are amusing themselves is not my place."

"On the contrary, Henri, it is precisely because Monseigneur le Duc d'Anjou is about to give some fêtes that you should remain at Château-Thierry."

"It is impossible."

"Because of your wish for retirement, and of the austere projects you have in view?"

"Yes."

"You have been to the king to solicit a dispensation?"

"Who told you so?"

"I know it to be the case."

"It is true, then, for I have been to him."

"You will not obtain it."

"Why so, my brother?"

"Because the king has no interest in depriving himself of such a devoted servant as you are."

"My brother, the cardinal, will therefore do what his majesty will be disinclined to do."

"And all that for a woman?"

"Anne, I entreat you, do not persist any further."

"Ah! do not fear that I shall begin over again; but, once for all, let us to the point. You set off for Château-Thierry; well, instead of returning as hurriedly as you seem disposed to do, I wish you to wait for me in my apartments there; it is a long time since we have lived together. I particularly wish to be with you again, you understand."

"You are going to Château-Thierry to amuse yourself, Anne, and if I were to remain there I should poison all your pleasures."

"Oh! far from that, I do not care for them; I am of a happy temperament, and quite fitted to drive away all your fits of melancholy."

"Brother——"

"Permit me, comte," said the admiral, with an imperious air of command, "I am the representative of our father here, and I enjoin you to wait for me at Château-Thierry. You will find out my apartment, which will be your own also; it is on the ground floor, looking out on the park."

"If you command me to do so, my brother," said Henri, with a resigned air.

"Call it by what name you please, comte, desire or command, but await my arrival."

"I will obey you, my brother."

"And I am persuaded that you will not be angry with me for it," added Joyeuse, pressing the young man in his arm.

The latter withdrew from the fraternal embrace, somewhat ungraciously perhaps, ordered his horses, and immediately set off for Château-Thierry. He hurried thither with the anger of a vexed and disappointed man; that is to say, he pressed his horses to the top of their speed.

The same evening, he was slowly ascending, before nightfall, the hill on which Château-Thierry is situated, with the river Marne flowing at its feet.

At his name, the doors of the château flew open before him, but, as far as an audience was concerned, he was more than an hour before he could obtain it.

The prince, some told him, was in his apartments; other said he was asleep; he was practising music, the valet-de chambre supposed. No one, however, among the attendants could give a positive reply.

Henri persisted, in order that he might no longer have to think of his service on the king, so that he might abandon himself from that moment to his melancholy thoughts unrestrained.

Won over by his perseverance, it being well-known, too, that he and his brother were on the most intimate terms with the duke, Henri was ushered into one of the salons on the first floor, where the prince at last consented to receive him.

Half-an-hour passed away, and the shades of evening insensibly closed in.

The heavy and measured footsteps of the Duc d'Anjou resounded in the gallery, and Henri, on recognising them, prepared to discharge his mission with the accustomed formal ceremonies. But the prince, who seemed very much pressed, quickly dispensed with these formalities on the part of his ambassador, by taking him by the hand and embracing him.

" Good day, comte," he said; " why should they have given you the trouble to come and see a poor defeated general?"

" The king has sent me, monseigneur, to inform you that he is exceedingly desirous of seeing your highness, his majesty will himself come and pay a visit to Château-Thierry, to-morrow at the latest."

" The king will be here to-morrow!" exclaimed François, with a gesture of impatience, but recovering himself immediately afterwards.

" To-morrow, to-morrow," he resumed; " why, the truth is that nothing will be in readiness, either here or in the town, to receive his majesty."

Henri bowed, as one whose duty it had been to transmit an order, but whose province it was not to comment upon it.

" The extreme haste which their majesties have to see your royal highness has not allowed them to think of the embarrassment they may be the means of occasioning."

" Well, well," said the prince, hurriedly, " it is for me to make the best use of the time I have at my disposal. I leave you, therefore, Henri; thanks for the alacrity you have shown, for you have travelled fast, I perceive. Go and take some rest."

" Your highness has no other orders to communicate to me?" Henri inquired respectfully.

" None. Go and lie down. You shall dine in your own apartment. I hold no reception this evening; I am suffering and ill at ease; I have lost my appetite, and cannot sleep, which makes my life a sad, dreary one, and which, you understand, I do not choose to inflict upon anyone else. By-the-by, you have heard the news?"

"No, monseigneur; what news?"

"Aurilly has been eaten up by the wolves—"

"Aurilly!" exclaimed Henri, with surprise.

"Yes—yes—devoted! It is singular how everyone who comes near me dies a violent death. Good night, count; may you sleep well!"

And the prince hurried away rapidly.


## CHAPTER LXXXIII

### DOUBT

Henri descended the staircase, and as he passed through the ante-chambers, observed many officers of his acquaintance, who ran forward to meet him, and, with many marks of friendship, offered to show him the way to his brother's apartments, which were situated at one of the angles of the château. It was the library that the duke had given Joyeuse to reside in during his residence at Château-Thierry.

Two salons, furnished in the style of François the First, communicated with each other, and terminated in the library, the latter apartment looking out on the gardens.

His bed had been put up in the library. Joyeuse was of an indolent, yet of a cultivated turn of mind. If he stretched out his arm he laid his hand on science; if he opened the windows he could enjoy the beauties of nature. Finer and superior organisations require more satisfying enjoyments; and the morning breeze, the songs of birds, or the perfumes of flowers, added fresh delight to the triplets of Clement Marot, or to the odes of Rousard.

Henri determined to leave everything as it was, not because he was influenced by the poetic sybaritism of his brother, but, on the contrary, from indifference, and because it mattered little to him whether he was there or elsewhere.

But as the count, in whatever frame of mind he might be, had been brought up never to neglect his duty or respect towards the king or the prince of the royal family of France, he inquired particularly in what part of the château the prince had resided since his return.

By mere accident, in this respect, Henri met with an excellent cicerone in the person of the young ensign, who, by some act of indiscretion or another, had, in the little village of Flanders where we represented the personages in this tale as having halted for a moment, communicated the count's secret to the prince. This ensign had not quitted the prince's side since his return, and could inform Henri very accurately on the subject.

On his arrival at Château-Thierry, the prince had at first entered upon a course of reckless dissipation. At that time he occupied the state apartments of the château, had receptions morning and evening, and was engaged during the day stag-hunting in the forest; but since the intelligence of Aurilly's death, which had reached the prince without its being known from what source, the prince had retired to a pavilion situated in the middle of the park. This pavilion, which was an almost inaccessible retreat except to the intimate associates of the prince, was hidden from view by the dense foliage of the surrounding trees, and could hardly be perceived above their lofty summits, or through the thick foliage of the hedges.

It was to this pavilion that the prince had retired during the last few days. Those who did not know him well said that it was Aurilly's death which had made him betake himself to this solitude; while those who were well acquainted with his character pretended that he was carrying out in this pavilion some base or infamous plot, which some day or another would be revealed to light.

A circumstance which rendered either of these suppositions much more probable was, that the prince seemed greatly annoyed whenever a matter of business or a visit summoned him to the château; and so decidedly was this the case, that no sooner had the visit been received, or the matter of business been despatched, than he returned to his solitude, where he was waited upon by the two old valets-de-chambre who had been present at his birth.

"Since this is the case," observed Henri, "the fêtes will not be very gay if the prince continue in this humour."

"Certainly," replied the ensign, "for everyone will know how to sympathise with the prince's grief, whose pride as well as whose affections have been so smitten."

Henri continued his interrogatories without intending it, and took a strange interest in doing so. The circumstance of Aurilly's death, whom he had known at the court, and whom he had again met in Flanders; the kind of indifference with which the prince had announced the loss he had met with; the strict seclusion in which it was said the prince had lived since his death—all this seemed to him, without his being able to assign a reason for his belief, as part of that mysterious and darkened web wherein, for some time past, the events of his life had been woven.

"And," inquired he of the ensign, "it is not known, you say, how the prince became acquainted with the news of the death of Aurilly?"

"No."

"But surely," he insisted, "people must talk about it?"

"Oh! of course," said the ensign; "true or false, you know, people always will talk."

"Well, then, tell me what it is."

"It is said that the prince was hunting under the willows close beside the river, and that he had wandered away from the others who were hunting also, for everything he does is by fits and starts, and he becomes as excited in the field as at play, or under fire, or under the influence of grief, when suddenly he was seen returning with a face scared and as pale as death.

"The courtiers questioned him, thinking that it was nothing more than a mere incident of the hunting-field.

"He held two rouleaux of gold in his hand.

"'Can you understand this, messieurs?' he said, in a hard dry voice; 'Aurilly is dead; Aurilly has been eaten by the wolves.'

"Everyone immediately exclaimed.

"'Nay, indeed,' said the prince; 'may the foul fiend take me if it be not so; the poor lute-player had always been a far better musician than a horseman. It seems that his horse ran away with him, and that he fell into a pit, where he was killed; the next day a couple of travellers who were passing close to the pit discovered his body half eaten by the wolves; and a proof that the affair actually did happen, as I have related it, and that robbers have nothing whatever to do with the whole matter is, that here are two rouleaux of gold which he had about him, and which have been faithfully restored.'

"However, as no one had been seen to bring these two rouleaux of gold back," continued the ensign, "it is supposed that they had been handed to the prince by the two travellers who, having met and recognised his highness on the banks of the river, had announced the intelligence of Aurilly's death."

"It is very strange," murmured Henri.

"And what is more strange still," continued the ensign "is that it is said—can it be true, or is it merely an invention?—it is said, I repeat, that the prince was seen to open the little gate of the park close to the chestnut trees, and that something like two shadows passed through that same gate. The prince then introduced two persons into the park —probably the two travellers; it is since that occasion tha the prince has retired into his pavilion, and we have only been able to see him by stealth."

"And has no one seen these two travellers?" asked Henri.

"As I was proceeding to ask the prince the password for the night, for the sentinels on duty at the château, I met a man who did not seem to me to belong to his highness's household, but I was unable to observe his face, the man having turned aside as soon as he perceived me, and having let down the hood of his cloak over his eyes."

"The hood of his cloak, do you say?"

"Yes; the man looked like a Flemish peasant, and reminded me, I hardly know why, of the person by whom you were accompanied when we met out yonder."

Henri started; the observation seemed to him in some way connected with the profound and absorbing interest with which the story inspired him; to him, too, who had seen Diana and her companion confided to Aurilly, the idea occurred that the two travellers who had announced to the prince the death of the unfortunate lute-player were acquaintances of his own.

Henri looked attentively at the ensign.

"And when you fancied you recognised this man, what was the idea that occurred to you, monsieur?" he inquired.

"I will tell you what my impression was," replied the ensign; "however, I will not pretend to assert anything positively; the prince has not, in all probability, abandoned all idea with regard to Flanders; he therefore maintains spies in his employ. The man with the woollen overcoat is a spy, who, on his way here, may possibly have learned the accident which had happened to the musician, and may thus have been the bearer of two pieces of intelligence at the same time."

"That is not improbable," said Henri, thoughtfully; "but what was this man doing when you saw him?"

"He was walking beside the hedge which borders the parterre—you can see the hedge from your windows—and was making towards the conservatories."

"You say, then, that the two travellers, for I believe you stated there were two——"

"Others say that two persons were seen to enter, but I only saw one, the man in the overcoat."

"In that case, then, you have reason to believe that the man in the overcoat, as you describe him, is living in the conservatories."

"It is not unlikely."

"And have these conservatories a means of exit?"

I

"Yes, count, towards the town."

Henri remained silent for some time; his heart was throbbing most violently, for these details, which were apparently matters of indifference to him, who seemed throughout the whole of this mystery as if he were gifted with the power of prevision, were, in reality, full of the deepest interest for him.

Night had in the meantime closed in, and the two young men were conversing together without any light in Joyeuse's apartment.

Fatigued by his journey, oppressed by the strange events which had just been related to him, unable to struggle against the emotions which they had aroused in his breast, the count had thrown himself on his brother's bed, and mechanically directed his gaze towards the deep blue heavens above him, which seemed set as with diamonds.

The young ensign was seated on the ledge of the window, and voluntarily abandoned himself to that listlessness of thought, to that poetic reverie of youth, to that absorbing languor of feeling, which the balmy freshness of evening inspires.

A deep silence reigned throughout the park and the town; the gates were closed, the lights were kindled by degrees, the dogs in the distance were barking in their kennels at the servants, on whom devolved the duty of shutting up the stables in the evening.

Suddenly the ensign rose to his feet, made a sign of attention with his head, leaned out of the window, and then calling in a quick, low tone to the count, who was reclining on the bed, said:

"Come, come!"

"What is the matter?" Henri inquired, arousing himself by a strong effort from his reverie.

"The man! the man!"

"What man?"

"The man in the overcoat, the spy!"

"Oh!" exclaimed Henri, springing from the bed to the window, and leaning on the ensign.

"Stay," continued the ensign; "do you see him yonder? He is creeping along the hedge; wait a moment, he will show himself again.    Now look towards that spot which is illuminated by the moon's rays, there he is; there he is."

"Yes."

"Do you not think he is a sinister-looking fellow?"

"Sinister is the very word," replied Du Bouchage, in gloomy voice.

"Do you believe he is a spy?"

"I believe nothing, and yet I believe everything."

"See, he is going from the prince's pavilion to the conservatories."

"The prince's pavilion is in that direction, then?" inquired Du Bouchage, indicating with his finger the direction from which the stranger appeared to be proceeding.

"Do you see that light whose rays are trembling through the leaves of the trees."

"Well?"

"That is the dining-room."

"Ah!" exclaimed Henri, "see, he makes his appearance again."

"Yes, he is no doubt going to the conservatories to join his companion? Did you hear that?"

"What?"

"The sound of a key turning in the lock."

"It is singular," said Du Bouchage; "there is nothing unusual in all this, and yet——"

"And yet you are trembling, you were going to say?"

"Yes," said the count; "but what is that?"

The sound of a bell was heard.

"It is the signal for the supper of the prince's household; are you going to join us at supper, count?"

"No, I thank you, I do not require anything; and, if I should feel hungry, I will call for what I may need."

"Do not wait for that, monsieur; but come and amuse yourself in our society."

"Nay, nay, it is impossible."

"Why so?"

"His royal highness almost directed me to have what I should need served to me in my own apartment; but do not let me delay you."

"Thank you, count, good evening; do not lose sight of our phantom."

"Oh! rely upon me for that; unless," added Henri, who feared he might have said too much, "unless, indeed, I should be overtaken by sleep, which seems more than probable, and far more healthy occupation than that of watching shadows and spies."

"Certainly," said the ensign, laughingly, as he took leave of Henri du Bouchage.

Hardly had he quitted the library than Henri darted into the garden.

"Oh!" he murmured, "it is Remy; it is Remy! I should know him again in the darkness of hell itself."

And the young man, as he felt his knees tremble beneath him, buried his burning forehead in his cold damp hands.

"Great Heaven!" he cried, "is not this rather a phantasy of my poor fevered brain, and is it not written that in my slumbering and in my waking moments, day and night, I should ever see those two figures who have made so deep and dark a furrow in my life?"

"Why," he continued, like a man aware of the need that exists of convincing himself, "why, indeed, should Remy be here in this château, while the Duc d'Anjou is here? What is his motive in coming here? What can the Duc d'Anjou possibly have to do with Remy? And why should he have quitted Diana—he, who is her eternal companion? No; it is not he."

Then, again, a moment afterwards, a conviction, thorough, profound, almost instinctive in its nature, seemed to overcome all the doubts he had entertained.

"It is he! it is he!" he murmured, in utter despair, and leaning against the wall to save himself from falling.

As he finished giving utterance to this overpowering, overwhelming thought, which seemed to crush all others in his mind, the sharp sound of the lock was again heard, and, although the sound was almost imperceptible, his over-excited senses detected it instantly.    An indefinable shudder ran through the young man's whole frame; again he listened with eager attention.  So profound a silence reigned around him on every side that he could hear the throbbings of his own heart.  A few minutes passed away without anything he expected making its appearance.  In default of his eyes, however, his ears told him that someone was approaching, for he heard the sound of the gravel under the advancing footsteps.  Suddenly the straight black line of the hedge seemed broken; he imagined he saw upon this dark background a group still darker moving along.

"It is he returning again," murmured Henri.  "Is he alone, or is someone with him?"

The objects advanced from the side where the silver light of the moon had illuminated a space of open ground.  It was at the very moment when, advancing in the opposite direction, the man in the overcoat crossed this open space that Henri fancied he recognised Remy.  This time Henri observed two shadows very distinctly; it was impossible he could be mistaken.  A death-like chill struck to his heart and seemed to have turned it to marble.

The two shadows walked quickly along, although with a firm step; the former was dressed in a woollen overcoat, an at the appearance of the second apparition, as at that of the first, the count fancied he recognised Remy.

The second, who was completely enveloped in a large man's cloak, seemed to defy every attempt at recognition.

And yet, beneath that cloak, Henri fancied he could detect what no human eye could have possibly seen.

He could not control a deep bitter groan of despair, and no sooner had the two mysterious personages disappeared behind the hedge than the young man darted after them, and stealthily glided from one group of trees to another, in the wake of those whom he was so anxious to discover.

"Oh!" he murmured, as he stole along, "do I not indeed deceive myself? Oh! Heaven, can it really be possible?"

## CHAPTER LXXXIV

### CERTAINTY

Henri glided along the hedge, on the side which was thrown into deep shade, taking care to make no noise either on the gravel or against the trees.

Obliged to walk carefully, and while walking to watch carefully over every movement he made, he could not perceive anything. And yet, by his style, his dress, his walk, he still fancied he recognised Remy in the man who wore the overcoat.

Mere conjectures, more terrifying for him than realities, arose in his mind with regard to this man's companion.

The road which they were following, and which was bounded by a row of elms, terminated in a high hawthorn hedge, which separated from the rest of the park the pavilion of the Duc d'Anjou, and enveloped it as with a curtain of verdure, in the midst of which, as has already been observed, it entirely disappeared in a remote corner of the grounds of the château. There were several beautiful sheets of water, dark underwood, through which winding paths had been cut, and venerable trees, over the summits of which the moon was shedding its streams of silver light, whilst underneath the gloom was thick, dark, and impenetrable.

As he approached this hedge, Henri felt that his heart was on the point of failing him. In fact, to transgress so boldly the prince's orders, and to abandon himself to a course of conduct as indiscreet as it was rash, was the act, not of a royal and honourable man, but of a mean and cowardly spy, or of a jealous man driven to extremities. But as, while opening the gate, which separated the greater from the

smaller park, the man he followed moved in such a way that
his features were revealed, and as he perceived that these
features were indeed those of Remy, the count's scruples
vanished, and he resolutely advanced at all hazards. Henri
found the gate again closed; he leaped over the railings, and
then continued his pursuit of the prince's two strange visitors,
who still seemed to be hurrying onwards. Another cause of
terror was soon added; for the duke, on hearing the footsteps of Remy and his companion upon the gravel walk,
made his appearance from the pavilion. Henri threw himself
behind the largest of the trees, and waited.

He could not see anything, except that he observed that
Remy made a very low salutation, that Remy's companion
courtesied like a woman, instead of bowing like a man, and
that the duke, seemingly transported with delight, offered his
arm to the latter, in the same way as he would have done to
a woman. Then all three advanced towards the pavilion,
disappeared under the vestibule, and the door closed behind
them.

"This must end," said Henri, "and I must seek a more
convenient place, where I can see everything that may pass
without being seen."

He decided in favour of a clump of trees situated between
the pavilion and the wall, from the centre of which the
waters of a fountain gushed forth, thus forming an impenetrable place of concealment; for it was not likely that in the
night-time, with the freshness and humidity which would
naturally be found near this fountain, the prince would seek
the vicinity of the water and the thickets. Hidden behind the
statue with which the fountain was ornamented, and standing
at his full height behind the pedestal, Henri was enabled to
see what was taking place in the pavilion, the principal
window of which was quite open before him.

As no one could, or rather, as no one would, venture to
penetrate so far, no precautions had been taken.

A table was laid, sumptuously served with the richest
viands, and with rare wines in bottles of costly Venetian glass.

Two seats only at this table seemed to be awaiting two
guests.

The duke approached one of the chairs; then, leaving the
arm of Remy's companion, and pointing to the other seat,
he seemed to request that the cloak might be thrown aside,
as, although it might be very serviceable for an evening stroll,
it became very inconvenient when the object of the stroll
was attained, and when that object was a supper.

Thereupon the individual to whom the invitation had been

addressed threw the cloak upon a chair, and the dazzling blaze of the flambeaux lighted up, without a shadow on their loveliness, the pale and majestically-beautiful features of a woman whom the terrified eyes of Henri immediately recognised. It was the lady of the mysterious house in the Rue des Augustins, the wanderer in Flanders; in one word, it was that Diana whose gaze was as mortal as the thrust of a dagger. On this occasion she wore the apparel of her own sex, and was richly dressed in brocaded silk; diamonds blazed on her neck, in her hair, and on her wrists, and thereby made the extreme pallor of her face more remarkable than ever, and in the light which shone from her eyes, it almost seemed as if the duke had, by the employment of some magical means, evoked the ghost of this woman, rather than the woman herself. Had it not been for the support afforded by the statue round which he had thrown his arms, colder even than the marble itself, Henri would have fallen backwards headlong into the basin of the fountain.

The duke seemed intoxicated with delight; he fixed his passionate gaze upon this beautiful creature, who had seated herself opposite to him, and who hardly touched the dishes which had been placed before her. From time to time François leaned across the table to kiss one of the hands of his silent guest, who, as pale as death, seemed as insensible to his kisses as if her hand had been sculptured in alabaster, which, for transparency and perfect whiteness, it so much resembled. From time to time Henri started, raised his hand to his forehead, and with it wiped away the death-like sweat which rose on it, and asked himself: " Is she alive, or dead?"

The duke tried his utmost efforts and displayed all his powers of eloquence to unbend the rigid beauty of her face.

Remy, the only attendant, for the duke had sent everyone away, waited on them both, and, occasionally, lightly touching his mistress with his elbow as he passed behind her chair, seemed to revive her by the contact, and to recall her to life, or rather to the position in which she was placed.

Thereupon, a bright flush spread over her whole face, her eyes sparkled, she smiled as if some magician had touched a spring unknown to this automaton-like figure, seemingly endowed with intelligence, and the mechanism of which had drawn the lightning glance from her eyes, the glowing flush on her cheek, and the sparkling smile to her lips. The moment after, she again subsided into her calm and statue-like stillness. The prince, however, approached her, and by the passionate tone of his conversation, seemed as if he had succeeded in warming into animation his new conquest.

Thereupon, Diana, who occasionally glanced at the face of a magnificent clock suspended over the prince's head, against the opposite side of the wall to where she was seated, seemed to make an effort over herself, and with her lips bedecked wtih smiles took a more active part in the conversation.

Henri, concealed in his leafy covert, wrung his hands in despair, and cursed the whole creation in the utter wretchedness of his sore distress. It seemed to him monstrous, almost iniquitous, that this woman, so pure and rigidly inflexible, should yield herself so unresistingly to the prince, because he was a prince, and abandon herself to love because it was offered within the precincts of a palace. His horror at Remy was so extreme, that he could have slain him without remorse, in order to see whether so great a monster had the blood and heart of a man in him. In such paroxysms of rage and contempt did Henri pass the time during the supper, which to the Duc d'Anjou was so full of rapture.

Diana sang. The prince, inflamed by wine, and by his passionate discourse, rose from the table for the purpose of embracing Diana. Every drop of blood seemed to curdle in Henri's veins. He put his hand to his side to see if his sword were there, and then thrust it into his breast in search of a dagger. Diana, with a strange smile, which most assuredly had never, until that moment, had its counterpart on any face, stopped the duke as he was approaching her.

"Will you allow me, monseigneur," she said, "before I rise from the table, to share with your royal highness one of those tempting-looking peaches?"

And with these words she stretched out her hand towards a basket of gold filagree work, in which twenty peaches were tastefully arranged, and took one.

Then, taking from her girdle a beautiful little dagger, with a silver blade and a handle of malachite, she divided the peach into two portions, and offered one of them to the prince, who seized it and carried it eagerly to his lips, as though he would thus have kissed Diana's.

This impassioned action produced so deep an impression on himself, that a cloud seemed to obscure his sight at the very moment he bit into the fruit. Diana looked at him with her clear steady gaze, and her fixed immovable smile.

Remy, leaning his back against a pillar of carved wood, also looked on with a gloomy expression of countenance.

The prince passed one of his hands across his forehead wiped away the perspiration which had gathered there, and swallowed the piece that he had bitten.

This perspiration was most probably the symptom of a sudden indisposition; for while Diana ate the other half of the peach, the prince let fall on his plate what remained of the portion he had taken, and with difficulty rising from his seat, seemed to invite his beautiful companion to accompany him into the garden in order to enjoy the cool night air.

Diana rose, and without pronouncing a single word, took the duke's arm, which he offered her.

Remy gazed after them, particularly after the prince, whom the air seemed completely to revive.

As she walked along, Diana wiped the small blade of her knife on a handkerchief embroidered with gold, and restored it to its shagreen sheath.

In this manner they approached the clump of trees where Henri was concealed.

The prince, with a passionate gesture, pressed his companion's arm against his heart.

"I feel better," he said, "and yet I hardly know what heavy weight seems to press down on my brain; I love too deeply, madame, I perceive."

Diana plucked several sprigs of jasmine and of clematis, and two beautiful roses which bordered the whole of one side of the pedestal of the statue behind which Henri was shrinking terrified.

"What are you doing, madame?" inquired the prince.

"I have always understood, monseigneur," she said, "that the perfume of flowers was the best remedy for attacks of giddiness; I am gathering a bouquet with the hope that this bouquet, if presented by me, will have the magical influence which I wish it to possess."

But, while she was arranging the flowers, she let a rose fall from her hand, which the prince eagerly hastened to pick up.

The movement that François made was rapid, but not so rapid, however, but that it gave Diana sufficient time to pour upon the other rose a few drops of a liquid contained in a small gold bottle which she drew from her bosom.

She then took from his hand the rose which the prince had picked up, and placing it in her girdle, said:

"That one is for me, let us change."

And in exchange for the rose which she received from the prince's hand, she held out the bouquet to him.

The prince seized it eagerly, inhaled its perfume with delight, and passed his arm around Diana's waist. But this latter action, in all probability, completely overwhelmed the already troubled senses of the prince, for his knees trembled under him, and he was obliged to seat himself on a bank of green turf, beside which he happened to be standing.

Henri did not lose sight of these two persons, and yet he had a look for Remy also, who in the pavilion awaited the termination of this scene, or rather seemed to devour every minute incident of it.

When he saw the prince totter, he advanced towards the threshold of the pavilion. Diana, on her side, perceiving François stagger, sat herself down beside him on the bank.

The giddiness from which François suffered continued on this occasion longer than on the former; the prince's head was resting on his chest. He seemed to have lost all connection in his ideas, and almost the perception of his own existence; and yet the convulsive movement of his fingers on Diana's hand seemed to indicate that he was instinctively pursuing his wild dream of love. At last he slowly raised his head, and his lips being almost on a level with Diana's face, he made an effort to touch those of his lovely guest, but as if unobservant of the movement, she rose from her seat.

"You are suffering, monseigneur," she said; "it would be better if we were to go in."

"Oh! yes, let us go in," exclaimed the prince in a transport of joy.

And he arose, staggering, to his feet; then, instead of Diana leaning on his arm, it was he who leaned on Diana's arm; and thanks to this support, walking with less difficulty, he seemed to forget fever and giddiness too, for suddenly drawing himself up, he, in an unexpected manner, pressed his lips on her neck. She started as if, instead of a kiss, she had received the impression of a red hot iron.

"Remy!" she exclaimed, "a flambeau, a flambeau!"

Remy immediately returned to the salle-à-manger, and lighted, by the candle on the table, a flambeau which he took from a small round table, and then, hurrying to the entrance to the pavilion, and holding the torch in his hand, he cried out:

"Here is one, madame."

"Where is your highness going to?" inquired Diana, seizing hold of the flambeau and turning her head aside.

"Oh! we will return to my own room, and you will lead me, I venture to hope, madame?" replied the prince, in a frenzy of passion.

"Willingly, monseigneur," replied Diana, and she raised the torch in the air, and walked before the prince.

Remy opened, at the end of the pavilion, a window through which the fresh air rushed inwards, in such a manner that the flame and smoke of the flambeau, which Diana held, were carried back towards François' face, which happened to be in the very current of the air. The two lovers, as Henri considered them to be, proceeded in this manner, first crossing a gallery to the duke's room, and disappeared behind the fleur de-lizéd hangings, which served the purpose of a portière.

Henri had observed everything that had passed with increasing fury, and yet this fury was such that it almost deprived him of life. It seemed as if he had no strength left except to curse the fate which had imposed so cruel a trial upon him. He had quitted his place of concealment, and in utter despair, his arms hanging by his side, and with a haggard gaze, he was on the point of returning, with life ebbing fast, to his apartment in the château, when suddenly the hangings behind which he had seen Diana and the prince disappear were thrown aside, and Diana herself rushed into the supper-room, and seized hold of Remy, who, standing motionless and erect, seemed only to be waiting her return.

"Quick! quick!" she said to him; "all is finished."

And they both darted into the garden as if they had been drunk, or mad, or raging with passion.

No sooner did Henri observe them, however, than he seemed to have recovered all his strength; he hastened to place himself in their way, and they came upon him suddenly in the middle of the path, standing erect, his arms crossed, and more terrible in his silence than anyone could ever have been in his loudest menaces. Henri's feelings had indeed arrived at such a pitch of exasperation, that he would readily have slain any man who would have ventured to maintain that women were not monsters sent from hell to corrupt the world. He seized Diana by the arm, and stopped her suddenly, notwithstanding the cry of terror which she uttered, and notwithstanding the dagger which Remy put to his breast, and which even grazed his flesh.

"Oh! doubtless you do not recognise me," he said furiously, gnashing his teeth; "I am that simple-hearted young man who loved you, and whose love you would not return, because for you there was no future, but merely the past. Ah! beautiful hypocrite that you are, and you, foul liar, I know you at last—I know and curse you. To the one I say, I despise and contemn you; to the other, I shrink from you with horror."

"Make way!" cried Remy, in a strangled voice; "make way, young fool, or if not——"

"Be it so," replied Henri; "finish your work, and slay my body, wretch, since you have already destroyed my soul."

"Silence!" muttered Remy, furiously, pressing the blade of his dagger more and more against Henri's breast.

Diana, however, violently pushed Remy aside, and seizing Du Bouchage by the arm, she drew him straight before her. She was lividly pale; her beautiful hair streamed over her shoulders; the contact of the hand on Henri's wrist seemed to the latter cold and damp as the dews of death.

"Monsieur," she said, "do not rashly judge of matters of which Heaven alone can judge. I am Diana de Méridor, the lover of Monsieur de Bussy, whom the Duc d'Anjou miserably allowed to perish when he could have saved him. Eight days since Remy slew Aurilly, the duke's accomplice, and the prince himself I have just poisoned with a peach, a bouquet, and a torch. Move aside, monsieur—move aside, I say, for Diana de Méridor, who is on her way to the Convent des Hospitalières."

With these words, and letting Henri's arm fall, she took hold of that of Remy, as he waited by her side.

Henri fell on his knees, following the retreating figures of the two assassins, who disappeared behind the thick copse, as though it had been a vision from hell. It was not till fully an hour afterwards that Du Bouchage, overpowered with fatigue and overwhelmed with terror, with his brain on fire, was able to summon sufficient strength to drag himself to his apartment, nor was it until after he had made the attempt nearly a dozen times that he succeeded in escalading the window. He walked to and fro in his room several times, and then staggered towards the bed, on which he threw himself. Everyone was sleeping quietly in the château.

## CHAPTER LXXXV

### FATALITY

The next morning, about nine o'clock, the beautiful rays of the sun were glistening like gold on the gravelled walks of Château-Thierry. Numerous gangs of workmen, who had the previous evening been directed to be in attendance, had been actively at work from daybreak upon the preparations in the park, as well as in the decoration of the apartments destined to receive the king, whose arrival was momentarily expected. As yet nothing was stirring in the pavilion where the duke reposed, for he had the previous evening forbidden his two old servants to awaken him. They were to wait until he summoned them. Towards half-past nine two couriers rode at full speed into the town, announcing his majesty's near arrival. The civic authorities, the governor, and the garrison formed themselves in ranks on either side of the road, leaving a passage for the royal procession. At ten o'clock the king appeared at the foot of the hill; he had mounted his horse when they had taken their last relays. He never neglected an opportunity of doing so, especially when entering towns, as he rode admirably. The queen-mother followed him in a litter; fifty gentlemen belonging to the court, richly clad and admirably mounted, followed in their suite. A company of the guards, followed by Crillon himself, a hundred and twenty of the Swiss, and as many of the Scotch guards, commanded by Larchant, and all the members of the royal household who accompanied the king in his excursions, mules, coffers, and domestic servants, formed a numerous army, the files of which followed the windings of the road leading from the river to the summit of the hill. Lastly, the cortége entered the town amidst the ringing of the church bells, the roar of cannon, and bursts of music. The acclamations of the inhabitants were enthusiastic; for a visit from the king was of such rare occurrence at that time that, seen thus closely, he seemed to be a living embodiment of divine right. The king, as he progressed through the crowd, looked on all sides for his brother, but in vain. He only found Henri du Bouchage waiting for him at the gate of the château.

When once within the château, Henry III. inquired after the health of the Duc d'Anjou from the officer who had assumed the high distinction of receiving the king.

"Sire," replied the latter, "his highness, during the last few days, has been residing in the pavilion in the park, and we have not yet seen him this morning. It is most probable, however, that as he was well yesterday, he is well also to-day."

"This pavilion is in a very retired part of the park, it seems," said Henri, in a tone of displeasure, "since the sound of the cannon does not seem to have been heard."

"Sire," one of the duke's two aged attendants ventured to remark, "his highness did not, perhaps, expect your majesty so soon."

"Old fool," growled Henri, "do you think, then, that a king presents himself in this way at other people's residences without informing them of it? Monsieur le Duc d'Anjou has been aware of my intended arrival since yesterday."

And then, afraid of casting a gloom over those around him

by a grave or sullen countenance, Henri, who wished to appear gentle and amiable at the expense of his brother François, exclaimed: " Well, then, since he has not come to meet us, we will go to meet him."

" Show us the way there," said Catherine, from the litter. All the escort followed the road leading to the old park.

At the very moment that the guards, who were in advance, approached the hedge, a shrill and piercing cry rent the air.

" What is that?" said the king, turning towards his mother.

" Great Heaven!" murmured Catherine, endeavouring to read the faces of those around her, " it sounded like a cry of distress or despair."

" My prince! my poor master!" cried François' other aged attendant, appearing at the window, and exhibiting signs of the most passionate grief.

Everyone hastened towards the pavilion, the king himself being hurried along with the others. He arrived at the very moment when they were raising from the floor the Duc d'Anjou's body, which his valet-de-chambre, having entered without authority, in order to announce the king's arrival, had just perceived lying on the carpet of the bedroom. The prince was cold, stiff, and perfectly inanimate, and it was only by a strange movement of the eyelids and a nervous contraction of the lips that it could be observed he was still alive. The king paused at the threshold of the door, and those behind him followed his example.

" This is an ugly omen," he murmured.

" Do not enter, my son, I implore you," said Catherine to him.

" Poor François!" said Henri, delighted at being sent away, and thus being spared the spectacle of this agonising scene.

The crowd, too, followed the king as he withdrew.

" Strange! strange!" murmured Catherine, kneeling down by the side of the prince, or rather of the corpse, no one being in the room with her but the two old servants; and while the messengers were despatched in every quarter of the town to find the prince's physician, and while a courier galloped off to Paris in order to hasten the attendance of the king's physicians, who had remained at Meaux with the queen, Catherine, with less knowledge, very probably, but not with less perspicacity than Miron himself could possibly have shown, examined the diagnostics of that singular malady which had struck down her son so suddenly.

Her experience was by no means indifferent, in the first place, therefore, she interrogated calmly, and without confusing them, the two attendants, who were tearing their hair and wringing their hands in the wildest despair.

Both of them replied that the prince had returned on the previous evening about nightfall, after having been disturbed at an inconvenient hour by Monsieur du Bouchage, who had arrived with a message from the king.

They then added that when the audience had terminated, which had been held in the château itself, the prince had ordered supper to be prepared, and had desired that no one should venture to approach the pavilion without being summoned; and lastly, that he had given the strictest injunctions not to be awakened in the morning, and that no one should enter without a positive summons.

"He probably expected a visit from a lady?" observed the queen-mother, inquiringly.

"We think so, madame," replied the valet respectfully, "but we could not discreetly assure ourselves of the fact."

"But in removing the things from the table, you must have seen whether my son had supped alone?"

"We have not yet removed the things, madame, since the orders of monseigneur were that no one should enter the pavilion."

"Very good," said Catherine; "no one, therefore, has been here?"

"No one, madame."

"You may go."

And Catherine was now left quite alone in the room. Leaving the prince lying on the bed where he had been placed, she immediately commenced the minutest investigation of each symptom or of each of the traces to which her attention was directed, as the result of her suspicions or apprehensions.

She had remarked that François' forehead was stained or dyed of a bistre colour, his eyes were bloodshot and encircled with blue lines, his lips marked with furrows, like the impression which burning sulphur leaves on living flesh.

She observed the same sign upon his nostrils and upon the sides of the nose.

"Now let me look carefully," she said, gazing about her on every side.

The first thing she remarked was the candlestick in which the flambeau which Remy had lighted the previous evening had burnt away.

"This candle has burnt for a length of time," she said, "and shows that François was a long time in this room. Ah! here is a bouquet lying on the carpet."

Catherine picked it up eagerly, and then, remarking that all its flowers were still fresh, with the exception of a rose, which was blackened and dried up:

"What does this mean?" she said; "what has been poured on the leaves of this flower? If I am not mistaken, I know a liquid which withers roses in this manner."

She threw aside the bouquet, shuddering as she did so.

"That explains to me the state of the nostrils and the manner in which the flesh of the face is affected; but the lips?"

Catherine ran to the dining-room. The valets had spoken the truth, for there was nothing to indicate that anything on the table had been touched since the previous evening's repast had been finished.

Upon the edge of the table lay half of a peach, in which the impression of a row of teeth was still visible. Catherine's attention was drawn to this in a particular manner, for the fruit, usually of a rich crimson near the core, had become as black as the rose, and was discoloured by violet, and brown spots. The corrosive action was more especially visible upon the part which had been cut, and particularly so where the knife must have passed.

"This explains the state of the lips," she said; "but François had only bitten one piece out of this peach. He did not keep the bouquet long in his hand, for the flowers are still fresh; the evil may yet be repaired, for the poison cannot have penetrated very deeply.

"And yet, if the evil be merely superficial, why should this paralysis of the senses be so complete, and why indeed should the decomposition of the flesh have made so much progress? There must be more that I have not seen."

And as she spoke Catherine again looked all round her, and observed, hanging by a silver chain, to its pole, the red and blue parrot to which François was so attached.

The bird was dead stiff, and the feathers of its wings rough and erect.

Catherine again looked closely and attentively at the torch which she had once before already narrowly inspected, to satisfy herself that, by its having burnt out completely, the prince had returned early in the evening.

"The smoke," said Catherine to herself; "the smoke! the wick of that torch was poisoned; my son is a dead man."

She called out immediately, and the chamber was in a minute filled with attendants and officers of the household.

"Miron, Miron!" cried some of them.

"A priest!" exclaimed the others.

But Catherine had, in the meantime, placed to the lips of François one of the small bottles which she always carried in her alms-bag, and narrowly watched her son's features to observe the effect of the antidote she applied.

The duke immediately opened his eyes and mouth, but no glance of intelligence gleamed in his eyes, no voice or sound escaped from his lips.

Catherine, in sad and gloomy silence, quitted the apartment, beckoning to the two attendants to follow her, before they had as yet had an opportunity of communicating with anyone.

She then led them into another chamber, where she sat down, fixing her eyes closely and watchfully on their faces.

"Monsieur le Duc d'Anjou," she said, "has been poisoned some time during his supper last evening; and it was you who served the supper."

At these words the two men turned as pale as death.

"Torture us, kill us, if you will," they said; "but do not accuse us."

"Fools that you are; do you suppose that if I suspected you, that would have already been done? You have not yourselves, I know, assassinated your master, but others have killed him; and I must know who the murderers are. Who has entered the pavilion?"

"An old man, wretchedly clothed, whom monseigneur has seen during the last two days."

"But the woman——"

"We have not seen her—what woman does your majesty mean?"

"A woman has been here, who made a bouquet——"

The two attendants looked at each other with an expression of such simple surprise that Catherine perceived, by this glance alone, how perfectly innocent they were.

"Let the governor of the town and the governor of the château be sent for," she said.

The two valets hurried to the door.

"One moment!" exclaimed Catherine, fixing them in their places by this single word as they approached the threshold. "You only and myself are aware of what I have just told you; I shall not breathe a word about it; if anyone learns it, therefore, it will be from or through one of you; on that very day both your lives shall be forfeited. Now, go!"

Catherine interrogated the two governors with more reserve. She told them that the duke had received from some person or persons a distressing intelligence which had deeply affected him; that that alone was the cause of his illness, and that if the duke had an opportunity of putting a few further questions to the persons again, he would in all probability soon recover from the alarm into which he had been thrown.

The governors instituted the minutest search in the town, the park, the environs, but no one knew what had become of Remy and Diana.

Henri alone knew the secret, and there was no danger of his betraying it.

Throughout the whole day, the terrible news, commented upon, exaggerated, and mutilated, circulated through Château-Thierry and the province; everyone explained, according to his own individual character and disposition, the accident which had befallen the duke.

But no one, except Catherine and Du Bouchage, ventured to acknowledge that the chance of saving the duke's life was hopeless.

The unhappy prince did not recover either his voice or his senses, or rather, he ceased to give any sign of intelligence.

The king, who was immediately beset with the gloomiest fancies, which he dreaded more than anything, would very willingly have returned to Paris; but the queen-mother opposed his departure, and the court was obliged to remain at the château.

Physicians arrived in crowds; Miron alone guessed the cause of the illness, and formed an opinion upon its serious nature and extent; but he was too good a courtier to confess the truth, especially after he had consulted Catherine's looks.

He was questioned on all sides, and he replied that Monsieur le Duc d'Anjou must certainly have suffered from some seriously-disturbing cause, and had been subjected to some violent mental shock.

In this way he avoided compromising himself, therefore, which is a very difficult matter in such a case.

When Henri III. required him to answer affirmatively or negatively to his question: "Whether the duke would live?" he replied:

" I will answer your majesty in three days."

" And when will you tell me?" said Catherine, in a low voice.

" You, madame, are very different; I answer you unhesitatingly."

" Well?"

" Your majesty has but to interrogate me."

" On what day will my son die, Miron?"

" To-morrow evening, madame."

"So soon?"

"Ah! madame," murmured the physician, "the dose was by no means a slight one."

Catherine placed one of her fingers on his lips, looked at the dying man, and repeated in an undertone this sinister word: "Fatality!"

## CHAPTER LXXXVI

### LES HOSPITALIERES

The count had passed a terrible night, in a state bordering on delirium and verging on death.

Faithful, however, to his duty, as soon as he had heard the king's arrival announced, he rose and received him at the gate, as we have described; but no sooner had he presented his homage to his majesty, saluted respectfully the queen-mother, and pressed the admiral's hand, than he shut himself up in his own room, not to die, but to carry determinedly into execution his long-cherished project, which nothing could any longer interfere with.

Towards eleven o'clock in the morning, therefore—that is to say, as soon as, immediately after the terrible news had circulated that the Duc d'Anjou's life was in imminent danger, everyone had dispersed, leaving the king completely bewildered by this fresh event—Henri went and knocked at his brother's door, who, having passed a part of the previous night travelling, had just retired to his own room.

"Ah! is that you?" asked Joyeuse, half-asleep; "what is the matter?"

"I have come to bid you farewell, my brother," replied Henri.

"Farewell! What do you mean? Are you going away?"

"Yes, I am going away, brother, and nothing need keep me here any longer, I presume."

"Why nothing?"

"Of course, since the fêtes at which you wished me to be present will not take place, I may now consider myself as freed from any promise."

"You are mistaken, Henri," replied the grand-admiral; "I have no greater reason for permitting you to leave to-day than I had yesterday."

"I regret that it is so; but in that case, for the first time in my life, I shall have the misfortune to disobey your orders, and to fail in the respect I owe you; for from this very moment I declare to you, Anne, that nothing shall restrain me any longer from taking my religious vows."

"But the dispensation which is expected from Rome?"

"I can await it in a convent."

"You must positively be mad to think of such a thing," exclaimed Joyeuse, as he rose, with stupefaction depicted on his countenance.

"On the contrary, my dear and honoured brother, I am the wisest of you all, for I alone know what I am about."

"Henri, you promised us a month."

"Impossible."

"A week, then, longer."

"Not an hour."

"You are suffering so much, then, poor boy?"

"On the contrary, I have ceased to suffer, and that is why the evil is without a remedy."

"But, at all events, this woman is not made of bronze; her feelings can be worked upon.   I will undertake to persuade her."

"You cannot do impossibilities, Anne; besides, even were she to allow herself to be persuaded now, it is I who could no longer consent to love her."

"Well, that is quite another matter."

"Such is the case, however, my brother."

"What! if she were now willing, would you be indifferent? Why, this is sheer madness."

"Oh! no! no!" exclaimed Henri, with a shudder of horror, "nothing can any longer exist between that woman and myself."

"What does this mean?" inquired Joyeuse, with marked surprise; "and who can this woman really be?  Come, tell me, Henri; you know very well that we have never had any secrets from each other."

Henri trembled lest he had said too much, and that, in yielding to the feeling which he had just exhibited, he had opened a channel by means of which his brother would be able to penetrate the terrible secret which he kept imprisoned in his breast.  He therefore fell into an opposite extreme; and, as it happens in such cases, and in order to recall the imprudent words which had escaped him, he pronounced others which were more imprudent still.

"Do not press me further," he said; "this woman will never be mine, since she belongs to Heaven."

"Folly!—mere idle tales!  This woman a nun!  She has deceived you."

"No, no, this woman has not spoken falsely; she is now

an Hospitalière. Do not let us speak any further of her, but rather let us respect those who throw themselves at the feet of Heaven."

Anne had sufficient power over himself not to show the delight this revelation gave him.

He continued: "This is something new, for you have never spoken to me about it."

"It is indeed quite new, for she has only recently taken the veil; but I am sure that her resolution, like my own, is irrevocable. Do not therefore seek to detain me any longer, but embrace me, as you love me. Permit me to thank you for all your kindness, for all your patience, and for your unceasing affection for a poor heart-broken man, and farewell!"

Joyeuse looked his brother full and steadily in the face; he looked at him like one whose feelings had overcome him, and who relied upon a display of feeling to work upon the feelings of others. But Henri remained unmoved at this exhibition of emotion on his brother's part, and replied in no other way but by the same mournful smile.

Joyeuse embraced his brother, and allowed him to depart.

"Go," he said to himself, "all is not yet finished, and, however great your hurry may be, I shall not be long before I shall have overtaken you."

He went to the king, who was taking his breakfast in bed, with Chicot sitting by his side.

"Good day! good day!" said the king to Joyeuse. "I am very glad to see you, Anne; I was afraid you would lie in bed all day, you indolent fellow. How is my brother?"

"Alas! sire, I do not know; I am come to speak to you about mine."

"Which one?"

"Henri."

"Does he still wish to become a monk?"

"More so than ever."

"And will he take the vows?"

"Yes, sire."

"He is quite right, too."

"How so, sire?"

"Because men go straight to Heaven that way."

"Oh!" said Chicot to the king, "men go much faster still by the way your brother is taking."

"Will your majesty permit me to ask a question?"

"Twenty, Joyeuse, twenty. I am as melancholy as I can possibly be at Château-Thierry, and your questions will distract my attention a little."

" You know all the religious houses in the kingdom, sire, I believe?"

" As well as I do a coat of arms."

" Is there one which goes by the name of Les Hospitalières, sire?"

" It is a very small, highly distinguished, excessively strict, and severe order, composed of twenty ladies, canonesses of Saint Joseph."

" Do they take the vows there?"

" Yes, as a matter of favour, and upon a presentation from the queen."

" Should I be indiscreet if I were to ask your majesty where this order is situated?"

" Not at all; it is situated in the Rue de Chevet Saint-Laudry, in the Cité, behind Le Cloître Notre Dame."

" At Paris?"

" Yes."

" Thank you, sire."

" But what the devil do you ask me that for? Has your brother changed his mind, and, instead of turning a Capuchin friar, does he now wish to become one of the Hospitalières?"

" No, sire, I should not think he would be so mad, after what your majesty has done me the honour to tell me; but I suspect he has had his head turned by someone belonging to that order, and I should consequently like to discover who this person is, and speak to her."

" Par la mordieu!" said the king, with a self-satisfied expression, " some seven years ago I knew the superior of that convent, who was an exceedingly beautiful woman."

" Well, sire, it may perhaps be the very one."

" I cannot say; since that time, I, too, Joyeuse, have assumed religious vows myself, or nearly so, indeed."

" Sire," said Joyeuse, " I entreat you to give me, at any rate, a letter to this lady, and my leave of absence for a couple of days."

" You are going to leave me!" exclaimed the king; " to leave me all alone here."

" Oh! ungrateful king," said Chicot, shrugging his shoulders, " am I not here?"

" My letter, if you please, sire," said Joyeuse.

The king sighed, but wrote it, notwithstanding.

" But you cannot have anything to do at Paris?" said Henri, handing the note to Joyeuse.

" I beg your pardon, sire, I ought to escort, or, at least, to watch over, my brothers."

"You are right; away with you, but return as quickly as you can."

Joyeuse did not wait for this permission to be repeated; he quietly ordered his horses, and having satisfied himself that Henri had already set off, galloped all the way until he reached his destination.

Without even changing his dress, the young man went straight to the Rue de Chevet Saint-Laudry. At the end of this street was the Rue d'Enfer, and parallel with it the Rue des Marmouzets.

A dark and venerable-looking house, behind whose walls the lofty summits of a few trees could be distinguished, the windows of which were few, bad, barred, and a wicket at the side, completed the exterior appearance of the Convent des Hospitalières.

Upon the keystone of the arch of the porch an artisan had rudely engraved these Latin words, with a chisel:—

MATRONAE HOSPITES

Time had partially destroyed both the inscription and the stone.

Joyeuse knocked at the wicket, and had his horses led away to the Rue des Marmouzets, fearing that their presence in the street might attract too much attention.

Then, knocking at the entrance gate, he said: "Will you be good enough to go and inform madame la supérieure that Monsieur le Duc de Joyeuse, Grand Amiral de France, is desirous of speaking to her on behalf of the king."

The face of the nun who had made her appearance behind the gate blushed beneath her veil, and she shut the gate.

Five minutes afterwards a door was opened, and Joyeuse entered a room set apart for the reception of visitors. A beautiful woman, of lofty stature, made Joyeuse a profound reverence, which the admiral returned gracefully and respectfully.

"Madame," said he, "the king is aware that you are about to admit, or that you have already admitted, among the number of the inmates here, a person with whom I require to speak. Will you be good enough to place me in communication with that person?"

"Will you tell me the name of the lady you wish to see, monsieur?"

"I am not aware of it."

"In that case, then, how can I possibly accede to your request?"

"Nothing is easier. Whom have you admitted during the last month?"

"You either tell me too precisely, or with not sufficient precision, who this person is," said the superior, "and I am unable to comply with your wish."

"Why so?"

"Because, during the last month I have received no one here until this morning."

"This morning?"

"Yes, monsieur le duc, and you can understand that your own arrival, two hours after hers, has too much the appearance of a pursuit to enable me to grant you permission to speak to her."

"I implore you, madame."

"Impossible, monsieur."

"Will you merely let me see this lady?"

"Impossible, I repeat. Although your name was sufficient for the doors of this house to be thrown open before you, yet in order to speak to anyone here, except indeed to myself, a written order from the king is necessary."

"Here is the order you require, madame," replied Joyeuse, producing the letter that Henri had signed.

The superior read it and bowed.

"His majesty's will shall be obeyed," she said, "even when it is contrary to the will of Heaven."

And she advanced towards the courtyard of the convent

"You now perceive, madame," said Joyeuse, courteously stopping her, "that I have right on my side; but I fear I may be under a mistake, and therefore may be abusing the permission I have received from the king. Perhaps the lady may not be the one I am in search of; will you be kind enough to tell me how she came here, why she came, and by whom she was accompanied?"

"All that is useless, monsieur le duc," replied the superior, "you are under no misapprehension for the lady, who arrived only this morning, after having been expected for the last fifteen days; this lady, I say, who was recommended by one who possesses the greatest authority over me, is indeed the very person with whom Monsieur le Duc de Joyeuse must wish to speak."

With these words the superior made another low courtesy to the duke and disappeared.

Ten minutes afterwards she returned, accompanied by a hospitalière, whose veil completely covered her face. It was Diana, who had already assumed the dress of the order.

The duke thanked the superior, offered a chair to her companion, himself sat down, and the superior quitted the room.

closing with her own hands the doors of the deserted and gloomy-looking apartment.

"Madame," said Joyeuse, without any preface, "you are the lady of the Rue Des Augustins; that mysterious person with whom my brother, Monsieur le Comte du Bouchage, is so passionately and madly in love."

The hospitalière bowed her head in reply, but did not open her lips.

This affectation appeared to Joyeuse almost like an act of rudeness; he was already very indifferently disposed to his companion, and continued:

"You cannot have supposed, madame, that it is sufficient to be beautiful, or to appear beautiful; to have no heart lying hidden beneath that beauty, to inspire a wretched and despairing passion in the heart and mind of a young man of my name, and then one day calmly to tell him: 'So much the worse for you if you possess a heart. I have none; nor do I wish for any.'"

"That was not my reply, monsieur, and you have been incorrectly informed," said the hospitalière, in so noble and touching a tone of voice, that Joyeuse's anger was in a moment subdued.

"The actual words are immaterial, madame, when their sense has been conveyed. You have rejected my brother, and have reduced him to despair."

"Innocently, monsieur; for I have always endeavoured to keep Monsieur du Bouchage at a distance."

"That is termed the art of coquetry, madame; and the result proves the fault."

"No one has the right to accuse me, monsieur; I am guilty of nothing. Your feelings of irritation are aroused against me; I shall say no more."

"Oh, oh!" said Joyeuse, gradually working himself into a passion, "you have been the ruin of my brother, and you fancy you can justify yourself with this irritating majesty of demeanour. No, no! the steps I have taken must show you what my intentions are. I am serious, I assure you, and you see by the trembling of my hands and lips that you will need some good arguments to move me."

The hospitalière rose.

"If you come here to insult a woman," she said, with the same calm self-possession, "insult me, monsieur; if, however, you have come to induce me to change my opinion, you are wasting your time, and can withdraw."

"Ah! you are no human creature!" exclaimed Joyeuse, exasperated. "You are possessed of an evil spirit."

"I have answered already; I will reply no further. Since that is not sufficient, I shall withdraw." And the hospitalière advanced towards the door. Joyeuse stopped her.

"One moment! I have sought you for too long a period to allow you to leave me in this manner; and, since I have succeeded in meeting with you—since your insensibility has confirmed me in the idea which had already occurred to me, that you are possessed by the foul fiend himself, sent hither by the enemy of mankind to destroy my brother—I wish to see that face whereon the bottomless pit has written its blackest traces; I wish to behold the fire of that fatal gaze which bewilders men's minds. Avaunt thee, Satan!"

And Joyeuse, making the sign of the cross with one hand, as if he were exorcising her, with the other tore aside the veil which covered the face of the hospitalière; the latter, silent and impassible, free from anger or ill-feeling, fixed her sweet and gentle gaze upon him who had so cruelly outraged her, and said: "Oh! monsieur le duc, what you have just done is unworthy of a gentleman."

Joyeuse's heart was smitten by her reply.

"Oh! madame," he murmured, after a long silence, "you are indeed beautiful, and truly must Henri have loved you. Surely Heaven can only have bestowed upon you loveliness such as you possess to cast it like perfume upon an existence devoted to your own."

"Monsieur, have you not conversed with your brother? or if you have done so, he cannot have thought it expedient to make you his confidant; had not that been the case, he would have told you that I have done what you say—I have loved; I shall never love again; I have lived and must die."

Joyeuse had never taken his eyes from Diana's face, and the soft and gentle expression of her gaze penetrated the inmost recesses of his being.

Her look had destroyed all the baser material in the admiral's heart: the pure metal was alone left, and his heart rent asunder, like a crucible which had been riven by the fusion of metal.

"Yes, yes," he repeated, in a still lower voice, and continuing to fix upon her a gaze from which the fire of his fierce anger had disappeared—"yes, yes, Henri must have loved you. Oh! madame, for pity's sake, on my knees implore you to love my brother."

Diana remained cold and silent.

"Do not reduce a family to despair, do not sacrifice the future prospects of our race; be not the cause of the death of one from despair, of the others from regret."

Diana, still silent, continued to look sorrowfully on the suppliant bending before her.

"Oh!" exclaimed Joyeuse, madly pressing his hand against his heart, "have mercy on my brother, have mercy on me!"

He sprung to his feet like a man bereft of his senses, unfastened, or rather tore open the door of the room where they had been conversing, and, bewildered and almost beside himself, fled from the house towards his attendants, who were awaiting him at the corner of the Rue d'Enfer.


## CHAPTER LXXXVII

### HIS HIGHNESS MONSEIGNEUR LE DUC DE GUISE

On Sunday, the 10th June, towards eleven clock in the day, the whole court was assembled in the apartment leading to the cabinet in which, since his meeting with Diana de Méridor, the Duc d'Anjou was dying by slow but sure degrees. Neither the science of the physicians, nor his mother's despair, nor the prayers which the king had desired to be offered up, had been successful in averting fatal termination. Miron, on the morning of this same 10th of June, assured the king that all chance of recovery was hopeless, and that François d'Anjou would not outlive the day. The king pretended to display extreme grief, and turning towards those who were present, said: "This will fill my enemies full of hope."

To which remark the queen-mother replied:

"Our destiny is in the hands of Heaven, my son."

Whereupon Chicot, who was standing humbly and reverently near Henri III., added in a low voice:

"Let us help Heaven when we can, sire."

Nevertheless, the dying man, towards half-past eleven, lost both colour and sight; his mouth, which, up to that moment, had remained open, became closed; the flow of blood which for several days past had terrified all who were near him, as the bloody sweat of Charles IX. had similarly done at an earlier period, had suddenly ceased, and hands and feet became icy cold. Henri was sitting beside the head of the couch whereon his brother was extended. Catherine was standing in the recess in which the bed was placed, holding her dying son's hand in hers.

The Bishop of Château-Thierry and the Cardinal de Joyeuse repeated the prayers for the dying, which were joined by all who were present, kneeling, and with their hands clasped reverently together. Towards mid-day, the dying man opened his eyes; the sun's rays broke through a cloud and inundated the bed with a flood of light. François, who, up to that moment, had been unable to move a single finger, and whose mind had been obscured like the sun which had just reappeared, raised one of his arms towards Heaven with a horror-stricken gesture.

He looked all round the room, heard the murmuring of the prayers, grew conscious of his illness as well as of his weakness, became aware of his critical position, perhaps because he already caught a glimpse of that unseen and terrible future, the abode of certain souls after they have quitted their earthly prison.

He thereupon uttered a loud and piercing cry, and struck his forehead with a force which made everyone tremble.

Then, knitting his brows, as if one of the mysterious incidents of his life had just recurred to him, he murmured: " Bussy! Diana!"

This latter name had been overheard by none but Catherine, so weakened had the dying man's voice become before pronouncing it.

With the last syllable of that name François d'Anjou breathed his last sigh.

At this very moment, by a singular coincidence, the sun, which had gilded with its rays the royal arms of France, and the golden fleurs-de-lis, was again obscured: so that the fleurs-de-lis which had been so brilliantly illuminated but a moment before, became as dark and gloomy as the azure ground which they had but recently studded with constellations almost as resplendent as those whereon the eye of the dreamer rests in his upward gaze towards Heaven.

Catherine let her son's hand fall.

Henry III. shuddered, and leaned tremblingly on Chicot's shoulder, who shuddered too, but from a feeling of awe which every Christian feels in the presence of the dead.

Miron placed a golden spatula on François' lips; after a few seconds, he looked at it carefully and said:

" Monseigneur is dead."

Whereupon a deep prolonged groan arose from the antechamber; like an accompaniment to the psalm which the cardinal murmured:

" Cedant iniquitates meæ ad vocem deprecationis meæ."

" Dead," repeated the king, making the sign of the cross as he sat in his fauteuil; " my brother, my brother!"

" The sole heir of the throne of France," murmured Catherine, who, having quitted the bed whereon the corpse was lying, had placed herself beside the only son who now remained to her.

"Oh!" said Henri, "this throne of France is indeed large for a king without issue; the crown is indeed large for a single head. No children! no heirs! Who will succeed me?"

Hardly had he pronounced these words when a loud noise was heard on the staircase and in the apartments.

Nambu hurriedly entered the death chamber, and announced:

"His Highness Monseigneur le Duc de Guise."

Struck by this reply to the question which he had addressed to himself, the king turned pale, rose, and looked at his mother. Catherine was paler than her son. At the announcement of the horrible misfortune which mere chance had foretold to his race, she grasped the king's hand, and pressed it, as if to say:

"There lies the danger; but fear nothing, I am near you."

The son and mother, under the influence of the same terror and the same menace, had comprehended each other.

The duke entered, followed by his officers. He entered, holding his head loftily erect, although his eyes ranged from the king to the death-bed of his brother with a glance not free from a certain embarrassment.

Henri III. stood up, and with that supreme majesty of carriage which, on certain occasions, his singularly poetic nature enabled him to assume, checked the duke's further progress by a kingly gesture, and pointed to the royal corpse upon the bed, the covering of which was in disorder from his brother's dying agonies. The duke bowed his head, and slowly fell on his knees. All around him, too, bowed their heads and bent their knees. Henri III., together with his mother, alone remained standing, and bent a last look, full of pride, upon those around him. Chicot observed this look, and murmured in a low tone of voice: "Deiiciet potentes de sede et exaltabit humiles"—"He hath put down the mighty from their seat, and hath exalted the humble and meek."

**THE END**

Printed at Parkgate Printing Works, Dublin, by Cahill & Co., Limited, and Published by Mellifont Press, Limited, 1, Furnival Street, London, E.C.4., and Kingsbridge, Dublin.